THE GAMAL

THE GAMAL

A NOVEL

CIARÁN COLLINS

BLOOMSBURY

NEW YORK · LONDON · NEW DELHI · SYDNEY

Published by Bloomsbury USA, New York

All papers used by Bloomsbury USA are natural, recyclable products made from wood grown in well-managed forests. The manufacturing processes conform to the environmental regulations of the country of origin.

LIBRARY OF CONGRESS CATALOGING-IN-PUBLICATION DATA
Collins, Ciarán, 1977–
The gamal / Ciarán Collins. — First U.S. edition.
pages cm
ISBN: 978-1-60819-875-7 (alk. paper)
1. Youths' writings—Fiction. 2. Psychotherapy patients—Fiction. 3. Youth—
Psychology—Fiction. 4. Friendship in youth—Fiction. 5. Bereavement in youth—
Fiction. 6. Psychological fiction. I. Title.
PR6103.O447G36 2013
823'.92—dc23
2012046539

First U.S. Edition 2013

3 5 7 9 10 8 6 4 2

Typeset by Hewer Text UK Ltd. Edinburgh
Printed and bound in the U.S.A. by Thomson-Shore Inc., Dexter, Michigan

Once Upon A Time

Once upon a time and a long time ago. Well not that long. 5 years. Long enough. 1/5 of my life isn't it? That means I'm twenty-five now, in case you're thick at sums. There were two lovers called Sinéad and James. One sec now. Just to clarify a few things here from the start.

Reading Shit

Don't be expecting any big flowery longwinded poetic picturesque horseshit passages in this book explaining the look of something. If I have to go into that much detail I'll take a photograph or draw a picture. This is for people like myself who hate reading. I always hated reading and never bothered with books even though I knew I would have no imagination if I didn't read a lot as a child. I listened to music or sometimes I watched telly with my father. You didn't have to use your imagination but I didn't care. *Charlotte's Web* and Enid Blyton and the whole lot were only a load of bollicks as far as I was concerned. One time when my teacher was helping me with my spellings she got me to say over and over and over and over again, the letters C O L D C O L D C O L D C O L D C O L D. Then she asked me what does that spell and I said, 'Tractor,' and the whole class were laughing at me. And I asked her what were they laughing at and she said, 'They're laughing at you.' And I said 'Why?' And she goes, 'You're even too silly to know why they're laughing at you.' I just nodded and sat down. I knew she wouldn't call me back. I was a hopeless case. Pray to St Jude, patron saint of hopeless cases. Had we anything better to be doing anyway only reading shit? That's what I said to her then when I sat down. The whole class laughing and giggling and shaking their heads and Mrs Fatty Fitzhenry sending me down to the master and I can't remember the rest. Lines I suppose. Fifty lines and a letter home that the mother couldn't read.

Mrs Fatty Fitzhenry used to be the whole time at me to leave Sinéad alone and not to be following her around the place but I wasn't. Fat bitch.

Anyhow that was me when I was small and this is me now. I'm not old but I'm older than I was then and I'm after making it out of a scrape or two and I'm still in one piece.

I became obsessed with her as well, I'm told. This shrink I saw lately. Dr Quinn does be sending me to other shrinks too. Dr Quinn is my main fella. But this fella was telling me that people with personality disorders often grow obsessed with people they encounter in their lives. But he never knew Sinéad. Everyone who ever knew Sinéad became a bit obsessed with her. Young and old. And not just men. Women too. *The women were talking wherever she went. Like a bell that is rung or a wonder told shyly.* I robbed that last bit from some ancient poet fella. Old Master Higgins taught us it. *The men who had seen her drank deep and were silent. Few in the candlelight thought her too proud. For the house of the planter is known by the tree. When night stirred at sea and fire brought a crowd in. They say that her beauty was like music in mouth.*

One Thousand Words

One thousand words, that's my aim aim aim. I was told by Dr Quinn that fellas who want to be writers should write one thousand words a day day day day day day day. Imagine if all the world loved reading telephone books. I could just write a telephone book. A fictional telephone book full of made-up people. Six hundred and twenty-six words so far. Now it's six hundred and thirty-three. I could finish my thousand words by going on like that.

Another Thing

Another thing is that you won't like me. I promise. I would have explained this in the first line but I wanted you to buy the book. And I reckon a lot of you bookworm types wouldn't have the balls to take it back to the shop and the chances are you'll probably just read it anyway seeing as you're after buying it. Anyhow, sorry and all that shit, but I need the money cos I want to get out of here after all the things that happened. When they get me well. You see I got something in the post one time off Sinéad. It was a map of America. On it she was after writing.

—Just follow the music Charlie. You'll find us there. Love, Sinéad. And Charlie, thank you.

You won't like me. Mainly because you know I don't care whether you like me or not, and people don't like that do they? They might say they do but they don't. Saying means nothing cos it could just as well be lies. I will tell the truth at all times. A lot of people around here won't like that either. So read on and don't be needing to like me like you would with all them other lick-arse books. I'm no lick-arse. I says it like it is. And like it was.

A Good Area

I live in a very good area. When I'd be working in Cork before everything and they'd ask me where I'm from and I'd say Ballyronan they'd say,

—Oh very nice, or

—Nice area down there, pay a fair penny for a house down there nowadays, or

—Ballyronan? No. Never heard of it.

Not the kind of place you expect people to be getting killed anyhow.

Here's a map of it. My house is up the hill. Up the bottom right corner of the map. Up past the Catholic church. I got sick of colouring in bits with my biro. It's not finished but I think it's finished enough.

Under the Bridge

There was a body found once under the bridge.

The Bridge

This is a picture of the bridge.

Under The Bridge

This is a picture of under the bridge.

There wasn't as much water though cos it was summer when it happened and I took the picture in the winter cos today is in the wintertime.

Read Another Book

I know you'd probably prefer a few pages painting the picture with words but you can read another book if you want to. There it is there. Look at it. That's where I seen.

Roads

I can go from the back of my house to down under the bridge by going out the back of my back garden and climbing a fence and walking down behind the new houses and through the north woods all the way down to the other side of the football pitch right down to the river and along the bank to the bridge. When the river's low I can go through the archways of the bridge to the other side. I can cross the bridge without touching the bridge. I go under it. Mostly I don't bother with roads cos they're shit so I let all the rest of people be following each other on the roads like fools and I go my own way. I go through fields and ditches and dikes. I go through back yards, under bridges, along river banks, through wasteland. I know short cuts. Over walls. Through briars and wires. Through a scrap yard. No. Two scrap yards. And two quarries as well. And one of them has a fierce big cliff. I go over outhouses. And in behind places. Where there's no clean paintwork or flower pots. No frilly blinds or net curtains. Clothes lines and rusty gas drums and mossy stones instead. Places where rats scamper and tomcats pace. But mostly it's fields. Fields and woods mostly. I seen badgers and owls and hedgehogs and hares and stoats and rabbits and pheasants and shrews and mice and squirrels and frogs and crows and rats and things that live under barrels and old tractor tyres and old carpets and damp smelly sofas like woodlice and slugs and snails and beatles. And ants if it's on concrete. And I never gave a fuck about them much. Any of them. But sometimes I might see a person and I'd watch them for a bit all right if they weren't after seeing me. One time I watched an old farmer for four hours. He used to nod to himself every now and again like he was agreeing with himself. People are definitely the best to be looking at. Except for when I see a kingfisher down by the river. They're my favourite cos they stand out and they're not trying to hide and blend in same as every other living thing. Brave they are. Kingfishers don't give a fuck. Anyhow, first thing my mam ever does when she sees me is look at my shoes to see is there shit all over them from the fields and the woods. At home or at Mass or in the shop or in someone's house she does be terrified I'll disgrace her by destroying some grand clean floor.

Read this too. It's about a thing called Post-Traumatic Stress Disorder.

PTSD

PTSD is not diagnosed unless the symptoms last for at least one month. The symptoms are severe and interfere with normal social functioning. A person with PTSD will have the following types of symptoms:

Re-experiencing Symptoms

Re-experiencing symptoms involve reliving the traumatic event. Memories of the traumatic event can return unexpectedly or can be triggered by a distinct reminder such as when a combat veteran hears a car backfire. This can cause a 'flashback' where the patient reacts emotionally and physically in a similar way that he/she did during the original trauma.

Arousal Symptoms

Patients will have increased emotional arousal (hyperarousal), and it can cause difficulty sleeping, outbursts of anger or irritability, and difficulty concentrating. They may find that they are constantly 'on guard', alert and on the lookout for signs of danger. They are often easily startled.

Avoidance

The hyperarousal and the re-experiencing symptoms become so distressing that the patient strives to avoid contact with everything and everyone which may arouse memories of the trauma. The patient isolates themselves and can experience so-called emotional detachment ('numbing').

Dissociation

Dissociation may arise from feelings of depersonalisation and detachment, where there is a disconnection between memory and effect. The patient will appear to be 'in another world'. In severe forms this can involve 'losing time', where a patient may have no recollection of his/her actions. This 'losing time' may involve

multiple personalities or may be a result of emotional detachment
or 'numbing'.

That's a cut and paste job from the internet. I was diagnosed
with PTSD. But I think Sinéad might have had it too only no
one ever bothered to notice. Maybe everyone has it a bit after
shit happens to them. Reminded me of Old Master Higgins
saying that the people of Ireland got an awful shock. Sometimes
people just kind of go autopilot isn't it? Old Master Higgins got
fired cos he cursed in class. I was there when he did it. Some
poor child asked him why Queen Elizabeth banned the harp long
ago and he went on a drunken rant cursing and blinding for five
minutes. I wasn't there when they buried him about four months
ago. I was probably the only one in the whole parish not at the
funeral but I couldn't go cos I wasn't well and even if they asked
if I wanted to go they wouldn't have got an answer.

But I'm getting better now. I'm probably better now than I ever
was. I've done away with some of my daft old ways. Like I don't
sleep upside down any more. Before the stuff that happened I used
to listen to music the whole time. Well not the whole time. But
nearly the whole time. Except when I was hanging around with
Sinéad and James. But usually we were listening to music anyway.
If they weren't making it. After the bad stuff I became kind of sick.
I didn't do nothing for two years. I was awake but I was in a coma.
I used to always be sleeping upside down on the bed before though.
My head used to be where your feet are supposed to be. You see
my stereo was down the end of the bed cos there was no room for
it any place else. So I slept upside down. I'd them long earphones

and the music could reach my ears if I was lying upside down on the bed. That way I could always listen to my music loud as I liked even when the mother and father were asleep. I'd listen to Sinéad too. Tapes of her.

But I don't listen to music now any more. And my concentration is better now too. If you were talking away to me now with your normal boring everyday shit I'd probably be able to listen to you and my mind wouldn't be gone off thinking about Sinéad or some tune or Sinéad singing the tune or just the look of her.

The door next to my bedroom is the door of the spare room. It has a hole in it the shape of my foot cos my father thought he could get me out of the bed if he played some music that I used to listen to in the spare room. The father has cardboard covering the hole in the door now. Stuck on with duct tape. He must think that looks better than the hole. Anyhow that was the end of my father's stupid schemes and I went back to bed for another twelve months or more.

But that's the father to a fucking tee. Thinks he knows everything just cos he has a head full of correct answers. Quizzes and questions and rivers and wars. We used to watch *Quiz Time* on the telly together the whole time and I small.

—What is the capital of Portugal?

—Don't give a fuck, says I.

—Lisbon, says the father.

—In which year was the Treaty of Versailles signed?

—Don't give a fuck, says I.

—1919, says the father.

Read This Too

In children with Oppositional Defiant Disorder (ODD), there is a distinct pattern of uncooperative and defiant behavior toward figures of authority. The conduct disorder seriously interferes with normal day to day functioning.

The child should be seen by a child psychiatrist who can evaluate the child's behavior. Along with a diagnosis the psychiatrist will work with school professionals and others to have specific educational tests done to clarify if a learning disability exists and to design a more appropriate educational programme for the child. Medication may be prescribed for hyperactivity or distractibility.

Oppositional Defiant Disorder

The disorder is seen in children below the age of 10 years. While there is an absence of severe aggressive, violent or dangerous acts against others, continuous disobedient, provocative and defiant behavior toward authority figures will be present.

Diagnostic Guidelines

The essential feature of this disorder is a pattern of persistently negativistic, hostile, defiant, provocative, and disruptive behavior, which is clearly outside sociocultural norms. Social, occupational and educational functioning will be impaired.

Diagnostic Criteria

A period of six months or more, during which four (or more) of the following are present:

often deliberately annoys people

often loses temper

often actively defies adults' requests

often ignores rules

often blames others for his or her misbehavior

is often hypersensitive

is often vindictive

is often easily annoyed by others

often argues with adults and shows resentment toward them

is often angry

Two hundred and thirty-two words, ha? How do you like that cabbage? That's the bones of a day's work nearly. Just like that. Magic. I like the internet. 'Tisn't total dossing either like, so don't be getting all thick, cos it's important for the story so you better have read it. If you didn't go back and do it now and stop being so lazy.

Everyone wants to be part of the gang. I couldn't give a flying fuck about no gang. My father said what's wrong with me is that even as a small child I never wanted to be liked. He said it was a serious fuck-up and the root cause of my trouble. He said there's a part of the brain that makes people want to be liked but that that part of my brain was fucked. Says he noticed it first when I was about two. See when people are very very small. Say, between the ages of nought and one. People don't have to be nice. Or make an effort to be liked if they want things. They just have to cry. And then they get fed, or get changed, or get more clothes put on them or get people to shut up around the house so they can sleep. Then you see when people are about two they have to learn to be part of the gang. They can't just cry for what they want any more. But they automatically learn how to get what they want. By being nice. Doing as you're told. You see people all want stuff. The little baby wants milk so he automatically cries. Without even having to think about it I suppose.

You come to realise that all this crying business that you're so good at won't get you so far any more. You realise that your mammy and daddy aren't going to be slaves for you for ever. That you'll have to start doing things for yourself. But it's not so bad because we are made in such a way that we begin to be able to do things for ourselves at just the right time. So your hands are starting to get handy enough so that you can spoon-feed yourself. And soon you learn to hold your bottom so that mammy or daddy won't have to be changing your nappy all the time. Of course all this goes on unknown to yourself. It's automatic. And you also learn that to get things for yourself you have to start behaving in a way mammy and daddy will like. And in a way that everyone will like. You can't be kicking your mammy or biting people. You have to be a good little boy in order to get what you want. Start saying, 'Yes please', and 'No thanks'. Start saying, 'Sorry', before you get the sweets.

This is where my father first noticed the difficulty with me. I was such a terrible two-year-old my mammy and daddy brought me to the doctor who hadn't seen anything like it before. I refused to do anything for myself and cried the whole time. The more they tried to bribe me into being good with sweets and toys and affection and approval, the more I cried. Then they tried not doing anything for me to see would I start being good and stop biting people and breaking things and screaming and roaring and crying. They stopped giving me food. They tempted me to be good. If I behaved for a little while they'd give me food. I wouldn't behave and went throwing things. Then they gave me food in case I'd starve and I threw it at them. We all used to go to sleep together then and I'd cry myself to sleep while they'd cuddle me and pamper me. I loved my mammy and daddy but I couldn't believe they wanted me to be good. I think I must have been very disappointed at that time.

Even after I had started school I was still going to see these doctors who were doing all sorts of special tests and experiments. In these experiments they realised that I wouldn't do anything if I knew that someone wanted me to do it. Even if I wanted to do it myself I wouldn't do it if I knew someone else like the doctors wanted me to do it. Not even the smallest thing. I wouldn't even look at something they asked me to look at. I wouldn't even say a single word that they wanted me to say.

There was this one test that the mother told me about that they did. I was four and I really wanted more than anything else in the world a toy tractor that you could sit on and drive with pedals. So unknown to me my father bought me one of these. A real nice one. They'd it all planned. Himself and the doctor. So this one day when I went to the doctor for the tests what was inside in the doctor's room only the tractor. Over beside the desk. Then the doctor explained to me that I could have the tractor if I just did one tiny thing for him first. All I had to do was look at a picture on the wall for one second. I wouldn't do it so he gets the picture off the wall and tries to bring it down in front of me so I'd have to look at it. I knew what he was at so I closed my eyes and put my two hands over them. I wouldn't take my hands away from my eyes for the whole session with the doctor. Three-quarters of an hour. Then my mother came to collect me and I still wouldn't take my hands down and open my eyes. I didn't open them until I was getting out of the car to go in home. And even then my mam says I opened one eye a tiny bit first to make sure the picture they wanted me to look at wasn't around. Fuck the tractor. That's what I said to my father. So that was my problem. I'd do anything in the world except what people wanted me to do. Then I started school and that all changed. Kind of.

—But you'd better watch it, the father used to say.

—The nail that sticks out gets hammered in.

—The Japanese know their shit Charlie.

My father knew from the word go though that I wasn't interested.

—Will you ever quit the fecking shit?

—Get with the programme man for the love of Christ.

He gave up on me then.

A Man Apart

So that lark was keeping all the experts off the streets and was keeping me from being expelled. At the end of the day I reckon they secretly knew that the real problem was that I didn't give a fuck.

They had my teachers reading about ODD so I was let away with murder. I was being praised left, right and centre. Any tiny bit of work at all that I decided to do next thing I was the best thing since sliced blah.

—Well done Charlie.

—Charlie that's excellent.

—Brilliant work Charlie.

Anyhow the beginning and the end of it all was that I didn't
have to do work in school any more if I didn't want to. I wouldn't
learn where the river Boyne was or which county was Antrim and
which was Armagh. Or what the capital of Canada was. Or who
came after Henry VIII. Or how the Irish made such a bollicks of
fighting off the English for eight hundred years. Or what was the
speed of sound. Or the Irish for cousin. Or how to spell pneumo-
nia. All the useless shite that they try and squeeze into your head.
I didn't have to pay a single ounce of attention to any of it. But I
had to be in a classroom somewhere until I was sixteen cos that
was the law.

So as long as I stayed half quiet and let the rest of them get on
with learning shite I was free as the wind. Well as free as you can
be, while sitting in a desk facing a blackboard. I was always sitting
at the back of the classroom. When I was put up the front I
created havoc. It never took teachers long to learn that 'twas best
if I sat at the back. A man apart. That's what my father calls me.
'Get the salt there like a good man,' he'd say. I'd get it then and
he'd say, 'You're a man apart.' Been saying it to me all my life,
he has.

Old Master Higgins

Met Dr Quinn today and he read my stuff so far. He wants me
to introduce Old Master Higgins properly. Old Master Higgins
was the teacher who I mentioned already who was made to

retire early cos he cursed and the cursing was probably on account of his drinking. And I don't think he was teaching what the government wanted him to teach. He used to still come in to the school now and again after he'd left to be telling us old stories about the parish long ago and the Greeks a zillion years ago. Another thing he said in the pub once was that what the people in the East are afraid of is us in the West boring them all to death with Powerpoint presentations. Master Coughlan took over from Old Master Higgins. They were different animals. I was sorry Old Master Higgins left cos he was interesting but I was glad he left too cos he suspected I was really clever and only pretending to be a dunce. I was weak once and I wrote the answers of a test on toilet paper cos he didn't bother handing out paper to me cos he knew I wouldn't do the test. Then he found the toilet paper on the ground and tried to say it was no other student's handwriting so it had to be mine. I said no. When Master Coughlan was taking over after they got rid of Master Higgins he let Master Higgins say goodbye to us. Master Higgins tried to explain to Master Coughlan that I was clever and Master Coughlan patted him on the back and said, 'Charlie? Charlie is a pure genius.' The whole class starts laughing then and Master Higgins mutters away, 'No actually he's actually very bright. He just has social issues don't you see,' and Master Coughlan leading him out the door as if he was after causing a disturbance, 'All the best now Master Higgins. Say bye to Master Higgins everybody.'

—Bye Master Higgins, they all goes.

I stopped acting up a good bit too when I realised they were going to put me on drugs to keep me from being bold long ago. Drugged up to the fucking gills I was a few times and I small. That's when I stopped being very bold in school. I stayed quiet now as long as they didn't make me do the stupid work that the other kids were doing. Anything was better than them tablets. Like the nightmare with the witches with green faces but it wasn't no dream.

Witches With Green Faces

I used to have a nightmare about witches with green faces who had a hold of me in a shopping centre and wouldn't let me go. And I could see my father and my mother and my sister but they couldn't see me. And the worst thing was my voice wouldn't work and I couldn't call out to them.

Friends

I never had any real friends long ago. I didn't want any. Friends have to be friendly. Sometimes I've no mind for being friendly. Except with Sinéad and James I suppose. They were the only ones I ever knew that it felt right always to be friendly to.

Like People

I started to like people a lot more, now that they were leaving me alone at the back of the class. Teachers, other students, everyone really. I used to love just sitting back having my noticings watching them all. Mental to be looking at them all and the heads on them pure wild.

But really like I think the truth is that the father kind of missed me around the place. You see, after the thing that happened I did nothing for a long time. Nearly two years altogether isn't it? I just was.

But I got up then when I was ready and it had fuck all to do with music. I'd get up out of bed for a bit in the evening time. Maybe it was Dr Quinn's anti-depressants that did the trick. But it wasn't music. My father just shouted up if I wanted to go to the match now. What match I don't know. Anyhow I said no. Still won't stop him asking next time. I used to love going to the big matches for the shouting. I shouted every chance I got. It's the only place I could do it and not get in trouble.

—Move the fucking ball.

—Come on lads wake up.

—Mark up lads for fuck sake.

—Lads will ye get into the game in the name of fuck.

—Ref you're a bollicks.

—Ya blind fool ya.

—Put on a blue jersey ref ya prick.

Sometimes I wouldn't watch the game at all. I watched the men beside me instead. And I'd try to tell by their faces when they were going to shout and I'd join in.

—Come on ref in the name of fuck.

I'd be cursing away like mad at the matches and no one only strangers took any notice. Most of the time anyhow. One time all right when it all went quiet I shouted,

—Referee you're only a big dirty knacker.

And they all saying,

—Ah Jesus Christ Charlie that's a bit much.

—Cop yourself on Charlie in the name of God, the man is doing his best.

Some few would always mutter under their breath,

—Bleddy gamallogue.

—Fucking loolah.

And some would be looking at each other and shaking their heads or throwing their eyes to heaven and saying,

—God help us.

That's what people say when I do stupid things. Some nod their heads once with a sad disappointed look on them when they say it.

—God help us.

And they'd say it to describe the like of me too. If someone was describing me they'd say,

—He's a bit of a God help us.

A God help us is another way of saying gamal. My name is Charlie but people call me the gam or the gamal. It's from an Irish word. Gamalóg. Gamallogue in English. Don't even know what exactly it means but I've a fair idea. Master Coughlan gave me that name after the famous relay. The name stuck. Not gamallogue. Just gam or gamal.

I never had the discipline to learn any sport properly. I'd just kick the ball as hard as I could any chance I'd get. And I didn't care what direction I'd kick it in either. Usually I'd kick it out of the pitch altogether. And then they'd give out to whoever kicked the ball to me in the first place.

—Charlie, Jesus Christ. Will you get away off the pitch. Get up on your tree in the name of God and stay up there 'til the bell goes. Jesus suffering Christ.

That'd be Master Coughlan. Anyhow, that was the last bit of football coaching I ever got. And probably the best as well. That was the end of my footballing career. But 'twasn't the end of my athletics days – even though that day wasn't far off either.

I was a fast fucker. When I say fast I mean fast. I mean beating the fastest by three or four yards in a sprint.

Anyhow, weren't the Cork County Sports coming up and Master Coughlan was in a right tizzy about them and the whiff of glory in his nostrils was putting an almighty spring in his step. The year before he threw any old team together the day before the races during lunchtime. But this year he was like a man possessed. Two months before the races he had us out training. Myself, James, his own young fella Gregory, and Dinky.

I was the fastest by a long way. Then James was the next fastest by a long way as well. Greg and Dinky were the next fastest in the class, but they were fairly slow. Anyhow, Master Coughlan figured, rightly as it turned out, that between the four of us we had the winning of the first County Relay Final in the school's history, no less. And who'd be triumphantly crossing the line for the school and for the parish, only Master Coughlan's own son, Gregory.

James started and was winning by a mile when he passed the baton to Dinky. Dinky held his own, fair play, and passed it to me. I took off and left them all wishing they were as fast as me. I was a mile ahead when I reached poor Gregory to pass the baton, only hadn't I gone back to my bad old ways again.

You see, I seen the whole school up on the stand going off their heads, standing on their seats and screaming their heads off. I seen Master Coughlan and he boxing the air and shouting. I felt like I was in danger of being the parish hero or something. Me, James, Dinky and Gregory doing it for the parish. We'd get a mention at Mass and everything. And our names would be on the Parish Bulletin. Maybe even the *County Star*. With a photo maybe even.

So there I was ready to hand the baton on to poor Gregory and he standing there shitting himself afraid he'd fuck it all up and cause his father to kill himself.

What I did next I swear on my mortified soul I had no control over. My outstretched arm wouldn't hand over the fecking baton to poor Gregory. I jogged along with the poor fella and I seen the tormented confused frustrated look on his face. He'd make a grab for the baton and I'd raise it, he went up for it then and I lowered it. I just circled the poor lad's hand with the baton until all the others had passed us out. And off he went, Paddy Last, and the tears rolling down his face and there were a few in his father's eyes too.

I know. I'm ashamed. Ashamed. Shamed. Ashamed. I'm not joking. I know. But I swear I had no control over my hand. My head was to blame. My heart would have given him the baton. My head was to blame.

Anyhow, Master Coughlan shouted at the top of his voice,

—What kind of a bleddy gamallogue are you to do that? and the spit and dribble coming out of his quivery lips and they as red as his face.

I'm the gamal since.

So anyhow. At the matches you have to gauge it right. You have to shout the right insults. At the right time. Otherwise you'll be the odd one out. I don't mind being the odd one out. I think I like it.

—Ah ref you're an awful fucking cunt.

I bang doors. They all turn around in shock and then just look back at each other. God help us. And I burp loud. Only thing louder is me shouting afterwards,

—'Scuse me.

Gives people a right good fright again. Might let out another small burp then after I shout that. Wear my jumper back to front the odd time too. No one ever said it to me once. Sometimes I forget to wear socks. When I eat I hold my fork in my fist and I bring my head down to meet my fork. I try to carry more than I should and stuff falls. People see the crack of my ass when I pick stuff up. God help us. In Mass when people go up to receive the Body of Christ they go up the middle aisles and down the side aisles to avoid a jam. I get it wrong a lot and people have to get out of my way and I going against everyone. I spill my Lucozade on my chin and my chest sometimes in the pub. In funerals I say the wrong things. I say match things like,

—Hard luck.

—No fault.

—Did your best.

My grand-uncle died when he was a hundred and two and I said to his son,

—It was a terrible shock, and the whole place starts laughing mad.

I don't talk much but when I do I talk loud and I say the wrong thing. I'm a pity, God help us.

Dr Quinn was kind of annoying today asking about girls. Once I was about fourteen and realised I liked girls so much I knew I was in an awful stupid situation. I knew I'd no chance of ever being with a nice girl where people knew me. Or where they thought they knew me. That's when I realised that I'd be doing a disappearing act out of Ballyronan at some stage in the future. Up and out to fuck. I'd been acting the gam for my whole life. I suppose I started caring even less what people thought of me once I realised that I'd be leaving for ever when I grew up. And sure that only made me worse. But he kept asking me about Sinéad,

—As far as I can make out Charlie, Sinéad was practically the only girl you ever spoke to as a teenager.

I just shrugged my shoulders. How fascinated he was by this. I'd say he didn't even get to talk to one girl when he was a teenager. Fucking eyes on him waiting for me to say something. Then he goes,

—What do you think of that Charlie? Looking back on your teenage years now. What do you think of how you were as a teen-ager?

I just shrugged my shoulders again.

—Do you think you missed out on having normal relationships Charlie? Do you think you missed out?

I just goes,

—Yeah. I suppose.

He went asking me about how I was sleeping then and the usual stuff about my tablets and my dry mouth. I think I've done enough words for today. Holy shit I've done two thousand, one hundred and thirty-two. That'll make up for me doing nothing yesterday or the day before. Another couple of thousand before I see Dr Quinn next week will keep him happy.

I didn't write anything yesterday but I did over two thousand the day before anyhow. Had to have a big wash there earlier. I seen a rabbit in the middle of the road that was after being hit by a car. Was still alive. Panting he was. Easier for it to be dead. Hobbling off it was but I caught up with it and I smashed his head with a rock. Bang bang. Blood and brains splattered all over me. Wiped my face with my hands and my sleeve to take the blood off. Thought it was gone but then I could feel my skin harden and get all tight. And the smell of it and the taste of it all irony and butchery. On I goes and next thing Detective Crowley passes me on the road and stops and reverses and asks me how I am and I say fine and he says,

—Is that blood Charlie?

—Yeah.

—What's it from?

—A rabbit.

—Are you sure?

—Yeah.

—What did you do to it?

He made me hop in to the car and I'd to tell him where the rabbit was and he drove there to check that the rabbit existed.

Took a minute to find it cos I was after kicking it over to the ditch. He stood over it and looked at the rabbit and looked at me and looked at the rabbit again. Then he dropped me home. Washed and washed and washed but it never went away. Have to be careful you don't get spattered with blood. There's a lot more blood behind skin than you'd think. 'Course when I was finished my washing Detective Crowley was still hanging around downstairs.

Detective Crowley was a disaster. A thick-looking fucker if ever you seen one. Big fat cabbage and bacon head up on him. He was on the missing list one time twenty odd years ago. He'd told his wife he was at a detectives' conference for a couple of nights up the country. She contacted his colleagues after she'd been called to the hospital because she couldn't contact him. She found out then that there was no conference. When Detective Crowley rang home later that evening from the so-called conference, his sister-in-law told him the news. That the whole country was looking for him. That his wife needed him. That their four-year-old son had been knocked down. That they couldn't save him in Cork University Hospital.

That was years ago now. First funeral I remember. He was in school with us in Ballyronan. In junior infants class. His hair was dark brown. His coffin was white. He was five I suppose. Shane, his name was. They didn't have any other kids. Detective Crowley's wife was never the same. They say he never fooled around on her again. Not that it mattered much to her now I suppose. My mother says she died with her son and her marriage. Still Detective Crowley and herself stayed together. Maybe she didn't have the energy to kick him out. Maybe she still loved him. Anyhow they were still together twenty odd years later.

Mother said Detective Crowley was fierce handsome back in the day. And how he used to be smartly turned out before his son got killed. Nowadays he looks like shit. There's a lot of him to dress though, size of a mountain he is. A fat wobbly mountain. They say they made him detective because they couldn't find a uniform to fit him any more. But of course he was a detective before he got fat. 'Course then someone would say that when Old Master Higgins got drunk below in the pub he said Crowley was the cleverest child he'd ever seen in forty years of teaching. That he'd begged his parents not to send him into the guards, that he'd be wasted in the guards. But the boy had an uncle a guard and that's all he ever wanted to be. He wasn't wasted in the guards anyhow.

Just wasn't clever enough to dress himself I suppose. He always wore a tie though. I'd say he had to. It looked like his mammy put it on him and he was after spending the last half hour trying to pull it off. They were the only house around that didn't have a television, himself and the wife.

—She do be reading books, my auntie said to my mother, with a face on her like she was after getting a smell of shit.

—She's deep, my mother said.

—God help us, my auntie said.

No wonder she's a bit fucking mental if all she does is be reading books. I'd go mental if I read four pages of one. One thing

Detective Crowley didn't find in my room was books. He was in there one time looking around.

Benign
Adj. 1. kindly; having a kind and gentle disposition or appearance 2. favourable; mild or favourable in effect 3. harmless; neutral or harmless in its effect or influence 4. *med.* not life-threatening; not a threat to life or long-term health, especially by being non-cancerous [14thC. Via French *bènigne* from Latin *benignus* of uncertain origin: probably from, ultimately, *bene gunus*, literally 'well born', from *bene* 'well' + *-genus* 'born'.]

Detective Crowley was a benign sort of a fella. But he could've killed with the size of him. People didn't have much good to say about his wife though.

—Worst thing he ever done was marry that one anyhow. Fucking weirdo she is.

—Yera that one is away with the fairies.

—She had an uncle out in Macroom killed hisself you know. Pure sign of weak in a family. Pure sign of weak.

Detective Crowley saw something nice in her anyhow.

He spent a fair while trying to figure me out back along. He didn't know if I was to be protected by him or if he needed to protect people from me. I could see him wondering in his eyes and he talking to me. What to make of me. He got it right anyhow, as it all turned out. After my wash I could hear himself and the father talking below.

—Ah things have settled down a lot. He's good really. Considering. Gets upset now and again. Goes walking like you know. Down to the river and stuff. We worry a lot.

—'Course you do.

—What he might do you know.

—I'd say if he was going to, he'd have . . . you know by now.

—Hopefully anyway isn't it?

—That said, you can't ever be sure.

—He seems to be getting on well with this Dr Quinn anyhow.

—Isn't that great.

—He'd a rocky start with him now like. He's after opening up a small bit now though like you know. You see he wouldn't talk about all that happened like. Not even to Dr Quinn.

—Really?

—Ah but sure, that's the kind he is. He was like that ever. Even as a child like, you know. Preferred to be away in his own world. Sinéad and James were the only people he'd ever talk to sure really like you know. And that doesn't look like changing much.

—But he's still meeting Dr Quinn is he?

—He is. Dr Quinn came up with a way to get him to ah . . . to get him to like . . . to . . . process things like you know . . . without having to let anyone in close to him like you know?

—How so?

—He has him like . . . so it seems anyway like, even though I don't think even Dr Quinn has seen much of it like, but he's writing his story like you know.

—Dr Quinn is?

—No no, Charlie. He's after learning how to type and everything sure. Dr Quinn does it above in the hospital like. Runs kind of writing classes for like, the mental . . . like people with mental problems like you know. As a kind of therapy you see.

—By God.

—Seems to be after doing the trick for Charlie anyhow. 'Tis definitely bringing himself out of himself a bit.

—Jesus, that's great altogether.

—Now don't get me wrong now like. There's still times when he takes to the cot and he mightn't get out of bed for the bones of a week. Sometimes you can hear him typing in the middle of the night. A lot of the time, nothing though. Might go for a walk before dawn and then he'd disappear back to bed when the rest of us are up and about. But Christ he's a million times better than he was a year ago like you know. Million times better.

—Is he working any bit?

—No. Dr Quinn doesn't think he's ready yet but I think 'twould be the best thing for him to be honest. Even a day picking spuds or something.

—I suppose the doctors know best.

—I suppose they do. He's probably washed up now I'd say. Will I give him a shout?

—Ah sure do, 'twould be nice to say bye to him.

The father shouted up for me. He didn't really need to. I was sitting at the top of the stairs listening to them. I went back into my room to answer.

—Yeah?

—Come down.

—Ha?

—Come down.

—Ha? For what?

—Come down and thank Detective Crowley for sorting you out today and giving you the lift home.

—Ha?

—Come down.

I went down.

—All cleaned up Charlie?

—Yeah.

—Good man, good man. Your father tells me you're doing great anyway.

—Yeah.

—And you're doing a bit of writing are you?

—Yeah.

—That's great. And you're up and about a bit now and stuff.

—Yeah.

The father goes then,

—Listen, I'm going to make a cup of tea. You'll have a cup?

—I will.

—Charlie you'll have some too will you?

—Yeah.

Out went the father.

—Your father tells me you're getting on great with Dr Quinn.

—Yeah.

—You're writing about all the stuff you've been through are you?

—Yeah . . . small bits only.

—Still . . . I think it's a great idea . . . You still have hard days your father tells me. Is it an dubh?

—Yeah . . . I suppose.

—Are you on tablets?

—Yeah. Father keeps them. Leaves a dose out for me like.

—I met Frank Deasy in court the other day.

Frank Deasy is my lawyer. He helped me during the trial.

—He was asking about you.

—Yeah.

—He's very busy since the case. Says he's a lot busier . . . after being on the telly and all. You know the way fellas are.

—Yeah.

—Like to feel important. Having a lawyer that was on the telly and all. You know . . .

—Yeah.

—It's good to see you again Charlie. I think about how you're doing a lot. You went through a lot.

—Yeah.

—Yeah.

We sat there and listened to the sound of my father fighting with the kitchen over a few cups of tea.

Then Detective Crowley said,

—My wife you know . . . Veronica . . . she's not well. Gone back again she is.

—Yeah.

—She's not reading or anything these days.

—Yeah.

—I think maybe for her sake we should have left Ballyronan long ago. Away from the house. Away from where he was knocked down. Just away. It's like she can't let go. Or forget.

—Yeah. Dr Quinn maybe could help.

—Won't see him.

—Yeah.

—I try to cheer her up. Put on the radio like. Bit of pop music. Open the curtains. Say all the nice things we could be doing. She just lies there and stares into space. Ignores me. Sometimes all right she'll tell me to, 'Fuck off', but most of the time it's like she doesn't even hear me.

—Yeah.

—What could I do Charlie? Have you anything you could suggest to help her get out of it?

—No.

—OK.

—Sad music maybe. Slow, sad music might speak to her more.

—Jesus Christ . . . are you sure?

—No. But maybe . . . Yeah . . . make her feel not so alone maybe.

—Christ. She does love the music. Think I might try it. Do you think it will work?

—No. Not for a long time nothing'll work.

The father came in then with a tray of tea and biscuits. They talked about the football team and the budget and saying how they'll always take care of the big noises with all the money anyhow, whatever about the ordinary man on the street.

Words

That's eight hundred and sixty-two words. That's me done for today.

Piss

I'm just in from a piss. Listened to the mother and father from the top of the stairs for a bit. They were below in the kitchen. Heard him saying to the mother that he's not too sure about Dr Quinn and if all his old writing therapy is only a load of old mickey mouse codswallop. The mother says,

—I dunno.

And I could see her shrugging her shoulders even though I couldn't see her.

The father always just looks at me sometimes for a few seconds then goes back reading the paper or watching television. Seen him do that a million times out the corner of my eye. The mother understands me better cos she doesn't be trying to understand me. The mother takes me as I am. And as I'm not isn't it?

'Course the mother's big secret is that she can't read. She even fooled my father who was married to her before he realised that she used only be pretending to be reading her women's maga-zines or that she was reading the subtitles of the foreign films he took her to. I seen pictures of my mother when she was young. She was very pretty and she looks like she could definitely read and didn't look like a thick. She doesn't even know that I know she can't read. I used to watch her face all expressions and shock when she was reading my letters home long ago for being bold in school.

—Charlie. I'm surprised at you Charlie.

Even though the last thing she was was surprised.

—Wait 'til your father sees this. Won't be one bit happy Charlie.

She calls in to me sometimes when I'm writing. She knocks on the door and says can she come in and then when she's in it's clear as air that she has nothing to say and forgot to even think of something all the way up the stairs. Then she'll just say a blandness like,

—Have you washing?

—No.

—How are you feeling?

—Grand.

—Anyway come down if you want a snack or something. How's the writing going?

—Grand.

I'm not being mean. I'm fond of her but she calls in to me about ten times a day and her loneliness makes me feel sad about her and about the world isn't it? Remember one time on a school tour to Dublin I bought her a cheap Aretha Franklin tape. She made such a fuss over it I never got her anything ever again. It meant too much to her and that made me realise what an awful useless cunt I am.

I could say more about my family but it's not really part of the story. I've an older sister too and she's normal. She's married. When she heard I was writing the story for a book she said,

—You better not have me in it anyhow, Cha, or I'll break your face.

She calls me Cha. She moved away out of Ballyronan and I think it was cos of me cos I'm an embarrassment. She does love me but my existence mortifies her. She's a lot older than me. I was an accident. A bad accident. I was carnage. She calls a lot, my sister does. Her husband does be away a lot with work. She used to come up to my room when I was in the coma but awake.

—I really hope you're going to be OK Cha. Isn't the same without you around. Even if you never say anything.

She used to rub my head softly sometimes when she came up. She's kind of busy now though. She has one little girl of two and she's pregnant now again I think. Emily is her little girl. My niece.

The Story

I'm having difficulty figuring out how to start my story. Or where to start. Dr Quinn was on about characters and character development and plot and climax and all this. If the characters are the people, well I'm one. And I'm the narrator also. Then there's Sinéad. Then there's James. I'll mention others along the way, but that's the main three anyhow. The story is mainly about people. And the things they do to each other.

Music

Sometimes music used to get me so I had to stop whatever I was doing. Sometimes it was the words as well but most often it was just the music. Or the music and words together maybe too. I washed a whole car one time in the garage cos of a song. It wasn't even what the boss had asked me to do. He asked me to stack the gas cylinders but there was a song coming out of a car at the petrol pumps that I couldn't stop listening to and he explaining what he wanted me to do.

—Whose fucking car is that?

—Ha?

—What are you washing that fucking car for? Who owns it?

—You.

—I do not. That's a customer's fucking car. It's not for sale. Leave it alone. I told you to stack up them fucking gas cylinders. Jesus Christ.

The song I could hear at the petrol pumps was a Neil Young song and I told Sinéad and James about it and they learned it. This is the words of it. It's nice not to have to come up with all the words for my book anyhow. A thousand a day is torture.

_____

_____

_____

_____

_____

_____

_____

_____

_____

_____

_____

_____

Did you notice that there was nothing there instead of the words of the Neil Young song 'Out On The Weekend'? I'll explain why there was nothing there now.

I wanted to include the words of songs but Dr Quinn was talking to his lawyer friends and they said I'd have to pay the people who made up the songs millions to put the words of them in my book. That's a disaster and I'll tell you why it's a disaster now. It's important that you know the world of Sinéad and James in order to understand my story. And the world of Sinéad and James isn't just bridges and rivers and a castle and houses and roads and fields and rooms and places and people. It's songs too. Songs were part of their world just as much as anything else or maybe more than anything else. And I can't just draw a picture of a song and I can't just describe the words of them and I can't play them to you so that means you have to do it yourself.

And you might say the words aren't important. Well they are. Sinéad and James learned how to make songs from words. They carved and moulded them into verses and choruses. Sinéad scribbled the words of songs she loved everywhere. The backs of schoolbooks and her pencil case and her copies and her journals cos she had journals and she learned the form you see. The forms of songs and the form of songs. Practised it and learned it.

I'll mention the name of the songs cos the names of songs are free but you'll have to get the words of them yourself and write them in. I'll leave a space blank for you to do it like I did with Neil Young. And do it in neat handwriting so it doesn't look shit. I put in lines and all for you. And listen to the songs too. You'll like listening to them but writing in the words will be a pain in the hole but the words are important too cos they were a fairly big part of the brains of Sinéad and James cos most singing needs words. And any other sounds people sing are words too. Important words that don't mean anything except a feeling in you. But some songs I won't have to leave blank cos they're Sinéad and James' songs and they wouldn't take money off me for using them. Other famous songs I might be able to put in cos the people who wrote them are dead ages and money only bores the dead.

It Happened
It's an awful story and it's a true story. It's a sad story and it might make you cross and it might make you sad and it happened and there's people in it. And some of them are dead people now.

Time
Time is cruel.

Pissed Off
Sometimes people piss you off. You can either let it piss you off or not isn't it?

God
Most people believe in God. I never did, God help me.

Protagonist

I dunno who the protagonist is. Me or Sinéad I suppose. Or James maybe. I meant to ask Dr Quinn if there's an antagonist and protagonist in stories that are true, but I forgot. He writes for a hobby. Actually enjoys it like. Said I should write down the story. That it would be therapeutic. He runs writing workshops once a week in the nuthouse in Cork. Said I could come along if I wanted. I said no. Bad enough to be hanging around with loonies. But this crew would be nerds on top of that. Anyhow I'm not doing this for therapy I'm doing it for money. Hope to God it'll make me some. I need to get out of here.

Dr Quinn showed me some writing today from a fella in his writing class that he thought was good. This star pupil kept using the word as. As he looked at me from across the table, as the steam rose from the coffee, as he spoke about this good writer fella he had in his class, as he blinked every few seconds, as he spoke, as I listened, as he handed me this piece of writing that he thought was really very, very good, as he sat back down as the chair swivelled slightly, as he spoke to me again about the having to pay for the words of songs I wanted to put in my book situation, as he shook his head and said I should just forget about the song lyrics as he explained that people would find it boring reading song lyrics as I looked out the window and tried to imagine the kind of fucking cunts that wouldn't want to read the words of the songs that Sinéad and James loved and learned from, as the sun broke through the clouds and found a bit of the redbrick hospital wall that was the best thing about the miserable view from his window, as I thought of all the other depressed headwrecked patients of Dr Quinn who had to look out at that miserable view and try to feel good about themselves and the lives they have, as I breathed and continued to think different thoughts as Dr Quinn tried to make me think other thoughts, as I just nodded and looked out the window and continued with my own thoughts about the way things were as the sun fucked off again as Dr Quinn stared at me waiting for me to respond to what I hadn't listened to, as I said,

—Yeah.

—OK, then. Good. That's good. I'm happy with the way things are going Charlie. I have to say, I'm happy with your progress. Well done. How do you feel about it? Do you think you're making progress?

—Yeah.

This writer fella that Dr Quinn thought was great used loads of the LY words too. He used them generously and superfluously and copiously, all these fucking LY words. As he walked hurriedly to the bus stop, as he decided decisively not to get that bus which had arrived punctually, but to stroll happily and lazily over to the shopping centre indifferently and look around, as resignedly, he crossed the road, carefully, deciding to do nothing much for another hour as he waited patiently and lovingly for the next bus to come punctually or belatedly, it made no difference to him. Him being me. I just read some of this star pupil of Dr Quinn's fancy writing over at the shopping centre and then I threw it in the bin.

Talk To Ourselves

My cousin married a Frenchwoman. She loves the Irish but she says we talk to ourselves.

School

I found school hard at first. Rules drove me mad. Mad.

Objective

Adj. 1. free of bias; free of any bias or prejudice caused by personal feelings 2. based on facts; based on facts rather than thoughts or opinions 3. *philos.*; existing independently of the individual mind or perception [14thC. From medieval Latin *objuctum* 'thing presented (to the sight)', ultimately from Latin *obicere* 'to present, throw against', from *jacere* 'to throw'.]

Only humans could come up with a word like that. I mean for fuck sake. Objective. By bollicks. Who did they think they were kidding like? Themselves maybe.

Dictionary

I read the dictionary now. I meant to say that. Only book I ever read. Big thick ancient one we have at home. Only book I ever held in my hand that didn't have some fucking agenda. My book doesn't have one either. And words are better than music anyhow. You know where you are with words. Words don't take you over.

Book

I just looked at a book. I counted the words on one page and multiplied that number by the number on the last page. The answer was one hundred and twelve thousand, five hundred and sixty. And that wasn't even a big thick book. I haven't a hope of writing that much but I'll do as much as I can. I might take more photographs. I could fill a lot of the pages with photographs. Would you mind? Could show you exactly where stuff happened, like I did with where the body was found. I only have eleven thousand, one hundred and eleven words done at the moment. Long way to go. But I haven't really started telling my story yet so that's OK.

But the main problem is that I keep remembering things in the wrong order. Dr Quinn tells me yesterday after reading the bit I've done that I must write the story in the order that it happened. But my brain isn't in charge of what it remembers and when it decides to remember it. I told him I can't help remembering some bits sometimes. I think I can remember everything exactly right but just not in the right order. Like thinking about Sinéad sleeping.

I watched her sleeping. All was on was the telly in the room. Different coloured lights dancing around her face. Looked different and beautiful all the time. Dunno if you ever looked at the sea in the changing sky but it looked nothing like Sinéad asleep in front of the telly but my eyes liked looking at the vision just the same. Dinky was asleep on the couch. Snoozie was on the floor. I'll tell you who they are another time. But Sinéad was cradled in the arms of James, whose chest rose Sinéad softly with every breath. Snoozie with his big dopey head would start snoring every few minutes so I'd have to walk over and give him a light kick. He'd groan and turn his head.

I wondered what Sinéad was dreaming about. James maybe. But I hoped that maybe I made some appearance in there too. It's not that unlikely you know, no matter what people say. She was fond of me you know. Fair enough, I'm not sure what she really thought of me but I know it was a hell of a lot more than anyone had ever thought of me before or since. She knew I wasn't the gamallogue I let on to be. And she trusted me. Told me things she never even told James. 'You're a dark horse Charlie,' she'd say to me. 'But your secret is safe with me.' There was one of them children's shrink lads long ago reckoned I was definitely on the autistic spectrum, cos I wouldn't look at the big stupid eejit for long enough when he was talking to me. Anyhow, had a staring match with her one time so I did. With Sinéad. I won. She was useless.

See I shouldn't have remembered all that now cos that's near the end of my story or maybe the middle but not near the start. I should be remembering the first time I met Sinéad so that's what I'll do.

Court Transcripts

I haven't wrote a word in a very long time and Dr Quinn is cross with me cos he says I'm not interacting with people. As if I ever did. And I missed two appointments cos I went for a walk around the hospital instead. Seen people crying down near the intensive care unit. A young father was in an accident. Anyhow Dr Quinn wants me to write again and I don't want to but he said I won't get better if I don't face up to the things that happened.

Sometimes you don't want to think about some stuff. So you'll talk about anything else. I'm like that sometimes. I'm afraid of telling you what happens cos I still can't believe it myself and I don't want it to be true. Like when the stuff was on the papers. Makes it real to me. Cos I'm still kinda waiting to wake up and for it all to be a bad blah. I don't want to write it cos I'm afraid and I don't know what of. There's nothing else to be afraid of at this stage only myself and you can't be going around the place afraid of yourself. Can you? Anyhow I've lost my way so I'm just going to shut up and tell you what happened. Been trying to put it off long enough. Am I getting a bit giddy? Did you ever want to laugh at bad news? Someone dead and you laugh. No I'll shut up. I'll go out for one smoke and I'll continue with the story proper when I come back in. I'm sick of my own thoughts at this stage. Smoking is probably the only thing I was ever good at. When I come back I'll tell you about the first time ever I met Sinéad proper.

Sorry I never did go back to it actually that time last week. Was at Dr Quinn today again and he went mad altogether and says I must get on with the story cos he says I'm getting stuck. Today, for the first time I actually told him what I was really thinking about and he got annoyed with me.

—Just the child was on the news.

—What child?

—The one that died.

—How?

—Like . . . out walking with his father and his sister. And he goes out near a cliff-top and his father goes to him to stay back and the child all showoffy turns around and walks backwards and he smiling and the father warning him and doesn't the sod go from under him and the ladeen falls to his death.

—I heard about the child that fell to his death. An eight-year-old in Sligo. But that's all we know. That's all they said on the news Charlie. That's a little while back now Charlie.

—Mother and father were on about it. Was an article in the paper about what happened. He was doing the fool and the sod gave way under him and his father watched the shock on the ladeen's face and he disappearing down.

—Charlie. Why are you thinking about this?

—It's just what I was thinking about when you asked me.

—But what use is it? I'm sorry. What I mean to say is . . . everybody could get consumed thinking about these things all the time. We could all be thinking about these things all the time.

—So what?

—So what? But we don't. That's the point. We don't think about these things too much.

—So what?

—What use would be served Charlie? If everyone thought about that? It's pointless Charlie. Do you realise that? It gets us nowhere.

—So what?

—It's not healthy.

—So what?

—We must accept that bad things happen and move on.

—OK, I said.

But he wasn't one bit OK with me saying OK.

—It doesn't serve you thinking about that boy falling to his death.

—I'm not.

—But you were.

—I wasn't.

—You told me you were.

—I was only thinking about the split second.

—What?

—Like one sec is all.

—What?

—Split second. Just when like . . . he realised . . . regret like . . . and the unfairness like . . . and the father and the daughter watching . . . fucking pity like . . . couldn't help him then . . . split second . . . unfairness isn't it? . . . and regret . . . and pity . . . perfect like . . .

—What?

—Like. Perfect.

—Perfect?

—Like picture like.

—What?

—Just like . . . perfect split second if you could see it only. With the cliff and the rocks and the sea and the faces.

—What?

—That's the truth isn't it? Pulls the rug from under you. Or the earth. Out from under all of us and all our shit. Pure mean, isn't it?

—Charlie I'm going to be harsh with you now. This rambling and these kinds of thoughts have got you . . . if you just stick to the task Charlie. You were progressing so well before. The task is to write your story and process it. Weekly. Next week you need to have moved on in your story. You need to explain how you met Sinéad. Say who she was properly. Do the same with James. You're avoiding it. Then you must talk about the other people in the story. We call those secondary characters.

I said I wanted another shrink and he told me I'd have to go to Dublin and I said fine and he said enough. Then he goes out and he comes back in with a big box full of papers.

—Charlie I think these will help you face up to things more successfully at an emotional level.

He said it would make me introduce my characters properly because if I've to use the transcripts I can't run away from talking about them any longer. It'll get me to face things, he says. His own brother is some big shot lawyer in Dublin and he got them for him.

He started reading one of the court transcripts. The evidence of someone in the trial it was. And I remembered it cos I was there that day so I joined in from my memory. He stopped and read silently and I saying the words on the page cos I could remember what was said. He was kinda stunned.

—Quite astonishing actually. Quite astonishing.

He said I've the equivalent of a photographic memory for audio information. He asked me was I the same with music I heard. I said yeah.

—Quite extra-ordinary.

He said he'd do a bit of research on it, but he was sure this talent of mine was quite rare. Quite rare indeed Charlie. But anyhow the transcripts are handy for the bits I wasn't there for.

Dr Quinn can talk and talk so it's OK going to see him really most of the time. I just agree with whatever shit he's saying and that keeps him from upsetting the mother and father saying to them I'm not making progress or that I didn't turn up to the appointment. So now I have to read some of these pages to keep him away from the mother and father.

You see, I was a witness in a court case once in the Central Criminal Court in Dublin. The case went on for nearly four weeks.

So I'm to show ye some of the pages that matter to my story. The pages all look the same. There's a number on every line so you couldn't change anything after it was written. There's twenty-five lines on every page. I'm going to see if Dr Quinn can scan the pages for me. But I won't see him until next Tuesday so I'll come back to this shit next week.

It's next week now and Dr Quinn said he'll get his secretary to scan them in. I won't see him until next Tuesday again so bye until next week.

It's next week and I got the scans. This is what they look like.

18	caused her a great deal of sadness. At this stage I changed her medication
19	from sleeping tablets to anti-depressants.
20	MR. COLE: I see. What was she taking then?
21	MR. MOONEY: I put her on Prothiaden. It's a mood-lifter. Unfortunately
22	there's a lot of trial and error involved as what will work for one patient may
23	not work for another.
24	MR. COLE: I see. And did Prothiaden help her?
25	MR. MOONEY: No. Not in my estimation, no. Two months later I put her

Hovenden Recording Services

Dr Quinn's secretary made a bit of a bollicks of the scanning. I think she's too old to work the scanner. That's what it looked like. They're the wrong size and there's tonnes of them so I'll type out the important bits. It'll give me words to fill up the book with anyhow. Some parts of the story are rotten so the transcripts can tell them parts.

Anyhow the court wasn't like on telly inside but it was on the outside with the big old stone building with fifty steps leading up to it and the big stone pillars. But inside it looked all new and modern. Our courtroom was only about the size of a tennis court. Another thing that was like telly was the judge cos he was an old fella with a big fat face. But he talked like Irish people which wasn't like the telly. He was up highest all on his own. Up behind him on the wall was a bronze plaque with a harp on it and Éire written under it. Éire is Irish for Ireland. The harp is a symbol of Ireland. Used to be on all the coins before we got European money called euros. When someone tossed a coin they said head or harp. They still say it. Actually the harp is still on the euro coins, I just checked. It's the heads that are different. No heads any more. Just a little map of Europe instead of someone's head. Maybe soon we'll be saying map or harp instead of head or harp. Guinness use the harp sign too but it's facing the other way cos drunks are on the wrong side of the law.

Anyhow beneath the judge then there were two people who had computers in front of them. A man who was the registrar of the court. And his helper. A nice-looking young woman. Then at the next level down there was the lawyers. The lawyers had the silly wigs on and all. Grey curly wigs with two rats' tails hanging down the back in the middle. They had black gowns on as well. One crowd of lawyers on the left side, the others on the right. They had two rows of seats. Then there was four rows of seats behind them. But there was a three-foot wall down the middle of this section. The accused was to the left side surrounded by eight guards. On the right side then you had the victim's family. There were a few guards with them too but only a few. Some journalists were in that section as well. Then behind that section was the public and the rest of the journalists. And a few guards. Nice easy job for the guards when they're in a court case isn't it? At least when they're not giving evidence.

The jury then have their own section. They're at the same height level as the registrar and his helper but the jury were over at the side. Up at the front of the courtroom at the right-hand side in two rows of six. Eight women, four men. I was thinking of saying what they looked like and all that but it would be boring. They were all ages and one woman used to put her finger through a tissue and pick her nose making it look like she was only wiping it. She was old enough too. And scrawny. One of the men was about forty and had long greasy hair tied back in a ponytail with streaks of grey in it and I'd say the court case wasn't keeping him from much of a job. I could describe a few more but it just isn't interesting is it? Maybe the woman who was always looking up at the skylight and biting her fingernails but no, not really that interesting.

They'd have only seen the left side of the judge's face. Didn't matter anyhow, was exact same as his right side. Fat and pink and old. And they only saw the side of the lawyers' faces too, except if the lawyers were talking to them. But whatever witness was in the stand they'd have been facing the jury. So the jury would see all of the witnesses' faces. So the lawyers were talking to a witness who was never facing them. The witnesses had to turn their heads to the side to look at them. Sometimes that made them seem snotty even if they weren't. Like they couldn't be bothered listening to the lawyer or something or like they were bored of him. I didn't say him or her cos all the lawyers that were asking questions or talking in the court were hims.

Anyhow the court case wasn't for a long time. Just be knowing that the court case is talking about stuff that happened a few years ago.

Anyhow so back to Sinéad and I meeting her first. Dr Quinn says to me to use the first bit of my evidence. That would introduce her for me and get me started. He showed me how to make the writing look like typewriter writing and all. Seen a picture of his family when I went around to see his computer and he showing me how to change the look of the type. He has a wife and two daughters around twenty. They all looked fierce tanned and happy and their teeth were fierce white.

My Evidence

—Charlie, do you believe in God?

  —Yeah.

  —Do you know what being under oath is?

  —Yeah.

  —Could you tell me what it means?

  —Yeah.

—Will you tell me now then, please?

—Yeah. It means God is watching and you have to tell the truth.

—OK. That'll do. Thank you Charlie. OK, swear him in now then please.

—Do you swear to tell the truth, the whole truth and nothing but the truth, as God is your witness?

—Yeah.

—Say, 'I do', Charlie.

—I do.

—OK, proceed. Be seated, Charlie. You can sit down now, Charlie.

—Charlie.

—Ha?

—Were you friendly with Sinéad?

—Yeah.

—When did you start to be friendly with her?

—When I was small long ago.

—Were you in primary school? In school in Ballyronan, is it?

—Yeah.

—Do you remember how you became friendly with her?

—Yeah.

—Could you tell me about it?

—Yeah. She started talking to me.

—Go on . . .

—She started talking to me up in my tree.

—In your tree?

—Yeah. I used to climb up on a tree during lunchtime and one day she come over and talked to me.

—Was she kind to you?

—Yeah.

—You liked her, did you?

—Yeah.

—Were you very fond of her?

—Objection . . . leading.

—Sustained. Rephrase.

—How fond of her were you?

—Fierce fond of her.

Problem with the transcripts is that you only get what the people said. But people don't always say what happened. Not all of it anyhow. And not the true version. Especially in court cases. But I'll tell you in my book isn't it? And transcripts don't show you the look on people's faces or the tone in their voice or when people murmured or shifted in their seats.

Anyhow back to Sinéad and I meeting her first. I was very small. She was even smaller. Mrs Fatty Fitzhenry was huge. I seen Sinéad and looked at her and watched her times before this but this is the day I met her. She was new in the school. It was senior infants class. That means we were five or six. I was seven cos I was kept back one year to do junior infants all over again cos of my behaviour troubles.

I was in trouble with Mrs Fitzhenry a million times but this one time sticks out in my mind cos it made me meet Sinéad. I tore Anthony Murphy's jumper by accident eejiting around in the queue to go back into the classroom after lunchtime.

—Is this the kind of carry on we can expect in Ballyronan Primary School? In a nice area like this? You wouldn't get the likes of you in a school for gypsies. Thugs like you tearing the clothes of decent children? And you've your poor mother and father's hearts broken with the carry on you have. Decent hard-working honest to God people and look at the son they have? A tearaway. And your sister and your cousins went through this school. And never an ounce of trouble from a single one of them. Lovely people, the whole lot of them. And then there's you. Where in the name of God did you come out of at all? A thundering ruffian. You don't care about your schoolwork and you don't care about the other children. Do you care about anything? Or anyone?

Her big long nose was inches from my face and her spit was spraying on me. I knew she was best friends with Anthony Murphy's mother. I seen them go walking together in the evenings and they were in charge of the choir in Mass too, the two of them. I felt like boxing her in the face but I didn't want her to stop. I'd never seen anything like this before. I gave her a little smirk to see if I could get her head to explode.

—Are you smiling? My God. Do you think this is funny? You may have your learning problems but plenty of boys and girls have learning problems too and they don't go around being the greatest little brat that God ever put life into. Your poor parents. What in the name of the good Lord will you amount to at all at all? Well? I'll tell you. Nothing! That's what you'll amount to. Anthony will get his jumper fixed. And he'll do very well in life. But will you? You'd want to get your mind fixed first you little tearaway brat.

The nostrils were flaring and she was after going the colour purple.

—Miss.

—Sit down and don't interrupt.

It wasn't me that was after interrupting.

—Miss.

—I said sit down!

—Miss you shouldn't say those things.

—Sit down I said.

—No miss. I don't think you should say those hurtful things to Charlie.

—Sit down.

—It's not right for you to talk like that to him. Those things you said could hurt his feelings.

She went down and marched the little girl out of the room and stood her facing the wall in the corridor. When she came in she was out of breath. She said,

—Charlie McCarthy get back down to your seat out of my sight.

In my seat afterwards thinking about all the things she said to me. That's when the tears started rolling down my face. They all went on with their lessons. Every once in a while someone would turn around for a look. I'd pull a face at them or mouth at them to fuck off or I'd kill them. At small break I sat under the oak tree and scratched the earth with a stick. Then I heard a girl's voice that I recognised. It was the girl that spoke up for me.

—Don't be sad. I think you're a nice boy, Mrs Fitzhenry was wrong to say them things.

I looked up at her and she smiled a little to me and then she turned around and walked away. Sinéad.

She was only five or six then. About a year later when we'd a different teacher Mrs O'Riordan Sinéad arrived in the door of the classroom in the morning and she half an hour late about. She was all out of breath and her hair was a mess and her face was white and she'd no tie on and she'd runners on her feet instead of shoes and she had no socks on. Everyone in the class turned around and stared at her. Mrs O'Riordan asked her if she was OK. Sinéad said yeah and started crying. Then Mrs O'Riordan walked back and guided her back out of the classroom. She stayed with her and Master Coughlan came in to us instead. We didn't see Sinéad until small break. She stood alone at the gable wall. Leaning against it she was with one knee bent so the sole of her runner was flat against the bottom of the wall. None of the girls went over to her. I went over to her. I asked was she OK and she nodded that she was. Her eyes were puffy from crying. She took a deep breath every now and again and just looked at something far away or maybe at nothing I'm not sure. Then she'd look at something or nothing for a bit in the other direction. She squinted a bit as if the sun was in her eyes every now and again too but there was no sun only clouds. I wanted to be superman and pick her up and fly her away. Anyhow it wasn't too long after that when James arrived.

I'm going for a walk now.

I went for a walk that time earlier on. I went down along the river. I was sitting on the river bank. A couple who live up in the new houses passed me. They were out for a walk. I could hear the woman saying to the man as they came closer,

—I think he's upset.

The man didn't want to know. 'So what?' he said. 'I'm sure he'd prefer to be left alone.'

—Do you know who it is? It's the boy from the

—Yes I know. Just leave it.

Then they walked passed me. 'Hiya,' said the man. I said 'Hi,' back. My voice squeaked a bit on account of my crying. They walked on anyway. Next thing I hear footsteps coming up behind me and the man saying, 'Fuck sake,' under his breath.

—I know you.

It was the woman.

—You're the boy from . . . her friend . . . isn't that who you are? Charlie, that's your name isn't it? You poor fellow. Is that why you're crying?

She put her arm on my shoulder.

—Is that why you're crying?

—Yeah.

My words barely squeezed out of me, whatever horrible place they were coming up from. Place of horrors. I didn't tell her all the stuff that I was thinking of. All the stuff that I knew. All the stuff that I'll keep trying to tell you. If my brain will let me. Little bit at a time, Dr Quinn says. Small steps. Instead I said to this woman,

—I'm just a bit lonesome today, that's all.

She asked her husband if he'd a clean hankie. He took a fabric one out of his pocket and looked at it for a second before handing it to his wife, who gave it to me. He said,

—Go on, use it, I've tonnes of them.

Just as well he did cos I was destroyed with tears and snots and your one's pity was only after making me worse. I started doing that hiccup crying. You know the one. Makes it hard to talk cos you can't catch your breath and your shoulders jump like you're being touched with a cattle-prod. I thought it only happened to kids but fuck it didn't I get a right fit of the hiccup crying myself after this one put her arm around me.

Before Sinéad

It's not that I can't remember my life before Sinéad. I can. But there's nothing to say. I may as well have been dead or never born. I never spoke to anyone except maybe a small bit at home if they asked me a question that I could answer. Like,

—Was school OK today Charlie?

—Yeah.

—Charlie will you come down for your dinner pet?

—Yeah.

—Charlie are you coming to the match?

—Yeah.

So when I wasn't answering questions or at a match with my father I just watched television and when I wasn't watching television I just put on my mother's records and tapes in the sitting room. Sometimes I'd go down to the shop with my mother and everyone would be saying hello to me cos it's nice to say hello to fellas like me.

—Hello Charlie.

—Hello.

—How are you doing Charlie boy?

—Hello.

—Helping mammy with the shopping Charlie?

—Yeah.

—Good man.

And then at night time I'd go to bed. And then the next morning I'd go to school and it would just go on like that the whole time. Not much to say about the time before Sinéad.

But then Sinéad was my friend and it was different then. Cos even when I wasn't with her I had her to be thinking about. I remember thinking God was lucky I didn't believe in him, the abuse I'd give him. I'd really have hated him. Cos I knew that some day Sinéad would have to die, same as everybody else and that was the wrongest unfairest meanest thing ever. One time Sinéad goes that if she ever died she'd like Katell Keineg singing 'The Gulf of Araby'. I wish I never thought of that now. Or the words of it. Forget about that. Cunt of a song. I'm going for a walk.

At lunchtime in school I used to climb up on the big oak tree at the top end of the slopey football pitch out the back of the school and Sinéad used to come over. She'd stand under the tree. Or sit down if the grass was dry. Sometimes she'd sing. There'd be no one to hear way up by the oak tree only myself and the tree.

—What do you think of that Charlie?

—It was nice.

—Do you like my voice?

—I do. I think your voice is fierce nice.

One day I brought her in a record for her to listen to. Roy Orbison it was. She said they'd no record player at home. I brought her in a tape of Elvis Presley. She said they'd no tape player at home either.

—No Charlie. I'm not taking gifts from you OK?

They weren't gifts anyhow. It was no big deal. I just wanted her to have them. To have something I gave to her. At home. In her own room. Next to her even and she sleeping. And it to be music. And if she was listening to Elvis or Roy Orbison she might think of me. Music kind of hypnotised Sinéad.

Like the time of her Holy Communion. That's when Catholics receive the body of Christ for the first time. It happens when you're in first class, so she'd have been six or seven. I got my Holy Communion when I was eight though cos Father Scully didn't think I knew my catechism. Who made you? God made me. Who is God? God is the creator of Heaven and Earth and of all things. Why did God make you? God made me to show His goodness and to make me happy with Him in Heaven. What does God know? God knows sweet fuck all cos he doesn't even exist. A fly knows more. Anyhow all the girls were in white dresses and Sinéad was too except she had on a red coat over it that she forgot to take off in the church. Anyhow up they all went about three-quarters way into the Mass. Up to the altar in a line. The boys on the left, the girls on the right. The boys in suits like small little car salesmen and the girls like baby brides. While they were going up someone started playing 'Ag Críost An Síol' on the violin cos the children couldn't be singing then in case the body of Christ would fall out of their mouths. I turned around to see the person playing it up on the balcony. A woman it was. She was standing in front of the big window so the bright grey clouds made a black silhouette out of her. A magic shadow making this sound. Made the church same as a ship. Or a spaceship. Gliding or something.

After a bit I turned around again to see them all getting their Holy Communion for the first time. Then I seen Sinéad in her red coat still in her seat by the wall and she looking back up at the balcony where this music was coming from. Next thing they all starts coming back in a lovely neat line with their hands joined in prayer at the breastbone, fingers pointing up to the heavens like they were taught. And Mrs O'Riordan's lips like she was sucking up a string of spaghetti and her nostrils flared like she just got a whiff of a terrible stink but wanted another sniff to see if 'twas really that bad and her eyes opened wide and they darting from child to child making sure that they'd all be a credit to her in front of the whole parish and not disgrace her in front of the whole parish. Next thing Mrs O'Riordan sees poor Sinéad. Or poor Mrs O'Riordan sees Sinéad. Or poor Mrs O'Riordan sees poor Sinéad. Sinéad was in her own world facing the back of the church looking at the violinist up on the balcony. Mrs O'Riordan closed her eyes fierce tight for a second and turned around and walked back to the altar to call the priest back for to give one more child the bloody body of Christ. The priest came and stood holding the chalice while Mrs O'Riordan went back to Sinéad with her head tilted forward and to the side like Father Scully was after hitting her on the back of her head. She wore a smile like she'd a pain and a face on her as red as Sinéad's coat. She ushered Sinéad off up and sat back down. Couldn't see Mrs O'Riordan's face any more now but I'd say it was very red cos her two ears were. Very. Anyhow she didn't scream, 'Fuck this shit,' and her head didn't explode. It stayed still, just tilted forward still and a little to the right side. Sinéad was less fazed by her lonely journey up to Father Scully. She didn't look at Mrs O'Riordan on her way back, just up at the moving outline of the violin player up in the balcony where the music was coming from. James didn't even know her then. But the next year he did. Cos they were eight when they met.

Sound

The sound of them was how they met. This one day she never came over to me at the oak tree out on the school field. I was watching a dog all serious watching nothing the stupid way they do. I was thinking about Sinéad and if she was taken home lunchtime or what and I was hoping she was feeling happy wherever she was. Or maybe the other girls were being nice to her and letting her play with them. One girl used to be nice to her that time. She was called Jane. She's still called Jane today and she's all grown up and working and driving and going shopping and going on holidays.

See Sinéad didn't start school in Ballyronan. She started in another school three miles away and only moved to Ballyronan school when they got the council house in the village. She didn't get invited to birthday parties or anything a lot of the time. Jane did invite her. Jane was nice to her. Anyhow I was up on the tree thinking all this and next thing I hear her. Thought I was only imagining hearing her cos that used to happen the whole time. But no I was hearing her proper. She was singing her favourite song. She was at the back corner of the school where the big old smelly oil tank was where no one could hear her sing. I closed my eyes so I could concentrate on trying to hear her instead of the fucking lads shouting for the ball. It was the frog song from the telly she was singing. Paul McCartney wrote it. I know that now. I didn't know it then. You can write out the words of it here but you'll never hear Sinéad's young voice singing it in the far off the way I did.

'We All Stand Together'

_____

_____

_____

_____

_____

_____

_____

_____

_____

_____

_____

_____

So I was listening away anyhow. And next thing I hear a toad. I looked over and around the corner of the school from Sinéad I seen this new boy and he leaning on the windowsill singing the harmony part. The toad's part and he putting on a big deep voice.

Bong bong bong

Bong bong bong

Bong bong bong bong bong

Bong bong bong

Bong bong bong

Bong bong bong bong bong

If Paul McCartney charges me for that bit he's only a cunt. Bong is only one word and it's not even a word really. Anyhow Sinéad kept on singing her bit and started to walk towards the voice she was singing with. The new boy walked towards the voice he was singing with too. Their duet made a triangle with the corner of the school. The triangle got smaller with each step they took. They were just finished and then they met face to face at the corner. The boy said something. Probably hello. Sinéad said something back. Probably hi. They smiled at each other. I could see the smiles.

—James. James.

It was Master Coughlan roaring from the middle of the field.

—Are you playing or not?

—I don't know the rules sir.

—Get over here.

James looked back and gave a small smile and said something to her with the look in his eyes. He walked back on to the field of play. Sinéad just stood there looking at him. James kept looking back at her too. Sinéad came over to me then and it was never the same again. She was happier. Million times happier isn't it? That's the truth and I said I'd tell the truth always.

I Seen Sinéad Cry

I seen Sinéad cry times. Mostly in her life she looked happy. This was a time she cried though. Herself and James were always in the same room in primary school. Our class was small. Seventeen students. Most classes were nearly thirty. I think our little class were all conceived the year Dallas was on the telly. The whole parish was too busy watching it. And wondering who shot JR. Instead of making babies. Anyhow that meant that our class was sometimes split up into two different rooms cos the school didn't have enough teachers to be devoting one whole teacher to seventeen kids. In fifth class for example the clever ones were put up with sixth class and the rest were put in with fourth class. This was the year they separated Sinéad and James. And it wasn't cos one of them was thick and one of them was clever. It was cos they thought it was unhealthy for them to be so attached to each other. So that's what they done. James was in with Master Coughlan. I was in there too cos Master Coughlan wanted to keep an eye on me. Sinéad was in with Ms O'Connell.

—James what did you get for number six? . . . Don't have the day long James. Number six, what answer did you get? If I've to come down to you now there'll be trouble . . . Number six, what answer did you get? . . . Right!

Master Coughlan with a big red head up on him stormed down to where James was sitting.

—Your copy book isn't even open. Or your book.

He picked up his copy book.

—You've no work done. What's the meaning of this? On strike are we? Right.

He picked up James hard by the arm and marched him out of the room.

—You'll stand there now boyeen until you get a bit of sense. Understand?

No answer. Master Coughlan came in and started back to the lessons all smug. About half an hour later we were doing History. Someone was trying to read our history text-book.

—In. The. After. In the after. Mass.

—Math. In the aftermath.

—In the aftermath. Of. The. Kive. Kiv.

—Civil.

—Civil. War. Indie. Indie. Indipat . . . I'm stumped sir.

—Sorry. Independence. In the aftermath of the Civil War Independence seemed less a priority to Jesus Sweet Suffering Christ.

Master Coughlan was after getting stumped himself. He was looking out the window. Out at the tarmac yard which amounted to one basketball court. He was looking out at the very middle of the basketball court. The centre circle. Where James and Sinéad sat facing each other. Master Coughlan marched out. Dinky hushed up the room so we could hear what he was saying to them through the open windows.

—What in God's name is the meaning of this? What are you doing out of class Sinéad?

—Ms O'Connell sent me out to the corridor for not doing my lessons sir.

—And what has you out here in the yard?

—I wanted to be with James.

—And how did you know James was out here? . . . Well?

—I dunno. I just thought he might be out there if I went out.

—Jesus tonight, never in my life. Sure that doesn't make any sense. Are ye on strike or what?

James spoke then.

—We just want to be in the same room sir. We don't mean any harm. We just need to be together.

—My dear boy you've a bit of growing up to do yet before you'll be needing the company of any girl.

—I don't need any girl. Just Sinéad.

—Get on your feet now, both of you.

They got up. He grabbed James by the arm and led him away, telling Sinéad to go back to the corridor outside her classroom. She did.

Master Coughlan dug his heels in. Their parents were called in. Neither James' or Sinéad's parents were too bothered about their close friendship. They'd gotten used to it. It was a normal part of life. James' parents liked Sinéad and Sinéad's parents never knew much about where she'd be or who she'd be with anyhow. But Master Coughlan was adamant. The school could never yield to a demand like this. The school's authority must be upheld. It was decided that they wouldn't be allowed to hang around together after school or at the weekends. James' parents didn't have the will to enforce this on either of them. Fact is they'd grown to love Sinéad like a daughter. Sinéad's parents didn't really care. That time the Kents was like a free babysitter for them.

So now Sinéad and James were mute as myself in school. Things came to a head then when Father Scully came on one of his monthly visits to hear the choir practise with no Sinéad and watch the boys practise football at lunchtime with no James. Could see Master Coughlan and Father Scully having it out over on the sideline out of earshot of the kids.

In Ireland the parish priest is in charge of the primary schools in his parish. They're in charge of hiring teachers as well. He was related in some way or other to Master Coughlan so he got him the job in the school. But there was no way he was going to go to the Ecumenical Choir Celebration in Cork with a shit choir like they had without Sinéad, let alone watch his school get hammered in the football school blitz without James at midfield. Next morning Sinéad and James were both in Master Coughlan's class along with myself. They had to write out a hundred lines. Easiest lines that were ever wrote by school children.

The colour was back in their faces, Sinéad's and James'. The colour was gone from Master Coughlan's but he wasn't long getting fairly fond of the idea of having Sinéad in the class anyhow. Joy as she was to teach and listen to and watch her body and mind grow before your eyes. We were all a big happy family then with Master Coughlan.

Earache

Jesus I think I'm getting an earache. I've the sheet from my bed wrapped around my neck now and it feels better. Less drafty. It's half four in the morning.

Headaches

I gets savage headaches. Pounding at my brain coming and going like a siren. And I used to get pains in my stomach. That was gastritis. I used to cough blood sometimes. Black stuff. Never thought it was blood until I brought a cup-full into the doctor after she told me to. She stuck a bit of paper in it and told me it was blood. I got tablets that took the pain away. There's tigers in a zoo too have gastritis so bad they're dying of it and it's only the ones in the zoos ever get it. I watch stuff about animals and humans on the telly now sometimes. There was two small kids living in a tribe in some jungle. A girl and a boy and they were feeding their grand-parents. Their grandparents were two crows now. The boy said the big one is granddad. They flew off then and the girl and the boy called after them,

—Bye grandma.

—Bye granddad.

Dr Quinn asked me did I have pains in my head or my tummy before the things that happened. I said no and he just stayed looking at me saying nothing. I think he might have fallen asleep for a few seconds with his eyes open.

Dinky and Teesh

Dinky and Teesh are central to my story but I don't want to talk about them two pricks now.

Religion

At twelve o'clock the Angelus bell would ring out from the church across the road and with the will of Christ we'd drop our pens and put away our sums or Irish books or English readers or whatever horrible shit we'd be at and stand and say the Angelus. Everyone got a turn to lead the prayer.

—The angel of the Lord declared unto Mary.

—And she conceived of the Holy Spirit.

Then we'd sit down and have a doss talking about how to be good for half an hour until lunchtime. I asked Master Coughlan once in religion class if maybe the Protestants could be right and we could be wrong. He said no.

Protestants

So Ballyronan was bigger than Newport or Mullinahone. Once upon a time. That's why the Protestants came here the time of the Plantations. There was a ford at the river. This was a shallow place where people could cross the river before bridges were invented. People came from far and wide to do business at Ballyronan. Goods of all kinds crossed the river at Ballyronan. And there was this small island in the middle of the river at the ford. The island belonged to Ronan because the townland near the ford is called Innishronan. The Irish for it is Inis Rónáin, Ronan's Island. The Irish for Ballyronan is Baile Rónáin and that means Ronan's place. When the English came they changed the names. This small island can be seen to this day and when the tide is low it is a favourite spot for the fishermen. And then there's Dunronan Castle. Old Master Higgins taught us the poem.

Where the Bannow swiftly flowing meets the Crandon's rapid tide,
The waters, ere they mingle, wash the Castle's rugged side,

Whose ivied walls and ruined tower still beautiful and grand,
Sad remnants of the greatness of our once proud native land.

That's only one verse. There was millions. Old Master Higgins told us the story of the king. Or chief as the kings were known in Ireland. The Irish for chief is Taoiseach and that's what we call the prime minister of Ireland nowadays. We like to hang on to things like that to remind us that we're different to them English pricks across the water. Anyway he told us about this chief of Dunronan Castle who made this competition for the men. The prize was the princess's hand in marriage. But the princess didn't want a competition as she was already in love with a grand lad from the area. But the father insisted that the competition went ahead. And the competition was this. The first man to climb the castle with a rose and to give the rose to the princess at the top would be allowed to marry the princess. The fella she was in love with anyway was winning hands down and he was about to hand over the rose to his sweetheart at the very top only the dopey bollics fell to his death. The princess was having none of that so over she went too down down down splat stone dead.

That Dunronan Castle story was the saddest bastard of a thing to happen in Ballyronan until my friends Sinéad and James came along. That Dunronan story is supposed to be true but my story about Sinéad and James is truer cos I was there and I seen it all happen in front of my own two eyes.

There was the posh school for Protestants and rich Catholics who wanted to be like them in Four Crosses, but his parents felt it would be nicer for him to know and make friends with the kids of

Ballyronan, cos that's where he lived. He didn't have to say the Angelus at twelve o'clock. Or any of the other prayers at morning and afternoon but was part of the religion class all right cos that was only about Jesus and being good and the Protestants were all for Jesus and being good as well.

James was the first Protestant that most of us had come across. His father and mother were Mr and Mrs Kent. They had moved home from Dublin to restore the ruin of Kent Castle which had been handed down to them through the generations.

There's a big wood around Kent Castle and 'twas there we all spent many a summer killing Indians and other baddies and making bows and arrows. There was Sinéad, James, me, Dinky and Racey and sometimes Gregory, Master Coughlan's son who was only let out sometimes cos he was the whole time learning violin and Irish dancing and sailing and elocution lessons and every kind of thing you ever heard of and anyhow he was the whole time falling and cutting his knees and crying. It got even better then when the Kents started doing up the castle. The castle was theirs which meant it was ours for exploring and killing baddies. Mostly the girls were Indian maidens or white girls captured by the Indians that needed to be rescued. Mostly I was just a prisoner. Or a dead body. Or an Indian they captured who couldn't speak English. Or other times I just climbed up on the scaffolding or up on a tree and watched them all play and fight and play again. Then when the tennis court was made we played that too. And there was a basketball net on one end of it. Sinéad loved the tennis best cos she was quick on her feet. She was as good as Dinky but not as good as James. Racey was not sporty.

She wouldn't ask the score, she'd ask how long more. In doubles matches it was Sinéad and Dinky against James and Racey but James always won and he'd be winking at Sinéad when Dinky would have tears in his eyes and fling his racket at the wire at the end of a match. James wasn't being mean, it was just to calm Sinéad down cos Dinky's temper used to frighten her. Dinky used to get so mad at himself you never saw anything like it. You'd see the marks on his leg when he hit himself with the racket sometimes. Sometimes Sinéad would go over and hold the racket to try and stop him.

—Stupid, stupid, stupid, stupid, stupid, he'd say and he belting himself with the racket every time.

James' mother was a Catholic from Dublin and her brother had played football for Dublin but she lost her religion and became a pagan so she married a Protestant. You'd see her in the shop some-times or out walking with James' father and she like a hobo with paint all over her. That's what she did. She painted. Morning noon and blah. She wore baggy trousers that were more like curtains. And she was plump.

There was a farmer once bought a horse off a tinker and when the farmer got the horse home and let it out of the trailor the horse took off and ran full speed straight into a wall and dropped dead. The farmer went back and found the tinker and goes,

—You rotten scoundrel, you sold me a blind horse.

—That horse wasn't blind at all, says the tinker, it just didn't give a fuck.

If there was anyone else in Ballyronan bar myself who didn't give a fuck it might have been James' mother. Only other thing about her was that she loved hugging people. She used to always hug me and Sinéad when we'd call up and she was hugging James' father the whole time and he'd say,

—Watch the paint dear.

—Yera whisht boy and give me an old squeeze, she'd say. We'll be dead long enough.

She had an exhibition sale one time in the hall. I helped James and his father bringing the paintings down. Thirty-six of them. And I helped them bring them back too afterwards. Still thirty-six of them. The paintings just baffled most people as to how anyone would have the cheek to ask someone to pay money for them. And they were called things like, Afterwards and Few and she had a one called Missing too. She got cross with James' father for not knowing which way was the right way up when we were hanging them.

She adored Sinéad. Sinéad was good at art but that wasn't why she adored her. She just adored her. And Sinéad loved her too.

One time there was this nun came to the school and she collecting money for some art gallery she was trying to set up in Africa. But she seen Sinéad's paintings and wanted to buy some but Sinéad was very embarrassed and went all red and said she couldn't cos they were going to be album covers. The nun was nice and said that was fantastic and asked if Sinéad would do one for her like the one that was her favourite. She said, it would be a commission. Fifteen euro. Sinéad couldn't believe it. There was tears in her eyes with joy. Or disbelief. Or belief. Dawning, isn't it? The painting was of the human brain. Prawny pink-looking slugs and it faded away into darkness and there was some kind of a living thing up at the top right corner kind of like a seahorse and a bird at the same time and there was a bit of some planet showing in the bottom left corner all bluey and pinky and the rest of it then was all blackness. It was like the other stuff she'd be looking at the whole time in the book she had of paintings by a fella called Joan Miró. All I knew about painting and paintings ever was that it made Sinéad happy and that was a trillion times more than enough for me. I remember looking at it when the nun unwrapped her commission. She kept looking at it, the nun did, for ages just saying,

—Wonderful. Just wonderful.

I couldn't see what she was seeing cos my brain was in the way. To me it was just blaggarding same as Joan Miró and James' mother used to be at, but the nun was moved. Sinéad gave the fifteen euro back to the nun for her art gallery but the nun would only take a fiver back. Sinéad bought me and James a choc-ice with the tenner after school. She got a tape of Billie Holiday and a record of Edith Piaf in the second-hand bookshop in Cork Saturday. It was called The Second-Hand Bookshop but mostly it was young people were in there, up the top floor where the second-hand music was. Sinéad kept her album covers and the rest of her art in James' mother's studio for safe-keeping in case her mother and father threw them out. They thought the painting was just a waste of time and just James' bad influence. They used to say the Kents have fierce high and mighty notions of themselves.

James had flowing locks when all the rest of the boys had tight haircuts. He played rugby, the posh boys' game. James spoke in a strange accent. He was quiet in himself for the first few weeks. He was the cause of them all having a great laugh the first time he played Gaelic football. That's an Irish sport played in a field. Fifteen against fifteen and you can catch and kick the ball or hand-pass it with the fist. Anyway, the first time he played in the school at lunchtime he threw it to a fellow. What a laugh. Then, next time he got it he took off running about thirty yards to score a try at the endline and sure you can't do that. You have to score goals or points. What laughing. Any other lad would have been embarrassed I suppose but James just laughed away at himself. The other lads didn't know what to make of this new fella.

Once he got out of the habit of throwing the ball he turned into a fine footballer and before the year was out Master Coughlan had handed over the free-taking duties from Dinky to himself. Dinky wasn't too pleased about it. I seen the tears in his eyes and he walking into class after lunchtime. He'd be all pally pally with James after school though. But I seen the tears in his eyes. He was not a happy boy. Everything would have been fine if James had never come to Ballyronan. That's what Dinky's eyes said and he looking over at James that time.

I remember seeing the same expression on Dinky's face one time years later in the pub after he'd been telling James some big long important load of shit and asked him what he thought then at the end of it. 'Sorry I wasn't listening,' James said. 'I've that new Pearl Jam song in my head.' 'You're fucking unbelievable, you know that?' Dinky said, and the tears welling in his drunken eyes and he looking up at the ceiling and licking his top lip trying to keep things under control, and he twenty years of age. All because James wasn't listening to him going on and on and on with the greatest shit you ever heard.

'Fuck are you looking at Gamal?' Dinky snarled at me for staring at him and he trying to hold back the tears that time. That was another thing about acting the gamal. That's a phrase. In Ireland if you're making an eejit out of yourself people will tell you to stop acting the gamal or acting the gam. But no one thought I was acting. Anyhow you could stare at people away when they thought you were a bit simple. When you're not a bit simple you can't be staring at people. Usually people don't mind cos they know you're special. Except Dinky when he's trying to hold back a tear or two in peace.

So anyhow James he was a mighty fielder too – that's when a player jumps high into the air and plucks the ball out of the sky with both hands. 'Tis few players have the gift for it but 'tis a sight to behold. James was fast too. When he got away they didn't even bother to run after him, some of them. Some of them would fall and hold their ankle like they'd sprained it or something.

The new boy. The quiet boy. The Protestant. The fella who didn't know how to play football. Soon he was seen as those things no more. By fifth class he had got big – bigger than he was supposed to get and I don't mean the size of him I mean the way of him. He wasn't the usual new boy. Grateful for acceptance. He never felt the need to hold back, new boy or not.

Master Coughlan couldn't really control him because he was too clever and funny. Coughlan didn't mind lads being funny as long as no one was funnier than him. As long as he had the last laugh. But he never did with James. I suppose Dinky was used to being the lad that got the most laughs but that all changed when James arrived. Dinky knew not to piss Coughlan off too much. Dinky knew where the line was. James knew where 'twas too but didn't care. It was only school.

Headaches starting again. I'm going for a lie down now.

Work

So I'm not working these days on account of me being unwell. When I do work I can do anything. Wash cars in Dennehy's garage in the village. Draw blocks and mix mortar for the bricklayers up at the new housing estate. My favourite was being a helper to the gardeners up at UCC. University College Cork if you don't mind. Other times local farmers call if they need a helping hand. Stacking bales of hay or shovelling shit or helping to build a new shed or picking spuds or weeding fields of cabbage. Other times people might call if they're doing up their house. Like one time I sanded a whole wooden floor and stairs. Or stripping wallpaper. I've done that tonnes of times. I can do anything. People know I'm a gamal so they feel good about giving me the work. But I've done fuck all work now really for the bones of a few years.

1

That 1 up there is a chapter symbol. Chapter 1. I've decided to use chapters. Came across a book in a bookshop in Cork today. Fifty-three chapters it had. And only three hundred and seventeen pages. Reckon he got ten pages out of it isn't it? Between having an excuse to go on to a new page without having the last one finished and the fancy chapter numbers taking up half the next page he got at least ten pages out of it. Maybe fifteen or twenty, I don't know. Anyhow I'm definitely doing it. It has to be done. Hope you like chapters. You'll have a new chapter every six or seven pages from here on.

Not The Same

It's not the same as before now. We borrowed each other all three of us for a while. But then we had to give each other back isn't it?

My Boy

Funniest was James' father long ago though. James' father didn't get it right at the football matches at all. You can only be praising fellas that's not your own son at the matches but James' father didn't understand. If it's your own son you're shouting at you're only supposed to shout things like,

—Will ya wake up for fuck sake.

—Contest the ball man for the love of Christ.

—Will ya tackle man for the love of God.

—Ah mark up for Jesus' sake.

And they have to criticise him to others saying stuff like,

—My fella's away with the fairies today.

—I dunno will I bother feeding him any more, 'tis only a waste.

—I dunno is there any chance he'll take his head out of his hole in the second half?

—He's playing fucking thick anyhow.

James' father was different,

—Brilliant James.

—That's the style James, outstanding kick.

—That was a beautiful catch James, majestic.

Then he'd turn to the other men,

—My boy is having a super game.

—James is right on the money today isn't he? Right on song.

—Wasn't that a spectacular catch by James though. My God, the way he got up for it.

I think it really gave the other men a pain in their holes. You'd imagine their insides twisting and turning in discomfort. Their necks getting hot with annoyance. Them blinking hard when they'd really like instead to lie down and writhe on the ground and scream or else hit James' father a box in the back of the head but instead they had to make do with a good hard blink. They'd look at each other sometimes to acknowledge their shared suffering but James' father never noticed this. One time old Jack Ballyhale says,

—Fucking yeoman,

and all the other men around him skitting laughing and rubbing their eyes and shaking their heads. James' father was not a noticer of things like that. It would just never have occurred to him isn't it? But he wasn't boasting. He was only stating the facts. Rejoicing isn't it? The Prods do be rejoicing. Even in the chapel you'd hear them across the road belting out their happy tunes.

Anyhow, soon a few of the fellas started calling James My Boy. Not to his face or in front of his father but when they were talking about him among themselves. You'd hear them in the pub saying things like,

—Where was My Boy playing?

or

—Jesus that was a great goal My Boy got, in fairness.

I dunno if James was ever embarrassed about him. I doubt he was. I think Sinéad was definitely embarrassed by her parents though.

Her father was the meanest alcoholic in Europe. Himself and Sinéad's mother would go on holidays and he'd come back with plastic cutlery he took from the plane. And one time when Sinéad got a lamp for her room so she could study he took the bulb out of the ceiling light to compensate. He was the only man of his generation in the area not to have a car. They lived in a council house. That's a house the council give to poor people for half the price of an ordinary house. Her mother didn't want to move into a council house but her father was mad to get one. Pretended he had a bad back and couldn't work around the time they got married in order to get his hands on one. Then sent his wife out to work. Then went off to work himself once he knew they couldn't take the council house off him. They used to joke that the Kents wouldn't be rich enough for any daughter of his. He didn't drive a car cos he was too mean maybe or maybe he just preferred to be able to drink wherever he went.

—If he's to pay for the wedding it'll be below in Roundy's.

—Tight-arse fuck!

Sinéad's father went around the world trying not to be noticed. His daughter's lack of fear for standing out made him nervous. Suspicious of her even. He was embarrassed by Sinéad hooking up with James from day one. Betrayal he thought it was.

—Fine thing you fucking stick to your own.

Lads in work would mock him about it. Henry Lee said to him in the pub once that if all went well with James and Sinéad he could become the landlord's lieutenant. They were all laughing. Saw the same fella, this Henry Lee, blame James one time. James kicked a ball to a fella but it was a bad pass and the other team worked the ball back up the field and got a goal. This fella was cursing James after the match even though James was the best player on the field and scored seven points and set up another seven. And they wouldn't have been within an arse's roar of the final in the first place without James winning all the other matches for them. Henry Lee.

Sinéad's mother did the office for a big panel-beating garage in Fermoy. Left early in the morning. Came home late. Sometimes she didn't come home at all. There was trouble at home a lot in Sinéad's house.

€20

Found the euro sign. Button with Alt Gr on it and 4 if you're ever stuck for it. Dollar sign is easier. $. People take care of their own. Anyhow the reason I wanted to say €20 was cos I was saying wouldn't it be grand if you could just ring me and I could tell you what happened. For €20. Seems stupid now. Not even worth the trouble. But this writing lark is still sickening my hole. I'm going for a walk.

Closure

Dr Quinn sent me to another head doctor as well this week. This fella agreed that the writing would help me form closure. He wanted a hundred snots, but I had no money on me. I told him I was going to the bank and that was the last he saw of me. I'm still having the dreams though. And the headaches. I like writing at night. I see through the bullshit better. It's like when you're tired you remember the bad things as well. When you're wide awake and full of life everyone's great. Even the fuckers. Dinky and Teesh were some fuckers. 'Tis dark and quiet now and there's a dog barking. The only other sound is the laptop. See in the daytime you'd think a laptop is quiet. 'Tis only at night you notice these things. The senses are rawer. And the mind is brave.

Why Did Crying Evolve?

I dunno. Sometimes. Sometimes it's like I can think of nothing else only what happened. My headache's at me all day now and it's only getting worse thinking about telling my story. Not today anyhow. My eyes are watering mad now too. You'd wonder with all this evolution crack why did crying evolve?

Thinking

Sometimes I could spend the whole day thinking about something like what has jealousy got to do with betrayal. And what has love got to do with vengeance. Or what has hatred got to do with laughter. Heard some yank on the radio the other day saying that laughing evolved from the apes to tell each other that the lad who fell off the tree was OK and wasn't after breaking his hole. I could think about laughter for ever. Like what has it got to do with pain. And how it can be an attack or it can be a defence. Laughter.

But mostly now I can concentrate with the tablets. I can sit and watch television for hours and not be thinking about Sinéad or not have some tune of hers in my head or some tune of somebody else that would only remind me of Sinéad cos it was someone else singing. Telly used to upset Sinéad. She used to say it was like death. Like how it sapped the life out of you. Like a hypnotist making you forget that you're alive. Or like a traveller doing the three card trick. Bamboozled you. But you didn't lose your money.

You lost your life. The time of your life. Telly made her think of her death I think. So I missed a lot of telly when I was hanging around with Sinéad and James but now I can watch it away with the tablets and no thoughts of Sinéad upsetting my head. It was a madness is what it was isn't it? To be thinking about music all the time. Sinéad and James and me that time I'm thinking now we were a small bit mad definitely. If they had these tablets they might have fitted in better. Been able to talk to Racey and Dinky and Teesh and everyone about *Friends* or *Home and Away* or *Coronation Street*. Or watch videos with them in Snoozie's house like *Police Academy 6* or *Wayne's World*.

Humpty Dumpty

We had this young teacher in fourth class long ago, Mr Costigan, for a few months. He was in from the teacher training college and he was always up for a laugh. We did a Rose of Ballyronan Contest in class one day. Sinéad wasn't in school that day.

Course she'd have won if she was there. Then we had a Man of Ballyronan Contest. The teacher interviewed and the lads answered the questions. Most were all shy smiles, looking down at the ground and blushing and shrugging their shoulders saying, 'I dunno,' to every question.

—Hello and what's your name?

—Ahmn . . . Tony.

—Tony what?

—Tony Desmond.

—And tell me a little about yourself Tony.

—Ahm . . . Like what?

—Well for instance what sport do you like?

—Ahm . . . Football.

—I see. And why do you like football?

—Ahm . . . I dunno.

—And who are your favourite team?

—Cork.

—And who's your favourite player?

—Larry Tompkins.

—Larry Tompkins. By God yer all big Larry Tompkins fans. And tell me Tony what would your ideal woman be like?

—Ahm . . . I dunno.

—You don't know?

—Ahm . . . Good-looking.

—Good-looking. Very well Tony. Can you think of any famous girl that you think might be good-looking?

—Ahm . . . that one in The Bangles. Susanna.

—Susanna. Is that the girl that all the other lads said as well?

—Ahm . . . yeah!

—My goodness, I'll have to check out this band The Bangles. The whole class laughed then all lick-arsy.

—And tell me Tony, have you any party piece you'd like to do for us?

—Ahm . . . no.

—Very well then Tony. Well done. You can go back to your seat. Good man yourself.

Tony went off back to his seat, head down smiling and the sweaty red face on him. The whole bleddy lot of them were the same. Smiling and looking down at the ground and shifting their weight from one foot to the other. No one took up an offer to do a party piece like all the girls had before half ten break. Most girls did a poem. A few sang. Just made everyone think of Sinéad not being there. Three girls did a few Irish dancing steps. But the lads were just too cool for any of that. Then it was Dinky's turn.

—Hello what's your name?

—Denis.

He had both hands in his pockets and he was just staring out the window, half bored-looking with his lips pursed. A few of the girls giggled.

—And tell me about yourself Denis.

—What can I say? Play a bit of football. Bit of a lady's man.

The class laughed mad at this.

—Very good. And tell me, what would you like to be when you're big?

—I think I'd like to be an actor or join the army.

—Very good. Do you know anyone in the army?

—Yeah my uncle is in the army.

—Is he?

—Yeah.

—And does he serve with the UN? The United Nations?

—Dunno.

—Does he go out foreign?

—Yeah sometimes he does be gone a good while.

—Very good. And what do you think is the best thing about being a soldier?

—Having a gun of your own.

A little giggle came from the class again.

—And tell me Denis have you a party piece for us?

—Not a chance, Dinky says.

The class all laughed when Dinky gave a peace sign walking back to his seat.

Next was James.

—Hello young man.

—All right man, how's tricks?

The whole class laughed at James grabbing the chance to be all casual talking to the teacher.

—Not so bad, thank you. And tell me, what's your name?

—James Kent.

—Kent. That's not a very common name around these parts.

—There are fourteen in the phone-book in the whole of Cork. I checked it out. So no, it's not that common in Cork.

—And where does the name Kent come from?

—England. Sure everyone knows that England is full of Kents!

Even Mr Costigan gave a flicker of a smile that time. The class were in stitches.

—OK, right! Settle down. If I don't get silence now the Man of Ballyronan contest is over.

That shut them up.

—And tell me James, do you have any hobbies?

—I like knitting!

More laughs.

—Right OK, settle down. Any other hobbies?

—I like playing flog.

—Flog?

—Yeah flog. It's my favourite sport.

—Flog? Never heard of it. Tell me about it.

—Yeah. I made it up myself. It's golf backwards. You start at hole eighteen and work your way back to one.

More laughs.

—Right, that's very good James. Tell me have you any party piece?

—I do. I would like to sing.

—What would you like to sing?

—I'd like to sing a song called 'Humpty Dumpty'.

He sang 'Humpty Dumpty' as a sincere slow plaintive lament. Doesn't seem too funny now, but to a roomful of ten-year-olds it was the funniest thing ever.

Out of sixteen girls James got fourteen of the votes. Didn't think anything of it at the time, but I should have. That a certain per cent of the girls didn't like James' funny antics or his good looks or his jokes should have got me thinking at the time. It wasn't only the lads who resented James, it was some of the girls too.

Sometimes even when they knew he was right people would disagree with James. I seen that too always. Just for the sake of it. Gang up on him even. Even stuff that didn't even matter. Like the score of a match. Or whether some show was good or not. I seen people change their minds just to disagree with him. As a group. I seen it a million times. I won't tell you the million.

But James had a weakness. Like the time on the Ballyronan under-eighteen team when James started letting Dinky come up from corner back to take the penalties even though James was one of the best penalty takers in the county and was taking them for the county team. A team that Dinky wasn't within an arse's roar of making. And the coach who was Roundy, the other publican in the village and the other players delighted to be taking James down here with the rest of us. See James thought no one ever could pose a threat to him. Dangerous thing it is to have no fear. Fear is what keeps us safe isn't it? He usen't realise it at the time but fellas would be seeing if James was. What's the word you'd say? Challengeable. Little things like. And little fellas. Not all types. The littlest mostly. And I don't mean the size of them to look at. I mean the size of who it was they were as men. Or as boys. Because that kind of size never changes. A man apart. That's what the father'd call James, maybe. And some lads who recognised this about James wanted to bring him down in small ways. The worst thing for them though was that James would only be nicer to them. He'd yield in whatever way the challenge was because in the great scheme of things he discounted the little things as having no importance. He was wrong to do this. Like letting Dinky have his moment and take the penalty just cos it meant more to Dinky than him.

When a fella sizes you up you should leave him knowing you're not one to be fucked around with. Should let him know for sure too. Instead of being nice to him and feeling sorry for him. Sometimes I think James thought he was some kind of saint or something. Fucking eejit. Never thought anyone could ever pose a challenge to him. Maybe that was his main trouble. He never saw anyone as a threat. James was nice to everyone. He went out of his way to be nice to people. People didn't expect it from him. Some people distrusted him because of it. Thought he must have been fucking around with them in some way or form, somewhere in the dark black monkey parts of their brains. They didn't trust his niceness.

Does that make James good? I dunno. I wonder what has goodness got to do with fear.

Do you know what? Maybe James just wanted to fit in. The odd kick in the face sure or stab in the back was a small price. Dunno. I wonder what has fear got to do with charity? Or what has admiration got to do with envy? Or what has pity got to do with disdain?

Followed

I was followed around by people once. People and photographers. People who wrote in newspapers. People who wrote hints. Who had ways of saying things that wasn't saying it at all. Or sometimes they'd say a lot of things so that you'd be left thinking about what they didn't say or what they couldn't say.

An dubh

An dubh is on me today. Dubh means black. An means the. Not too bad today but bad enough. I'm not crying like a baba no more these days. Not everyday anyhow. That's when I started coming out of it first really. When I started crying all the time. Before that I was made of stone for a long time. Think of stuff sometimes though all the time. I mean like sometimes I can think of nothing else. Absolutely nothing else. Not even like eating or drinking or washing or dressing or answering the mother. Makes me feel like

I'm dead. And my eyes water a bit still for no reason. And the nightmares. I get nightmares sometimes when I'm awake. Sorrows notice me.

People

Some people don't care about other people.

Matches

Today I bought fourteen boxes of matches. They were three euro fifty cents. I counted all the matches. Then I did it again. Then a third time just to make sure. Then I went outside and burned them all. First, one by one. Then I did it box by box. I needed something to keep my brain occupied. 'Twas at me. And I liked watching them burn.

Sisters

Sinéad's skin was darker than her sisters'. She didn't look one bit like them. She didn't act like them either. They didn't have her spark. But sure I suppose no one I ever met did.

Whispering

Dinky and Teesh were doing a lot of whispering in her ear once. They knew she was vulnerable isn't it? But forget about it until we come to that part.

Ice It

'Twas the first and last time anyone ever saw James cry. Except for me. But I seen more than anyone. Anyhow he was in fifth class.

The second last year of primary school when you're about ten or eleven. Master Coughlan picked the teams for lunchtime. As daft a pair of teams that was ever picked by a schoolteacher. All the good players on one team. All the poor useless lads on the other, except for James. James started to protest, 'Ah but sir?' 'What?' said Coughlan, looking at him as if he was all puzzled and all. 'Nothing,' was all James could say cos he realised that he couldn't say, 'Why are you putting me in with all the shit fellas?' And Coughlan knew he would never have it in him to insult the useless fellas like that. Every goose that tried to play football was with James. He told them where to play, and took up the midfield slot himself. I was up on the big oak tree keeping an eye on proceedings like I always did.

James took them on. All on his own he took on the other team. Racing forward and racing back. Scoring. Stopping scores. Intercepting. Spoiling. Catching. Blocking. Scoring again. He looked like a man among boys. In the middle of the second half though he stormed off the pitch with the tears streaming down his face. The game stopped inevitably, cos no one on his team could even kick a ball out of their own way, let alone get a score. James went straight for the jacks and locked the door. Dinky and Gregory, the Master's son, and the rest of them followed, waiting at the door asking, 'What's wrong James?' letting on like they were all concerned and all, and puzzled and all, 'James are you OK?' they were asking. Master Coughlan stayed out on the pitch and had a smoke for himself for a while. Eventually James came out of the jacks holding his shoulder. He said he thought he might have dislocated it. But that was the greatest bullshit you ever heard. And the lads knew that. And James knew they knew that there was feck-all wrong with his shoulder. And Coughlan knew, even when he held James' arm aloft and watched James' fake grimaces. 'You gave it a good jolt all right James lad. You'll have to ice it at home. The ligaments got stretched. But you'll be fine.'

So Master Coughlan and the lads and James himself partook in this great farce about an injury that never happened. Well an injury to the body didn't happen anyhow. James would go on to have many injuries in his future playing career, but looking back on it, the injury that happened to him that day was the worst of them all. Up on the tree by the sideline I could hear the jibes of the other players as he lorded it over them against all the odds. But most of all I could see their faces. Their eyes. They were all ganging up. Little wolves. Brought together by something they didn't even understand. They were out for blood. Poor James was confused that day. I wasn't one bit confused. He'd come face to face with the animal. That made him fear for his young life. Even though that day his life was never remotely in danger. But if there was a sign of things to come that was it.

He was a quiet boy in class that afternoon. And Coughlan didn't ask him nothing either. Just let him stare out the window for the whole afternoon without as much as opening a book. Looking out at the sun sending waves of heat spiralling off the soft tarmac. Looking out at the basketball ring with the no net. Looking at the small goals and the square with no grass left. Looking out across the road up at the Catholic church steeple rising high above the Protestant one in the distance. Looking at the faded lines of the basketball court. Looking out at the field where the smallies play football at the front of the school.

Truth is I don't know what James saw when he looked out that window that sunny June afternoon. I don't know cos I'm not him. All I'm saying is that he looked out there. What did he see? What was he thinking? Your guess is as good as blahdeblah. I'd say there's a good chance he wished he was only a middling kind of a player anyhow. Or maybe he was just wishing Sinéad was in school that day. Sinéad missed a lot of school on account of her helping out at home.

After school he laughed and joked with the lads, same as usual. And explaining that he got this shock up through his arm that was the sorest thing he'd ever felt in his life. The lads nodded, looked at each other and looked away. Dinky told him he should definitely ice it when he got home.

Not So Good

I can't remember what I was thinking about. I remember now. Hard to explain. It's like in the nature programmes. And the cameraman watching the poor small animal being killed by the lion or tiger. The deer say or whatever. And he's waiting the cameraman is. And he knows what's going to happen. And he doesn't stop it. Cos it's nature's way. And that's how he's telling the story. By letting it happen. Showing us. Except in my story it isn't some stupid deer or whatever like. If it was a deer I wouldn't give a fuck. I wouldn't care cos I'd say it's nature's way. But if it was nature's way that the people died that died. Then things aren't so good. They're just not so good like isn't it?

Sometimes

Sometimes I think I'm like the cameraman who let it happen. Other times I know I'm not. I didn't let nothing happen. And I did nothing. I know it. Swear to God.

Ancient History

You'd think ancient history is ancient history. It isn't. Not in Ireland anyhow.

A Desperate Hammering

Fella in Four Crosses got a desperate hammering in the pub there one night by a fellow who was beaten up by his father sixteen years before. Fellas have a memory when it comes to blood isn't it? When it suits them they have anyhow.

Walking

I think I might go for a walk. I walk around a lot now. It's one of my favourite things always. It could have been along a dirty dark street or along The Long Strand. The longest nicest beach in the world. I wouldn't care either way. I'd like it just the same.

Secondary school was a bit embarrassing at the start for me. I got a special needs assistant. That's some grown-up who the government pays to wipe my hole and tie my laces like I wasn't able to look after myself in school. You see they changed the law so now fellas like me had to have a hippy with them in school. And the one I had was the biggest pain in the hole anyone every met. All We fucking this and We that.

—And if we're not engaging Charlie we don't make progress.

And if we don't make progress Charlie we don't reach our potential. Each child has a right under the law to reach their potential. That's why I'm here Charlie but we must engage if we're to succeed.

Like most people I ever met in my life, I never spoke one word to her. But of all the people I never spoke to, she replied the most. On and on and on. Only time she'd stop talking and coaching me from her bollicksology textbook was to take a bite of some fucking celery or raw carrot or a drink of water from her glass bottle with the rubbery top. Longest few weeks of my life it was with that one following me around the place in case I'd fucking trip over myself. She had a fucking clipboard with her always in case anyone would find out that she did sweet fuck all. In the end she went to the principal about me not engaging. The principal got her helping other fellas with their reading and sums but I still had to meet her once a week so she could fill in her report and lie about my engagement and progress so she'd get to keep her job and could buy her celery.

But I was left alone eventually and she was given the road after first year off to some other poor bollicks some place else. No one ever mocked me cos of James being around. I wasn't in all of James and Sinéad's classes cos they were doing honours English and Maths and Irish and them subjects were split up into different levels. I hated being without them. Even other girls that weren't Sinéad made me puke with their sucking up to the boys and trying to be popular with them.

Only girl I thought was kinda nice was Julie. She liked to dance. Her mother taught ballet and music and cleaned the school in her spare time. Julie was hippyish looking and walked tall. Sinéad hadn't really met anyone like her and they became good friends in first year. Sinéad started wearing hippyish scarves and didn't bother with make-up. Racey and the others would be covered in make-up. They'd go to the toilet together to be touching it up. But Julie never bothered with that. Neither did Sinéad. Julie made it easier for Sinéad to be not doing stuff that Racey and them were doing.

But then before the holidays they moved away and Sinéad never saw her again. And neither did we. Cos they moved to Australia. So then Sinéad just tagged along with Racey and the other girls then instead.

I remember Dinky long ago when we were in first year and we'd get off the bus in Ballyronan after a day's school and we'd all go home but Dinky would follow James back to the castle to be hanging around with him. James said to Sinéad that he doesn't help him doing his jobs, he just sits there watching and talking. The castle was rebuilt by then but James always had lots of jobs to be doing in the garden and stuff.

When he was finished his jobs then Dinky would follow him in and he'd join the Kents for the dinner. His mother used to joke that they should just adopt him. James' father would send him up to do his homework then and Dinky would have to go home. James would be glad to be rid of him by then I think. That's the impression I got anyhow, not that James ever said it. James would ring Sinéad most nights. Until she was old enough to be allowed to call up herself. That didn't happen until they were about sixteen. She'd call up in the evening time. Sometimes they'd do the homework together and I'd be putting on records for them. In the library in the castle. I might tell you more about it later. Yeah I will. I loved the library more than any place else ever. They had a record player in the library and my mother had tonnes of records that I used to bring up. I used to walk up with Sinéad a lot of the time. We'd just be listening to music mainly and they'd be working on songs too. They made up songs. The tunes of them and the words of them. That kind of bored Dinky so he stopped coming up then. He started hanging around a bit with the older lads. Especially with Teesh and Snoozie. Licking their holes.

Dr Quinn says I've to introduce my secondary characters properly before I say another word about Sinéad and James and the library and their music or anything else cos I'm making a bollicks of the story. He told me who the secondary characters are. They are Dinky, Snoozie, Racey and Teesh. This is a description of each of them and their ages. I wrote out their names ten times so you can read it out loud ten times and get to know the names and know which is which. Plus it's words for my story. Fifty.

Dinky = a rotten cunt. Male human. Same age as Sinéad and James. Dinky. Dinky. Dinky. Dinky. Dinky. Dinky. Dinky. Dinky. Dinky. Dinky.

This is Dinky's nose.

This is Dinky in court.

Dinky's Evidence

—Could you tell the court please, are you Denis Hennebry?

—Yes.

That's Dinky's real name.

—And you reside with your parents at 43 Main Street, Ballyronan. Is that correct?

—Yes.

—And when did you first get to know Sinéad?

—I went to school with her. Primary school. And secondary school. I've known her through my whole life really.

—I see. And how about James?

—The same like. He joined our class in primary school when they moved to Ballyronan.

—By 'they' do you mean the Kents?

—Yes.

—James and his mother and father, is it?

—Yes.

—Sinéad and James entered into a relationship with each other sometime in their teenage years, is that correct?

—Ahm. Into a relationship yes. They were always together like. The two of them were always hanging around, even in primary school but they were in secondary school then and they started going out like.

—Were either of them ever in a relationship with anybody else while in secondary school?

—In secondary school no. They were only with each other then.

—I see. And tell me this, Denis, please, if you wouldn't mind. Were you ever fond of Sinéad during this time?

—No. Like what do you mean fond? She was sound like. We were friends. Everyone was fond of Sinéad like.

—Did you ever have stronger feelings for her while she was going out with James?

—Ahm . . . no like. Not like that, no.

—Did you ever want to be in a relationship with her at the time?

—No. I didn't, no.

—Your parents are quite friendly with Sinéad's parents, aren't they?

—They are, yeah. Well, my father anyhow. Her father and my father went to school together and they worked together in the precast yard once like. Started on the same day.

—Did you ever feel that it might have been nice for them if you and Sinéad had been a couple?

—No, like. It didn't come up like. Cos she was always with James. As far back as anyone can remember.

—Isn't it true that your father used to tell you that Sinéad was the girl for you?

—Who told you that?

—Answer the question please, Denis.

—He might have said it like, and I growing up like, just like half messing like.

Langer

They called Dinky Dinky cos he's supposed to have a small langer like your baby finger. They started calling him Dinky when he got the trials for the divisional side. They were having a joke calling some fella who was hung like a donkey Truncheon when one of the lads points at poor Dinky and calls him Dinky. The name stuck like a fly to cowshit.

By the way for anyone who's not from Ireland a langer is a willy. A penis. But it can mean dickhead or idiot or fool or wanker or a generally disliked fella. Can mean drunk too. But always a fella.

—Ya fucking langer.

—What a langer.

—You're some langer.

—What kind of a langer are you?

—Drank fourteen pints last night, I was fucking langers.

—You're a fucking useless langer.

—You may as well be at home playing with your langer.

—You're an awful langer.

—The stupid langer forgot his ticket.

—Bit of a fucking langer, you are, aren't ya?

—You're only a langer, you.

—Langer.

Langur

N. a slender, leaf-eating monkey of Southeast Asia with a long tail, bushy eyebrows, and a chin tuft. Genus: *Presbytis*. leaf monkey [Early 19th C. Via Hindi *langûr* from Sanscrit *langula* 'having a tail'.]

Long ago when the Irish were poor as fuck they went off to fight the wars for England for a few quid. But one of them wars was in India and they had a type of monkey called the langur so when the war was over the lads who lived came back to Cork calling each other langers. Nowadays if you're out of favour in Cork you're a langer. Anyhow sorry I went off track there. Yeah so James would have been there at the divisional trials as well. James and Dinky were only young lads of seventeen. The other lads were all in their twenties. James was the only one in Ballyronan that never called Dinky Dinky.

Dinky
Adj. small and compact; small and compact or neat (*informal*).
N. *S African*; beverages; a small bottle of wine; usually containing 250ml (*informal*) [Late 18th C. Formed from Scots dialect *dink* 'finely dressed, trim', of unknown origin. The original sense was 'neat, dainty'.]

When he was in primary school Dinky's head was always looking around. Not out of interest in people but out of fear of them. Dinky thought that if people didn't like him they'd kill him. He was canvassing always for people to be liking him. Balancing things up always.

Snoozie = a stupid cunt. Male human. Three years older. Snoozie. Snoozie. Snoozie. Snoozie. Snoozie. Snoozie. Snoozie. Snoozie. Snoozie. Snoozie.

This is Snoozie's eyes.

Snoozie's Evidence

—Do you know if Sinéad ever cheated on James?

—She did, yes. With the Rascal.

—OK. Was this common knowledge?

—Yes. Everyone knew it.

—And when James took her back, so to speak, when they rekindled their relationship, was she loyal to him then?

—No. She went with the Rascal again. Went off in his car with him. Used to be at it the whole time. He'd collect her when she'd finish work in the pub. Roundy's. Fellas would joke about his car being outside.

—I see. Are you sure of this? How can you be certain?

—The Rascal said it.

—And you believe him?

—Well, he had an Afghan scarf around his neck that he said Sinéad gave to him as a present. James had given it to her way back along as a present. That's how James found out. He asked him where he got the scarf and Rascal told him out straight. James went to hit him but Dinky and Teesh pulled him away. Told him he needed to talk to his girlfriend.

—I see. Thank you.

That fella Rascal was called the Little Rascal. He used to do a bit of block-laying up in the site with me. He was a handy corner forward too. Tough little cunt. But that's what he was. A little cunt. He used to play guitar and sing the usual shit in pubs for a few extra bob and he was a small bit of an alcoholic. He used to be at work bright and early every morning but when he went for lunch in the pub you never knew if he was going to come back. He was paid different to the rest of us. By the amount of blocks he laid, not by the hour. But he could work faster than the other fellas. He was hardy. He was the same age as Teesh and Snoozie and was friendly enough with them when he was around. He did a lot of travelling though. Over to Spain singing to drunken Irish people on holiday. He's not doing any more shite singing nowadays. Not doing much at all so he's not. Anyhow, don't mind him a while. I could go talking about that time when Sinéad was working behind the bar in Roundy's but actually I can't. There's probably stuff in your life you couldn't talk about either. I dunno. But I definitely can't talk about that time in the pub now cos I'd be afraid I'd do harm to myself. I can talk about Snoozie all right I think.

Snoozie didn't have a lazy eye. He had two of them. And looked pissed as a lord the whole time whether he'd drink on board or not. And. He. Spoke. Incred. Ibly. Slow. Ly. People thought he was pissed or slow in the head. He was neither a lot of the time. Think he invented that way of being to give his brain time to think of what to say next. 'Twas a droll front that worked for him most of the time. If I think of him now I can see him. He nods his head once, slowly, up and down. Stares straight ahead. His face is blank and dead. And he says, 'What. A. Fuck. Ing. Eejit. Ha?' Snoozie was a cornerback in football too. Once

James said, 'God invented cornerbacks because God loves a tryer. He invented the colour grey, the same day.' Snoozie resented it, even though he laughed with the rest of us, 'You're. Some. Fuck. Er. Ha?'

Snoozie and Teesh were a few years older than ourselves but Dinky liked them so we got to know them. When Snoozie was nineteen he became the owner of a business that his brother had set up. It was a metal engineering firm that made gates and small trailers and railings and stuff. They were doing very well. Then his brother died in a car crash and Snoozie got the business. This gave him a bit of status around the place. It was around this time that Dinky started hanging around with him. Snoozie had got a big BMW and used to drive Dinky around the place. I suppose they became friends around then.

Snoozie's father owned a pub. He used to be a farm labourer who got a farmer's daughter pregnant. He married her, sold her farm and bought the pub. Snoozie's father didn't like James. I know because he called him Sir James any time he saw him. And if he was talking about him he'd call him My Boy. James didn't know he didn't like him but I did. The pub was called The Snug. That's where they did their underage drinking. There and Roundy's, the other pub in the village. Teesh wanted to get his hands on The Snug so he was always trying to go out with Snoozie's sister cos she was going to get the pub. Snoozie spoke with a bit of a lisp too.

Teesh

Teesh = a lousy cunt. Male human. Three years older. Teesh. Teesh. Teesh. Teesh. Teesh. Teesh. Teesh. Teesh. Teesh. Teesh.

Teesh was all legs.

Teesh was short for Taoiseach. That means chief like I said before. And it's what the prime minister of Ireland is called. His lackey Snoozie was always around too. Teesh used to play midfield with James. Teesh was six foot six but he used to drive the old fellas daft cos he was too afraid to go up and catch the ball in case he'd get a knock. Instead he used to just punch it. Teesh had a farm behind him when his father died but he had his eye on The Snug too like I said before. This was the shape of him.

Teesh's Evidence

—You are known as Teesh? Is that right?

—Yes.

—Why?

—Short for taoiseach.

—And why would you be called taoiseach?

—I dunno. Maybe...

—Yes?

—Well... My parents were told I had leadership qualities when I was in school long ago. But I dunno who started calling me taoiseach first. I think it started in secondary school.

—Very good. I see. You obviously impressed the people around you.

—I suppose.

—Very good. Could you tell me about your relationship with Denis Hennebry, please.

—Yes, yeah. Didn't know him very well, he's a few years younger than me. But he drank with us in the pub.

—What pub?

—Roundy's like and The Snug.

—In Ballyronan?

—Yes, yeah. Most people calls it Roundy's. That's what the owner is known as. Seán. People call him Roundy.

—I see. But you became good friends with Denis Hennebry, is that correct?

—Ahm . . . well like . . . we drank in the same pub like . . . he was there a lot of the time that I was there so I suppose we became kind of friendly all right. He hung around with me like, as opposed to me hanging around with him. To be honest.

—Can you clarify what you mean please.

—Nothing really, like. Just like, mainly he'd come along and join myself and Snoozie and whoever else in the pub. Or if we were going to the Four Crosses he might come along like. I wouldn't say we were best friends like. He tagged along is all. He was probably better friends with Snoozie. They used to be driving around and that. Snoozie had a car like fairly young. Dinky. I mean Denis. Denis was a few years younger like but Snoozie would take him for a drive around when they'd nothing to do. And he'd come in to the pub to us like too, Dinky would. I thought he was a grand fella.

—I see. That will be all for the moment. Thank you.

Racey = a liardy bitch. Female human. Her real name was Tracey. Same age as Sinéad and James. Racey. Racey. Racey. Racey. Racey. Racey. Racey. Racey. Racey. Racey.

Racey's nose was like it was pushed back in her face or something.

Racey was born to be probably reasonable-looking but she let herself go before she even knew she was gone. Out of sight. Before going on a night out she'd get all dolled up to the last. Same as cramming before an exam, isn't it? Too late. She wasn't in vanity for the long haul anyhow. She was fond of boys and didn't show it in a subtle way. That's why they called her Racey. She lived between Ballyronan and Mullinahone.

Racey's Evidence

—How did you get to know Sinéad?

—Well like, Sinéad would have been one of my best friends like. Since we were children like.

—Were you in primary school together?

—Yeah like.

—And were you close with Sinéad throughout your childhood?

—Yeah like. Like . . . I wasn't to know she had this like darker side.

God love her like, you know. Heart of gold in her like. She might have had her problems like but God love her like she could be wild at times but like deep down like . . . heart of gold I swear to God like.

—You used to drink with her, is that correct?

—Used to, yeah like. We were friends like, yeah. She used to be out and about normal like drinking and having the craic. She could be wild like but no harm in her I swear to God like. Was like quite normal that time. Just could be like . . . a small bit wild like. The girl made mistakes like but sure who doesn't like? We had great fun in The Snug like. That's where we hung out when we were in secondary school like. Fifteen, sixteen, seventeen kind of way like and back then like she was just normal like, sound like, you know?

They just never knew that it would pass. That it would all go and work out the way it did. Write out 'Country Fair' here. It's Van Morrison's.

_____

_____

_____

_____

_____

_____

_____

_____

_____

_____

_____

_____

_____

_____

Sinéad used to sing the second line in the last verse as, 'Sad life-times slipping though your hand', but it's totally different. She heard the words of songs wrong sometimes and learned a line that wasn't in it at all. I liked when she did that. Another bit of her isn't it? Her mind as well as her voice.

I don't think it's possible for me to give you the feeling that we had. Like in The Snug long ago. Because I can't give you the feeling of being a nice warm happy cosy drunk just by you reading a book. I can't give you the feeling of being sixteen or seventeen. I can't give you the feeling of being sixteen or seventeen and you're in a place with no parents. No teachers. No old fucking shit. I can't give you the feeling of a bar lounge that was all ours. I can't give you the feeling of how new it was for us all to have our own little bit of money and to be free to waste it on drink and happiness. I can't give you the feeling cos you weren't there. I seen them. I seen each slug of beer or Guinness or lash of vodka and coke or shot of whiskey on the rocks or peach schnapps or rum or Malibu or Tequila or Bacardi fuel them. They became greater versions of themselves isn't it? In the right dose. Became funnier, happier, bolder, stronger, louder, flirtier, nicer, trustier. Have misneach. Irish word that. Means courage maybe or spirit or bold-ness maybe. Heart isn't it?

With music played that was our own CDs. Our music. I can't give you the feeling of happy faces all around. The faces that you love the most. And they're so happy you're there, even if you're me. And you're so happy they are there. And people are sweating and laughing and shouting and singing. And you're watching them all.

Anyhow the warm glaze of alcohol made them happy and not give a fuck and made them love each other and love themselves. And I think they all knew even then that all times wouldn't be as good. They couldn't be isn't it? Agendas and plans were still strangers to them then though. They didn't give a fuck because they were drunk and because there was so much they didn't know. Most of all they didn't know themselves.

But I don't drink any more. It doesn't suit me. People sat me down and had a talk with me and told me that it was best I stayed away from the alcohol or else I wouldn't be allowed to hang around with Sinéad any more. Drink made me inappropriate. I don't remember. But Sinéad was nice about it. And James was sound about it too. Just called me a messy eejit. Messy is the word for very very drunk carry on.

Sinéad could dance too. Disco dance like, the real thing. Beats became part of her and threw her around the place, she let herself become part of it. And she was the whole time looking up to the heavens, unless she was dancing with James.

Anyhow I must get back to the story before Dr Quinn has a stroke. There was just a terrible racket downstairs. Like someone throwing a couple of saucepans on the ground in the kitchen. And that's what it was I'd say. My mother is lonesome or bored so she tries to trick me to go down to her. She already asked me twice in the last half hour if I wanted coffee. Fuck it, I'll just go down to her.

2

Something Else

Was crying in bed last night. So the headaches were bad enough this morning. Sometimes when I think of her. I dunno. I think of her the most at night. The last time I saw her she whispered thank you and squeezed my hand and then let go and she had a smile as she looked at me and then the smile went away. I can't even think of it without the tears streaming down my face. Like they are now so I'll think about something else to be talking about awhile.

Pain And Justice

Sometimes I wonder should I have killed myself. Maybe after I tell my story I will. I'll see. But if there's the remotest tiniest chance that there might be justice in the world this story has to be the fucking starting point. And I'm the one who has to tell it cos no one else knows. And I will tell it. I suppose that's what keeps me going isn't it? Just have to get my fucking head around things, that's all.

Time

Makes me think about time. I think maybe time might be the cause of my headaches. That's what I told one of Dr Quinn's junior doctors at the start. Dr Quinn asked me to talk to him. Young fella with a fat neck. He looked at me like I was after farting. A sideways glance and wrote me a quick prescription for glorified paracetamol. And that the distance between the time we're in now and where we should be. Where is that? Is that a place in time? Where does regret go in time? And the way it should have been? Was there always a way that it had to be? That's the closest I can fucking get to what I'm trying to say. Fuck him and his useless pills. I prefer Dr Quinn.

—I'm a great believer in time, Dr Quinn is always saying, and he telling me how my mind is doing.

Confession

You feel lighter coming out of Confession. That's what my mother always says. Everyone needs to talk to someone now and again about their troubles. Weight off your shoulders.

Friends

I spend times sometimes just thinking about what friends are. What's the difference between friendships and alliances? What happened has made me wonder are they just two words for the same thing. The word friends makes us feel better about it. At the end of the day all the friends I've seen in the horrible story I've to tell ended up only being allies. Or worse. The word friend was only invented to have a word for someone who wasn't out to kill you in the battles long ago. You were a friend or an enemy. Instead of 'friend' we should use 'person not out to kill you' isn't it? But that wouldn't be true of every friend either.

Everdone

Things that are everdone are a fucker. Even good things too cos if you're thinking about them it's cos things aren't so good for you now and that's bad. Like me thinking about Sinéad and James. Now is the worst time ever. All the time.

Thoughts

I never knew thoughts could hurt so much. Dr Quinn sent me to a fella that does a thing called Cognitive Behavioural Therapy as well. It kinda goes like, 'Hey, what's troubling you isn't the awful things that happened. It's the thoughts and memories you have of them that's troubling you. You can learn ways of dealing better with these thoughts and memories.' It's all fine like and stuff but it doesn't take the pain away. It doesn't make the truth go away. It doesn't make the past go away. It doesn't change what happened. No therapy in the world is gonna stop me being in pain over what happened. The only thing that could do that for me is a noose around my neck. And that's not therapy. That's fucking stupid. Death is fucking stupid. If this story tells you nothing it'll tell you that. Anyhow I asked the shrink if he knew Sinéad and he said no. So like I mean, what the fuck was he on about in the first place? If he knew her he'd have just been happy to give me the sleeping tablets so I could get a night's sleep. That was the best I could hope for and it was all I wanted from the eejit. Anyhow Dr Quinn sorted me out with sleeping tablets in the end so I didn't really mind. This other fella just didn't understand isn't it?

Afghan Scarf

That's a photocopy of an Afghan scarf that's a big important part of my story. I went down to the village for a walk down as far as the river but the bus to Newport was at the corner and I hopped on to it. The bus driver knew I'd the free travel cos he seen me before. I was only there for about an hour cos there was only one bus back cos it was already evening time even though I was only just out of bed. I seen this scarf in one of the second-hand hippy shops and I got it. It's a different Afghan scarf but it's like the one in my story and I want you to be able to see it in your mind. If a thing can be cursed then that scarf is cursed. Wherever it is now. Sinéad used to wear it. Was a present from James. James got it off his grandfather. I think his grandfather was in Afghanistan working one time. But one time a bad person stole it off Sinéad. And it wasn't cos he liked the scarf. It was cos he wanted to fuck them up. I know this is the wrong order cos the scarf part is later in the story but if I didn't tell ye I got it today then it wouldn't be the truth and the truth comes first but I don't want to be telling you any more about it now cos I just don't.

3

I looked at people in Newport for a small while the day I got the scarf. Newport people would remind you how ridiculous people are with the heads on them and the lanky walk of them and the way they sit on a bus or in cars or in queues all facing one way and the long stiff stupid backs on them and the two hands on them doing nothing half the time just hanging there dangling and the confused embarrassed faces on them and the heads stuck on to their necks looking around for clues and to see what other people are thinking of them and the way they think they look nice in some clothes but not nice in other clothes and the way they have different rooms in their houses and the way they paint these rooms cos they think it looks nice and the way they feel pride for the things they have and want other people to admire them and the way they have to cut their fingernails and their toenails cos they keep growing and the things they do to hide from the rain and the cold and the way they use tissue paper to wipe their noses and the way they write newspapers and make news programmes where one of them tells the rest of them about bad things that have happened to some of them and how they feel sorry for them and how they're relieved it didn't happen to them and how some people hurt other people cos they want to and how some people cause other people pleasure cos they want to and the way they misplace things and spend time looking for what they've lost but can't remember what they did with it and how sometimes they drop something and it breaks and they say a special word for such occasions that's called a curse word and how they teach their young never to use such words but to use other words instead and how they understand that some time they're going to die and this makes them afraid and sad and how they all each and every one of them is different and how they can be jealous of the differences and how they all use their own special differences to keep on keeping on best as they can and how they fall in love sometimes with someone who doesn't love them back and how they have personalities and how their personalities change if you take away food from them or love or friendship or admiration or if people are nasty to them and the way sometimes they misread the intentions of the people around them and cause themselves stress or cause other people stress and how this same stress can make them less likeable to other people and how some people are more forgiving than other people and how some people find it too hard to forgive and how other people find it too easy and how sometimes they remember something that never even happened and forget something that did and how their babies are born totally helpless and need a lot more care than calves and how they get more time to live than most other animals and how they can't for the life of them figure out what time is or where they came from and how they kill each other for greed and how they get itches on their skin and how their skin holds them together.

Signs

Dinky was cornerback but he had a long kick so he used to take the kick-outs instead of the goalkeeper. Then James used to be midfield. There are two midfielders in Gaelic football so for the kick-outs one would go on one side of the pitch and the other on the other side. Loads of times Master Coughlan had to insist that Dinky would kick the ball out to the side that James was on, at least some of the time, but preferably all the time cos James was one of the best young fielders of the ball in the county. If I was looking for signs at the time that was definitely one.

Remorse
N. 1. guilt; a strong feeling of guilt or regret 2. pity; compassion or pity [14th C. Via Old French *remors* from, ultimately, Latin *remordere* 'to torment', from *mordere* 'to bite'.]

I feel remorse yes.

Ultimately. Ultimate.
Some words make you think of other stuff.

Ulterior
Adj. 1. underlying; existing in addition to or being other than what is apparent or assumed 2. lying outside; lying outside or

beyond a point or area [From Latin, 'further', formed from assumed *ulter* 'beyond'.]

Ulcer

Watched a nature programme once. Monkeys getting ulcers and suffering from nervous disorders. When they feel left out by the rest of them or when all the other monkeys are mean to them. Monkeys can be fierce mean.

Ugly

Adj. 1.offensive or repulsive to the eye; disagreeable to look at 2. loathsome; vile especially **a.** morally offensive or repulsive; base **b.** very bad or disagreeable; offensive to the ear, nose, etc.; nasty 3. likely to cause trouble; threatening; dangerous 4. US (*informal*) given to or displaying violence, extreme irritability, etc.; very ill-natured [From Scandinavian (compare Old Icelandic *uggligr* dreadful <*uggr* fear).]

Same as Sinéad's mother. It was more her treatment of people was ugly though.

Uilleann pipes

A type of Irish bagpipes played by squeezing the bellows under the arm [Early 20[th]C. From Irish *píob uilleann* 'elbow pipe', from *uille* 'elbow', from Old Irish *uilind*.]

Like the ones they played at the side of the grave. Everyone started crying. The uilleann piper played 'Ar Éireann Ní Neosfainn Cé hÍ.' Means 'I'll Never Reveal Who She Is'. Or 'For Ireland I Won't Tell You Who She Is.' It's some ancient Irish love song. And there's an ancient Romanian song too with the exact same air. Travelled somehow. The tune of it would bring tears to a stone it would. Brought tears to everyone who wasn't already crying at that funeral so it did. Except myself. I was after climbing up on the flat part of the roof of a house looking down at them all going about the business of the burial. Ritual. Rite. The difference between the bagpipes and the uilleann pipes is the difference between a shout and a cry. Anyhow everyone was crying except myself. I started vomiting. Nobody could see me cos I was off away from the crowd on my own. Then I think I passed out. Came round and they were in the middle of the Rosary. The Rosary is a prayer. Or more like a load of prayers repeated in some special order. The coffin was going down into the ground. Interred. In earth.

Words

It's easy to say words and not mean them. Can't fake the kind of singing Sinéad did. It's either in you or it's not isn't it?

'Blue Moon' was one of their songs too. Whatever way they made the record it sounded like Elvis was right in the fucking room with you.

'Blue Moon'

_____

_____

_____

_____

_____

_____

_____

_____

_____

_____

_____

_____

_____

Walk to Newport

One time when we were in secondary school there was the walk to Newport for charity. A sponsored walk for Mother Teresa. There was a school from Newport and two schools from Mullinahone, St Brendan's and the Tech. The Tech was a Christian Brothers school and that was all boys and the school from Newport was a convent and that was all girls. Our school, St Brendan's was boys and girls.

The nuns in the convent wanted all the girls to be kept separate from the boys until the beginning of the walk so Sinéad and all the girls from our school had to go on a separate bus from us boys. When the buses and buses of girls descended on Ballyronan you could see that the organisers were starting to shit themselves. They had all us lads from St Brendan's and the Tech inside the wall of the grotto, watching the more than four hundred young girls in hoisted school-skirts and perfume and make-up and fake tan and real tan and opened buttons and ties. The nuns had the girls all covered up as much as they could but it was pointless cos the hot sun and the girls had other ideas. They had the girls standing across the road from the grotto.

They weren't one bit happy, them nuns. Would have struck us blind there and then if they could. A roar built up then all of a sudden, that stayed going for probably a whole minute. Hundreds of teenage boys and girls just screaming. Eventually they shut us all up so we could hear our principal speaking on the megaphone. He congratulated us all for all the money we raised and invited the first years to start walking together. Then second years, then third years and then us. Fifth and sixth years behind us then.

They had nuns and Brothers and old fusspot parents along the whole nine miles every hundred yards to stop any boys and girls going away into the countryside for a shift. A shift is a kiss.

Something gave the air a kind of an electricity that day. Youth. Sun. Dunno. Probably it was the best day of my life.

After a few miles we were coming up towards Pontoon Castle. Pontoon Castle stands on the wooded valley of the river Crandon between Ballyronan and Newport.

—We have to escape, said James.

—Yeah, said Sinéad, it'll be raining tomorrow.

—We need a distraction, said James.

—Yeah said Dinky, someone to get shot or something.

We walked on. People and parents and concerned citizens and volunteers and whoever else walked along with us in pairs. Pair of these fifty-year-olds walking along with us every fifty yards about. A yard for every year. A fly landed on Sinéad's forehead and she made a fierce nice and funny face and she brushed it away from her fierce quick and shook her head a little bit. Next thing at that very exact moment something miraculous happened.

—What's going on above?

—What the fuck?

Two fifty-year-olds did a fat-ass run to where the crowd was gathering up ahead of us. Girls were screaming. James ran ahead and Dinky followed and I followed then.

—Antoinette O'Riordan is after fainting.

—Is she all right?

—She's fine.

Antoinette O'Riordan was the whole time fainting the poor thing. Fainted before exams. Fainted during them. Fainted after them. Fainted in Mass. They were all helping her to her feet when James grabbed me and Sinéad by the arm and said to come on. He went first, helping Sinéad over, and I hopped over beside them, landing on Dinky who was after hopping over it already with Racey.

—Fuck ya Charlie, Dinky goes and they all giggling mad.

Biggest fear was standing on branches cos the crackling would be heard by whoever was on the road above us. We crouched and stayed silent while the fifth and sixth years passed. The sparkling river way down in front of us. Tempting us through the trees.

James climbed up again and said the next group was a hundred yards back the road so if we ran to the far side of the castle we could run into the woods and down to the river. We went for it and we made it. We sat down then, leaving the grey stupid obedient road behind us. When the last of them were gone we got up to stretch our legs.

—We're gonna be killed you know, Racey said.

—We won't be killed, said Sinéad, I promise we won't be killed. We'll get in a world of trouble but they won't kill us.

We laughed all nervous and giddy.

—Will there definitely be a roll call in Newport ye think? asked Dinky.

—Dunno. Maybe not, went James.

—Well that's our only hope, Dinky said.

—What if we're expelled? Racey asked then.

—We'll be suspended but we won't be expelled, said Sinéad. They'd never expel the lot of us.

We walked down the path through the woods down, over the wooden footbridge over the waterfall and then the river appeared like you were at the cinema and it was on the screen all bright in the dark. At the other side of the river there was a small dock and a big red rowing boat.

—Pity that boat is on the other side, said Dinky.

—Pity we're on this side, James said.

James lay down on the soft grassy river bank and Sinéad lay at a right angle to him with her head on his belly looking up at the sky. Racey lay her head on Sinéad's tummy then and Dinky lay his head on hers. This was them.

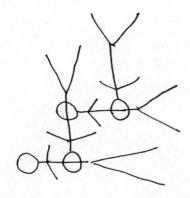

This was me.

They all watched the blue sky and spoke about what kind of trouble they thought we were going to get in and I skimmed stones and then they were planning how to get to Newport without being seen.

—We could go down to the village and hitch a lift to Cork and then hitch a lift to Newport on that road, James said. That way we might get there before roll call.

—How long does it take to walk nine miles?

—Quarter of an hour a mile so that's about two hours. Be lucky to make it.

There was silence then for a long time.

—I wonder is that river deep?

—Don't be getting any crazy ideas James, Sinéad said.

—Seriously though.

—Stop.

—What do you think Charlie?

—I dunno, I said. Maybe.

—What ya reckon? he asked Dinky.

—Deeper than a spit, said Dinky.

—I must go for a wee, said James.

He went off down the river a bit and into the woods. He was gone a while and next thing we heard a bit of a splash and there's James wading through the water in his boxer shorts.

—James, said Sinéad. Come out of it.

—Aaagh, said James, it's freezing.

—Please come out James, she said.

—I've seen fishermen out here when the river's a lot rougher, he called back.

—Please come out James.

—I will in a minute, he said.

He looked back at us and gave us a big mad grin.

—Jesus Christ James, Sinéad said.

We were all laughing nervously as he went deeper and deeper. Next thing Dinky stands up and starts stripping off too.

—What are you doing? said Racey.

—I'm goin' in too.

Dinky stripped to his jocks and waded in too.

—Oh, he said. Tá mo liathróidí fuair.

That means my balls are cold in Irish. Halfway across the river James was up to his chest in water but then he started rising up out of it again over to the other side. He waded up towards the boat. Next thing Dinky was nearly halfway across when he froze. James looked back at him.

—You all right? James asked him.

Dinky didn't answer.

—What's wrong with you? Racey called to Dinky.

Still no answer.

—I think he's in shock, James said. Just stay there Denis, I'll come and get ya.

When James got on the boat he was looking around.

—There's no bloody oars, he said.

He jumped out on to the bank at the other side and looked around. He grabbed two big long heavy sticks, broke the twigs off them and threw them in the boat. He bent down and pulled up something from under the seats of the boat. He raised two orange life jackets and grinned across at us. He released the boat. It was about two hundred yards down river by the time he got to the other side of the river in the boat. He used one of the long branches to push the boat from the river bed as it was taken downstream. Sinéad had his clothes. Dinky was still frozen shitless in the middle of the river.

—I can't, Dinky said.

James threw me the rope and I pulled the boat up on the river bank. He handed the girls the two life jackets. I had to clean them with my jumper cos the girls wouldn't put them on at first cos they were too dirty. There was a third life jacket too but none of us wore it.

Then James walked up the bank to where Dinky had gone in from.

—I'm coming, he said.

Dinky was still saying,

—I can't.

The girls just watched on and James waded back in and got Dinky by the arm and coaxed him back the way he went in. Dinky was white as a ghost. Led by the arm same as an old woman getting help across the road. The lads got dressed then. The girls weren't laughing, just looking at each other and shrugging. I walked up to the lads.

—Dunno what happened there James, Dinky was saying. I just . . . fucking lost it. Got it into my head there was a hole in front of me and I was gonna die.

James laughed. Then Dinky laughed a little bit too.

—You saved my life man, Dinky said. We should be blood brothers.

When James was getting dressed Dinky got a small key ring pinknife off his jeans and stabbed the tip of his finger with the knife and drew blood. Then he stood in front of James, handing him the knife and showing him his bloody finger.

—What the fuck? said James.

—Blood brothers, Dinky said. I have to save you some time too. That's the rule.

—Go 'way to fuck boy. What are we nine? said James, and turned and walked back to the girls, pulling his jumper over his head.

—What are ye doing? Racey called.

—Nothing, James said. We're coming now.

James walked on and I followed him. Dinky caught up then and we jumped on the boat and we were on our way. Dinky and James steered us with the two sticks. I tried to row a bit with my hands. But there was no need so I stopped. We took turns then with the sticks. One of us took a break every now and again. Racey asked Dinky what happened to him and Dinky goes,

—I just wanted to stop for a little bit and enjoy the moment, and they all laughed.

The sailing together gave the five of us a nice feeling. Down river. Green and shadows. And dark brown earth. The underside of fields. It all moved past you slow and content. Lying back. Sun. The sound of water. When the stick plunged in you heard the deep fat roundy gulp and then the high-pitched splash at the top. The flighty playful drops up top. Away from the business end of things. The working water. Floating is definitely very different to walking. Can make you giddy. Especially when it's supposed to be walking you are isn't it? Drifting away together. The river was our accomplice.

We got out before the bridge across the river before it opened up and went out to sea. We tied the boat to a tree and ran across a field that brought us out on to the road. Easiest nine miles we ever walked. We walked across the bridge that would bring us into Newport from the south side. The walkers would be coming in from the north side because that was shorter. When we reached the waterfront we could see there was lots of them already there. All over the place, eating ice creams that were given out for free. We went around a block and joined them from the town side. First the two girls. Then us three lads. About an hour later the roll was taken in the bus back to the school.

I dunno if you wish you were there with us but if you don't it's because I made a balls of describing it. I had it in my mind that this was going to be a great part of the story, but it wasn't was it? Nicest day of my life maybe. Dunno why it doesn't seem so great now. Probably cos it's only words on a page. Not the real thing isn't it?

Isn't it not? Like a film that's supposed to be great and turns out to be shit. I think I made a balls of describing it. I have to admit that to myself and to you. I made a balls of it. Made the best most exciting day of my life sound cat to the world. But that's the best I can do. I'm not a writer am I? I'm an onion picker and a gardener and a petrol filler and a car washer and a stairs sander and a wallpaper scraper and a floor mopper but I'm not a writer. I'm very disappointed with how the boat trip turned out. Very disappointed. They're worth better than that, James and Sinéad are. And that day was worth better. Like as if there was a shit eulogy at the funeral of JFK or Princess Diana. Didn't do them justice isn't it? What good am I? What's the use of me? If I can't manage to tell this story right I'm only a waste of blah.

Similes

All good writers use similes to describe stuff. That's what Dr Quinn says to me too today. He showed me some in a book. I think they're thick. Waste of time.

Listen to this.

> It was a glorious, oh, truly glorious spring sunrise, all Egyptian creams and golds under a Renoir sky of silver blue, the beach sun-dappled and still, seeming not so much itself as its own image in a faded photograph from some years ago.
>
> The streams on the distant hills were like cracks and crevices in the earth's surface, revealing a moving mercury sea underneath.
>
> The redbrick façade, although tumbledown, is really rather attractive when looked at with a forgiving eye, the surface of each brick

worn, their edges rounded, some protruding oddly, the years of rain coalescing the rusty browns and maroons, comforting somehow, like the appearance of a favourite old cardigan say, or a winter's fire.

The lad who wrote that stuff won some big book prize. Must be good so. I just don't get it unfortunately. As far as I'm concerned the lad who wrote that has a way too much time on his hands to be coming up with shit like that. Anyhow I'm gonna get all my similes out of the way in one go. Get them over and done with to fuck. Cos I hate them.

The book was like a page followed by about three hundred other pages and they were all stuck together along the side.

The car was like a jeep but in the form of a car.

Snoozie was like a piece of a jigsaw. And a piece hiding in the middle where he wouldn't ever be noticed. A piece as far away from the edge as he could be. Could never live on the edge. If he had wings, he'd walk.

Being in primary school was like being a daddy-long-legs that someone pulled the legs off.

In secondary school you realised that all the other daddy-long-legs had their legs cut off too but now the legs were starting to grow back again and it felt good and the assholes that cut them off were starting to get a bit worried and were trying to placate you and lick your arse and entice you with stuff and the promise of more stuff to make it all OK again so that you might come round in the end to join them pulling the legs off the younger ones.

That last simile was like a baby's first steps that he couldn't bring to a reasonable stop before crashing.

Or a drunk's speed-wobble that he couldn't bring to stop before stumbling into people and making an eejit of himself. Embarrassing.

Dinky was like a tree in the shade of others. He grew all wonky and weird and out of shape in order to get a bit of the sunshine. Surviving fucked him up. Like the rest of us. But he did survive. Like the rest of us.

Death did them part. Like a divorce. Only final.

Watches are like a slap in the face telling you to do what you're told the whole time. That's why I never wore one. I still pretend not to be able to tell the time from the face of a clock.

Fire is like all we have isn't it? Like life. My favourite word. Fire.

Music is like the only bit of quiet I used to get. Shut out all the voices I've heard through my life. Don't need music any more for that.

I wrote another shit simile there like I give a fuck.

I write similes like a fella that can't write good similes.

Jealousy sat on James' shoulders like mighty new big lumps of cancer.

Jealousy was new to him like the new way a man looks at life after he's been told he has fuck all time left.

Jealous like a fella on his deathbed.

He hadn't a clue, like he spoke a language all along that had no word for jealousy.

There's things you can't be saying too. Like saying a fella's

family were relieved he killed himself cos he was such a troublesome sort of a prick. That he didn't really fit in anyhow and life
would be a lot better without him. Or someone saying Jesus Christ
that's a ferociously ugly child you have. Or saying the reason she
doesn't leave him really is cos she's addicted to his violence. Same
as a gambler.

Had to ditch some similes – kill them off like the farmer drowned
the kittens with no home.

Similes are like empty retches between vomits.

He was mean like a baby. Babies don't give two shits about all
this sharing is caring business.

James' father looked out the window of the castle like an alien.
It was like this fella was on the wrong planet or something. First
time I ever seen him look stupid. Like the monkey in space.

The body was lying there wasted like Pompeii. Seen Pompeii
on the telly one time and I very small long ago and never forgot.
Seen the shape of them.

Waste is a sad word like innocence but it isn't sad in the same
way.

The body was cold and stiff like a Christmas turkey in the
butcher's isn't it? The mouth was open in a gamallish kind of way.
Anything could crawl into it overnight. One eye was fully open.
The other one closest the ground was a small bit less than half
open. Lying on the left side, half naked. Couldn't have looked
more different. A body is no comparison to the person anyhow
isn't it? Especially what I seen. In the dreams. No comparison.
Should have evaporated or something. Or been turned into a
diamond statue standing all graceful or something. And there

should have been music maybe. But what I seen and the mouth open. No. No. In my dream. Nothing. Worst dream ever isn't it?

Where the body was was nice like a postcard. The look of the body wasn't like a postcard.

The tears in his eyes made it hard to read the words he was typing. Was like looking through an empty bottle.

Sad like looking into someone's eyes knowing that they're trying to figure out if you're lying to them or telling them the truth and it means so much to them but they've no way of knowing and they can only hope hope hope.

A miracle like Sinéad channelling Kurt Cobain and she singing 'Pennyroyal Tea'. She didn't bring him back. But she brought back how he felt isn't it? How he felt was alive now in someone else. I was there. I seen it happen. Heard it.

There's a million different ways from A to B but most people only know a few. Knowing all these ways is like being a human that can fly. Or like being the invisible man.

Sometimes I black out. Like when you're reading something and you realise you were thinking of something else all the time and have to go back and read a whole page again. Except with me the page is gone and you've nothing to go back to. I never really get caught out though cos no one ever expects me to know anything anyhow.

Nothing is like no music. Same as death. And who cares?

Regret is like more than enough punishment for the mistake.

His love for her was like medicine or bandages or a cure for her.

I'm like the laptop with a broken screen that everyone thinks is useless but the computer's working fine.

That's the end of the similes. Over and done with. I asked Dr Quinn was there any chance they could perforate the pages with the similes so you could tear them out and wipe your ass with them. He said 'twould be very expensive. Maybe you could use a scissors or something.

My nose is running like nobody's business.

He burst into the room like nobody's business.

The car was green like nobody's business.

I never got it. Nobody's business? What's that about? I think in Ireland we say nobody's business when we don't know what something is like. Anyhow that's the last three similes for you. I couldn't think of any more. Just like that. Nobody's business.

5

Mind for Faces

Some people have a mind for faces. Other people have a mind for names. Other people remember things they see. I remember things I hear. Always did. I could hear a song once and I'd know it. Or a conversation in a pub. I remember these things word for word. Sometimes I wish I didn't cos when I think of things or people sometimes it's like voices in my head.

Laugh

I made people laugh. I don't know if it's cos I hated them or loved them. I'd get myself into all sorts of tangles and look at their faces then and they all laughing mad at me. Head full of blood on them, pushed up from within with the height of heaving. Make you wonder what has laughter got to do with disdain. Or what has disdain got to do with loyalty.

Seen it the time I got stuck. When I was thirteen I was the

water boy at some big under-fourteens' match and the ball hopped over the gate of the fence that was around the pitch. Cos of the bank it rolled back near the gate so instead of trying climbing it I tried to reach through it and I got my head stuck in the gate. They sent some fella off to get his angle grinder cos every time they tried to get my head loose I let an almighty roar out of me. At half time people were going over to the chip van and the shop and they were all asking me was I all right so I said I was fierce hungry so they came back with some chips for me. They put them down on the grass in front of me where I could reach them.

—Are you all right now Charlie?

—Yeah, says I with a big mouthful of chips and I trying to look up at them best as I could with my head two foot from the ground stuck in the gate.

And they all walking on laughing and shaking their heads saying,

—Jesus Christ, he's some pity, ha?

—God help us.

We won the match. They got one of the subs to be running on with the water for the rest of it instead of me. The whole crowd stayed on at the end of the match to watch when the man with the angle grinder came and cut me free. And the big cheer then. Bally-ronan's supporters and the other team's supporters. They were all for me, and they were against the gate and they all laughing and joking together. Not like during the match when they didn't like each other at all.

6

Next thing then was we all went to Irish college. Sinéad studied Irish like mad so she'd get a scholarship and she did. She was mad to get away from home for a few weeks cos things weren't so good at home. The gardaí had been to the house over her mother and father fighting and her mother had gone to stay somewhere else a few nights leaving her on her own with her father. She used to hang around with me and James in the evening until she knew her father was gone out to the pub. Then we'd walk her home and maybe have a cup of tea with her in her house and they'd work on some lyrics or a song or just listen to some tunes before going home. They worked on 'Evening Shadows' around that time.

James used to sing it cos the voice in the song was a man. Anyhow enough fucking talk. We'll have the song now from James Kent. Wouldn't doubt ya James. Good man James.

She like some kinda Marilyn Monroe type
Or some girl out of a Shane McGowan song

Dunno I must have eaten something rotten cos I vomited that time yesterday. I'd to take sleeping tablets then to sleep.

I'm thinking there's stuff the world doesn't deserve isn't it? Like the songs. Sinéad and James'. I've recordings of theirs.

You should hear the way this one took off to another level when Sinéad would join James for the chorus.

And the evening shadows fall yeah
Rolling summer evenings slow
And the evening shadows fall yeah
Maybe it's time that you let go

The tune of the verses was fierce safe, and James sang it just right. Safe. But this made Sinéad's input in the chorus blow your fucking blah. The way with music isn't it? Just the right amount of safety and risks. And in music you've less to lose. Just time. And you lose that anyhow cos there's no choice.

The end of the song never got wrote far as I know. Lots of songs never got finished. But I have the recordings and I have their notes.

Anyhow, I suppose I'll have to explain to you what the summer Irish colleges are before I go any further. Irish is a language. Yeah we had our own language before the English came and beat it out of us. So anyhow after eight hundred years didn't we finally beat the cunts and Ireland became no part of

Britain no more. So there we were with our own country again at last only wasn't the whole country after forgetting how to talk Irish. The crowd in charge then were trying to figure out how in the name of God to get people talking Irish again. They realised then that there were people in the arsehole of nowhere way out in the west of Ireland and in the little islands on the west coast who were still talking Irish every day. 'Twas how the English had no interest in these places cos there was no good land there worth stealing, only rocks. So for eight hundred years they escaped a right good battering and having to talk English. By the time Ireland was free these places were the only places still full of Irish speakers and diddly-idle-dee music and Irish dancing and weird old-style singing called sean-nós.

Anyhow. Right. So the government started setting up Irish colleges in these places and paying for youngsters from all over the country to spend a few weeks with families there or in the dormitories of the colleges and go to classes where they'd learn Irish. In the night then there'd be a céilí which was like a disco only no flashing lights and no disco music, just diddly-idle-dee music and Irish dancing. Just other youngsters and time. Three weeks of it.

It's a magical place cos there's a load of young people who are neither children nor grown-up humans and they are freer than they ever been before. With no one pushing them forward or holding them back. Free to love and be loved. Reject and be rejected. Dream about and be dreamed about. Trust and be trusted. I went on a bit. But that's what it was. That's exactly what it was for the young people.

The world was full of pain but that didn't matter to them cos just like all the grown-ups who ever went before them, they now had perfected the same language too and the same words. And the thoughts these words permit conspire to allow the pain of others to be ignored. We are all proof of that isn't it? But them thoughts never got into their heads. They had Coca Cola and Tommy Hilfiger and Lynx and Nirvana and seeing how they were figuring up alongside other people their own age. They had how they looked and how they spoke to be thinking about. And they had attractions to pursue or keep under control. And they had fun. More fun than they ever had before, most of them maybe. And I loved seeing every second of it all and even though I was on the sideline of life I wasn't jealous of them. I was rooting for them all and they fighting alive and fire in their bellies.

I said very few words in Irish college myself. Made people think I was tough and cool in the beginning but at the end of three weeks they probably just thought I wasn't right in the head. At least they didn't know I was the village gamal back home. And they weren't going to find out either with James around. Mostly I just said nothing and people got used to ignoring my presence. James said at the start,

—That's Charlie. He doesn't talk. Finds it all too boring. He listens to music. But he's cool. Charlie's all right man.

I used to have headphones on all the time. Hardly ever had batteries in the walkman but no one knew the difference.

There was an old fella who was teaching Irish dancing and old Irish music. He was kinda funny and everyone liked him

and were nice to him, even the bold kids, but he was a bit
obsessed with Sinéad's singing. He was in charge of the choir at
Mass too and he had Sinéad doing all the solos. Sinéad really
liked it. I don't think she was used to all the praise she got.
Local old women used to come up to her after the Mass to
thank her and to ask her where she was from and who her
parents were as if she should've been related to some famous
singer in the area a hundred or two hundred years ago. But they
couldn't trace her. Only Halloran one of them knew went to
America long ago and she said that he had the voice of a bullock
and they were glad of the peace when he left. Sinéad was just
smiling and nodding her head and blushing a little too but only
at the start.

—Beautiful.

—Go hálainn ar fad.

The old Irish dancing teacher caught her eye and gave her a
proud nod, as much to congratulate himself too. He knew he'd
done good. Charming the young shy talent out of her. The talent
beginning to believe in itself. James was happy in the background
playing the guitar or the keyboard. He knew this confidence
would help her to fly isn't it?

He used to like watching her dance too – the old dance
teacher. Sinéad wasn't the best Irish dancer of the girls or
nowhere near but had something else that the other girls could
never have even if they could seem like the ground was electricity shocking them a foot into the air every time their feet
touched it. Sinéad had something different. The best was when
she made a mistake – she'd frown and smile all at the same time.

The old dance teacher had me in charge of the tape recorder cos I was fucking up all his dances the first day.

—Maith thú, a Sheárlas, he used to say. Good man Charles.

—Píosín ceoil a Sheárlas marsin, le do thoil. A little bit of music so Charles, if you please.

—Bhí sé sin go hálainn ar fad a Sheárlas, Maith an fear. That was beautiful altogether Charles, good man.

As if I was playing the accordion and not just pressing the play button on the tape recorder. Maybe he thought that he could even give a fella like me a bit of confidence. Old teachers think anything is possible cos maybe they seen it done. I'd say this old fella definitely, he believed in miracles.

In the last day of dance class he asked Sinéad to sing for himself and the class. She agreed. She sang the old Irish song called 'Ar Éireann Ní Neosfainn Cé hÍ'.

There was just silence after for a bit when she finished and wherever it brought the old teacher it made his voice break a bit when he thanked Sinéad.

—Go hálainn ar fad.

I could have given ye the lyrics of the song for free cos they're ancient and the fellas who wrote them songs a hundred or two hundred or three hundred years ago were only tramps and beggars who walked the byroads, cos the Irish chiefs were all after getting beaten. It's the same song I mentioned earlier that was played on the uilleann pipes at a funeral one time. But Dr Quinn said no one would understand it cos it's Irish and ye wouldn't be interested.

Anyhow Dinky used to be doing monkey impressions in Irish college to make people laugh. He'd stick out his chin and somehow pull his bottom lip up as far as his nose. Then he'd bend over, tickle his armpits and go,

—Ooo-ooo, ooo-ooo, ah-ah, ah-ah, ooo-ooo.

People found it funny and stupid.

James told him he didn't think he should do it any more and Dinky went spitting thick.

—Fuck you James. I know what you're at all right. I fucking know what you're at all right. Lord Haw Haw.

James just looked at him and said nothing. Dinky went ranting.

—Think you can tell me what to do. Is it? Do you think you can fucking tell me what to do? Who the fuck do you think you are like? Think you're fucking great that's your problem.

James still said nothing. That night in the céilí everyone was asking Dinky to do his monkey impression. Especially the older lads so they could be taking the piss out of him and get a laugh off the girls. Dinky was known for the rest of the week as the lad who does the monkey impressions and if it wasn't for the fact he was always around with James, the nickname Monkeyface would've stuck. James caught one of the bigger Dublin lads by the scruff of the neck and told him if he heard him call Dinky Monkeyface again he'd kick him back to Dublin. Threw him on the bed then and called him Jackeen.

The Dubs used to call the country lads boggers and we'd call the Dubs Jackeens. That's from the time the Queen of England was let into Dublin long ago and all the Dublin lads got free Union Jack flags and didn't they wave them like mad all along O'Connell Street and she passing. Fucking Jackeens.

Anyhow, Dinky got on fine in Irish college after. Just had a bit of a hairy start but people soon forgot about calling him Monkey-face and got to like him as James' best friend. One of the Tipperary girls that was there asked him about it at the end of the course.

—Hey Denis.

That's what people called him before he was Dinky.

—Yeah?

—What possessed you to do that monkey thing?

—I dunno. I think I did actually get possessed by a monkey.

—Everyone thought you were crazy you know.

—I thought everyone else was crazy from where I could see them up on my tree.

—You're funny.

—I think I did it for my nephews who thought it was hilarious but they're only five or six.

—Ha! Really?

—Yeah.

—That's mad.

—Yeah.

—I'd say your nephews just think you're a bit of a fool, she said.

Dinky blushed and laughed along with everyone else.

On the third day we heard a commotion in the dorm next door to us. When we went in there was a fat younger kid on his knees crying. Pink head up on him same as a big old balloon that lost some air. Dimpled from the fat. Few other young lads scampered back to their bunks when we came in. The fat lad was all snots and tears but he managed to answer James eventually,

—They were calling me skunk.

Started sniffling and panting again then and wiped his nose with his sleeve and said,

—And they kept saying I was farting and I wasn't. Whenever they see me they block their nose and roar 'Skunk' at me.

Then he got fierce angry and shouted at his tormentors, 'Fuckers!' and started banging his thighs hard with his fists, wild angry face with tears streaming down his face. And then he pointed at two of them and shouted,

—And they call me lagging jacket.

The two bullies were a bit shocked by this outburst. James put his arm around the fat boy and told him that as long as we were around it would never happen again. James took hold of the boy's wrists to stop him hitting his chubby thighs in rage, all the while saying,

—Easy. Easy.

Then he said,

—Come into our dorm for a while, will ya?

The kid didn't answer. I think he thought James wasn't being serious.

—Come on. We're listening to the new Nirvana album. Have you heard of Nirvana?

—No.

—Well then it's time to commence your education. Come on.

He followed us out. James stuck his head back into the dorm at the end and said,

—Anyone else mocks my cousin they're going to have us to deal with.

James put his arm on the fat kid's shoulder and said,

—*Never mind.*

—I know, said the fat kid, snorting like a little pig.

—No. *Never mind.* It's the name of the Nirvana album.

He tossed him the CD cover and laughed. The fat kid smiled.

—What's your name cous'?

—Henry, said Henry.

—Hey scumbags, James roared. I wanna introduce an honorary member of Nirvana.

Nirvana was what we called our dorm as well.

—Henry is his name.

All the lads who were around on bunks shouted out a hello to Henry and went back about their business. Poker, computer games, car magazines. One lad had a tabloid.

—He's staying in dorm three but they all keep farting in there, Dinky said.

Henry laughed. There was another chap. A big lanky Dub that hung around with us all the time as well. He was the biggest Nirvana fan you ever saw. He'd sit on the bed and play the imaginary drums along to the songs. Then there was Sinéad and her friends.

So. We went on like that. Three weeks. A kind of freedom. Except for the teachers who as long as you stayed put and didn't go killing or hurting anyone they left you alone. And you had to make an effort to talk Irish when they were around of course. So it was a bigger version of freedom than any of us were used to.

And every year everyone cried leaving Cape Clear, same as all the other Irish colleges. I watched them all. The trying to be hard men, the young beauties, the spotty self-conscious, the lucky confident, the young eyes filling with their first knowing tears. For the friends they'd never see again. They knew it now. That the truth of the world was the truth of leaving isn't it? New to them all, the old was. And how they might never see the Naomh Chiaráin ferry boat again or the little roads and the old people who watched them being young and the hills and the sea within a mile in any direction. Even me they'd miss and my weird self so hopeless and strange and sad to them. They knew too that life gets hard and cancer and big stuff happens and they'd change and have to work and change into people that could succeed and survive and wear suits or uniforms and behave all appropriate always so they'd succeed and survive. And they knew they'd never be like this again isn't it?

Could go through the whole three weeks there but it's not really part of the story so I'll just go straight to the last night. Some stuff I tell is just so you can kind of know the people isn't it? Important that you know the people.

The last night was always mental on the island. It was the tiring middle-aged teachers versus the teenagers who were sprouting wings in the dark hours. The worst that can happen is they're sent home but everyone is going home the next day anyhow. The plan was to escape from the dorms at four in the morning and meet the girls by the ruin for sunrise.

—Henry I'm sorry you can't come.

—What? Ah come on.

—No. Anything happened you we'd be in fierce shit. You're too young.

—Nothing will happen.

—We could easily get caught.

—I don't care. I'll risk it.

—Not going to happen.

—Who'd wake you Henry?

—I'll set my alarm.

—You'd better not Henry.

But there was the last céilí first. Went on longer on the last night and there was a disco for an hour after the Irish dancing. Sinéad loved the song 'You Are Not Alone' by Michael Jackson. Was on the radio the whole time that time. The DJ was only a teacher. A young bittertwisted fella of about twenty-five called Ó Cinnéide who took a strange dislike to James from day one. Anyhow James asked him to play 'You Are Not Alone' when the slow songs were on in the disco but Ó Cinnéide said he didn't have it but James saw it on the desk and said you do have it and then Ó Cinnéide told James to get lost. James told Sinéad she'd hear it before the night was out but even though James went up twice more to Ó Cinnéide, he still wouldn't play it.

The last time James went up and asked him to play 'You Are Not Alone' Ó Cinnéide had a right good rant and shouted at him not to ask him again. James turned around and walked away but he was after stealing Ó Cinnéide's Michael Jackson CD unknown to anyone. Except me. I seen it. Ó Cinnéide was all business lining up his CDs and James just lifted it and stuck it into the belt of his trousers under his shirt.

Ó Cinnéide didn't know his problem. His problem was that he didn't like young people and he was after choosing a job that wouldn't ever let him get away from them. He didn't trust them. He was afraid of the fire isn't it?

Anyhow the girls' dorms were about fifty yards from the boys' dorms. By half one in the morning they were all in bed asleep or nearly. The teachers had stopped patrolling the corridors. That's when the wave came. The soundwave that woke the stillness for a dance.

Probably for the first time ever in the history of Cape Clear island or the island when it had no name at all but just was there. And probably for the first time for the goats with the beards. And for the first time for the old people who lived on the island. And the rabbits in the fields. They all woke or stopped dead on their tracks and tried to figure out what the sound meant. In the dorms the young people from the mainland sat up in their beds and knew it was Michael Jackson.

'You Are Not Alone'

_____
_____
_____
_____
_____
_____
_____
_____
_____
_____
_____
_____

It sounded good coming out over the intercom. Could hear Ó Cinnéide starting to shout. Ó Cinnéide was a zealot.

—Séamus Kent, tar amach as sin! Oscail an doras.

When I went down a few of the older teachers were pulling Ó Cinnéide away from the door cos he was wanting to break it down. They knew he was got the better of but Ó Cinnéide wasn't inclined to believe it. The teachers were busy dealing with Ó Cinnéide so I walked away out so as to hear what the music sounded like under the stars.

If you can imagine night-time and outside and no wind and an intercom and Michael Jackson playing out over the intercom then

you'll have a good idea of what it was like. No lights came on in
the girls' dorm and the only light coming from the boys' dorm was
the office. I could see the shadow of James. He was standing dead
still for the whole thing – just holding the mic to the CD player.
Everything different cos it was night. Stilly isn't it? And not stupid
with daytime business. Stones on the ground with the memory of
the sun. But Michael Jackson reinvented everything that night. All
was new. Even the stones could never be the same again. And the
air was new. All was new to the goats on the hill. Michael Jackson
made it so. Atmosphere. And I was new myself from it.

So. That was the last night on Cape Clear. James had to stand
outside the door of his dorm in his boxer shorts for the whole
night with Ó Cinnéide sitting in a chair watching him.

—Did he let you go to bed? I whispered when I heard James
getting into his bunk underneath mine.

—No. Ó Cinnéide fell asleep. We'll have to go out the window.

When James did stuff like that it was like he didn't know what
he was doing. The pros and cons of it didn't enter his head. Was
like he was stupid. Same as the tide comes and goes. Doesn't think
about it just does it. And if you tried to stop James these times you
might as well have tried to beat the tide back with a stick. Some
things are just going to happen no matter what.

It was just ourselves, the waves, the moon and the old ruin. At
half three in the morning we snuck out. We were just up the path
and we seen Henry coming out behind a bush. All you could make
out first was the teeth in his smiling head.

—About time, he said.

James got him in a headlock and rubbed his head,

—Doubt ya kid. Glad you made it scumbag.

—You too scumbag. What's with the gas drum?

—We're gonna light it and it'll fly out over the Atlantic like a rocket, James said.

—Oh cool, said Henry, the eyes wide in his head like the moon. Dinky and the Dublin lad laughed.

—When did you get out, the Dublin fella asked him.

—I got out about half twelve.

—Half twelve?

—You've been out here three hours?

—What have you been doing all the time?

—Waiting.

—Why'd ya leave at half twelve?

—That's when Ó Crualaí was down in the kitchen. I could hear him talking below so I knew I could sneak out the front door. If he was in his room he'd hear me leaving.

—Good thinking Sherlock. So you've been out here three hours.

—Yip.

—Jesus.

—Have you any provisions?

—What's provisions, like blankets? I have my sleeping bag here in the bag.

—No I mean food.

—No. I'd a packet of chocolate digestives but I ate them to pass the time.

The lads laughed.

—Seriously, I wasn't even hungry. Feel a bit sick after them.

He burped and the lad laughed again.

—Henry, Henry, Henry, said Dinky.

—Yes, yes, yes, said Henry, moving his bag to his left hand now, his fat little legs starting to struggle.

—All right there Henry? asked James.

—Yeah, said Henry.

—Good man, said James.

All the drink had been found by the people running the Irish college so we hadn't a drop. But James borrowed a gas cooker, a tea pot and a fist of tea bags. The worst was the big orange gas drum that we took turns carrying. That's what made us about fifteen minutes late. The walk was a laugh. Dinky dropped the gas drum on his toe and let a yelp out of him. I can hear the voices.

—You couldn't carry a fucking virus, the Dub said.

—I think my fucking toe's broke!

—Ya dick!

—Seriously, it's fucking agony.

—Walk on the other foot, we're nearly there. Charlie take the gas drum the rest of the way there will ya?

—Thanks Charlie!

—No bother. How's the toe?

—Broke.

Once we reached the final horizon the sight of the skeleton of the old ruin against the Atlantic and the moon's reflection way out south beyond was reward enough for our escape. But the faint sound of the girls below was even better. I can hear the nervous excited giggling. It told the night-time's eerie silence to go away and fuck off.

—Jesus Christ we thought ye were after getting caught.

—What have ye got there?

—Sure 'twouldn't be right if we couldn't have a cup of tea.

—James borrowed the kitchen and we helped him to carry it!

—Jesus Christ.

—Ye're gas.

—Jesus I'd murder a cup of tea.

Within twenty minutes everyone had a hot cup of tea in their hands. Sinéad was delighted she got to hear her Michael Jackson song and we all had a great laugh about it and thinking about Ó Cinnéide waking up and seeing James gone and going into the dorm to get him and seeing him gone again and his head exploding with rage. We sat around the gas ring of fire, duvets and sleeping bags over us.

—Thank fuck it's not raining.

—Chalk it down.

—We wouldn't have come out anyway if 'twas raining.

—Someone's watching out for us.

—God maybe. Maybe he wants us to have a great fucking night here on our last night on Cape Clear. Maybe he kept the airí asleep when we escaped.

—Getting cold now it is.

—That's why God invented fire.

—Let's find some wood.

—The fire would be seen.

—Sure let's face it, if they find out we're missing this will be the first place they'll look anyway.

—There's shag-all fire wood around anyway sure.

—There's the palm trees down the valley.

—You get them so.

I got them with James and the Dub. Two armfuls of palm branches and one whole palm tree that the Dub pulled clean out of the sandy earth. Fell back on his backside with the tree up on top of him. Pissed themselves laughing with the mad night sea air in their lungs. Different to the air we'd be breathing if we were asleep in bed where we were supposed to be. Sweeter isn't it? Everyone helped break up the tree and the branches for the fire. The seven of us sat around. Two half moons. Myself, Sinéad and James on the north side, looking south at the ocean. The rest more or less facing us, with their backs to the Atlantic. The fire crackled and cracked and hissed and sparked same as a jazz drummer competing with the human voice of our talk. Fits and starts. Sinéad liked random drumming like that. Like sparks from the fire, she said. Best thing was I was near Sinéad and I could see the tiny tiny image of the fire reflecting in her eyes and the warm colour of it on her face.

Mostly talking it was. There was a second round of tea made. Then the Dub suggested a party piece from everyone, as long as he himself was allowed to go first. Dubs are different.

He sang 'Boolavogue'. Never heard a Dublin accent singing it before. He was brutal but the accent made it nice. Bew-la-vowg was how he said the word. Sang it. He said he learned it off his grandfather. His grandfather was a Wexford man. He taught James the words of it.

And he taught James one called 'The Ould Triangle' too about a fella in prison in Dublin thinking of women. The other girl,

Michelle, after a load of coaxing said an ancient poem-prayer that we'd learned in class. 'Gile Mo Chroí.' Means light of my heart. The next time I heard it was at a funeral.

Sinéad then sang 'Táimse im Chodladh.'

No one could remember what the words mean but it didn't matter. The tune of it with Sinéad's voice and the sea and moon is what mattered. I didn't sing anything, and they didn't push me to either. James recited that thing he used to often be spouting, even in class before the teacher would come in, or walking along the street. You can write a few verses cos that's all James ever said. It's called 'Last Thoughts on Woody Guthrie'.

_____

_____

_____

_____

_____

_____

_____

_____

_____

_____

_____

_____

Henry recited some poem he'd learned in school called 'Mid Term Break'.

—Now look what you've done, joked James.

—Sorry Sinéad, Henry said.

—No, it's just so beautiful, said Sinéad, sniffling away her tears. I'm such a dork it's unbelievable.

—You're just nice, Henry said.

—Hey back off now, said James and they all laughed.

They were talking about Detective Crowley's little boy who was killed on the road long ago cos the poem reminded them of it. No one could really remember him in school. Just that his name was Shane and he had dark brown hair.

—Imagine, he could be here with us right now if he lived, James said.

—Maybe he is, said Sinéad quietly and her eyes welling up on her again, and she looking out to sea at the moon's reflection.

Lull then for a bit. Just the waves and the sky and the shadows from the moon and crackling fire. Some of them were praying maybe. Then Sinéad said,

—I'm going to sing again now, if that's OK.

We all went quiet. Ready for Sinéad to blow our minds and our hearts. She soaked up the attention for a moment, went all serious and then started singing 'Twinkle Twinkle Little Star.' We laughed and Sinéad did too but kept singing so we all joined in.

Then everyone sang some song one of the women teachers taught us. It was some Lionel Richie song and all the girls loved it. 'Love, Oh Love'. Except we learned it in Irish. Grá is the Irish for Love. Ó is the Irish for Oh. Just in case you want to write it out. But it's not essential. It wasn't a major part of their minds, this song, in any language, but it was really nice then and they all singing it together and they all huddled up together and the blankets and the fire and a hint of a tint of the sun and it about to rise up out of the sea on the horizon yonder.

_____

_____

_____

_____

_____

_____

_____

_____

_____

_____

_____

We watched the sunrise together before going back. Dazzling isn't it? In Ireland when people think of life they don't ever think of sunrise. People don't see much sunrises. I wonder did anyone ever say it had to be like that.

The Library

We lived in the library of Kent Castle that year. Especially in the summer holidays. This is a drawing of the candle stand that was in the library.

I could spend for ever trying to explain the look of it and you still wouldn't have it. I'm handy enough at drawing. Spent my whole life drawing at the back of the class sure. Anyhow some things I think you need to know the look of. Don't ask me why. I don't know myself. Anyhow the writers who describe things get pages and pages out of it so why shouldn't I get a few pages out of my drawings?

Sinéad would ask me to light the candles every time we went into the library. She'd say,

—Let out the dark there Charlie. It has no place here with us.

That meant light the candles. I'd say real quiet,

—Get out dark.

One time then she said,

—Get thee hence to endless night.

She had other candles over the fireplace and on the bookshelf and on the floor. Fat ones that stood by themselves and other little hour-lights – the ones the believers and the hopeful light in the churches for the souls of the dead and the bodies of the dying. I didn't bother drawing the candles. Or the flame. Can't draw fire anyway. No one can. Only a fool would try. Especially a fire that can burn no more. You can use your imagination for the flame. You can imagine the flame can't you? The fire? I hope you can.

When I'd the right half of the candle stand drawn I folded the page and pressed it over on to the left side, leaving an outline of it for me to trace. Mirror image. Be hard to get it right otherwise. Anyhow I think the candle stand is a credit to whoever made it a hundred or two hundred or three hundred years ago. The drawing left an imprint on the page behind it.

Some people leave things after them after they're gone isn't it?

The carpet and the curtains were the same kind of red that drying blood is.

The ceiling was fairly high so the light that hung from it doesn't really matter. James would be your man for a description of the ceiling, he spent half his time lying on the ground looking up at it.

The piano was a grand piano.

Grand pianos are hard to draw.

This was the doorbell of the castle. Still is. But it doesn't work any more. I tried it.

There were two big long windows in the library. I liked them. I used to stand at the window looking down at the village and the football pitch and the river and the woods while Sinéad and James were at the piano or guitar and making their music. It was nice. There's not much nice any more. This is one of the windows. I wanted to draw a bit of the roof and the castle walls too to give you an idea of where the windows were. I made the grey bits around the bricks by spitting on my finger and rubbing it. This was the last drawing I did. My biro ran out colouring in the roof.

This is the other window.

I used to be sitting in with Sinéad and James when they used to be making songs together. In the library room in the castle Sinéad would be sitting on the couch with her guitar. James would usually be lying on the floor. He'd jump up sometimes suddenly and go to the piano when he had an idea for notes to play in that part of the song. Other times they'd sing parts of the songs they worked on. James didn't sing much, just sometimes, but he was only singing in the way a grown-up would sing along with a toddler. To encourage them along isn't it? Sinéad needed encouragement after being told she wasn't worth a fuck by all belonging to her, all her life. I still know the songs they had. Some of the words were a bit babyish maybe. Sinéad singing about saving all God's children from hunger and shit like that. We can change the world with love, yeah yeah yeah kind of stuff. That was one of Sinéad's. James' efforts were a small bit more grown-up but they were only learning isn't it? They were still copying a lot of the shit that they heard on the radio. And a lot of that stuff is only shit.

But sometimes. Might be for a verse. Maybe even a whole song. But more often just for a few seconds in a song, the sound they would make. The sound that Sinéad's voice would make. With James on the piano. The sound they would make sometimes was something that rose above. The very very very rarest beauty it was. In sound form. Sometimes. I believe they'd definitely have become famous. I don't know that for sure of course. That's why I said I believe. I believe that anyone who heard Sinéad's voice would have wanted to hear more. Just like anyone who ever seen her wanted to see her again. And again. And blah. Sinéad was more-ish. In the same way, people find me less-ish.

There was this one song that they didn't sing, but spoke. They just spoke the lines with James playing a slow soft eerie tune on the piano. Sinéad had come up with the tune. Simple and magic cos it played tricks with your heart, the tune of it did. She'd hummed it to James, and James found it on the piano. The song was a conversation between two lovers who were dead. It was called 'Love Song from Beyond the Grave'.

It's weird, all along I've been avoiding thinking about James and Sinéad's singing and their songs all because of my headaches and in case an dubh would floor me again. But I've no headache now. I'm not crying either. Maybe I'm getting better. Maybe I'm getting worse. Maybe I'm not remembering them as good as I used to. I dunno if that's a good thing or not. Like the brain isn't bad at remembering but it's shit hot altogether at forgetting. Fuck it. Only thing worse than remembering is forgetting isn't it? Sadder. Seems very fucking unjust isn't it?

Just
Adj. 1. fair and impartial; acting with fairness and impartiality 2. morally correct; done, pursued, or given in accordance with what is morally right 3. reasonable; valid or reasonable [14ᵗʰC. Via French *juste* from Latin *justus,* from *jus* 'law, right'.]

It's a pity you can't hear Sinéad's tune for the piano that played softly behind their voices. Soft but resilient. Put up a good fight for life, her tune did, but faded away and died in the end, just like the couple in the song. This is the start of it. The first line was James, then Sinéad,

> —*So you're dead now too*
> —*No shit Einstein*
> —*Ha! . . . There were lies told*
> —*Damaging cruel lies babe*
> —*Do you miss your kids?*
> —*All the time. Do you?*

The voices talked about happier times and how wrong their whole lives felt cos they weren't together. But Sinéad and James' voices were too young for it. It needed old people's voices. But it was the over and back that would get you. Same as life and music. The communication isn't it? The effort. To really hear and to really be heard. And it impossible really and the way of things and the stupid daft heads up on us all. But the tune would leave you kind of stunned. This was the end of the song anyhow.

—*Think that's the deal now*
—*We evaporate*
—*Goodbye*
—*I loved you*
—*I loved you too*

Sinéad's tune evaporated too at the end, the way it faded. Fuck it anyhow. I just ran in to the jacks and vomited and I've this fucking headache. I'm going away getting tablets and some fresh air maybe. And something to get rid of the taste of vomit.

Shane McGowan
Shane McGowan said he only likes talking to bums and drunks. Cos they're the only people who take the time to stop and think about anything. Most people go through their whole lives without ever having a chance to stop and think about anything. Let alone everything. I'm like an alco that doesn't drink. When you're thinking about something, you're not thinking about something else isn't it? Most people always have to be thinking about something so they never have time to be thinking about the something elses. I spend loads of time just thinking. About the something elses. Like what has money got to do with

thinking? Or what has sex got to do with pride? Or what has food got to do with friendship?

I'd say I could get along with Shane McGowan if I could understand a word the bollicks says. Slurring a lot nowadays, he is. Do you even know who he is? Imagine not knowing who Shane McGowan is. Well if you don't, he's a famous drunk and singer and songwriter. That's who. Wise up.

He'd a band called Póg Mo Thóin but when they started to become famous they had to change their name cos Póg mo Thóin means Kiss My Ass and the BBC wouldn't play any song on the telly or on radio by a band called Kiss My Ass cos the queen would get offended cos she has no ass. So they changed the name to The Pogues so they could make money in England cos everyone knows that's where the money is. Money is money isn't it?

Anyhow Sinéad and James liked The Pogues' song 'Fairytale of New York'. Might have kinda given them the idea for 'Love Song from Beyond the Grave'. Two lovers talking. Talking away their regrets isn't it? You can write in 'Fairytale of New York' here.

I can hear the mother and father arguing below. She'll put on music and he'll storm off. Always the way. They're arguing about me. The father wants to act the hard man and tell me to stop feeling sorry for myself and my mother wants him to let me be.

My father never really likes the sight of the old records. They upset him. Some American fella my mother knew in America long ago got her into all the music. She lived in the Bronx in New York. Fella in the same apartment building was into music. My father said to me one time you never know what a woman is thinking. I said to him,

—Sure mam doesn't know what you do be thinking either.

—Sure I don't be thinking anything, my father goes.

My mother would dig out all her old records and listen to them if they were after having a falling out over something. Drive him daft, it would, thinking of this American fella long ago.

James had a music teacher for the piano. Sinéad kept it on as a subject through secondary school. But really everything they learned they learned it from each other. And sometimes from me. I swear. Especially early on when I played for them all my mother's old records. Elvis in Sun Studios. Bob Dylan's Bootleg series. Van Morrison's *Astral Weeks*. Nina Simone. Louis Armstrong. Seán O Riada. Marlene Dietrich. Aretha Franklin.

David Bowie. Edith Piaf. Emmylou Harris. The Beatles. John Lee Hooker. Leonard Cohen. Lou Reed. Maria Callas. The Jackson Five. Miles Davis. John McCormack. Simon and Garfunkel. Queen. U2. Neil Young. Willie Nelson. Odetta. Sam Cooke. Kate Bush. Frederic Chopin. Joni Mitchell. Tim Buckley. Roy Orbison. The Rolling Stones. Arvo Pärt. Cindy Lauper. Luke Kelly. Makem and Clancy. Claude Debussy. Not one person alive who had to go to school like we did listened to more music than the three of us. Mainly that was what school was. Time not listening to music. In our young lives we'd already listened to many many many lifetimes of music. Hours and hours and hours and hours that all added up would be years and months and weeks and days and more hours still probably. These words and any words are only a fucking paleness next to the sounds that we travelled in together. All the books in the world aren't worth a fuck. It's all languages to all people every place, same as the smile on your face isn't it? The music. I used to like Vaughan Williams, the English composer. They asked him if he believed in God. He said no. The one who asked him couldn't believe it and she asked what he thinks will happen when he dies. Said he'll just become music, that his spirit will dart all around the place in the notes and enter the souls of people everywhere. Sinéad really liked it. That idea. We all listened to *Fantasia on a Theme* up in the library. Got lost in it we did. She said after she could feel Vaughan Williams all over her and James and me laughed and she said shut up ye pervs. I just listened to them talking like I used to always then.

—What happens like? Sinéad said.

—What? said James cos he didn't know what she was talking about.

—In music. What exactly happens? Like . . . what's going on like? Where were we just now like? Where did we go? Felt like sailing or something.

There were tears in Sinéad's eyes.

—Or gliding.

—Yeah . . . like . . . what . . . like what's going on like? You kind of know the feeling being expressed. The like . . . ideas maybe . . . no not ideas . . . more vague than that . . .

—Sentiment . . .

—What does that mean?

—Not sure really.

—Like there's something being expressed and no words can describe it. Like it can't be translated into words.

James smiled at her like he kind of understood what she meant and he thought she was the most amazing person he ever dreamed could be.

—Yeah, he said.

—And like . . . the movement like . . . it's like I was in a thousand different rooms or landscapes or something like. Just floating.

—Yeah I know what you mean, he said. Like not a visual world.

—Exactly like but definitely like. A world with dimensions you know?

—Yeah.

—Like being a bat maybe. Negotiating terrain with sound. Some unseen magical terrain.

—Yeah.

—It's like there's the music of exploring and the music of coming home.

—Yeah like. And both are cool.

—Yeah. And need each other like. Like the bitter and the sweet.

She turned to me then.

—What do you think Charlie?

—I dunno.

—You do.

—No, I said.

—It's so unbelievable isn't it? It makes me feel so happy cos it's like this thing that God has given us to let us know he's there. That's what I think. All the scientists and all who say there's nothing like . . . they can't explain what happened with us just now listening to that. Like listening to that like . . . it communicated what language can only . . . language is just lost for words you know? You just know that at the end of the day, we're OK. We're not alone. Definitely we're not alone.

—Yeah, said James.

—Yeah, I said too.

She said,

—Remember the old woman from the documentary in school that said if Hitler could have stopped and listened to *Moonlight Sonata* how he might not have been so full of hate.

It was an old woman who was in the camps long ago and they lived on music. The Nazi guards let them have a choir and a piano cos it was so nice for the guards to listen to. When the old woman said that about Hitler and *Moonlight Sonata*, and then the camera pulled back and you could see she was sitting at a piano and she played it. She looked as old as the world.

—Will you play it there James, Sinéad said.

He played it nice and I seen Sinéad wipe tears from her eyes.

The mother has a Van Morrison song on below now. And it's after making me upset. I can think about music sometimes but hearing it is the worst. Sometimes I'd be doing fine and the mother would put on some tune and I'd go down hill fairly fast. It's best if I stay away from music. Makes me weak and I get the shakes sometimes. The terrors. All the fuss over music long ago seems a bit stupid really. Fine thing to be content with plain life same as everyone else.

Had to lie down that time and I ended up falling asleep. I don't know what time it is now but it's the middle of the night and it's fierce quiet thank God. No fucking music. Song the mother had on that upset me is called 'High Summer'. Sinéad used to say that that song says the most in the chorus. There's no words in the chorus. Just Van Morrison playing a sound over and over and over on the harmonica. The very same CD the mother had on cos I borrowed it long ago for Sinéad. Heard it a million times up in the library of the castle. Was the summer before James went to Dublin.

I always had a love of words. A fascination for them. The beauty of language delighted me always. The mystery of words. That's the way the writing nerds I met once went on. Dr Quinn had it all set up so that he could bring me to one of their sessions after my appointment. All these people reading bits of what they wrote about themselves and their problems. Making a shit story out of their shit lives. And telling each other how great their stories were then.

—I want to thank you for sharing that with us. It was really special and wonderfully crafted I thought.

They all go then, 'Yeah.' 'Really lovely.' 'It was.' 'Really good like.' 'Well done Margaret girl.' and the usual all fierce nice lick-arsy shit like that.

Then Dr Quinn goes,

—Did you find the process of writing that therapeutic Margaret?

—Ahm . . . well like . . . I suppose definitely like really, in fairness . . . I think it like helps you to take a step back from things, you know?

—That's a very interesting point Margaret makes, Dr Quinn goes. Any other thoughts? Anybody?

—Well I just think the part about your father's lying to ye all was really well done. Like you'd feel so much for ye all. Especially your mother like. Your heart would go out to her like.

They all agreed away mad, all fierce nice again.

—Well said Eric, Dr Quinn goes. I agree. And isn't empathy a big part of the healing we can find in this writing exercise too? We can empathise with people. Have sympathy for them. Feel sorry for them. And we can empathise and feel a bit sorry for ourselves too, can't we?

More fucking agreeing mad.

—Somehow we can own what has happened to us when we control it in our thoughts. When we structure our thoughts. And language is the key. Language is the key to help us find our way out of the difficulties our thoughts can give us sometimes.

—I agree, Dr Quinn, says a young fella of about seventeen, and he skin and bone. Books have always been an escape for me. Like friends.

—Yes, goes Dr Quinn. And what your own words can offer you too is

Then some fella of about fifty in a red dressing gown comes to life all of a sudden and interrupts Dr Quinn and the voice he had was so loud and high-pitched it made the interruption even better,

—Reminds me of one time when I was at the beach and we had this kite and the fucking thing ends up diving into the fucking sea and the fucking thing was pure destroyed and I'd the young fella crying beside me asking me why the fuck I didn't give it back to him and saying do I always have to fuck up everything.

There was pure silence then until Dr Quinn took a deep breath and goes,

—Thank you for that little anecdote Terence. Wouldn't it be great if you could write us something on that for next week?

—Well maybe sure. I'll try a few words.

—Thank you, that would be great, goes Dr Quinn.

Next thing the cunt looks over at me and all the nerdynuts turn their heads too.

—So what do you think Charlie? Would you like to join us next week?

I just looked at Dr Quinn and all the other stupid faces. They were looking at me and then back at Dr Quinn and then back to me again. Waiting for a response. Dr Quinn let it go on for a while but in the end turns back to the nerdynuts and goes on,

—Anyway. I'm sure he'll certainly think about it anyway. But thank you all for allowing him to observe our little group today.

This fella Eric goes then,

—You're welcome Charlie, and the rest of them all nodded in agreement all smiley kind faces trying to outdo each other with kindness again in front of Dr Quinn.

Then they went on about the power of language again. All misty-eyed ardent talk and reverence for fuck all.

Fuck off. Don't bore me. Pass the salt. I love you. Once you can say them things and tell a joke, what more do you want? They're all the same, the languages. Cos they have to be isn't it? They do the job sure isn't it? I gave Dr Quinn and them the slip anyhow during the next story and I fucked off. I got the bus into Patrick Street and strolled around for a bit and got the late bus. When I got home the mother told me Dr Quinn was after ringing twice. He rang again then but I wouldn't take the phone. I just says,

—You can tell him I'm going to no reading group.

But I can't stop thinking now about the poor madman who destroyed his son's kite. What do you do with the like of him? A pure God help us. Kindness is what Dr Quinn tries but sure once he leaves the hospital then he's back trying to deal with real people and kindness doesn't really figure isn't it? Anyhow I'll be back to you later on or tomorrow to carry on with my story and give you a lovely new chapter for yourself. It'll be called 8. I'm going off to see if a walk will get that poor fucker out of my head.

8

Thinking About It

I stopped thinking about your man but went back thinking about Sinéad and James then. They'd have been nice to him. Helped him if they could. I shouldn't be fucking thinking cos that's when I gets the headaches the worst. Thinking about it. I gets headaches. Said it before two or three times maybe. But I do. And they're very sore. But I have to keep going with the story cos who else will tell the fucking thing?

Cavity Wall

There was something between. No one could see it except myself. There was something between and Sinéad and James were on one side of it and the rest were on the other side of it. It was a wall. A cavity wall. You could put things into the wall. Things like dreams. And plans. And belief that you could do amazing things. With your voice and your mind and your thoughts. That's what went into the cavity in this wall. The cavity was as big as your mind could dream.

Social Welfare

I haven't ever once gone into the social welfare office without stealing something. The longer I have to wait the more I steal.

Poor Oul' Paddy Connell

—Let me do that because you don't understand. That's what poor oul' Paddy Connell used to say. Fuck it he was a beautiful man surely.

That's what Tim Joe Larkin says to my father yesterday when he was tying the seats from the church to the trailer. The club bought six long seats for the sides of the pitch. For the big matches for the subs to be sitting on.

Denis O'Mahony

Denis O'Mahony rang for the father earlier. When I told him the father was out he says,

—Yera, 'tis all right. I didn't want him for anything anyway.

Good luck so Denis.

No Holes

—Fuck Sake. Even fucking people who fucking think they've no fucking holes have to fucking talk through it some fucking times.

I heard Seán Casey say that one day. Seán Fuck everyone calls him. He was going out the front door talking about some crooked politician fella to the father.

Seen a fella walking up the road there and he reminded me of a time he was a sub at a match with Dinky. Dinky was taken off in a match cos he was playing shit. I went watching Dinky then for a bit. He took off his boots on the sideline and flung them one at a time at the wire mesh around the pitch, and all the other subs going,

—No fault Dinky.

—The goal wasn't even your fault sure.

—Dunno what they took you off for, it's crazy.

Dinky said nothing but tears welled in his eyes. Eyes that should have been too old for them kind of tears. He sat down eventually anyhow. Got the subs to make room in the middle. He liked to be in the thick of things, did Dinky, except when he was on the field of play. Anyhow here on the bench he'd a few fifteen-year-olds to lick the arse of him, just like he lick-arses the older lads. That's how it goes, isn't it? So anyhow I been watching all this and I decides to just watch Dinky and nothing or no one else. Watch the get up of him, the shapes he pulls. The sulking. The looking for notice. After about five minutes he spoke for the first time.

—Can't fucking believe it!

—It's unbelievable Dinky sure. You're the best defender we have and they take you off!

—Yeah like, you're one of our best players like.

—That goal could've happened to anyone. Can't blame you for it.

He did it again a few minutes later when the lads had stopped on about it.

—Fuck sake they haven't a fucking clue.

—No way should you have been taken off.

—Madness.

—Don't mind them Dinky boy, sure they haven't a clue.

So Dinky would make noise every few minutes looking for notice again and his new young lackeys would oblige. Was more like Dinky was the baby birdy and the young lackeys were its mammy dropping worms into Dinky's mouth every now and again to keep him happy.

So I'm watching Dinky anyhow. He seemed to have lost all interest in the game now that he wasn't playing. He wasn't following the action at all but he wasn't looking at the ground either. Or the sky. Dinky's eyes were glued to James. Wherever he went on the pitch, Dinky's eyes followed him, whether he had the ball or not, Dinky's eyes followed James everywhere like a cameraman told to follow one player only.

I remember being in Dinky's mother's car when he started driving first. He'd borrow it the odd day and we'd go for a spin. Snoozie, myself, and James were driving through Newport. We'd have been around seventeen and we stopped at traffic lights near a bunch of fourteen- or fifteen-year-old girls. Then the girls start screaming and jumping and holding each other. 'What the fuck is wrong with them?' James goes. And Dinky says,

—They're shouting because of you, you dope!

—What?

—Yeah!

—What are you on about?

—They fancy you, ya dopey bollicks!

—Go away to fuck!

—The girls saw you in the car and you made them get a tickle in their little fannies.

—Shut up Dinky will ya.

—I'm telling ya. You're after making them all wet!

—You're a sick puppy Dinky. A sick puppy.

—Only nature sure, Dinky goes.

Sometimes I think Dinky was jealous of James and Sinéad and I'm not sure who he was most jealous of sometimes. If he wanted to marry Sinéad he wanted James for a best friend maybe. I dunno. Dinky's father drinks with Sinéad's father and they live near each other and maybe life would have been nicer for Dinky if Sinéad liked him instead of James. They could all play happy families then. But you have to let a girl decide for herself isn't it? Every fella has to accept that.

Hold on a minute. The mother and father are arguing about me downstairs.

—Out in God's air picking spuds for ten hours. Then he'd sleep at night, the father says.

—Sure you're an expert aren't you? Dr McCarthy here.

—Very smart. I'm for the boy's good and all we're doing, all we've ever done is kill him with kindness. From day one we've been too soft on him.

—Keep your voice down or he'll hear you for God's sake.

—Christ, about time he did.

—Charlie's different John.

—Different. Sure we're all different woman.

—And he's been through a lot.

—Yeah. So have the fucking Serbians and they don't stay in bed all day and stay up all night.

—Dr Quinn knows what he's doing.

—Dr Quinn is only a padhsán.

Anyhow, Dinky. One thing Dinky could never figure out about James was why he actually enjoyed spending time with his family. Dinky's idea of family was probably the same as the one Sinéad grew up with. That they're just people who are related to each other, live in the same building but don't have a whole pile to say to each other. And if you weren't bringing in a few bob by the age of seventeen or eighteen you were selfish and ungrateful. Dinky used to make fun of the way the Kents treated dinner. Sat at the dinner table for a good hour and discussed anything ranging from how things were at school to international politics. Dinky used to call it the heated debate. James would laugh and Dinky would too. In the good old days.

He Who Dares

Another thousand words for ye now. I'm eating grapes. A bit bitter. I always steal a grape or two when I walk past them in a shop. Just grab one and gobble it up without anyone looking. Never got caught. Ever. He who dares wins. That's what James always said when the shit hit the blahblah. In a London accent. Just like Del Boy from the telly. He'd make everyone laugh and forget for a minute that things were gone fucked up on them. Like the time we stole Racey's father's car when she had a house party. Racey was Sinéad's best friend who was a girl. Her best friend was James. And me. Anyhow Dinky was driving her father's car and wrapped it around a tree. We were all sitting in the car in stunned silence. Then James pipes up with,

—He who dares . . . wins, and we all in stitches laughing.

The Cup

Heard Master Coughlan one time out in the yard telling Mrs O'Riordan that he'd bring James down to size and that he'd make a man of him yet. I thought of that years later when they went to the primary school with the cup. When the lads were about seventeen the club won the Junior Football Divisional Final. That was a right big deal for the parish. The team went up to the school to show the kiddies the cup and to make a big deal of it and all that kind of stuff. So it was a warm October day and Master Coughlan brought the kids out into the yard and had them all sit on the basketball court while all the players were introduced by name to the kids by the Master. I only went along cos I was involved with the team too. I was the water boy. Not cos I wanted to be the water boy. Just so as I could keep an eye on things. On James. And on Dinky. And on how they got on with the older fellas. James, Dinky and the Master's son were the only young fellas on the panel. Anyhow so the Master is introducing everyone and all the kiddies clapping and cheering away like mad. Then Master Coughlan came to James and pretended to forget his name.

—And aah, sorry what's that your name is again?

James only laughed.

—James, one of the lads said.

—O James Kent, of course, sorry James.

My hole he didn't remember his name. James' was the first name on the front of his mind the whole time. It was embarrassing for James in front of everyone, especially seeing as he remembered every other player's name. James was acting all hard and every-thing as usual, laughing the slight off like he didn't give a flying fuck. I often wondered when he'd stare into space, was it getting to him at all. I think he convinced himself 'twas all only innocent mistakes. He must have known though. Somewhere in the back of his mind he must have known that a lot of people didn't really like him at all, and wished he'd never have set foot in Ballyronan in the first place. Or worse.

Water boy

I was the water boy for that team so I was able to keep a fairly close eye on how things went. James was never too pushed about the pints with the lads after training and matches but it's what Dinky lived for more than anything. More than hanging around with us or the school crowd. More than chasing girls. More than anything. To be pinting with the older lads was the highlight of his life.

9

The Pub

Anyhow, Teesh and Dinky went to The Snug usually after train-ing cos it was across from the pitch. Dinky liked to be sucking up to Teesh and the other lads. That was something James never really cared about. Snoozie would show his face for a pint or two as well. That was more for business than anything else. Snoozie might have been bored by a lot of the old sucking up too, but that team meant a lot of business to his old fella so 'twas import-ant to keep them onside. Most of the time he made sure he was inside the bar serving the pints as opposed to on the other side. That way he didn't have to drink. His heart wasn't in the pub. He'd end up working with his brother anyhow. When Dinky dragged James into the pub after training there were always a couple of the older lads there first.

—How are the boys?

—Oho horse, how's things?

—Oho look who's in! The bould Dinky and the Landlordeen, Teesh goes.

—Oho, the future of the club!

—What's the club coming to, ha?

—Two young alcomyholics!

—All right My Boy, Teesh goes then in a posh English accent.

—What'll it be lads?

—I'll have a pint!

—How about yourself good sir?

—I'll just have an orange juice please, said James.

—You will in your hole! Two pints for the young lads please. And an orange for the gamal. Prince fucking William wanted orange juice!

—Ha?

—You could drink a barrel of that oul' orange sure and you still wouldn't get drunk.

—'Tis fucking soberer you'd get.

—Soberer! You're some gobshite. Will you talk proper English and don't be insulting the Landlordeen's language.

—We're only joking ya James boy, take no notice of that eejit either, his mother dropped him on his head and he a young fella.

—Better than being dropped on your face like *you* were.

—So what do ye think of playing in the big time, lads, ha? Christ 'tis no bother at all to you James boy, you're better than half of us already.

—Ah I wouldn't say that!

—Don't mind your false modesty at all boy, there's no place for false modesty in this pub. I knows I'm brilliant and I've no problems telling people!

—Dinky didn't do too bad in training there either boy. Fleming got a couple of goals off ya but the second one was lucky. You're doing all right Dinky boy, don't let any fella tell you any differ.

—I'm still a bit off the pace though.

—'Twill come boy, 'twill come. You're only seventeen and Rome wasn't built in a day.

—You'll get full marks for effort anyway Dinky boy, and that's what makes a player great, not what he's born with.

—Here here to that. I've seen many a talented player in this club go by the wayside because he didn't have it in his heart. Heart is everything boy.

—And Dinky, *you're* all heart, you might be fucking useless but heart will get you on the team!

—Sure talent is only a hindrance to cornerbacks. They'd only be trying oul' fancy flicks and dandy tricks with the ball instead of kicking it a mile out the field.

—Now you're talking. James you've too much of the oul' fancy stuff. Catch the ball and kick the fucking thing, end of story.

—Will you shut up and leave the lad alone. You're only annoyed that he roasted you in training.

—But the Rovers have always had a simple game plan. That's how we all know what the next man on the team is thinking.

—Trouble is the opposition know as well. Maybe we need to

vary things a bit. Keep them guessing. Maybe that's why we haven't won anything in fifteen years.

That was the bold James who spoke last. Silenced them for a while it did. Don't think no young fella had ever spoken to these parish godeens like that before. The two senior players he said it to were Teesh and Snoozie. Anyhow Snoozie and Teesh sat quietly for a little while after what James said about tactics. I just sat there looking at them and I let a bit of spit fall out of my mouth and I looked where it landed on my lap and I gave it a good hard rub and then I jerked my head back up and looked at them again for a bit of notice. Teesh noticed.

—What do you think Gamal?

—Ha? About what?

—Well said Gamal! About what indeed!

—Come here to me Gamal, are you washing them water bottles at all or what?

—I am yeah, why?

—There's a shitty oul' taste off the water.

—Don't mind him Gamal, in the name of God.

—I washes them with hot sudsy water after training every day.

—And do you wash the suds out of them?

—I do. I washes them with no sudsy water before I fill them with the cold water.

—Ha! By Christ Gamal, you're a beaut' if ever there was one. I washes them with no sudsy water! Ha!

—You wouldn't find it in a comic!

—Good lad Gamal, you're a good lad, and don't let anyone ever tell ya any differ. I washes them with no sudsy water, ha?

They were in tears laughing. I likes to keep the opposition guessing too.

Then Snoozie disappeared into the house behind the bar for a bit. Anyhow he came out to the bar then again after a bit. Sent out by the father to make sure they didn't get the hump and go drinking up the road.

—How. Are. Ye. Now?

—Nice shit Snoozie?

—Not. Too. Bad.

—Did you wash your hands with no sudsy water?

—No. Sudsy. Water! Ha? Doubt ya Gamal, *boy*!

— What do you think of what Prince William was saying about changing the way we play?

—Each. Man. To. His. Own. Ha?

—To his own, yeah!

—Dinky did all right in training didn't he?

—He. Did. In. Fairness. Yeah.

—Good for us old farts as well. Keeps us on our toes.

—That's. Right. It's vital sure.

—Vital, yeah.

It's Halloween. The 31st of October. No it isn't. It's the day after now. 00:44. But it was Halloween all day and this evening I could hear my mother telling children how scary they were and they calling to the door. My mother loves children. My father does too but he pretends not to cos he's a man so he stayed in the sitting room reading the paper but every once in a while he'd pretend he was going into the kitchen to get something so he'd pass the hall so he could see the little children who called to the door being ghosts and monsters and witches.

—Lord God aren't ye scary, he'd say.

—They're very scary, my mother would say and she filling their bags with sweets.

The children never said anything. I think they were scared. This would be a good time to tell of a Halloween from when Sinéad and James and me were younger. Not that young though. About sixteen.

The older kids were always out trying to scare the life out of the trick-or-treaters. Usually it was twelve-year-olds scaring littler ones but Dinky and Racey and Teesh and Snoozie were still doing it well into their teens and me and Sinéad and James weren't sure if we liked that so we came up with a plan. Music was one thing we had in common. Another thing we had in common was that we weren't afraid of graveyards. Dinky and Racey and Teesh and Snoozie were planning a big fright for all the kids and had a hose set up from behind the school to drench them too. They wanted us to come but Sinéad and James said no. We were sixteen and Teesh and Snoozie were nineteen. Anyhow, I'm not sure how to make this dramatic cos it wasn't really that dramatic at all. All we did was practised for a few nights in the castle. James took off the big brass cone-shaped speaker thing off the old gramophone in the library and Sinéad made this sound into it. James hammered the low keys on a xylophone really fast while Sinéad made the noise. It was a noise the like of you'd never really hear. In Ireland there's a spirit called the Banshee. She was heard only by an unfortunate few at night-time and if you heard it, it meant that one of your relatives was going to die that night. If you saw it that was very unfortunate for you cos that meant the person going to die was you. The sound Sinéad made was a screeching howling mournful wail and you'd never think someone so pretty could make such a sound. You'd think only the Banshee could make that sound. James' hammering on the low keys of the xylophone only made it all the stranger. It sounded like the most awful deathly sound and it made Dinky and Racey and Teesh and Snoozie run past the graveyard faster than they'd ever ran before or since. Snoozie's father lost a good hose that night too cos they never went back to get it and never spoke a word of what happened since. We asked them if they went scaring the trick-or-treaters and they said no.

It's the only sound Sinéad and James ever made that I don't wish you could have heard. Myself and James were crying laughing straight away when we saw them scampering but Sinéad was committed to the performance and kept the howling screech going for about twenty seconds. Sinéad could hold her breath under water for nearly two minutes. She could outlast the fella who sang lovelydaylovelydaylovelydaylovelydaaaaaaaaaaaaaaaaaaaaaaaaaaaaaaay so the wail didn't even test her.

Probably the only test ever for Sinéad was singing along with the Luke Kelly record of 'Rocky Road to Dublin'. If you listen to Luke Kelly singing it it's hard to think of where he might have stopped for breath but the people who were in the pub that it was recorded in swear blind that he drank a pint of Guinness and smoked a cigarette while he was singing it too. The performance of it was a lot of things and one of the things it was, was athletic.

It tested Sinéad physically more than I ever seen any song do. I seen fellas trying to sing that song nowadays on the telly. Bunch of four of them it took to get through it. They had to take turns same as a fucking relay race.

10

Anyhow Racey was in a state and Sinéad wanted to go after her to calm her down but James stopped her saying think of all the children we're saving from getting soaked to the skin. We watched them all passing up and down the road. The clueless little witches and ghouls. Some were ushered on by their older brothers or sisters whose mammies made them take out the little ones and look after them. Bored and embarrassed they were.

—It's weird, isn't it? Sinéad said.

—What is?

—Just like, the way . . . that like one time all the people who are buried here dressed up in little costumes and went trick-or-treating too. And all their grannies and granddads and all the other big people that saw them pretended to be spooked by them. Just for fun like. To make them happy and excited in their cute little ridiculous outfits. And they're all dead now, the whole lot of them.

—It's sad yeah.

—It's kind of awesome too though isn't it? Like . . . the honour of it. I hope they can hear us talking about them. I'm sure they can, Sinéad said. Her eyes filled up a small bit.

—Yeah I think so too, James said.

—What do you think Charlie?

—Dunno. I suppose they don't mind either way.

It was getting late now and all the trick-or-treaters were in bed with bellies full of sweets.

James messed around quietly on the xylophone and Sinéad hummed softly. James had his old duffel coat around her.

—I think we should write a song for all those who lie here, Sinéad goes.

—OK, said James. Like an ode to life maybe or something.

—What kind of song would they write if they could come back? Sinéad said, all quiet and whispery but with a tiny bit of voice too.

—I suppose about things they wished they could've seen when they were alive.

—Yeah, like. Be cool to see how we look to dead people. The living like.

Went silent for a bit then. Could hear the odd car in the distance on the main road. Sinéad spoke then again.

—That was so funny, the kid complaining about the apples.

Earlier on we heard a little lad complaining to his companions and we'd a laugh.

—How many fucking apples have ye in yer bags? That old bitch gave me another two apples. Sure we've loads of fucking apples at home.

Anyhow Sinéad went on.

—People count everything, don't they?

—I suppose, said James, and he still tapping quietly on the xylophone keys.

Sinéad sang quietly around James' notes. She was guiding them. Coaxing them into her melody.

> *Count the hours that you sleep*
> *Count the light years*

—That's nice, said James.

—What rhymes with sleep?

—Peep! Keep. Weep . . . deep.

—Keep playing that little tune a second.

> *Count the hours that you sleep*
> *Count the light years there to here*

—Cool.

—Maybe you could go up a bit at the end.

Sinéad hummed what she meant and James found it on the xylophone for her.

—Exactly that, said Sinéad.

There was the bones of a new song by the time we went away that night, whatever use it was to them or anyone else. It was one of the fairly shit ones.

I could get pages right now where she wrote down the words of that song. I have them. No good in them being in her room and the gardaí and her family going through them like any of it was their business. Detective Crowley found some of them in my room once. He goes,

—How did you get your hands on these?

—She gave them to me.

—I don't think she did, he goes. Did you go to her house and take them out of her room?

—No, I said.

—Someone got into her room and took stuff when there was no one at the house.

One thing I didn't like about Detective Crowley was the way he'd stare at you. He was fierce ignorant.

I've lots of bits now in my room in hiding places. Found an old newspaper with a picture of me in it. I was standing on the river bank looking out at the river. There was big writing on the page saying something not very nice about me but not saying I was a killer. And then under was the article. Bullshit isn't it?

'I think he was kind of obsessed with her,' one local added. 'He used to follow her around the place always. And when she was working in the pub he was the whole time there. It was unhealthy now to be honest, if you ask me like. I don't know whether or which but it was unhealthy, that's all I'm saying.'

Heard my mother that time telling my father that she thought it was Beatrice Coyle was after saying that cos she was a known backstabber and Norma Kelleher seen her talking to a stranger that looked like a journalist.

11

Saucis

Was weird the way music was to me then. When I think of it now I must have missed an awful lot of television for nothing except stupid songs. Programme on there today about all the different ways that animals see and smell and hear. Wondered if there was a better way of seeing than us humans have. Or do some people have a better way of seeing than other people? Some people are colour blind. Got on fine I suppose 'til they invented paint. When I taste an orange I wonder is it the exact same taste you get when you have one.

And saw a documentary about tribes. This old fella, the chief of the tribe told us all about the *Saucis* which is a kind of evil spirit that comes when people are asleep and sucks out their brain and their insides and replaces them with grass. Makes people evil and they cause other people around them to become sick or they can cause them to have no luck hunting for food. And the worst thing is they don't even know the *Saucis* has come and sucked out their brain so they're acting away all normal. It's only certain gifted people in the tribe who can see that they've been paid a visit by the *Saucis* and they inform the others so they can kill them and eat them. He said that human flesh tastes just like something but I can't remember what it was. I'd never heard of it anyhow.

But this chief said that he had the gift. He could tell. He'd got the tribe to kill and eat eleven people over the years. Some of them were from neighbouring tribes. Some from his own tribe.

Then they spoke to a fella of about thirty whose brother was visited by the *Saucis* and had to be killed. His girlfriend from a neighbouring tribe became sick and died and the leader of that tribe came and said that her boyfriend had been visited by the *Saucis* and would have to be killed and eaten. They had no option only to hand him over. There was tears in his brother's eyes when he was describing his brother being taken away. Nice carry-on isn't it?

The shit we know is unbelievable so it just shows you that half the bullshit we know is only so that we can feel right about living the way we do and truth don't have much to do with it or about just as much as the *Saucis* sucking people's insides out has to do with truth. I hope that sentence wasn't too long and confusing for you. Sentences are a pain in the hole and that's half the problem. Every word we ever invented and the ways we have to make them mean stuff is only there cos it made us live and feel right about the way we live. And all our clever words are really just the same as a dog barking when it comes to the truth. I seen Teesh in the pub yesterday cos I went in after a match with my father. Teesh was there like the whole parish just plain forgot what a cunt he is and he in the pub with other fellas having the craic and all I can see is monkeys grooming each other cos David Attenborough said once the stronger the alliances the longer they spend grooming and it's the same with lads in the pub.

I first knew for sure there was evil in this world when I woke up in Snoozie's house – I think Racey might have been there too or maybe she was above in the cot with Dinky or maybe she was with some other lad that night, they were always blowing hot and cold those two. Anyhow the rest of us were asleep in the living room of the house. I woke up anyhow and it was early. Probably about ten. The rest of them were still asleep. There was this documentary on and this woman was talking to the man. He was asking her about long ago when her little girl went missing. She was only ten years of age. And how the papers all thought her mother's second husband had killed her or something. Later on then they caught Myra Hindley and whatever her man's name was and this woman had to identify her child by the tape recording Myra Hindley and your man made when they were taunting her and torturing her and raping her and teasing her and she crying mad and calling out for her mammy the whole time. She had to listen to the tape that went on for sixteen minutes. The woman looked sixty about. Maybe older. Said all she wanted was to die. That's all she's ever wanted since she heard the tape and knew her little girl was dead and how she died. She just wanted to be dead and to be with her and she prayed every day for God to take her. Seemed unreal to me. I knew that no matter what happened in my life I'd never feel pain like that woman had. You'd wonder what has suffering got to do with pain. And how has the pain of one person got anything to do with the pleasure of another person. And can you feel other people's pain?

Sadism

N. 1. *psychol.*; hurting others for sexual pleasure; the gaining of sexual gratification by causing physical or mental pain to other people, or the acts that produce such gratification 2. being cruel for fun; the gaining of pleasure from causing physical or mental pain to people or animals 3 cruelty; great physical or mental cruelty [Late 19thC. From French *sadisme*, named after the Marquis de Sade.]

Amazing some of the things people needed to invent words for.

Is there a part of everyone that likes to see people suffering? Like people who buy newspapers. I remember my cousin when I was small hitting me with a golf club and just looking at me when I was crying, like 'twas entertaining or something. Kids like to see other kids get in trouble in school. Makes small little smirks appear that they have to smother with the muscles of their cheeks. I seen it a million times. A pretty little girl had her face beaten with stilettos in some place in Europe by other girls so she would stop being pretty.

Anyhow I suppose after watching that programme that morning and the suffering of the girl's mother and the evil of Hindley and your man, it changed the way I thought. Became watchful. Vigilant. Noticed more.

And maybe that's when I started to realise that all the music stuff with Sinéad and James was only silly in the face of real life.

Sinéad and James and me we spoke about music. It wasn't just listening to it or making it. Talking shit talk instead of getting on with our lives.

—Do you enjoy singing such a sad song and feeling so sad like? James goes one time in the library.

—Dunno. Kind of.

—Weird, isn't it though?

—I suppose yeah. Don't lose any sleep over it pet!

—Maybe it's like a problem shared kind of thing maybe. Even when you're on your own listening to it. It always comes from another, goes James.

—What about singing or playing a tune on your own?

—Oh yeah, said James.

There was silence for a bit while we were thinking, then Sinéad goes,

—Maybe there's always a chance that someone will hear.

Sinéad went to the record player then and puts on a Sam Cooke record and she grabbed James and went dancing. 'Twisting The Night Away' was the song. One of her shoes fell off when they were spinning around the place. It was weird to see the sole of it worn just like an ordinary person's shoes. At the end of the song they fell on the couch laughing and panting and the rhythm of their breathing was nice to listen to. Getting slower the whole time and the giggles coming and going until it was silence again except for the quiet crackle of the needle on the spinning record. I took the needle off the record then and then James goes,

—Some music is fearful then though.

—Maybe nice music is like . . . the opposite of fearful sound . . . like the opposite of the roar of a tiger or something.

—Yeah maybe.

—Couldn't imagine a tiger making beautiful sweet music before biting your head off.

—No.

—So like we're supposed to not like a tiger's roar cos it's dangerous.

—But it's a horrible sound anyway.

—Horrible to us, James said, cos that's how we survived. Any idiots who were attracted to a lion's roar would have had their heads taken off.

—So are you saying that it only sounds rotten to us but if you weren't made of meat it might sound nicer?

—Ha! I dunno . . . maybe.

—That's silly. It's a horrible sound anyway whether people hear it or not. But music was used like by warriors wasn't it? To like intimidate and scare the enemy.

—Yeah.

—Would make them feel closer together too like. As a group. Stronger like.

—Yeah.

—And like territorial. Like birds.

—I guess. Makes you want to move too. Like a march.

—Yeah.

—I wonder what's the opposite of a tiger's roar, James asked.

—Kate Bush, said Sinéad.

James found her favourite Kate Bush song on the piano and she sang. Write the Kate Bush song 'This Woman's Work' in here please.

_____

_____

_____

_____

_____

_____

_____

_____

_____

_____

_____

_____

I wondered where Sinéad summoned this sadness from and she singing this song. It was like she'd lived a thousand lifetimes. Buried a thousand daughters and a thousand sons. Maybe the sixteen years of her somehow had access to another memory. Through the music isn't it? A thousand thousand thousand lifetimes back maybe and maybe even more and to a different creature yet. Us once.

12

Mass

The mother's making me go to Mass now again. It's half five in the morning now and Mass is at eleven in the morning. But I'm not tired anyhow. In Mass I always go up the balcony so I can look down at the back of all their stupid holy heads praying away mad and picking their noses or their holes. I used to try and block out Father Scully's voice going on and on but it was hard cos he went on and on cos he was only an old bollicks. He'd shout and roar from the pulpit with the big angry red head up on him. When he wasn't throwing abuse at the Catholics of the parish he spent his days walking around the place reading the Bible. You could see him anywhere just reading it. Well if it was raining you couldn't see him anywhere reading it. But when it was dry you could see him sitting on the street bench across from Roundy's. Or walking around the churchyard taking slow small steps and never taking his head from the pages. Like he was a piano being pulled along by a rope. Our own moving statue. And all his stupid sermons were the same. He'd vomit out all the bits in the Bible that he'd read the week before but it was always the same bits that proved that the devil was a terrible fucker and tell them all how the devil had woven his evil ways into all their lives and God wasn't one bit happy with them and that there'd be hell to pay. In hell.

He didn't think much of young people. Vice had them. Vice grip.

He stopped me being an altar boy long ago cos I was shit cos I'm a gamal. The altar boy at Mass has to ring the bell at four very special times during the Mass. When I was on I forgot to shake the bell at the special times. But I remembered to shake it at the wrong times. At five wrong times. You should have seen the faces on all the people in the church and they trying not to laugh. Snorting same as pigs some of them and they trying to hide their faces by ducking behind the person in front of them or pretending to wipe their noses with their hankies.

Father Scully just waited patiently for the bell the times when I was supposed to ring it but never did. He tried to catch my eye but I was looking down at all the people or trying to see inside my fingernails so he carried on with the holy talk then when he realised I was only there in body. The body of Charlie, Amen. The times I rang it at the wrong times then he was patient too. Just looked sad is all, looking down at the ground and not at me at all. But the last time then he told me to move to another seat. And when I tried to take the big heavy bell with me he told me to leave it where it was.

Some of the people were laughing so much now that you could hear the shrieks. The shoulders of them rocking like they were hiccup crying.

But he'd lambaste them all for being such horrible rotten sinners. And everything was scandal with Father Scully. Every week the same old puke, woe is the man.

—Let us turn then to scripture.

—Woe to the man to whom the scandal cometh.

—Scandal is the word or act which gives occasion to the spiritual ruin of one's neighbour.

—After the death of a certain person who had given scandal, a holy man witnessed his judgement, and saw, at his arrival at the gates of Hell, all the souls whom he had scandalised, and they said, 'Come accursed wretch, and atone,' and they rushed upon him . and tore him to pieces like wild beasts.

—Now. You sit there and wonder. Can I be redeemed? Well you can. Great is the mercy of the Lord. Great is the mercy of the Lord.

—If thy right eye scandalise thee, pluck it out and cast it from thee.

I like being up on the balcony all by myself looking at the statues. But Father Scully ruins it. Sometimes I can never get his voice out of my head. Give you the holy spooks it would. Every poor eejit in Ballyronan had to listen to them same words once a week. He kept going on about scandal and the fucking wild beasts in Hell.

—Examine thine own heart.

Cape Clear Again

Seen Racey there pull into the petrol station with her father. She got out of the car and her father stayed in it. She came out with milk and bread. You're lucky I don't be describing things. Milk and bread. The milk looked white because it was. Anyhow I felt sorry for her. Even though she did wrong on Sinéad. Made me think of her in Cape Clear Irish college all self-conscious with the same fat ass she has on her today. Wasn't her fault she was no Sinéad. Inside or out. She doesn't have a mind of her own. The people around her always owned Racey's mind.

The night before the Leaving Cert Exam results came out we went to Cape Clear island again. The Leaving Cert is the state exam eighteen-year-olds do to see if their parents made them study enough to go to college. I failed all my exams. My mother and father pretended they never noticed when the letter arrived with my results. NG. No grade. When the exams were on I looked around and drew pictures instead of writing for a few hours. And in my art exam I just looked around. I liked watching them all anyhow. They all thought they were getting more out of it than just a pain in their hand. They were reading the shit on the exam paper and then writing their own shit in the answer book and then reading more shit and then writing more of their own shit. And I was glad I didn't have to read any of the mountains of shit being read or being written. And the man in charge was walking around the place trying his best to keep looking like he was in charge. The first day he came over and asked me was I feeling all right cos he seen me looking around and drawing on the answer book instead of writing. I said,

—Yeah.

—OK, he said, and the caring stupid head on him.

Anyhow the night before the results and we went to Cape Clear again. This time we were camping. We went back out to the island for old times sake, whatever that means. We watched all the kids at Irish college eejiting down at the waterfront like they were kids and we weren't. But we were. For another small while anyhow. All the tears that would flow when they all said goodbye to their new friends seemed silly to the others now. But I knew they weren't silly. Silly if life is only silly isn't it? Feelings are real at the time.

We camped right in against the wall of the old ruin this time to shield the campfire from the breeze. We could still see the sea that stretched out for America. Just not the other side of the ruin where it stretched off for England or France or some place. Dinky and Racey went off for a stroll somewhere off back the way we came, for a kiss and a cuddle. America Sinéad was thinking of.

—Charlie you should get out of here and start a new life. When we make it we'll set you up in America with an apartment and a job and the whole lot. But you'll have to stop acting the gamal.

—I will.

—Are you sick of how people see you?

—I suppose.

—I understand. You can start anew though. Somewhere no one knows you. Imagine New York?

—Yeah.

—Do you think we'll hit New York like Bob Dylan did long ago?

—No.

—Oh. Thanks! You do think we could make it though do you?

—Yeah.

—OK, cool. I'd love if you were with us Charlie.

—Yeah. Wouldn't be right without you boy, James said.

—Our chief roadie. Stage manager. Would you like that Charlie?

—Yeah.

—Yeah, said James.

—Yeah, said Sinéad. Cool.

—Dublin first though, James said.

—Yeah, said Sinéad, definitely Dublin first.

When Racey and Dinky came back they were both soft. That means a bit drunk.

—Imagine we're finished the Leaving Cert. We'll never have to study like that again.

—Fuck yeah! The adventure starts now. We don't have to do anything we don't want to any more.

—We're gonna be famous, aren't we Sinéad?

—'Course we are babe. Our music will make us famous near and far.

—I just don't see why ye have to go to Dublin to make it, to be honest, said Dinky.

—Jesus man, that's where it's all happening. Dublin is imperative, said James.

—Ye could make a name for yourselves here first, said Dinky.

—Be easier in Dublin. Trinity College have the best college music scene this side of the Atlantic. Not to mention the acoustic sessions happening in the city every night of the week. Best spot in the world, right now, and it's only a couple of hundred miles up the road. You're mad not to want to go too.

—What's wrong with what we have here?

—Nothing. There's just more in Dublin. It's only for a few years.

—I'll live and die for Ballyronan anyway.

—I know you will.

—You'll go far to find half as good a spot on the planet.

—I know. I'll take my chances.

—You're just never satisfied James. You're never just happy with what you've got.

—The future beckons.

—You're a snob James.

—You can accuse me of anything boy, but don't call me a snob. I was born into a few bob, big shit. I never let it affect me.

—Are you sure?

—'Course I'm not, but I was never a snob.

—Lads come on, Sinéad said.

—Leave it Dinky, Racey said.

Dublin

I didn't know what I was going to do when Sinéad and James went to Dublin. Be lost without them isn't it? Nothing to do and no one ever to talk to ever. James was going doing engineering in Trinity College and Sinéad was going to art college. But really they were going up there to be free and to become music stars. They were going to join the live music society in the college and play all the acoustic sessions in all the bars around Dublin. Imagine Dublin. I'd never been but I could imagine it I think. Sinéad and James there. Christ. Let loose.

—We'll knock 'em dead up there. What ya think Charlie?

—Yeah.

—Will you visit us Charlie?

—Ha?

—'Course he'll visit us. You can stay with me Charlie. Dunno where I'll be staying yet but you'll be staying with me. We're gonna stay in houses right beside each other.

James' parents thought they were too young to live together. Sinéad's parents didn't care.

—I think you'd love Dublin Charlie. Maybe you could get a job there and stay up with us.

—Ha?

—Yeah. Fuck yeah. You could do that. My dad knows some people in Dublin. Building people who could fix you up with a labouring job.

—Yeah. Dunno.

—He's right Charlie. Be a clean break for you wouldn't it?

—Dunno.

—You could help us gigging. Be like our stage manager or something. I'd say you'd like that Charlie. Would you?

—Yeah. I'd say I would.

—We'll suss out the scene for a few months above. Then we'll send for ya.

—A telegram.

—Message in a bottle.

—Or a pigeon maybe.

—Or we could send a messenger on horseback.

—You won't have to shoot him Charlie. He'll have good news. Your friends will have sent for you to come and join them as they meet their destiny in the capital city of Ireland.

—What ya reckon Charlie?

—Yeah.

—Yeah! You're kinda quiet in yourself today Charlie.

—Yeah!

—You're a cute whore Charlie. Ingenious.

Cute whore means clever rascal in Ireland.

—Yeah, I said and they laughed.

I did see Dublin in the end. And it was cos of Sinéad and James. But it wasn't in the way we thought.

Next thing around a month before James went to Dublin the father comes in the door at home with shiny new steel-cap boots.

—New boots, I said.

—They're for you, he goes. I was talking to Diarmuid above in the new houses. He's giving you a start.

I said nothing. I just felt sick. That's what happens when you see the next forty years of your life all at once.

—Bed early tonight, he goes. You've to be above before eight o'clock in the morning.

The site was only up the hill a bit. Only a few hundred yards. This Diarmuid fella is Teesh's brother. He was the foreman. I used to be doing the snag lists mostly. That's a list of stuff that has to be done before the new owners would pay for the house. Usually it was scraping hard concrete off the floor or scraping the spatters of it off windows and window frames. Or raking the earth in the garden for the grass seed. Or taking down scaffolding and taking out whatever loose blocks and planks and cut-off bits of sills and lintels and wood and pipes that the sloppy fuckers would leave after them. Diarmuid used to go through the list with me fierce slow cos I'm a gamal.

Mostly he was sound enough except when he used to pretend to lose his temper if some fella wasn't getting the job done or was fucking it up or if some delivery wasn't made. Then he'd roar and curse but you'd see his face then when he turned around and he wasn't really cross at all. Usually I was left on my own to tip away. I was the last to work in a house. All the tradesmen would be after moving on to the next house. That's how they did it. They used to all be having their lunchbreak together and the tea at eleven. But mostly I was able to stay in my own house. And not be listening to their boring shit and they laughing and winking to each other at the lunch the mother made me in a big A-Team lunchbox with sandwiches and all sorts of goodies and snacks and a flask of coffee and a bottle of orange. If I gave a fuck the mother would've embarrassed the hole off me my whole life. But she was the perfect mother for a gamal to have. Jumpers she buys me. I'd say she gets them in the middle-aged perverts' shop. V-neck ones with square or angular designs on them that school inspectors or trainspotters would wear at home in their slippers. And the cheap denim jeans she gets me that you'd think someone painted blue. And she never knew my size. The legs were always too short and the ass of them was always fucking huge. And black slip-on shoes she'd have on me and white socks under them. Except when I was working. Now I was a working man and wore a working man's boots. And I always have a pencil on my ear. So I'm like the workmen on the site who just look at me and shake their heads. God help us.

13

I should tell you about the bank holiday weekend of that summer too actually. It was the August bank holiday weekend and James had a big match on the bank holiday Monday but we wanted to go camping out at the Fleadh Cheoil an tSamhraidh in Dingle. That's the Summer Music Festival. Dingle is a town. Nobody in Dingle is passing through cos the other side of it is the Atlantic ocean. Everyone is there cos they went there and it's usually for the music. It's hours from anywhere and it doesn't mind one bit.

So we were going to head off Friday night cos James' last training session before the match was Friday evening. But then I think they got wind of our plan and they didn't want James sleeping in a tent and stuff in the days coming up to the big match so they changed the last training session to Saturday evening so that James couldn't go to Dingle at all. Dinky was the only one who knew we were going to go to the Fleadh and he told Teesh and they told the trainer then I reckon. And Kerby was the trainer but everyone said it was Roundy used to pick the team cos Kerby licked Roundy's ass always. Anyhow they changed the training so the best player couldn't go to the Fleadh.

Only trouble was James went anyway and decided to miss the training Saturday night. All it meant was that he could go earlier. So we all went Friday morning instead. We'd come back Sunday and James' final was on the Monday. We got the bus as far as Cork cos they'd have seen us hitching with the bags and the guitar. We got off near the roundabout by the Kerry road and me and James hid in the ditch and Sinéad stuck out her thumb. The third car stopped. James got in the front and me and Sinéad sat into the back. The man driving took a few minutes to come to terms with it.

—Ye're gas out, he says.

—Yeah we were taking turns hitching, you'd be wrecked from the standing, James said.

The man started laughing and we did too. He took us as far as Killarney and then we did the same again to get a lift on to Dingle. Lorry this time so it was a tight squeeze but the view out was worth it. The land out that way would make you think differently. One thing about hills and valleys and mountains and rocks is that it reminds you that all you have is one point of view. Keeps you humble and makes you giddy to explore a thousand other viewpoints for a thousand new rewards. And it all at odds with the ocean and it dead level and straight and for ever. Only way you could describe it all to a blind person is by playing some tune of it. Be even better for them cos they'd be like an eagle gliding through it isn't it? Or a bat cos they're blind and that's where sound came from in the first place I suppose. Let creatures with no eyes know where they were. And they moving through terrains. Sound waves isn't it? Sound was freedom. Sound was everything.

We arrived into some kind of a dreamplace. There was music everywhere. On the corner a girl of about our own age singing sean-nós. Old style. And twenty or thirty around her and they all so quiet that you could hear the girl draw breath for the next bit each time. On another bit and a young fella sitting on a crate playing the concertina and an old man standing beside him playing a wooden flute. Crowd around them too. Next was two old women singing sean-nós and a girl of about eight tapping on a bodhrán. It lined the streets as far as the eyes could see. Went for a piss in a pub and the inner room was crammed with people listening to a tin whistle player with a comb-over. Sinéad's face was best of the lot though. She was stunned. Smile would break out in her every now and again and her eyes were bright as flame taking in all the wonders.

We were camping and we'd only one four-man tent. It was my sister's. They'd no problem sleeping cos the nights were warm and the drink had them immune to the hard ground. We talked and then they fell asleep and I liked to listen to the two of them breathing and the sound of the sea.

On the Saturday night there we ended up in the bar of the hotel in the middle of the street. It wasn't that full but it was cosy and there was a good session on there. A session is where everyone takes it in turns to sing or play a tune. Sinéad started singing then. She sang a song called 'Carraig Aonair' that she learned out in Cape Clear and a change started coming over the place. The murmur stopped and people started coming in from the street to hear her. Crowds at the door looking in. The place erupted when she finished and they called out for more and she went shy and said,

—Ah no, someone else now, so they left her alone.

A few of the musicians started playing a reel then and this woman came over to Sinéad. A blonde English one of about thirty. She said she was a singer-songwriter and was always on the lookout for a great voice. They talked for hours. She told Sinéad how she started out busking outside a tube station in London and went on from there. She said her work is more popular in Japan, mostly piano-based. Some guy came over then and introduced this one to the crowd and asked her to play one of her own pieces on the piano. She said she would only if Sinéad would sing along and Sinéad went all apologetic and said she didn't know her music and your one just goes sing anything and coaxes her over to the piano beside her.

—Whatever comes to mind, just let yourself go, she said.

—God, said Sinéad, I'll try.

Your one started playing on the piano then. A fierce nice tune it was. Not complicated. And not slow. But it was kind of innocent or something. Remind you of a small stream. After a while she started to look at Sinéad to encourage her on and then Sinéad started. She sang some phrases from U2's song 'Bad'. The same ones over and over. Desolation. Isolation. Revelation. In temptation. Let it go. And so fade away. Over and over and over.

The electricity in the place went bananas. It was like a

phenomenon we witnessed. Same as some shooting star or some eclipse or some comet. After all the applause and people congratulating them the woman and Sinéad spent the whole night talking again. James was very drunk. Just smiling and muttering away to himself and saying,

—She's fantastic. Simple as that. Fantastic.

When we were leaving the woman wrote down Sinéad's name and address and gave her her own card and asked what we were doing the next day. Sinéad said,

—We're hoping to get to Mass at ten in the church cos there's these famous musicians playing O'Riada's Mass. It's like this Irish music Mass an Irish composer wrote. Really beautiful.

—My goodness, that sounds amazing. Where's the church?

—Just up at the top of the hill I think.

—Great, see you there then tomorrow. Ten is it?

—Yeah, said Sinéad.

We were a little bit late cos James was still very drunk. When we went in Sinéad saw her sitting down but was too shy to sit in beside her and walked on ahead. Then we heard,

—Pssst. Sinéad.

It was your one so we went and sat in beside her. She gave us a big wink and smiled. She was on her own. We enjoyed the Mass but the talking bits were boring. At least it was in Irish and we didn't understand so you couldn't find yourself listening even by accident. Afterwards your one insisted on buying us all breakfast and wanted to give us money for the bus when we said we were hitch-hiking home but we wouldn't take it.

—The bus would take twice as long anyway, James said.

—Well you guys mind Sinéad. She's rather precious you know.

—I know, said James and put his arm around her.

—I'll be in touch, she said. Have a good summer.

We did have a good summer but it's long since passed. I could tell you your one's name but she mightn't like it, I dunno. If you search hard enough you'll find who it was. Music is how you'll find her.

We were all giddy coming back. Especially Sinéad. Your one was touring for the summer but had said to Sinéad she'd love to bring her over and do some recordings in her house. She had her own studio. James could come too and me too if I wanted Sinéad said. Sinéad was finally starting to believe it about herself. That she was special.

We got back to Ballyronan Sunday night so James was fresh as a daisy for his match the next day. I went with my father. There was a big crowd at it. They had programmes and everything. I was inside the wire doing the water when I seen James coming over to the subs bench when the game was starting. Roundy and Kerby said they were starting Teesh instead cos he was more committed and didn't go off to a concert for the weekend. They'd beaten the hardest opposition in the semi-final thanks to James and now he was on the bench cos they knew that they'd win the final easily anyway cos the other crowd were only fair. And Teesh midfield the cowardly prick and he trying to punch the ball away from him instead of catching it in the air. After half time James was still on the bench so he got up and headed for the dressing room. Sinéad met him at the wire and walked him up. I knew James would be OK but I could see his father outside the wire and I knew that's who James was thinking about. The picture of the team was on the *South Cork Weekly* with the cup and no James and no mention of him either and all the smiley heads up on Teesh and Dinky and Roundy and Kerby and all the other fools too. James put a brave face on it all and acted like he didn't care but he did. And he knew it hurt his father. People said not very nice things about Sinéad in the pub too for taking him to Dingle. How she was a bad influence and all.

—He should have more sense anyway than be hanging around with that tramp. She's a bad influence and that's proof.

—She's a slapper anyway and she sharing the tent with James and the gamal over.

—Weird shit boy that.

—Isn't it?

—Weird shit yeah. Not right like.

—They're no good for each other them two, and the gamal inside in the middle of them then and the clueless head up on him. Name of Christ.

Sinéad's Father Sick

Next thing Sinéad's father decides to come down with some sort of sickness or other and the whole Dublin plan goes to shit. Cancer is a terrible illness. Good people get it. Nasty people get it too. Sinéad's father got it. Bollicks cancer. That's not cancer of the bollicks, that's testicular cancer. Bollicks cancer is the kind of cancer bollickses get. He got it in his stomach.

—Oh you're a nice one. Fuck off to Dublin just when your family needs you. You ungrateful little bitch.

I think Sinéad wanted me in the house in case her mother started trying to hit her. Stuff like that happened her before but I can't tell you about it cos she made me swear not to repeat a word about it. That stuff and worse stuff as well. Private kind of worse stuff that shouldn't happen to people any time but definitely not when they're only small. Cruel things.

Anyhow I used to hang around Sinéad's house in case she'd get hit or something. Nobody took any notice cos I'm a gamal. And anyhow, I did their gardening for them. Pretended I loved gardening. One time her father told her to fuck off out of it and take the retard with her. The retard was me. But really he liked the way I kept the garden.

—Am I supposed to give up my job now is it? Over my dead body will you go to Dublin you little fucking jade you.

That was her mother again. Truth is Sinéad's mother drank even more than her father sometimes. One of Sinéad's older sisters was off in Australia. The other one was married up in Northern Ireland somewhere. Teesh called them the ugly sisters. One of them was in Teesh's class in school long ago.

I still don't know why she didn't go to Dublin. James could have helped her with some money and she could have got a loan. But there was some hold over her. Some unnatural or natural hold over her. She loved the drunken old bollicks of a father I suppose isn't it? Bit of love from him would've meant a lot to her I think.

Roundy's

So Sinéad's father got her a job in Roundy's, the pub.

—You're not going to be sponging off us no more. Teach you what a day's work is.

Then there was the time James arrived down to my house after we all thought he was gone off to Dublin. That morning they took me for the spin up to the train station. Me, Sinéad, James and his father. His mother didn't come cos she doesn't like goodbyes cos all her brothers had to go away long ago to find work in America. Even the fella who played for Dublin and he was one of the best footballers in the country in his day. Came back later on and settled in County Wexford, he did.

—And I'm not saying goodbye. We'll see you again in a couple of weeks. Just mind yourself for God's sake.

That's all she said. James hugged her and then she said it. By the time James had sat into the car she was after going back in the front door and closing the door behind her.

—Your mother doesn't like goodbyes James, his father said.

—I know, said James.

In the car Sinéad was quiet in herself. James just entertained his father's ramblings about his own college days.

—And join the societies. That's where you'll meet people. Sinéad will go up to you next weekend. I'll give you a spin to the train station next weekend if you like.

Sinéad wasn't listening. James turned around with a smile for her. Then he noticed she was crying.

—Yeah she might take that lift dad.

His father adjusted his rearview mirror for a second to see Sinéad's face. When he saw her tears he readjusted the mirror and he said,

—Ah. I see. That's a new kind of pain you'll be feeling there now, the both of ye. The pain of leaving. Separation is hard for those in love.

James threw back his hand for Sinéad to hold. She squeezed it tight. She'd a crumpled tissue in her other hand. James' father went on.

—No distance in the world could come between the love you two have for each other. Ye'll see each other Friday night when you go up to him.

Silence then for a while. At least from human voices. The old Volvo the size of a house droned away up the road and Mozart or Beethoven or Carmen or whatever rusty old classical tape he had on fleeted and flittered and flitted away in the background. Only other sound now and again was Sinéad trying to stifle her crying.

At the station James' father spoke to me.

—Very good, very good, very good. Gardeners will always have work. In fact I might have a bit myself for you now that James is going. Would that suit?

—Ha?

—Would that suit you?

—Ha?

—A bit of work. I could give you some gardening work. Would that suit you?

—Yeah.

—Very good. Ah yes. Yes indeed. Mam and dad are both good?

—Yeah.

—Very good. I suppose you'll miss James too will you?

—Yeah.

—I'll miss him myself. As will his mother. You know, his mother now will be awful quiet in herself for a few days. Then she'll get used to the idea of him not being around. Went to Greece for a week without him when he was about two. Took her a few days to get used to him not being around then too. She'll be fine in a few days.

He stared at me suddenly then, half worried-looking, same as a child after dropping something and he goes,

—Do you think?

—Ha?

He stared off into the dark tunnel then where the trains go off to Dublin. Then half to himself he said,

—At least I hope she will.

Silence then again. He looked over to where James and Sinéad were. They were beside an old steam engine that the rail crowd had there for people to be looking at. James had her hands in his and was talking to her. They hugged and kissed. Talked. Hugged and kissed. Talked. James' father turned his attention back to me then.

—I hope he keeps up the football now in college. Good for the body. What's good for the body is good for the mind. Isn't that right Charlie?

—Yeah.

—Christ I dunno how he'll ever manage without her. They've been side by side ever since we came to Ballyronan. Doesn't seem natural somehow that they're parting. Such a shame. Such a shame she couldn't go. He'd settle much better with her up there you know. And she'd be a damn sight happier too, I fancy. I really don't know. Maybe I should have spoken to her parents. James told me not to, you know. Didn't think it was my place. Still.

They shouldn't be holding her back like that. We all have our misfortune. This is her hour. Her season. This is when Sinéad should come into her own. Dublin is the place for her. Art college is the place for her.

He looked at me then like he didn't recognise me for a second.

—Isn't that right Charlie?

—Yeah.

—Yes indeed. I go on Charlie. I do go on you know. Don't mind me.

I didn't mind him. He looked at all the people around. From head to head to head like he was looking for someone.

—Youth. Christ youth is important though isn't it? All we have is our youth. All we've ever lived for. Let them live damn it all. Let them live. That's what I say. What do you think Charlie?

—Yeah.

—He'll not get a seat on that train you know at this stage. I suppose he doesn't care. He'd stand for seven days for another minute with her I fancy, let alone the few hours' train journey. And who'd blame him Charlie. Am I right? Hmmm?

—Yeah.

—Still. They've five minutes. He'll have to go underneath the track in the tunnel to the other side to get on that train. He'll have to get a move on. Charlie would you ever go over to them and tell them it's five to six. Like a good fellow.

—Yeah.

There was a train on the near track as well as the one on the other side so we couldn't see him to wave goodbye as the train pulled off. Sinéad puckered up a little on the way home. James' father spoke nice words to her. Made her cry a little but made her feel better at the same time.

—Sinéad you're the best thing that ever happened to him. And he's the best thing to ever happen to you too I fancy. You'll be together soon. I'll bring you to the train station next Friday. You can go up to him for the weekend. Don't worry. Hundred years ago he could be emigrating to America. Or going to war. You'll be fine.

He dropped Sinéad home first. Then me.

14

About two hours later I was up in my room when I heard gravel hitting off my window. James it was.

—I forgot to get on the train! Bleddy thing went off without me.

—Ha?

—Ha yourself. I wanna spend another night with Sinéad. We need it.

—OK.

—Will you mind my bag? I'll collect it in the morning.

He threw it up and I caught it.

—Cool. I'll be over for it in the morning. Think I'm mad?

—No.

—Do you think your mother would miss a few roses from her rose bush?

—Probably. But she wouldn't mind if she knew where they were going. Where ye gonna stay?

—Dunno yet. Somewhere nice hopefully.

—Don't get seen.

—I won't. See ya.

—Bye.

Early in the morning same thing again. Gravel at my window. Looked out the dreary window at the dreary morning and I saw the smiling faces of Sinéad and James looking up at me. Two candles in the dark.

—G'morning Charlie.

—Gimme the bag and come on. We're getting the seven o'clock bus to the train station.

I threw on my clothes, went for a pee and went straight out the window to them. We'd the bus all to ourselves. We were down the back seat. James was leaning on the window at one side with Sinéad between his legs. I was leaning on the other side facing Sinéad and James.

—You'll mind Sinéad for me Charlie won't ya?

—Yeah.

—Do you swear?

—Yeah.

—Thanks Charlie, but we both know 'tis James needs looking after.

When he was gone Sinéad cried again for a bit. We had a wait up in Cork for a bit then before the next bus. She told me about a swimming final I never knew about. Sinéad was way out in front but tried so hard that she forgot to breathe and a few strokes before the finish line she panicked and nearly drowned. She lost the race. How she tried so hard and couldn't believe she was winning and was going to get a gold medal, a gold medal around her neck, and bring it home to show it to her mammy and daddy who couldn't go to the competition and that she'd be so special and loved when she won this and it would make everyone proud and when she knew she was winning she tried even harder harder harder so that she'd definitely win and next thing near the very end of the race she left it too long to breathe and panicked and then inhaled some water and was flailing around in the pool for air while all the rest passed her out and she came last instead of first. She was nine years old and she cried and she cried. Anyhow. People do be failing isn't it? We walked back to Merchant's Quay from the train station. We sat on the benches overlooking the dirty mossy green River Lee.

How oft do my thoughts in their fancy take flight
To the home of my childhood away
To the days when each patriot's vision seemed bright
Ere I dreamed that those joys should decay
When my heart was as light as the wild winds that blow
Down the Mardyke through each elm tree
Where I sported and played 'neath the green leafy shade
On the Banks of my own lovely Lee

Ballyronan is in County Cork. Each county in Ireland has its own song. The Cork one is 'The Banks of My Own Lovely Lee'. When the county team wins a big match everyone gets drunk and sings their county song. And other songs as well. We've a million songs. Most of them are about fighting off the English. Except the

Dublin song, 'Molly Malone'. That's about a prostitute. They'd a red-light district in Dublin before red lights.

Dunno what the song of County Leitrim or County Louth is cos they're shit at football. Maybe they're good at chess or draughts or something and get drunk and sing their song after a big chess match. Or maybe they're just shit at everything. Never heard of no one from Leitrim or Louth. I suppose they just don't give a fuck. I'd say Leitrim was the easiest county of them all to get back off the English cos they were probably sorry to be stuck with it in the first place.

Anyhow. Sinéad told me stuff. She told me stuff she didn't even tell James. Stuff I never told nobody cos she asked me not to. About when she was only small long ago.

But she calmed down anyhow watching the Lee like she learned something from the river just by looking at it. Cos the river didn't give a fuck, far as we could see. The last little cry she had I didn't know if it was for James gone away or for the troubled little girl she was long ago who inhaled some of a swimming pool instead of the air above it.

—You'd never let me down Charlie would you?

—No, I said. I would never do that, no.

We went upstairs in Merchant's Quay shopping centre and had some coffee and scones in the café up there. She went up to the till and paid before we even got the second cup off the girl. Felt strange. I always had money cos I'd be doing jobs. But now she had money too. I kinda didn't like it. Thought of her being a woman with a handbag. Saw her mother in her for the first time in my life. Wasn't the Sinéad my dreams were made of and I hoped it wasn't becoming hers. We sat across from each other over at the window. I was looking south down along Patrick Street, she was looking north across the river. Up over the hill of the north-side where the sky was clear and blue and stretched up towards Dublin and beyond. James' sky now isn't it?

—You'd never lie to me Charlie would you?

—No, I said.

—Do you think he'll forget about me?

—What do you mean?

—Do you think he could find someone else?

—No.

She bit her nails and stared at the few bubbles still whirling slowly in her coffee.

—Sometimes . . . it's like. I dunno.

—He'd never, I said. He'd never.

—Ah no, I don't . . . think like. It's just . . .

—Yeah.

We spoke about what it would be like in Dublin then, when she did get to join him. I said she could still go up before too long and just work somewhere until her course started again the follow-ing October. She said,

—Yeah . . . yeah.

But I was starting to see she was starting to doubt it would happen. The doubt was in her voice and in her eyes. I pressed on.

—Ye could get a gig in the Ruby Sessions.

—Yeah.

—Go to it some night first though. Meant to be like, intimate like.

—Yeah.

—And like in the college as well. Music like, there'll be loads going on for ye.

But she wasn't listening to me any more.

—Yeah, she said. Yeah.

—What time are you working tonight?

—Eight. Eight to close.

Her eyes welled. I wanted to say something good like James would but I just said,

—He'll be up around Limerick Junction now I suppose, or even further up maybe.

—Yeah, she said.

—Have you done anything since on that song?

'Faraway' was the name of the song.

—No. I think it might be kinda crap, she said.

It was.

—Still. Some of your lyrics were nice, I said.

—Thanks. I think James kind of likes it.

—He likes them all when they're new. Does be thinking too much about them. Keys and chord sequences. Only hears the melody when he's the thing learned.

She laughed and said,

—Yeah that's true. Gets all caught up in the mechanics of it.

She laughed again and said,

—He's just afraid that he'll forget it.

—Yeah I said. When he's the keys worked out he has a map to go back to. Some trail back to the tune.

—Yeah. Could you forget a melody?

—No, I said. Could you?

—No. Not a good one anyway.

She laughed again and said,

—He wouldn't have room in that head of his. My brain is a fat lump of a couch potato in comparison to his. Sometimes I think his mind is like a miracle. That it can do all the stuff it does like. Like sometimes I just can't believe he can do all the ordinary stuff like dressing himself and being able to write when there's so much other stuff going on like the football and the music and the studying and the plans for us and everything. He can do so much like, can't he? He's a miracle. Isn't he though?

—Yeah, I said.

—Like . . . sometimes I wonder like . . . and I know I'm terrified of it like but . . . if he did lose interest in me and found someone else . . . I'd still be like . . . I'd be heartbroken but I'd still have to be happy with God just for having him in my life for the time I did.

—Sinéad.

—I know. He loves me, I know, I'm just saying, that's all.

—Your gift is a million times rarer, I said.

She looked at me and there was a moment when our eyes met that had never happened before. Then she looked at me in some kind of disbelief. Hint of disgust even.

—I must go to the loo, she said, already on her way.

Things were a bit funny then for a while when she came back and I thought she was gonna ask to go away by herself.

—What I said was the truth, I said. Your gift is a million times rarer than his. Your voice. Your melodies. He knows that himself. I said I'd never let you down. I'd never let him down either, I said.

—I know, Jeez I know Charlie, she said as if I was making a mountain out of a blah.

I was still glad I said it though.

—You're the best friend we've ever had Charlie.

—Yeah.

When we got out of the bus we both knew that we were kind of saying goodbye in a bigger way than usual. That I couldn't be hanging around with her without James there too cos it would look strange cos we weren't kids any more and even if I was a gamal, gamals become men too isn't it? Only place I'd see her now when James wasn't around was in Roundy's, same as everybody else. I watched her for a few secs when she was walking home to the council houses. Handbag on her shoulder. New high-heel boots on her. Small quick unsteady steps. Comical kind of. Didn't find it one bit funny though. Looked like someone else to me.

Anyhow. Sinéad drew a crowd to Roundy's.

Roundy was in well with Teesh and the lads on account of him being one of them. He was much younger than Snoozie's father. I suppose he was about forty.

—He was some boyo in his day boy! the lackeys would say about Roundy.

—Remember the time he took the young one upstairs after closing hours one night and told us to watch the upstairs window from across the road.

—Oh Jesus Christ yeah.

—The light came on boy and next thing we see your one's bare ass on up on the windowsill and the bould Roundy giving her a service.

—He wasn't married then was he?

—Ah Jaisis no. Christ he only about twenty-five that time.

—Didn't stop him in The Groove one night though and she standing right beside him.

—Oh Christ yeah, I heard about that.

—One hand around the wife-to-be and she blind stocious and the other hand down another girl's pants that he was talking to.

—Jesus Christ ha?

—Oh unbelievable in his day, that fella. Don't say a word about that to anyone now, that's all a million years ago.

—'Course, sure who would I be talking to?

—Oh he's some beaut all right.

—Legend surely. The gamal won't be talking, will he? Did he hear ya?

—And who would the gamal be talking to? Is it joking me you are? The lights are on but there's nobody at home. Isn't that right Gamal?

—Ha?

—That's right.

—Ha?

—Nothing Charlie.

—Ha?

—Nothing strange Charlie?

—Ha? Not a bit. 'Tis wild windy out.

—Wild windy is right Charlie, good man you are.

Roundy still organised bus trips for the fellas who drank in his pub. Mostly the bachelors and the too young to be married. The bachelors loved him.

—Oh some pup he was.

—Pure laugh.

—Legend.

Roundy took all the midweek trade in the village now from The Snug. In Ballyronan the midweek trade was all men. Men who didn't want a wife or didn't like the one they had. They sat and hissed, something of the kicked cat about them isn't it?

15

After James' first week in Dublin the plan was that his father would give Sinéad a lift to the train station in Cork on Friday so that she could go up to James for the weekend. Between the jigs and the reels she couldn't go. Her father was after hitting the bottle hard and was vomiting mad on account of the cancer and her mother was working on the Saturday and was going to a hen party in Kilkenny on the Saturday night. James understood. James came down instead. He called over to her house Friday night. Sinéad's father answered the door.

—She's not here.

—What?

—She's not here. I don't know where she is but she's not here anyhow.

Her father was drunk. The eyes were bloodshot in his head and he didn't have nothing to say to his daughter's boyfriend. He went back in and closed the door in his face. James called to my house.

He had tears in his eyes telling how Sinéad's father was to him at her house.

—Where is she?

—Dunno.

—She said she'd be there like. To call. Do you think he was lying?

—Dunno.

—He wouldn't be after hurting her would he?

—No. Dunno. No.

—Charlie will you do me a favour?

—Yeah. I will.

—Come down with me and call to see if Sinéad is there.

—Yeah.

—I'll wait around the corner. Just in case she's there. See what he says to you anyway.

He opened the door to me eventually.

—Hello.

—What?

—Hello. Is Sinéad there?

—Who wants to know?

—Ha?

—Ha? Ha!

He closed the door in my face. I waited a few seconds and knocked again.

—Have you some kind of a problem have you? She's not here and if she was she'd be having fuck-all to do with the like of you anyhow you fucking simpleton. Fuck off and leave my daughter alone.

He slammed the door shut. Then it opened again.

—And tell Prince William to do the same, if he knows what's good for him, ye two stupid cunts. He shut the door again.

—Take no notice of him, he's only drunk Charlie. I'm going to have a word with him now.

I grabbed James by the arm to stop him. We headed back up to my house. James' father was after ringing my house. Sinéad was after ringing the castle. She was in Roundy's, my mother said. James was relieved first and uneasy second.

—Cool. She's probably just having a drink with Racey and co.

—Yeah.

—You coming down Charlie?

—Yeah.

When we went in Sinéad was behind the bar. Teesh and Snoozie were sitting at the bar. Teesh goes,

—Oho, look here. A knight in shining armour coming to rescue a damsel in distress.

That got a few laughs. Then Teesh again goes,

—And James is with him.

That got more laughs, and a few of them looked over at me and shook their heads. Then Teesh goes to James,

—The wanderer returns. How are you kid?

He stuck out his hand for James to shake. James obliged.

—So how's the big smoke treating you?

James was looking with a kind smile at Sinéad as he spoke,

—Grand. It'll take a bit of getting used to but I'd say I'll like it. Any sca here?

—Yera same shit different day, you know yourself, I was only saying to Sinéad there before you came in that . . .

Teesh found himself talking to the air that took James' place cos James was after going over to Sinéad's embrace. She closed her eyes and squeezed him tight. Teesh nodded and smirked to himself in his stupid silence like he knew something no one else did. He took a long draught of his pint, squinting his eyes to two slits that looked up to the ceiling for clues.

—I missed you so much, Sinéad said. So so so much.

—Me too.

—Two more when you're ready Sinéad, Teesh said.

—Yera keep the knickers on there Teesh, Sinéad said back, and the lads laughed.

Teesh smiled and shook his head and finished his pint, having another look at the ceiling with his eyes near closed again.

—I better let you give the lads their medicine. Will you pull me a pint too babe and a Lucozade for Charlie please.

—Lucozade Charlie?

—Yeah.

—I'm here 'til closing. Roundy rang the house and Dad answered and said I'd work. Something came up and Roundy had to go to Newport with Eileen.

—Not to worry. Do you still have to work tomorrow night?

—Yeah. Roundy and Eileen have a wedding up the country.

—Not to worry, James said.

He was worried. He put a fiver on the counter for the drinks, sat on a bar stool and massaged his forehead with his eyes closed. He pulled another stool to the bar between himself and

Teesh and motioned me to sit down. Sinéad was looking at him the whole time. She could see he was uneasy. She was uneasy too.

I went talking the greatest gibberish you ever heard then about my new job with the landscape gardener to let Sinéad and James have a chance to catch up.

—Any news anyhow Teesh?

He didn't answer me so I went on.

—I'm after getting a job for a few weeks with Jim Murphy from the Four Crosses.

—The landscape gardener is it? Snoozie asked.

—Yeah. Fierce equipment altogether. Fierce equipment. I was in charge of the shredder. Throw sticks and branches into it and it comes out the other end in bits and pieces. Do the same to your hand if you're not careful. Hand would be in bits and pieces. That's what Jim said to me. Bits and pieces. And where would you be then? Up in the hospital and I wouldn't have no time to take you to the hospital cos this job has to be done today. Whether your arms are in the shredder or not. Ha? Gas man Jim, ha? What do you think of that Teesh?

—Fascinating. Would your head fit in it?

—'Twould.

—Fuck sake Teesh, Snoozie said.

—Doing well for himself now boy, Jim is, Teesh said.

—Heard that all right, said one of the old fellas.

—Got the gardens of the four Fitsimmons hotels he was telling me. And fuck all to do, only a bit of weeding and trimming shrubs.

—Is that a fact?

—'Tis yeah, cushy number. Fucking thousands he's getting for it. Cute fucking whore him, ha?

—Cleverest cunt of 'em all. Did you see the house he's building?

—No. Nice?

—Six bedrooms. Two en suite.

—Jaysus, up in the home place?

—Yeah. The lower field.

—What did he put it down in that hole for?

—I'd say herself don't want to be too close to that mother of his.

—Who'd blame her for that?

—No sane man, that's who.

They went on talking then about some brother of Jim's wife who went to the States long ago. James and Sinéad were able to talk away themselves with Sinéad going over to pull pints every now and again.

—Couldn't really say no, seeing as I'm only here a week.

—I know babe. Do you think you'll hang on here for a while or will you look for something else?

—Dunno. There's isn't a whole lot around like, you know?

—Yeah . . . God I wish you were with me.

—Me too. Every minute of every day.

They kissed for a bit.

—It feels so wrong being away from you. I'm so so lonesome.

—I know. I know, I'm the same, James said.

She suddenly turned her back on James and walked into the

back room to wipe away her tears. Teesh was getting stuck in Snoozie about some soccer player.

—I still make off he was a more intelligent player than Cantona.

—You brainless cunt! You've just confirmed how stupid you are.

—You're so fucking ignorant. Could you not just disagree no?

—I could disagree that today is Friday. Would only make me as stupid as you.

Snoozie got up and walked past his taunter to the jacks with a thick angry head up on him, and Teesh calling after him,

—A fact is a fact. Cantona is a genius and you're a dunce. An ignorant harmless dunce and only your mother could ever love you.

—Get fucked you prick.

One of the old fellas piped up then,

—He's gone sour on you Teesh.

—He'll be fine. He'll have it all forgot when he comes back. Memory of a goldfish that fella. If he remembers to wash his hands 'twill be a miracle. Isn't that right Gamal?

—Yeah.

He turned around wildly and had a look at me, then he looked past me at James, then straight ahead at Sinéad who was back behind the bar. James was staring at his pint as was not usually his wont. Sinéad was staring at a telly with no sound on. Teesh took it all in with exaggerated stares.

—Someone fuckin' die or something?

James laughed.

—No. Nobody's dead, he said and he looked at Sinéad.

—Right Sinéad?

Sinéad looked at him and managed a little smile.

—That's right babe, she said.

One minute, time for a chapter. This next one will be called 16.

16

They look the job don't they? The real thing. I hope I'm getting this punctuation right with what people say and stuff. I hope it's not confusing for you. Punctuation is a right pain in the hole. Anyhow, Sinéad and James started getting involved in talking shite with Teesh and Snoozie and managed to have a laugh or two. Sinéad was dragged away by her duties then cos the place started filling up. Run off her feet she was. She was a bad barmaid that night. Many's the time she had to ask a customer what exactly was in the drink they just ordered. A White Russian is vodka, Kahlua and milk. She'd be looking around behind the bar for bottles then. The bottles stood patiently waiting for their locations and their names and their colours and their shapes to be introduced to Sinéad's mind.

—Wait now, I know where that is, she'd say.

Handing back a man's change she told him to count it and make sure she hadn't given him too much. He laughed. Another man asked for a bottle of Budweiser and she looked at him and pointed at him all serious.

—I know where that is.

She went straight to the fridge with the Budweiser and the Heineken in it and put the bottle on the counter in front of him,

—Voilà!

Then she snatched it back.

—Oh, better take the cork off it!

The man was still looking at her after she'd gone on to the next customer. The smile was still on his face. He'd never seen anything like her before in his life. I never seen him before or since but he still thinks of her. How do I know? I know. Cos you'd be the exact same if you were him. Let alone me. Let alone me.

I'm after putting on a pair of sunglasses here. I'm getting a pain in my eyes from the screen and I don't know how to turn down the brightness of it. Anyhow yeah, as the Yanks would say, she was a big hit, Sinéad was.

All the people who were kept waiting could do was admire her. Hypnotised. Dinky arrived in then.

—James. You weren't away long, Dinky said.

—I missed you too much.

—You'll just have to move on and no more about it.

—Any sca?

—Kerby said our attitude is shit.

—Nothing new then?

—No. Said it's backwards we're going since winning the championship. How was Trinity?

—Not too bad. Nice buzz around the place. Ocean of foreigners there.

—You'll fit in well so.

—I might.

—Any totty up there for a loser like myself?

—Met just the girl for you in the Live Music Soc.

—What's a soc?

—Society.

—Society. Indeed. Tell me more.

—Australian one. Blonde.

—Do fine. Why didn't you bring her down with you?

—I'd say 'twould be easier to get you up to Dublin to her.

—Wouldn't be too sure. Problem with Dublin is it's full of Dubs.

—Savage buzz. You'd love it. Seriously.

—We'll see.

—Unless you're back with Racey are you?

—No. No go. She's odd with me over something I did that I've no recollection of.

—The demon drink.

—Might be my saviour yet, if she keeps telling me to fuck off. What do you think of Roundy's new barmaid?

—Yeah.

—Seems to be settling in well enough anyway.

—Yeah.

—How's her father?

—Drunk.

—Useless prick. They made me vice-captain for the league.

—Great stuff. Congrats boy.

—Ah it's nothing really. They just wanted to give more of a voice to the younger lads. Probably would've been you if you were around. Pity you didn't go to college down here and not go all the way up to fucking Dublin.

—Ah sure . . . I'll be around weekends.

—You goin' dancin' later on?

—I hardly will. Might give Sinéad a hand cleaning up. Spend little enough time with her nowadays as it is.

—Under the thumb James. You're pussy whipped boy.

—Easy kid.

—Easy kid, is right.

They drank in silence for a bit. The different paths they were on now was sitting in between them. An invisible smug ignorant cunt between them that they both knew was there. Same as some unsayable secret that people steer around with moribund talk.

—Gonna head over to a few of these boys a sec.

That was what Dinky said and he getting up off his seat. He turned back to say something to James then but it never came out of his mouth. He just looked at him for a small bit longer than a second and turned away again and went over to Teesh and Snoozie and a few others.

James sat looking at his pint, looking at Sinéad serving drinks every once in a blah. The lads were with a few other lads whose faces I knew from the Four Crosses. The Four Crosses was a small town halfway between nowhere and somewhere else. Was four miles from Ballyronan. Was like Ballyronan's brother that he didn't get on with sometimes. Especially at matches long ago when they were children and the Four Crosses children were the devil who they had to beat in the matches. Dirty cheating rats, they were then, for some reason. James turned to me,

—What ya reckon Charlie?

—About what?

—Dunno.

—I know, I said. Hard to figure.

—I suppose I should go over.

—Yeah, I said.

Sinéad was keeping an eye on James between customers. Strange face on her. Same as a boxer's wife. James arrived over to the middle of one of Snoozie's stories. He was after telling a yarn about some girl who worked with him in the sweet factory a few years ago.

—She no more went down on you in the jacks now than the man on the moon, Teesh roared at him, looking sideways and nodding to one of the Four Crosses lads, as if to say, What a fucking eejit.

—Honest to God.

—You're so full of shit Snoozie.

—Fuck you an' all belonging to ya.

—Ya dumb shite.

Two or three Four Crosses lads acknowledged James' arrival saying,

—How ya!

And,

—How's James.

James greeted both by name. They'd have known each other from football. The third lad didn't greet him.

| | | | | \\\\\ ¬¬¬¬ !! "" £ℒ $$ %% ^^^ && ★★ (( )) _ ++
}}}}}}}}} {{{{{{{{{ @ @ @ "' ~~~ #### ::: ;;;;;;;
??????? ///// >>>>>>>>> ....

Would you ever have thought there were so many different symbols on the keys of a computer. I'd no spaces between them first but the computer said the whole lot was only one word the bastard of a thing. So I put spaces between them all and it gave me twenty-seven words for it. 'Tis something anyhow isn't it? Only the computer knows what the words mean. Anyhow, don't mind that shit. I'm only distracting myself on purpose. I was talking about James and the lads in the pub and I'm not even sure why but I know it's part of the story. You won't be shitting yourself with excitement reading this cos it's just lads in a pub. But when I was there I noticed some small things so in my story you'll have to read about small things too. It's dangerous to ignore the small things. Pay attention to all this or you'll miss the whole thing.

Teesh and Snoozie were sitting down facing the Four Crosses lads and Dinky who were standing. James had stood slightly outside the group near Dinky's right shoulder and said to Dinky,

—All right kid?

Dinky ignored him and didn't move over a bit to include James in the circle. It was one of the Four Crosses lads moved instead, seeing as Dinky didn't budge.

—What are you having there James? asked Teesh.

—No I'm fine. I'm on a round with Charlie over.

I was looking into space.

—I'll get the gamal one too.

—No honestly, no I'll stay with Charlie, cheers.

—Yera go away out of that don't be annoying me. Dinky what's James drinking there, Guinness is it?

—Yeah. The gamal drinks Lucozade, Dinky said.

James protested again but he may as well have been dead for all difference his efforts made. Sinéad landed six pints and a Lucozade on the counter. Teesh distributed the medicine he'd bought, saying to Snoozie,

—See will that do you any good. Take one of them every half hour for six hours and come back to me. See will you stop talking shit.

Snoozie got the next round. When Teesh told him what the round was Snoozie asked who the Lucozade was for and Teesh made a funny face with his tongue hanging out and Snoozie knew then that it was for me.

There was another couple of rounds bought then and then it was James' turn.

James came over to me.

—Have you much money on ya Charlie?

—Fiver only.

—Shit I'm stuck in a big round here with the lads and I've only fifteen quid.

He went over and asked Sinéad. She was going to borrow some out of the till but he stopped her. He came back again.

—Don't want her getting in trouble.

—Yeah, I said.

—I'll ask Dinky.

Over he went.

—Denis, any chance you'd spot me a twenty 'til tomorrow, I've only fifteen quid.

—Yeah no bother.

He gave him the money and James went to the bar. Dinky goes to the lads,

—Ah yeah! The lads who have the most minds it the most.

—That's true, fuck sake, said Snoozie.

—A fella don't get a castle by being flaithiúlach, Dinky said.

Flaithiúlach is the Irish for generous. Generous in a kind of carefree way. A flaithiúlach person wouldn't even know how much money they had and when they had it they'd spend it.

—Don't be taken advantage of Dinky, Teesh goes to Dinky.

—Look, you know me. I'll put my hand in my pocket, no fear. If another fella won't I won't be found stooping to the same level. We're here to enjoy a few pints, twenty quid won't put me up nor down. You know me. Seriously like, what is it only paper at the end of the day.

—Don't be taken advantage of Dinky, Teesh said again.

—Leave it Teesh. Leave it go boy, protested Dinky.

—You'd want to watch it, that's all. Wouldn't want to be making a habit of it, Teesh said.

—'Tisn't like it's the first time.

—Ah Dinky, you'd want to wise up to that. Not a nice trait. Fuck sake. You're a good friend of his and he shouldn't be sponging off ya. Wise up to it. Don't let it continue. It's wrong.

—'Tis all that, agreed Snoozie. All wrong.

—Who the fuck goes to the pub for a Friday night without money in his pocket anyhow? asked Teesh.

—A cute fucking whore, that's who, said Snoozie.

—Leave it lads, seriously, it's no big deal, protested Dinky again.

—Miserable.

—Anyhow, say no more, said Teesh.

—Just leave it, each to his own, Dinky said.

—Sure isn't he from a race of fucking thieves. All the airs and graces in the world can't hide a savage.

—Leave it Teesh, will ya.

James came back with the first few pints and handed them out. Teesh took his without saying a word. The others said thanks.

By midnight everyone was messy drunk. Faces were red and foreheads were beady sweaty. Spirits were good. The drink was making theorists of them all one minute, comedians the next. Things lads didn't give a fuck about sober, suddenly they felt very strongly about. Things they were cross about sober mattered no more. Things they knew nothing about sober, suddenly they knew everything about. All wise nodding, serious pursed lips and chin rubbing. Shy lads who would always avoid verbal and eye contact with their elders boldly called over to them,

—How's the form?

Backslapping affirmations and kneeslapping laughs, I'll let you be in my dreams if I can be in yours. Build each other up. Whatever it is that made me be sitting there drinking Lucozade and talking to nobody is the opposite of what I saw all around me. And what I saw all around me I'm thinking now is maybe what life is made of and it makes me sad to think of me there on that stool all by my lonesome. Make you feel like a ghost among the living isn't it? Dead to the world I been always.

At half twelve Sinéad flashed the lights on and off. In Ireland that means last call. Last chance to get a drink before the bar closes. Closing time is half past midnight Friday and Saturday night. It's half eleven all the other nights cos people have to go to work weekdays and the government prefers people to be able to go to work in the morning and as well as that, to be half sober. Sends the gardaí around every now and again to make sure greedy publicans aren't breaking the law and making extra money out of people's thirst for drink in the early hours.

Sinéad's cheeks were rosy red with the height of serving beers in the sweaty flesh-hot sticky air. When she flashed on the lights there was a roar of protest from the lads, led by Teesh.

—Oh. On the button at half twelve? Must be joking!

—What's that about like?

—Fuck sake!

All Sinéad said was that she was under strict orders from Roundy to close up on time.

—Ye can have one more and that's it.

Another round was ordered and served. By one the lads were holding empty glasses again and were thirsty for more.

—Jesus Christ if this isn't a chance of a lock-in I don't know what is.

A lock-in is when the doors are locked, curtains are drawn and the lights turned down low with customers drinking inside, ahide from the law.

—There'll be no lock-in tonight Teesh, I'm sorry.

—Unbelievable like. Golden opportunity like.

—Perfect night for a lock-in in fairness, says Dinky.

—Fuckin joke like in fairness, says Snoozie, and he shaking one of the Four Crosses fellas who'd passed out in the corner.

—'Tis only ourselves like in fairness, says Teesh.

—Disgrace, says Dinky.

—Ha? says the Four Crosses fella and he looking around cos he did not know where he was.

—Come on lads, Sinéad has orders from the boss, it is what it is, says James, and he collecting empties and throwing stools on tables for the exhausted love of his life.

—Fuck sake, says Dinky.

—You know she doesn't have a choice Denis, so be fair now.

—Oh yeah. The big man has spoke. Lads, we must be fair, the big man has spoke, says Dinky looking around for approval.

—Come on to fuck, says Teesh, grabbing Dinky by the jacket and pulling him out the door.

They were followed by the rest, last of all Snoozie who was leading the Four Crosses fella by the hand, same as a pair of toddlers they were, the drunk leading the blind drunk.

—You'll be fine, you'll be fine, you'll be fine, Snoozie kept saying to him, over and over and his eyes half closed, like a prayer for himself. You'll be fine, you'll be fine, you'll be fine.

James bolted the door behind them. Sinéad was coming out to the bar floor carrying a mop and a steaming bucket. I gently prised the mop and bucket off her and took a stool off a table by the bar for her to sit on. I gently guided her by the shoulders to sit. I started mopping and she goes,

—You're a star Charlie, thanks.

—Yeah, I said.

—Wasn't Dinky some prick there, said Sinéad.

—He didn't mean it. You know what he's like when he's drunk, James said.

—Still, she said.

—Drink talk only, said James.

James took absolutely no notice of any of it. I looks up at James and he's standing, leaning on the pillar by the door smiling at Sinéad. She was wiping the sweat from her brow with a napkin.

—You played a blinder tonight babe, he said.

I got busy mopping. James stood behind her and massaged her shoulders. I made quick work of the floor and went out to mop the jacks, with Sinéad protesting that that was her job.

—Stay where you are, I said.

James came out to me. I told him I didn't need any help but he insisted. He did the men's. Dirty work. Pool of piss on the floor. I did the women's. I was out in the beer garden having a smoke by the time he was finished.

—Men weren't created to piss indoors, he said.

—Yeah, I said. Go on back in see how she's doing, I'll be in in a sec.

When I went in Sinéad had a pint for James and a Lucozade for me on the counter. She was putting coins in money bags and sending them into a chute that led to a safe under the till. James went over to the piano around the corner out of sight. Sinéad would sing a few notes between counting money.

—Cool. I balanced the books on my first night on my own, she said.

—You're a winner.

—Roundy said I'll probably be out on my float the first few times cos I'll make mistakes with the till.

—You're a winner babe, James said again, then tinkered away on the piano again.

Sinéad threw a few quid in the till and got a bottle of beer for herself.

She sat beside me.

—You're a star for doing the floor and the toilets for me. Thanks a million.

—James helped me.

—You're never doing that again though. That's not fair. I owe you one, right?

—Yeah.

—He's playing well for a fella that's in a tangle isn't he?

—Yeah.

—I heard that, roared James.

Sinéad laughed.

—I'm not bitch you silly drunk, roared James.

Sinéad laughed. Then she goes,

—Did the lads tell you there's training tomorrow at five?

—Ha? said James. No. No one said it.

—I heard Dinky and Teesh talking about it. Five o'clock tomor-row.

James stopped tinkering with the piano and goes,

—Why didn't they tell me? Well I'll be there anyway.

—That's what I like to hear, said Sinéad. I might go down for a look. Will you go down too Charlie?

—I only do the matches.

—Sure come and watch with me. Don't mind the water bottles.

—OK so, I goes.

—Cool, she said and skipped around the corner to him. They giggled and I could hear them kissing.

—I'm going to head off, I said, getting tired.

—By fuck, you're not, said James.

—Stay right where you are Charlie, I mean it, said Sinéad.

—I'm going out for a smoke so, I said.

—OK, said Sinéad, that's allowed but if you go home we'll be up the hill after you.

—Yeah, I said.

—Yeah, she said.

—Yeah, said James and laughed.

I strolled away out the back door to the sound of wrong notes and Sinéad laughing and James saying,

—The keys of the piano keep moving. Stay still ye little fuckers.

Stayed out the bones of half an hour. Waited for the noise of the piano to start again and coughed loudly on my return.

—No need for all the coughing, we're respectable, said Sinéad.

—Speak for yourself, said James. I'm only respectable in the sense that I can be respected. It is possible to respect me. I am . . . respectable.

—Lost me babe, said Sinéad.

—Did I lose you Charlie?

—Yeah.

—Lost to the world I am so.

—You might have more luck making sense with the piano than your mouth. Play, she said, sitting on a stool at the bar.

He played some familiar riff on the piano.

—Cool, Sinéad said.

Sinéad rubbed the polished oak counter slowly with her index finger, watching the condensation from her skin appear and disappear in an instant when she moved it. Then she started singing. I'd the words of 'Time After Time' here cos that's what she sang.

_____

_____

_____

_____

_____

_____

_____

_____

_____

_____

_____

_____

—That's what I'm talking about, said James, that's what I'm talking about. World must hear you. Your next job now is knowing it too. Not only believing it. But knowing it. Am I right Charlie?

She went over and knelt beside him and said ssshhh and kissed him and said,

—My beautiful drunk man.

He shook his head and smiled at her and said,

—I'm still right babe. Amen't I right Charlie?

—Yeah. He's pure true Sinéad. You must know it yourself. Or else you could falter.

—Falter, said Sinéad, beautiful word. You're some gamal all right.

—Yeah, I said.

Sinéad sang slow,

> *Don't falter*
> *Don't falter please*
> *We've come so far*

—That was nice, said James.

He played Sinéad's new melody on the piano, and jinked around with it a bit and came back to it again. When Sinéad sang again, he played quietly along with her on just a few keys.

> *Don't falter*
> *Don't falter please*
> *We've come so far*

—That was OK was it? Sinéad asked.

—A tad brilliant maybe, James said.

—What did you think Charlie?

I could hardly listen to the talk cos I was still kinda lost somewhere between her voice and the tune. Still inside in the middle of it I was. I looked over and they were both looking at me for an answer,

—Yeah. I like it. Keep going with it, I said.

—You heard the man, said James, turning back to the piano and tinkering the tune out again. She sang,

Believe in

Believe in me

We've come so far

—Need to take it somewhere else now. A chorus that's . . .

Sinéad was trying to think exactly what she meant. James encouraged her.

—OK yeah . . .

—Like . . . dunno . . . ya know 'Tangled up in Blue' where like . . . it's like you get flashes of what's going on but aren't sure. Like you don't even know whose words you're hearing, you know?

—Yeah.

—Like so far like we're in the first person. Whoever's talking is saying don't falter. You'd presume it's like to a lover or someone wouldn't ya?

—Yeah.

—Well like . . . if we could like inject a bit of like mystery or something you know?

—OK.

—Like. There's yearning and there's fear, she said.

—Yeah, James said.

She sang some rambling lines then.

—Did you ever hear such puke? Sinéad said.

—I like it, said James.

—I can't find the chorus, she said.

—The sound was beautiful, I said.

—Thanks Charlie.

—And some of the words were fierce nice as well I thought, I said.

—What do you think James?

—I think it's amazing.

He was after going over and leaning behind the bar and grabbed the biro and the notepad Sinéad had used for adding the money up and he started writing.

Sinéad sang a few verses quietly and James wrote the lines. I was lying on the bench on the flat of my back with my eyes closed and when Sinéad couldn't remember the words of the new bit of song she'd just created, I called them out.

—That's incredible Charlie. Do you ever forget anything? Sinéad asked.

—Not that I recall, I said.

When they finished that they got to work on the chorus that they couldn't find.

—Good tidings . . . What's tidings?

—Like . . . news I think, said James.

—Cool. Good tidings. Bad tidings. No tidings.

I sat in the corner cos I was sleepy. Ideas bounced between them. Their quiet voices washed over me with the shy and blooming ideas entering the room we were in. From I do not know where. Their voices spoke and hummed and sang ideas at each other's minds. Of newborn. Of newborn dreams. Like children. Twins. Forecast. Outlook. Look out. Outpost. What prophecy is this? They took their wounds and cast them out to sea. Bleeding dreams. And all souls prayed for miracles. Yeah. Calm seas. Good tidings. The old man saving food for the young and dying instead of them. And secrets. Deathbed secrets made for all to save. Entrusted. Knowledge. Old man's sacrifice. That to him is no sacrifice. Yeah. Child's hand in his. The child is fascinated by something ordinary. Like tassels on the blanket. Yeah. Playing with the tassels while the old man dies and the others cry. Yeah. Old man says goodbye. You've come so. You've come so far. Go take the day. You've come so. You've come so far. Go take it please. We've come so far. Yeah I like that. What about? No, what about like the sea or something? A lighthouse.

When I woke up the dawn of day was beaming in through the chinks in the curtains. They'd put a jacket over me that some drunk had left behind. They were asleep huddled in the corner of the bench opposite, her head on his belly. Her legs were on the bench, his were on the table beside it. I went over and shook James by the shoulder, telling him to wake up but it was Sinéad who woke.

—What time is it?

—Quarter to six.

—Jesus.

She sat up. She eventually woke James out of his drunken coma. He didn't know where he was. She giggled.

—Good morning, she said.

—Ha? said James, looking wildly around.

We left. James was carrying the pages with the new song on it, rolled into a scroll. The morning sun was hunting the mist off like Sinéad kicking the lads out after closing time. I took off up the hill.

—See ye today, I said.

—Slán, said James.

—See ya later, said Sinéad, don't falter.

—Yeah, I said.

17

Sinéad called up to my house at about half four and she had some tea with the mother. She used to do that long ago when we were younger so it was kind of nice for my mother too. My mother put on some old Ray Charles record and was asking her all about life in Roundy's. We headed over to the pitch then a bit after five and sat down on the grass bank looking down at the pitch. The lads were playing a training match between themselves. James was marking Teesh in midfield.

Next thing we seen Sinéad's father and he walking all unsteady down past us. He walked down as far as the wire that's around the pitch below to where the other men were. He was half pissed already I'd say. He was kind of ignored, standing behind the men who didn't move when he reached them. After a while one of them moved and he moved towards the wire then. Sinéad watched him the whole time. Was like she was willing them silently with her eyes to be nice to him. She only sat back and relaxed when he seemed more part of the group. She caught me looking at her then and I seen there was moisture after resting on her eyelids. Tiny bit more and she'd have had tears proper. She goes,

—He's got goodness in him Charlie.

—Yeah, I said.

—No really, she said.

Silence then for a bit.

—One time when I was small he carried me the full length of The Long Strand cos I was tired.

The Long Strand is a mile long.

—He's suffered like . . . humiliations, you know?

—Yeah, I said.

—He does have goodness in him.

—Yeah. He's an alcoholic now though, I goes.

—I'd just so love to see him happy you know? Or even . . . respected a bit, you know?

—Yeah.

—I remember one time when I was small long ago. Must have been like only six or seven. And he took me to a match. We got a spin off someone. I can't remember who but we were both in the back seat. But anyhow, half time came and my father said he was going to the toilet so he brought me over to it and I waited outside. It was kind of high up in the back of the stand behind the goal. It was some kind of temporary toilet cos there was work going on there. The urinals were over a bit but they'd this weird little toilet up high at the back. But in he went anyway about his business. Then I notice everyone is turned around looking back at the toilet. It was some kind of canvas covering over it and the sun was shining so you could see the shadow or like the silhouette of him perfectly. Was like a shadow puppet show of someone like . . . you know . . . going . . . and all the young lads in the stand were having a fierce laugh and cheering his every move when he was like . . . going about his business. He came out then and the whole place gave him a big cheer. He grabbed me by the hand and walked straight out and went to the nearest pub. The people who brought us to the match found us and took me home and left him in the pub. There was some sort of a scuffle before I left. I remember a man holding him back and he trying to attack someone. Probably whoever had come to take me home.

—Were you crying?

—Yeah I was . . . Crap just seems to happen to him, you know? There was this other time. Am I boring you Charlie?

—No, I goes.

You'll have to decide for yourself if what she was saying was boring but she wasn't boring me. She couldn't have isn't it? She went on then about this holiday they went on.

—It was a big thing for my mother and father like. For the three of us I suppose. My sisters wouldn't go of course, cos . . . I dunno, I suppose they were just a lot older and didn't want to. But it was nearly like a proper little holiday anyway like, for the three of us. They'd been planning it for weeks. They borrowed a car off someone and all. We were on the road anyway . . . in the middle of nowhere and . . . my father of course got lost. My mother was all quiet and annoyed.

James just flattened Teesh on his hole then. Teesh still hadn't got one touch of the ball. Sinéad was all wrapped up in her story.

—So there we were, the three of us, in the middle of absolutely nowhere, could have been Donegal, could have been Clare. To this day I don't know. But it was the West. There was mountains and it was near the sea. But we were halfway up this mountain, on a grass road looking for our B and B and there's no sign of life for miles around. Next thing the crock of a car konks. My father was trying the ignition over and over again. Next thing my mam just shouted at him to stop. We all just sat there and no one said a word. Probably for five minutes but it seemed like for ever. I was just frozen there waiting for the fighting to start.

—Oh Christ, I said.

—But then my father turns around to me and he says, 'Jaisis Sinéad girl, what are we going to do?' I don't remember what I said . . . But they both burst out laughing. They were in stitches. And looking back at me. The two of them looking over at each other and laughing and smiling. Mam turned around and stretched back to me and gave me a big hug.

I was listening to her but I was just as interested in watching James make mincemeat of Teesh out on the pitch. Teesh hadn't even touched the ball once so far. Sinéad was still on about this holiday.

—Then we got out and had a picnic. And afterwards myself and dad went off picking wild flowers for mam. Then later on they took out this big bottle of whiskey.

—Christ, I said.

—No, like, it was OK. There wasn't anything happened. The three of us sat down and watched the sunset is all. Me in the middle with my coke. Mam and dad drinking the whiskey from the bottle.

Sinéad started rubbing her hands hard against each other then. Seen her do that times before and she telling me stuff.

—And we could see the sea. Not much of it, but we could see it. Down . . . d'ya know the way two hills cross in the distance to make a V.

She showed me with her hands.

—Well there was this tiny bit of sea visible where the hills make the V. And the sun was going down. And it was this . . . just one of those amazing things. A coincidence I suppose. Whatever angle we had with the two hills like and the little bit of sea we could see in between them. The sun went down right in between the two hills, right down the middle, on top of the water. And the sun met the tip of the water. It was like . . . like the old sun and the new sun. With the reflection, you know? The two suns. Does that make sense? It was like. Felt like a birth or something. A new beginning. Does that sound like puke Charlie?

—No.

—But do you know what I mean? Was like some sign or something.

You'd wonder what has delusion got to do with love? Or what has belief got to do with fear. Or what has sacrifice got to do with pity.

—Such a vivid image it was. Am I making any sense Charlie?

—Yeah, I goes.

—And we just sat there and I looked up, into my father's face. And he was looking over at my mam, kind of smiling but not really. Just staring at her. I knew by his face that right then he'd do absolutely anything for her. Then I looked over at my mam and there were tears running down her face. She wasn't looking at him, she was looking at where the sun was meeting the water.

James floored Teesh a second time. Teesh still hadn't touched the ball. No stopping Sinéad either. I looked at her cos she sniffed and I could see she was teary a bit, but she carried on anyhow.

—Oh God. I'm sorry. Dunno where this is coming from. I'm just tired I suppose.

—What happened then, I goes?

—Just remember the three of us watching the sunset. The two suns. So the sun went down and I pretended to fall asleep on the rug. The two of them got their coats out of the boot and put them over me. And I just listened to them for a while. Laughing, talking. Giggles and whispers and my mother humming that Carly Simon song 'Coming Around Again'.

Then she looks at me all of a sudden and says,

—That's it Charlie. Harry Hogan played that song on the radio earlier. That's why it's in my mind. Jesus.

—Ha, I goes.

—And you know . . . I dunno.

She was just thinking then for a sec and then she goes,

—I'm not sure if it really was that song she was singing now that I think of it. I think it might have just been the song that my mind associated with it. You know? Isn't that just . . . bananas. Just cos of the sound of the song you know? So weird. Does that ever happen you? Like where you just give a song a place and a time in your life?

I just smiled and looked at her and shrugged. It was nice to see her all excited about something again. Music. It was always the music.

—I'm sorry for being such a saddo Charlie. I'm just . . . I dunno.

—Maybe you should give the song a try yourself with James. The mother has some Carly Simon records, I'll bring them over to the library.

—Yeah. Maybe. But do you not think I'd get all weepy again?

—Sure so what if you do? Might help you leave it after you.

—Yeah might be nice anyway to give it a try.

She took a slow deep breath then, looking down at her father below. Then I goes,

—You know the two suns with the sunset and the reflection?

—Yeah?

—Is that what that painting is of? The one with the two orange balls that have a red bit in the middle?

—Yeah Charlie. Wow, well spotted. I didn't think you paid any attention to my paintings.

—Ah I do, I said. But I thought they were two boobs.

—What? Ya dirty eejit Charlie, she goes and she having a right laugh at me.

—Thought you were trying to be like James' mother and Picasso and them all with boobs every place.

—What? And what did you think the hills were?

—I thought they were like the backsides of two elephants or hippos.

—What? You did not, she goes and she laughing mad.

—Swear, I said.

—Ha, she goes.

We said nothing then awhile and then she goes,

—Is it my imagination or is James trouncing Teesh out there?

—Teesh hasn't touched the ball once, I said.

—Jesus. Go on James, she said in a little whisper.

Teesh was landed on his ass most of the time now and was making a fool of himself. Swinging a fist at a ball that James was after catching and going off with already. After about ten minutes then Teesh went down holding his back. He limped off holding it.

—Pulled a muscle, goes Teesh, and he heading off up to the dressing room.

Then Sinéad went away cos she'd to go to work.

In The Snug after training Teesh and Dinky sat drinking again. Snoozie was serving behind the bar.

—I'm dying, said Dinky.

—Not too good myself, James said.

—Sure you didn't even go dancing, said Teesh.

—How's the back? James asked him.

—Sore enough, goes Teesh, giving himself a rub.

James headed off then. I said I'd stay and finish my Lucozade. Wanted to keep an eye on the lads for a bit before going home myself. Dinky stayed in the pub with Teesh and then they went down to Roundy's and I went off up the hill home.

James was after telling me how Sinéad was scared working there, that Roundy was creepy to her and Eileen, his wife was horrible to her, throwing her dirty looks the whole time. James was troubled you'd say. He was more like a man of forty-five with money or family troubles than the James from before. Worried, he was.

James got the bus up to the train on Sunday night. His father was at a funeral up the country and Sinéad was working.

The next Wednesday a miracle was after happening Teesh and his back was cured. After training he didn't go to The Snug, only up to Roundy's and he started on Sinéad.

—Hey Sinéad, fair play to you, that's all I say.

—Why?

—No, no. Credit where credit is due. Most girls would hit the roof.

—Hit the roof about what?

—'Tis a fair distance in fairness. Can't expect him to be pulling his wire up in Dublin with you down here taking care of the locals.

—What are you on about Teesh? Seriously. What are you on about?

—I'm only joking.

He spoke to Snoozie and Dinky then, knowing that Sinéad could hear him.

—She doesn't even know.

—About what?

—About the Ozzy one.

—SSShh, for fuck sake Teesh.

—I didn't say nothing! Apparently she's like Ballyhale bottled spring water.

—What d'ya mean?

—Good to go.

The lads laughed. That was the advertising slogan for Ballyhale spring water. Good to go. The ads had happy people looking good and going off some place delighted out with themselves and the bottle in their hand. Good to go. Good to go means mad for it.

Sinéad's mind was ill at ease now. I can see her staring into the distance like the world couldn't know what she was thinking.

—Little birdy tells me he has an admirer down under!

—Teesh leave it for fuck sake, Snoozie said, and he smiling away mad.

—An admirer down under up above, said Dinky then.

They laughed. And laughed. And laughed.

I must use a semi-colon; makes it look like I know what I'm doing. Teesh started ringing her too around this time. The phone calls used to upset Sinéad no end. He attacked herself and James with his laugh. He'd ring her up in Roundy's and ask her if she was still calling herself James' girlfriend and when she said, 'Yeah, of course. Why?' he'd just laugh and hang up. I asked Sinéad why she didn't tell James about Teesh's nasty phone calls and she said she didn't want to upset him.

Power in Sinéad's voice singing the Roy Orbison song 'In Dreams' was. Well. She had a tenderness to her voice that made the power of it at times kind of shocking. Frightening, nearly. Wouldn't mess with a voice like that, you wouldn't. Strength of it. Floor an army it would. And it comes over first all sweet and inno-cent and girly. Then. Well. You'd have to have heard it to know isn't it?

The line, 'And if too pale the moon these things' we couldn't make out on the record so that's what Sinéad used to sing. James used to get kind of excited at this part of the song and hammer the shit out of the piano. This made something kind of extraordinary out of Sinéad and the sound of her and the look of her. She was measured still and restrained and her voice demolishing James' belting piano playing and she standing there still as a lamp and James like a fella getting a thousand volts a second. The sound was electric too isn't it? Shocking it was. It shouldn't have even been possible.

It's only bullshit talk, all that isn't it? Getting carried away about music like that. We'd all have been better off with no music really, I'm thinking now. I have to stop myself from falling back into my bad old music ways. There's stuff that matters and music isn't part of that stuff. I can see that now. Music is only eejiting around isn't it? Fucking eejiting.

Anyhow dunno when Racey gained the ability to influence Sinéad but she did. Even though Sinéad was working in Roundy's it was still Racey's territory. She drank there more than Sinéad worked there and had been drinking there long before Sinéad started. She was well in with the lads too. Monkeys grooming again.

It's ten to four in the morning. I just went out for a smoke there and I seen a fox. The fox was just strolling along at the edge of our driveway. Next thing a few things happened all in about one half of a second. A wild cat hadn't seen the fox and jumped off a wall and landed down beside it and let out an almighty screetch with the fright it got and tore off in the opposite direction again. I roared too with the fright I got, I'm ashamed to say. The fox got a fright too and let out a right loud yelp and the fucker took off in my direction. Then I let another roar out of me and the fox yelped again and ran off in the other direction. We all scared the shit out of each other. Was kinda glad to get back in home and close the door behind me. There's a reason why people like being inside nice and cosy when it's dark. Outside isn't our territory any more when it's dark. Felt like I didn't belong out there. Cos I don't. The street lights of Ballyronan don't make much difference. Only remind you that the sun is long gone.

Sinéad made the best of Roundy's by trying to be like the people in it. But she wasn't. And they knew that, even if she didn't. They all knew she was only there cos her father was sick and if she'd much choice in the matter she'd be two hundred miles up the road trying to make her daft dreams come true with her pie in the sky boyfriend. Sinéad would have on the music she liked but soon got tired of their moaning and put on whatever Racey and co wanted on. They didn't have any love for music. They were just marking their territory isn't it? They just weren't raising their hind leg to do it is all. Anyhow Sinéad put on whatever top-of-the-charts collection she was asked to play. Computery shit most of it. Polluting her precious ear. Just wrong.

Racey started at her.

—Jesus Sinéad girl, where in the name of God did you get the top?

—What?

—Like something an oul' hippy would wear.

—Why?

—I'm surprised at you girl. 'Tis wicked.

—Is it? Are you serious?

—Ah Jesus girl, 'tis terrible.

I'm no fashion expert but Sinéad looked beautiful. She was wearing a kind of a linen or cotton blouse or something. Kind of thing she often wore.

—I'll have to take you shopping love, Racey said.

Teesh pipes up then.

—You'll have to be at the cutting edge of fashion when you've classy clientele the likes of us!

—Don't mind him, Racey said. He's wearing his father's old Y-fronts!

The lads laughed.

—Don't be letting Dinky know about your tangles with my underpants. That's a sensitive area for him.

He looked at Dinky and wiggled his baby finger at him.

—Ah now, Racey said.

Dinky was the colour purple and shook his head to himself.

—He be all right, said Teesh. Only a bit of sport for fuck sake.

—You're a prick Teesh, Racey said, looking up at the telly with no sound.

—Prick, said Teesh, prick is it? At least I have one.

—Shut the fuck up Teesh, Racey demanded, still watching the silent telly.

Dinky just took a few deep breaths and waited for the torture to be over, his big nostrils flaring every now and again and his eyes opening wider than wide as if trying to figure out was this really happening or was it maybe a bad dream. Took a good while for a normal human colour to return to his cheeks.

—Sinéad throw on a few pints for us there, said Teesh.

Sinéad went about her business like a robot. Put the pints on the bar, took the money off Teesh, put his change on the counter in front of him, never looked at him or said thanks or anything. For a second I thought she was going to do something. Throw a pint at him or quit or something but no. Next customer came up she was nice as blah. Tomorrow's my appointment with Dr Quinn again. I think I've enough written for him this week. Last week he wasn't happy. He didn't say it out plain just said maybe I could get a bit more done. Hopefully tomorrow will be better.

Dr Quinn is after deciding to give out to me. Giving out doesn't come easy to him. He scratches his face and crosses and uncrosses his legs usually before saying anything. Was very bad today. Was like some kind of a weird dance.

—Well it's like this really Charlie. There's pages and pages and pages about people in the pub. But I mean, at the end of the day it doesn't really tell us much about Sinéad. I know more about Sinéad from talking to her own psychiatrist casually a few times than I do from reading what you've had to say about her. I think you're holding back a bit in the way you describe her.

I'm always speechless but this time I was speechless in the kind of way that you or any other normal person would be. I didn't know what to say. This fucking eejit was obsessed with Sinéad now too and instead of helping me I was going to have to figure out a way to help him and wean him off thinking about her the whole time. Useless eejit. I goes,

—How often did you speak about Sinéad to her shrink?

—Her psychiatrist. And that's neither here nor there really Charlie. I spoke to him once or twice. Plus a couple of times on the phone when we discussed several things. And on the train to Dublin one other time we discussed you, and Sinéad came into it, naturally.

—And what did this fella have to say about her?

—I can't go into it Charlie. We take an oath you know. It's highly confidential, as is anything you say to me. Or write, for that matter. I can't show your writing to anyone without your consent. Unless of course it's a doctor. You know that don't you? Everything here is between ourselves.

—What kind of stuff did her psychiatrist say?

—I can't say Charlie.

—Yeah I know but like what kind of stuff like was he saying? What was so good about what he said about her?

—My goodness. Nothing. I mean. I thought I just got another picture. Another insight into her. She seemed to have been a little more rebellious than you'd have described in your writing Charlie. A lot more rebellious really. When she was younger even. And that's not saying anything about what I was told. But that's the impression of her I was left with. A very rebellious youth.

I don't know what picture you have of Sinéad from all the things I've said but you should have a picture of Dr Quinn as a terrible annoying stupid cunt sometimes. Dr Quinn doesn't know what rebellious is. He probably thinks cos she got suspended from school and ran away from home that that makes her a rebel. He probably thinks she was trying to kill her father when she pushed him down the stairs and he smashed his knee and broke his nose. He probably thinks she was a rebel because she wouldn't waste her breath talking to his stupid shrink friend who was probably obsessed with her too.

But here's what happened. And don't go making up your mind now that Sinéad was a tramp like other ignorant lazy-brained people said about her behind her back. The picture I was giving you all along of Sinéad was the right one. The one that was the truth. I didn't tell you one or two things cos it gave a picture of Sinéad that wasn't true.

But now Dr Quinn is after fucking it up with his stupid prying. I'll explain how people thought Sinéad was out of control and would say mean things about her. But it drives me pure feral that I have to cos it wasn't the truth and I know how stupid people can be and you're no different I bet you.

There was a new girl came to the school when we were in transition year and she had an unusual hairstyle cos she was a Goth. Transition year is fourth year so they were all about sixteen. She wore black nail varnish and pale make-up. She had long black hair but she had cut her fringe down to absolutely nothing. Some girls started calling her Lego Man and being nasty to her. Next thing half the school were calling her it. Even though she was a year below Sinéad in school they used to talk about music sometimes and Sinéad would always be on to her to give up the smokes. So then when she realised all this bullying was going on Sinéad cut her fringe up at lunchtime just like the Lego Man girl and next thing others were coming up to Sinéad asking them to do it to them. By the end of lunchtime I'd say she'd a hundred and fifty fringes cut. Parents complained to the school then about Sinéad cutting their children's fringes and the principal suspended her for two days cos all he ever did was lick parents' holes anyhow. Only problem for Sinéad was she'd have been at home alone with her drunken lech of a father so she moved out for the two days and into a spare room in the castle unknown to James' father but his mother knew. Her parents rang the guards saying she was missing and I think Detective Crowley knew but pretended to be looking for her anyhow. The whole place was talking about how she was after running away with some fella. It was those days that Sinéad did some of her painting for her Leaving Cert exams. And James' mother teaching her. And then a couple of years later her father decides at one in the morning on a Tuesday night that he wanted to get in to his daughter's room and her mother was away so Sinéad pushed him away and he staggered backwards and fell down the stairs. And next thing you'd hear people saying things like,

—Sure that Sinéad Halloran one is tapped.

—She's off her game altogether.

—She's a bit of a knacker, her.

—She has a bad name, that one. Bit of a huzzy. Pure fucking wild.

The Holy Joes or the bitter people could have told Sinéad that life wasn't supposed to be a joyous thing always but Sinéad wouldn't have listened. She couldn't have listened. There were a zillion different thoughts that found their way into Sinéad's mind but reasons to be miserable never made it in. Sinéad was unafraid.

Sinéad used to ask the question,

—Sure what's to be afraid of? What can they do to us? They can't shoot us.

When someone would say something like,

—Oh my God we're in big trouble now. Or

—We'll be killed for this.

She'd go,

—Yeah, I don't even know where I want to be buried. We're so young to die, it's such a shame.

She was interested in people. Stupid reckless people a lot of them, who had no fear. She read life stories. Biographies. Especially of people when they were young. People like James Joyce and his wife Nora. Or Vincent Van Gogh. Bob Dylan. Billie Holiday. Kurt Cobain. People with no fucking cop on. And this did damage to her too.

I'm thinking of a painting she did for her Leaving Cert exam in those two days when she was painting with James' mother. It was huge. Size of a wall in a room in a house. It was of a net. And there was shapes. And none of the shapes were getting through. But then you noticed this one. This one shape that was blue. It looked like it might get through the net. Just one. Might. It was like the shapes became people and you felt for them. And you didn't know if the one that might get through was the lucky one or not. The net could be saving them from falling or capturing them. You didn't know if this blue one was going to fall or get free. Or both.

I can't do it. I can't remember how she made the shapes. How she gave them life. Cos they didn't have faces. But Sinéad was good at art and I'm only a doodler.

Everyone is kind of stupid but Dr Quinn is the same kind of stupid that most people are. His witness statement about the world would be supported by most people. Billions would have seen it all the same way as him. If you want to know Dr Quinn and the rest of them all just read one of them fancy Sunday newspapers the father gets, with the glossy bits and the serious bits and the funny bits and all the fucking bits and they all just right. Same as the right dose of tablets. People have their brains numbed along the way isn't it? But then you'll get the odd erring one. Who might have seen different.

And the truth of it is that a lot of people would have called Sinéad ignorant words like trollop or knacker or huzzy behind her back cos of them things that she'd no choice about but that doesn't mean you have to be the same as the rest of them. But chances are you would be isn't it? So in order to give you the proper Sinéad I had to not tell you some things but Dr Quinn messed it all up then with his bullshit rebel Sinéad talk. And he after talking to some stupid shrink who can only think in textbook. The picture I was giving all along is the right one of Sinéad.

All that stuff proves is that the world makes no sense same as the fox and the cat and myself all scaring the shit out of each other. Random and stupid isn't it?

Anyhow I'm going back talking about Sinéad in the pub. I don't care if it's boring. Dr Quinn is boring. That Wednesday night the place livened up a bit later on. Couldn't hear what they were saying over the far side of the bar but herself and Racey seemed to be having a bit of a laugh. They were talking about clothes. Sinéad looked down at her top, pulling it out to look at it. Racey covered her eyes and laughed and Sinéad laughed too and shook her head. Racey put her hands on her hips then and started saying something to Sinéad. Then Sinéad put her hair up with her hand for a second and turned to the side and Racey nodded approvingly and said something. Then another customer came to the bar and Sinéad said,

—Same again Gerry?

—Like a good girl yeah. There's a few in tonight Sinéad.

—There is isn't there? For a Wednesday night like it isn't bad in fairness.

—You're good for business Sinéad.

—Oh! I dunno about that! I'd say if 'twas tea I was giving out there wouldn't be many here!

—Ha! Do you know, I'd say there would.

—Oh go on out of that! There you are. Pint of the best.

—That's the girl.

She gave him his change and said,

—Thanks Gerry.

—Come here.

Sinéad leaned over to him but I couldn't hear what he said to her.

—Oh go 'way out of that Gerry, Jesus!

Gerry went off laughing back to his seat. Another bachelor. Gerry was about fifty and worked in the quarry. Was going steady with a Cork city one for a bit back along. Teesh said,

—She bled the poor bastard dry and gave him the flick. Bought her a car and everything sure, the fucking eejit.

Teesh and the lads called him Bitches cos that's what he mutters to himself when he's very drunk.

—Oho Bitches is in now!

—Watch out girls!

Roundy had warned Sinéad on her first night working there to watch Gerry when he's drunk. Gets violent towards women. That's all, she never had any trouble with him far as I know. Was just one of her customers. That's the last ye'll hear about him. Just thought I'd give him a mention, that's all. This was all part of her new world.

Sinéad went back over talking to Racey.

The lads were mad to get inside Sinéad's head. Later that night Teesh was telling Snoozie stuff knowing that Sinéad could hear him inside the bar.

—Heard he met some Australian one above, Dinky was telling me.

—Oh yeah, said Snoozie.

—Singer one. Gorgeous-looking thing.

—Oh yeah, yeah.

—That's what he said to Dinky here the other night. Savage-looking bird altogether. She's in some music society above in the college.

—Ssshhh, said Snoozie.

—Yeah, say nothing, said Teesh glancing over at Sinéad.

—Christ, ha? A dark horse, said Snoozie.

—Down under ha? said Teesh and he looking over at Sinéad and shaking his head and goes,

—Do you know what ninety-six is down under? Sixty-nine!

Snoozie slapped his knee and pretended to find it hard to breathe with the laughing and looked over at Sinéad and shook his head again saying, 'Oh Jesus Christ.' The lads laughed too. Sinéad didn't take her eyes off the telly. That was the end of it for the night except the lads kept saying random things in an Australian accent.

—Not on your nelly mate, stone the crows!

—Cor blimey!

—Struth!

—Fair dinkum!

—Cor blimey, that's a big didgeridoo.

—Struth!

I dunno was the mother or someone in my room doing a bit of snooping. Went for a walk and when I came back there was a thing on the floor that shouldn't be there at all. Should be away in the drawer with the rest of Sinéad's things. Even though it's mine. But it's like the one Sinéad got. Easiest way to describe it is to photocopy it. This is it.

It's called a Rosary ring. Detective Crowley asked me where I got it one time, the time he was up in my room. Cos Sinéad's went missing when her room was broken into. They took it off her key-ring and took it. Detective Crowley goes,

—Did Sinéad give you this?

—No, I said. It's my own always.

—Where'd you get it?

—The Bishop. He came and gave us all one in school long ago.

—And this isn't Sinéad's one?

—No.

—And do you go to Mass Charlie, you do?

—Yeah.

—Good man.

I don't know why he said good man cos himself or the wife never go to Mass. Even their little boy was buried some place up in Cork for burying pagans. Then he goes to me that time,

—Do you say prayers?

—Yeah. Before I goes to bed.

He was looking into my eyes then fierce concentrated. Just looking at my eyes. I turned away a bit but he comes around the side of me to look at my eyes. Wildest carry-on you ever saw. He was shameless about being weird and strange and ignorant, Detective Crowley was.

Sinéad had the sureness of God definitely one time. Most people were too cool to use the Rosary ring or they just didn't believe in it. The boys used it as knuckle dusters. But Sinéad still had hers years after. She had it in her hand with her keys the evening down by the river. She was pressing it into the palm of her hand so hard I thought she was going to crack it and cut herself. We were sitting on the river bank in that exact same place as in the picture from the paper that was being mean about me. We were crying and she goes,

—There's no God Charlie is there?

—I wouldn't think so no, I goes.

Sometimes I wonder if I ever should have lied to her it was then. Can you respect someone too much? We just sat there crying all evening looking at the world go dark. It was proper dark before she spoke to me again. I knew then that she knew I'd do anything for her. Anything. Anyhow that's for later in the story. You wouldn't be able for all that yet. I'll tell you a bit about it later on maybe.

For fuck sake. The mother has on John Lee Hooker below, I'm going away out again for a stroll.

That song yesterday it messed up my brain. John Lee Hooker. He has no regrets. 'Don't Look Back' has to go here now.

———————————————————

———————————————————

———————————————————

———————————————————

———————————————————

———————————————————

———————————————————

———————————————————

———————————————————

———————————————————

———————————————————

John Lee Hooker would say things over and over again and it was like a mother going to an upset baby that she comforts in her arms. Kinda singing-talking, same as John Lee Hooker. And the repeating the whole time. That's what Sinéad used to say anyhow.

I dunno to fuck. Daft talk really but that's what she used to say about the blues. That it was baby talk for grown-ups.

—I know, I know, the poor lovely baba. No, no, no, ah sure the poor baba, no, no, no. My own little peteen, no, no, no, the poor lovely baba, no, no, my lovely peteen, my own darlingeen, no, no, no.

I stopped crying after a bit of John Lee Hooker last night at about five in the morning and I fell asleep too.

You see it made me think of Sinéad too cos that same 'Don't Look Back' song reminded Sinéad of the mná chaointe long ago as well. Old Master Higgins told us about them. Women paid to come to funerals long ago and be wailing and saying the same stuff over and over again. Sinéad said you could see ones like them with the black shawls on them on the news and they crying over their dead sons in Palestine or Pakistan or Lebanon or some place. Some place hot and troubled anyhow. Wailing and saying something over and over and over again. And it wasn't about the price of carrots. It was emotion sounds. We listened to a lot of blues for a while. Thinking of how it started with the black slaves in the cotton fields hollering and singing over and back to each other in America long ago. And their sadness and they soothing each other with sounds. Sinéad thought the origins of a lot of music is in mothers and babies and soothing sounds.

—You know you're not alone when someone is making sound, Sinéad said. Like a baby crying in the wilderness is reassuring to a mother who can't see her baby. And the mother's baby talk reassures the baby like.

—Yeah, I said.

—Yeah, said James.

Sinéad lifted the needle and we listened to the record again. I don't know how I'm going to get better in this house with the mother's music fucking me up. My brain is fidgety today. Won't settle down at all. Thinking too much too fast isn't it? If I wrote all my thoughts 'twouldn't make much sense probably. Couldn't write fast enough anyhow. Regrets bouncing around my brain like fucking pin balls. They won't even slow down, just keep shooting all over the place in all directions inside my brain and 'twon't stop. I try to press my head but there's no pain on the outside, it's the inside of my brain that's sore. From regrets. Bouncing off the inside of my skull. Take a big bullet hole to let them out.

I was down the village again today. Went down for milk for the mother and had a little stroll. Seen Teesh below at the petrol station. He never looked at me in the eye since everything that happened. He never says hello, nothing. Maybe he never did but I notice it more now cos I'm watching him and hating him. Brazen head on him all talk and a smile and a joke with every fella. Fools. Even some of the women around are nice to him.

The Promise

'Twas a winter wedding so it was about six months after James went to Dublin. He wasn't invited to Laffey O'Brien's wedding. He must have been the only footballer in the parish not to be invited. It was a strange one. A sign. No one seemed to be asking where he was either. Another sign. And he wasn't invited to Séamus O'Mahony's either come to think of it. I was at both of them with my mother and father.

But James and Sinéad were invited to Teesh's. Teesh was twenty-two and was marrying Snoozie's sister, Anne-Marie. It was young to be getting married. Anne-Marie was a shy girl and didn't go to the pub. She didn't say much at the wedding but she said to James when he congratulated her at the wedding that she'd be lucky if Teesh stayed faithful to her for a month. Only place I ever saw the two of them together was when I seen them at the two other weddings I mentioned a sec ago. Teesh never spoke to her and as soon as the dinner was over he got up and left her on her own for the night. Anyhow, so James and Sinéad were at Teesh and Anne-Marie's wedding along with the rest of the parish.

They were sitting with Snoozie and the rich builder's daughter, Karen and Dinky and Racey. I was sitting over with the mother and father and other old people. But I was watching them and they were really enjoying themselves, having a right good laugh. Sinéad was getting on great with Racey and Karen. After a while James came over to me saying there were two empty seats at their table, cos some couple never turned up but I said no, and then Sinéad starts beckoning me to sit over with them too, then Dinky and Snoozie start, and they going,

—Sit over with us Charlie boy.

—Come over here Charlie.

And they being all nice to me, cos the whole parish were watching. My mother gave them a smile that meant, 'Thank you,' and said to an old one beside her,

—Aren't those lads great to my Charlie.

I went over then, and the big napkin flapping under my chin.

Teesh had asked Sinéad and James to perform a song or two at the wedding.

Sinéad was all excited.

—What'll we sing?

—One of our own, said James.

—No, I said. Wedding crowd. Give 'em what they want.

—D'ya think?

—Yeah.

—Maybe he's right, Sinéad said.

—Yeah. Maybe.

—Know your crowd, I said.

—Yeah, I suppose, said James.

—They'll adore her. She'll sing a song they all love better than they ever heard it before.

—You're right Charlie.

—Ah lads, said Sinéad, get real now like.

—What song?

—I dunno, I said. Some old Irish love song ballady thing. There's a lot of nice ones.

—Or what about 'I Got You Babe'? Sinéad said.

—What ya think Charlie?

—Yeah . . . maybe, I said. There's lots of songs.

We spent a day up in the library in the castle listening to old Irish love songs and ballads. Sinéad singing a verse or two of them all with James finding them on the piano trying to keep up with her. 'Dan Murphy's Meadow', 'The Dutchman', 'She Moved Through the Fair', 'The Voyage', 'Carrickfergus', 'Sweet Sixteen',

'The Lass of Aughrim', 'The Sally Gardens'. We ended up going with 'Silver Threads among the Gold' sung as a duet.

We listened to it a million thousand times on the record player. The song was on two of my mother's records. John McCormack and The Fureys with Davey Arthur. The McCormack version was like orchestra. But in a quiet kind of way, not like the usual show-offy orchestra. Let his voice do the flying it did. The Fureys with Davey Arthur record did a bit more with it. There was one of them lads could make the banjo talk to you. In a soothing kind of way. Finbarr Furey sang then. There was in his voice the tenderness of a ghost who was fierce fond of all the living. And he after smoking a million hundred thousand cigarettes and after drinking as many pints. In search of some different kind of wisdom isn't it?

At the wedding during the dinner Teesh came over to our table and started taking the mick out of James about something that puzzled him.

—This must be one of the biggest band break-ups since The Beatles, Teesh goes.

—What? James asked.

Snoozie and Dinky started skitting then.

—Where's the Little Rascal? Teesh says, looking around with a big grin on his face. Then he sees him and shouts over to him,

—All right kid? Viva L'Espagna!

Then the Little Rascal starts breaking his hole laughing and goes back,

—Viva L'Espagna, giving a big thumbs up.

Did I tell you who the Little Rascal was? Shite little pub singer fella used to work in the building site up the road from my house too and he used to sing in the pubs in Spain. And Germany too I think. One man band. One bad man.

Teesh and Dinky and Snoozie and Racey were all skitting laughing. Sinéad was blushing and said,

—Go away Teesh will ya.

And off he did go laughing mad back up to the top table and he looking back at the lads and over to the Rascal laughing away mad the whole lot of them. I couldn't figure out for certain if it was real or fake laughter. It was partly real and some of it was fake and maybe they were just all licking up to Teesh cos it was his big day, but I was as puzzled as James was. He turned to Sinéad and asked her,

—What was all that about?

—Oh just something stupid, she said. He asked me to go with him to sing in a pub in Spain.

—What? goes James, with a puzzled cross look on his face.

—It was just kind of a joke like but the lads won't leave it drop.

—Cheeky little prick, I'll break his face.

—Calm down James. Don't make a scene. Not today.

—Cheek of the little prick, James said again.

Then he looks at Dinky and Dinky just smiles and shakes his head and James stared at him until he stopped smiling. All this was news to me as well as James. It was impossible to keep an eye on things all the time. Sometimes I'd prefer to be listening to her on tape than watching her in the company of them fuckers. Next time Teesh came over he says all serious like, that they sounded very good together like. That their voices worked well together. James said nothing until he went away then he asked Sinéad did she sing with him in the pub.

—Yeah. Just one song. They were all saying to go up for one song. I had to. I hated every minute of it. He's rubbish.

James said nothing, just took a drink of his pint.

Anyhow, that was the end of the Rascal stuff for the rest of the night. Then later was time for The Promise to sing. The Promise is the name we called the band. It was Sinéad came up with it. She didn't want James to be seen as just her guitar player or the keyboard player so she insisted on a name. Another one she came up with was Elsinore, just cos she liked the sound of the word. James came up with No More Auction Block but that was too long. Only thing I came up with was Sinéad And James. They didn't like it. We all liked The Promise though. I feel so so sorry for you that you never heard Sinéad sing the lines,

Oh my darling, mine alone, alone
You have never older grown

cos it's the nicest thing I ever heard maybe. And I know now that a lot of the people at the wedding were affected by their perform-ance in the deep way and in the way that's so rare it's confusing. All powerful and all. Maybe. Maybe if I heard it now I wouldn't be as floored by it. I'm better now at dealing with music for what it is and not something that important.

I noticed she only ate two bites of dinner and was quiet at the table. The nerves were at her. The wedding band man lowered the mic for her and said, 'Testing, testing one.' She looked over at

James and gave him the nod. James' intro on the piano was fine. Robbed off The Fureys. At the start, Sinéad didn't take her eyes off James. Next thing Sinéad. She sang the first two lines of the song still looking over at him. Then she turned around to face the audience. Everyone at the bar stopped and turned around. People who were talking talked no more and looked up at Sinéad. I knew deep in my heart that this was something that couldn't be stopped now. This voice, which was now heard, was a force of nature and all who heard it. Well. Beguiled them isn't it?

I'm up right at the front of the stage over by the side cos I helped James with moving over the keyboard to where Sinéad could see him. Anyhow next thing I see a few people at the front turning around from the stage. Next thing another few did it. Just glancing back at the back of the hall. Then I heard what it was they were turning around for. Some people were laughing and heckling at the back of the hall. All in a huddle at the back of the hall were Teesh, Snoozie, Dinky, Racey and and a few more of Teesh's brothers and they all bent over laughing. Staring up at the stage and convulsing. Pointing. Nudging each other. Could hear Teesh roar something and they all laughed mad again. The veins popping out of their temples and their mouths all teeth laughing mad and the eyes on them that weren't laughing at all.

Sinéad sang through. James looked down the hall but kept on playing. Sinéad was singing still. By the time she got to the end of the song her voice had become something else. A quivering remnant. There was silence for a second after she'd finished. Then the clapping started with people still glancing to the back of the hall where the laughter continued, bold and strong. Dinky put a hand to his brow and shook his head that was laughing still. Teesh nudged him and they laughed some more. The wedding band singer spoke into the mic,

—The Promise, ladies and gentlemen, Sinéad Halloran and James Kent.

The crowd clapped again but Sinéad was after leaving the hall out the side door to the smoking area. James had to help a musician put back the keyboard. I looked one more time at the wild laughers at the back of the hall. All backslapping and head shaking. I didn't draw the rest of them but this was their faces.

Imagine if you had them faces up at you. And that they were your best friends. And you revealing the best and most secret part of you. Do you no good anyhow isn't it?

Outside Sinéad was crying and her father was in her face.

—I'm fucking ashamed of you, do you know that? Fuckin eejit of a young one.

Then he looks at me and says,

—Thinks she's fuckin Aretha Franklin that one.

Then he takes a second look at me and says,

—Jesus Christ! Ye're a fine pair. Pair of fucking dumbos. And Prince William as bad.

And off he goes. Sinéad was sobbing. I told her she was brilliant. She didn't answer, just shook her head. Then James came along.

—Jesus Sinéad what's wrong?

—I was shit, that's what's wrong.

—What? What? Charlie tell her.

—Told her.

—You weren't shit babe. You were class.

—They were . . . they were all . . .

—No.

—They were all laughing at us.

—Only Dinky and Teesh and a few of the pissheads babe. They're just drunk, they didn't mean it. They were only doing the fool.

—It was awful.

—Don't you see babe?

—See what? It was horrible.

—They're all only jealous of you. Racey? Jesus babe you can't take any notice of them. Teesh? Snoozie? Dinky? What do they know?

Sinéad was bawling crying now.

—They were in stitches laughing, she said.

—That's just them babe. Drunken jealous fools babe. You can't take any notice of them. The rest of the people loved us.

—My father said he was ashamed of me.

—But sure. You've heard that from him before.

—But sure what?

—He just cares what those pissheads think. Surely you don't babe. You can't. You were awesome.

—Yeah. That's what's true. That's what's true, I said.

—See? You know Charlie wouldn't say it if it wasn't true.

—Yeah. I wouldn't. James is right.

—Listen to him Sinéad. Please. Please babe . . . Believe babe.

—Wasn't real laughing Sinéad. Only the jealous type. Not from the heart. From some place else. Heartless.

—Charlie's right Sinéad. Believe in yourself.

She continued sobbing. Then I said,

—Yeah Sinéad. Believe in you. Not them.

James went away back to Dublin again. Was only a couple of weeks to Christmas so we wouldn't see him until then. He asked me to call into Roundy's often as I could, just to keep her company. He rang her every night himself anyhow, whether she was at home or in Roundy's. I called in in the evening after my dinner every night. One time the foreman sent me down for smokes to the village and I met Sinéad coming out of the doctor's and I said what's wrong with you? She said it was about her father's chemo. She asked me to meet her for lunch the next day. It was dry so we went for a walk down by the river. She had a sandwich she got from the shop and a paper cup of tea.

—Charlie, you're going to have to fix up your life you know.

—Ha?

—Like. You've got a lot to offer like you know.

—Yeah.

—That's what you always say. But you need a plan Charlie. You could get into the music industry or something. You must come up with a plan.

—I will.

—Would you like to be a roadie? Like for U2 or something. They say they really look after their workers.

—Yeah. I suppose.

—Like you can't just be waiting for me and James to make it cos it might never happen and where would you be then?

—I'd still be there. I'd help ye anyhow.

—Charlie you're too bright to be a sidekick all your life. Like you could get a job in a music shop even. Get to know people with the same interests as you.

She must have thought I got upset then or something cos she goes,

—Hey . . . Charlie . . . I'm not saying like that we don't want you with us any more. We love you Charlie. It's like what Bob Dylan said about Johnny Cash Charlie. Remember? He said Johnny Cash was like the North Star, you could guide your ship by him. You're our North Star Charlie. You been there showing us the way from day one. Best of times Charlie. So the best of times.

There was silence then for another bit.

—Like remember the hen party last year that stopped off in Ballyronan. And that girl you were with until Teesh and the lads started slagging her about you. She fancied you Charlie. And I know you fancied her cos I seen you looking at her across the bar. Teesh and them are only pricks and they'll drag you down always if you stay around here. And I know you could get your teeth fixed if you really wanted to and the social welfare would probably cover it. When was the last time you were at the dentist?

—Dunno.

—Have you been since primary school?

—No I'd say.

—It's amazing you even still have teeth Charlie. I could help you shop for some nice clothes. If you'd better teeth and nice clothes and got out of here Charlie . . . I'm telling ya . . . there'd be no stopping ya. You wouldn't even have to shave or cut your hair. Some girls love the wild look.

—Right, I goes.

—You just have to look after number one Charlie. As in like your future. I don't want you rotting away here for ever the butt of rotten jokes.

I cried for a bit after I walked her back to the pub. I wasn't sure at the time why I cried and I'm not sure now either.

Other than that I used to only see her in Roundy's. I'd call in around eight or nine and go home about eleven when she was closing up cos mostly Roundy or the wife would call in after closing to collect the takings.

But there was still some right nasty craic in Roundy's before James came back for Christmas. Craic is Irish for fun. Or stuff. Sometimes it was behind her back and other times they were mean to her face. I didn't really understand why she took it. I know they were mean to Racey too sometimes, in a joking kind of way, but still mean. Racey just laughed along. Racey was a sport. But Sinéad like. Maybe she took it cos she was stuck behind the bar and she needed the job. But she should have been brave enough to say stop to them. Maybe it's cos she was young too. Made me want to have a machine gun and blow them all to blah. She was still only becoming a woman that time isn't it? Fierce tender time.

—She'd be good to go I'd say. Good to lay pipe.

—Pipe? She take'd six foot of it a week I'd say.

—The conqueror's pipe.

—Thing like that wouldn't be fussy. All kinds of pipe I'd say. More the better.

—Good girl.

—That's the girl.

—Mighty little girl, what are ya?

—Flora.

—Spreads easily!

—Any chance of a Twix?

—No. No chocolate, sorry Teesh.

—Who said anything about chocolate? All I want is two fingers for thirty pence!

I'd just sit there imagining setting fire to them and they tied to a pole. Watch their faces melt. But I couldn't cos if I did no one would ever ignore me again. I didn't say anything to James cos I thought it would only cause aggro between them and he'd see for himself when he was down and he knew her better than me. Was supposed to anyhow isn't it? I got to know that Sinéad was a shy person. And words affected her mind. She was a different person altogether when James was around. Felt protected. I gave her no protection. Even if I wanted to I couldn't. I'm only a gamal and gamals only are. But that's why I seen isn't it? Only way I could ever have seen what I seen. There's small pictures and a big picture isn't it? A surgeon don't work on your hernia if you're having a heart attack. How could I ever know what happened if I went and became part of the story? No how. So that's the end of that. Anyhow when he came home for Christmas she was grand again so I knew I was doing the right thing.

In my noticings too I could see something else happen now when Sinéad and James were with them all. Like the times Teesh and the lads and Racey started on about someone in a nasty way, just for a laugh. They'd snipe and laugh and mock people behind their backs. Like when Mags Fitzhenry came into the pub one time for a bag full of ice cubes cos her mother was after twisting her ankle. The whole world knew her husband John was after having an affair with their au pair and how he'd his bags packed to go away with her and how she was seen crying, kneeling in front of his car one morning to stop him leaving and she shouting,

—What about Finbarr?

Finbarr was their son. Anyhow in Mags came for the ice and Racey goes to her,

—How's John Mags? and she winking at Dinky.

—He's grand out girl, sure you know him.

—We do all right, Teesh goes, squinting his eyes and he taking a swig out of his pint.

Sinéad was filling her the bag with ice and asking Mags about her mother's fall and Teesh interrupts again,

—Was he away for a bit Mags?

—He was yeah. He was away on business for a week there. Something about a new calibrator or something, you know now, 'tis all double-dutch to me.

—Speaking of Dutch, is that where that au pair of yers is from? Teesh goes.

—No, no. She's Spanish.

—How's she settling in? Dinky asks her then.

—Oh she's gone.

—Is she? Racey goes, and the all shocked face on her.

—How come? Teesh goes.

—Oh she was homesick, Mags says.

Sinéad handed her the bag then quick as she could so she could escape.

—I hope your mother will be OK now, Sinéad says. Take care Mags.

—Bye Sinéad, thanks a million.

Then of course Teesh goes,

—Christ Mags, that's a shame isn't it. John was saying how she was mighty altogether.

—I know but sure that's the way. Good luck to ye now, she said.

—Good luck Mags, said Teesh and the rest of them starting to snigger and Mags speedwalking out the door.

Then Teesh goes,

—And the big fat liardy hole on her, and they laughing away mad and shaking their heads.

James sat silently and met Sinéad's eye. Sinéad and James stood out cos they were silent and their faces were red. They wouldn't have been there only for that Sinéad had to work. But their silence made them more noticeable. It annoyed the others I think. Sinéad and James never said anything that if people heard it their feelings would be hurt. People weren't suspicious of you when you were talking. They knew you weren't scheming and they knew what your thoughts were. Or knew a lot of your thoughts anyhow isn't it? That the shit you were talking was mainly what was in your mind at the time and it didn't seem then that you were scheming. And if you were talking it showed you made an effort to be part of the gang. You have to be a gamal to get away with saying nothing. No one ever took any notice of me and the wet tongue hanging out of my mouth. They wouldn't look at me even.

Look at this.

I brought in Dr Quinn grand fresh leaves for him go get scanned for me only his secretary was out sick so he said she'd do it the next day and put it on a disc for me to collect the next week. So what I got back today was the leaves only they're a bit withered and look shit. She must have been out a few days.

They're from a copper beech tree that's part of my story later on. Or soon enough maybe I dunno. From the exact branch that's in the story. If you remember the page you can come back to here and look at it. I'm on page 313 now. If you can't remember that you can put a dog's ear on the corner of the page. If you can't do that you could some day maybe go to Ballyronan and look at the copper beech in the churchyard. If it wouldn't make you too sad. Dr Quinn said I'm doing fine now anyhow, just to keep going with it. He asked me were the court transcripts a help and I said yeah and he was delighted altogether with himself and I didn't have to listen to him much more just agree away mad when I'd get the face he makes when he wants me to agree away mad with him.

—Yeah. Yeah.

—Wouldn't you think Charlie?

—Yeah.

Some of the transcripts are just shit talk and the judge talking with the lawyers about procedure and what was done in other cases and drivel like that. But then now I just came across this.

More of Teesh's Evidence

—You say you drank in Roundy's. Sinéad Halloran worked there, didn't she?

—Yes.

—As a barmaid, is it?

—Yes.

—How well did you know her?

—Fairly well like, she'd have been working there a lot when we were drinking there.

—I see.

—How would you describe her? What kind of a girl was she?

—Ahm, she was pretty sound.

—Pretty sound. Isn't it true that you thought she was overly promiscuous?. . . Well?

—Ahm.

—Just answer the question please.

—Ahm.

—Just tell the truth. Simple as that. Well?

—What's promisc ... ?

—Promiscuous. What does it mean? OK. It means, someone who is sexually indiscriminate. Somebody who, in common parlance, sleeps around a bit. Is given to many different sexual partners. Do you understand what it means now?

—Yes.

—Isn't it true that you thought she was like that?

—Well like. . . that's. . . I couldn't say that. That's not right.

—Now. Let us reflect for a moment on our situation. You are speaking about a young woman. You are an honourable young man. Somebody your community has christened as, quite literally, a leader. You are, it seems to me, a pretty good guy. Honourable. Decent. Respectful. And it seems to me that, you, just like myself, would have a great deal of respect for women. And we don't like to speak of people who are not in a position to defend their reputation. You know what I mean?

—Yes.

—I must remind you then, that you are in a court of law, and respect or fear of causing embarrassment has no place at all here. Because the only thing that's appropriate in this courtroom is the truth, no matter how unpalatable. No matter how hurtful. No matter how disrespectful. The rules outside in the community are different. The rule in here is you tell the absolute truth. Do you understand?

—Yes. Yes, I do.

—Good. Now. Isn't it true that you once described Sinéad Halloran as being, and I quote, 'Mad for pipe'. . . Well?

—I'd have been only . . .

—Answer the question please, yes or no. Your Lordship . . .

—Please answer the question you are asked only. If the court requires you to elaborate, you will be specifically asked to do so. Quite simple, yes or no, do you understand?

—Yes.

—Continue.

—Now. Did you once describe Sinéad Halloran as being, and I quote, 'Mad for pipe'.

—Yes.

—By pipe, were you referring to penis?

—Yes.

—And further, you said that Sinéad would take seven foot of pipe a week. What did you mean?

—Just that she'd have a lot of sex.

—You had a nickname for her too, is that not the case?

—Yes.

—What was her nickname?

—Well, it was just what a few of us called her for a laugh.

—Again, just answer the question.

—Flora. The nickname was Flora.

—Why?

—Spreads easily.

—Meaning she would readily agree to have sex, is that it?

—Yes.

—Thank you.

Seen her mother and father after. Walking around like zombies like their brains were fried. The whole world hearing about Sinéad being thought of as some kind of a sex nut. The confused embarrassed sad heads on them. They didn't even know if it was bullshit or not cos they didn't even know their own daughter. Stupid fuckers isn't it? I wouldn't let myself feel sorry for them, even a tiny bit. Hated them fools nearly as much as my own useless self.

More of Dinky's Evidence

What Dinky speaks about here happened in the pub one of the nights between Christmas Day and New Year's Day. It's stuff that I was looking for in the transcripts for a while. I couldn't find it. Dr Quinn says to me maybe I didn't want to find it. I didn't say anything, just looked out the window with the shitty view of a wall. Anyhow, this is it.

—Now, could you tell me what you thought of Sinéad?

—I thought she was a nice girl.

—Did you think she was promiscuous? You can answer truthfully. You have to answer the question.

—Yes. I thought she was. Especially since it got out that she'd been with the Little Rascal after closing time in the pub she worked in back home.

—Who's the Little Rascal?

—Oh. He's a travelling musician. Used to come around to all the pubs. Singing like. Young fella like. From Four Crosses. Worked in a building site in Ballyronan too.

—And he lived in Four Crosses, did he?

—Yeah. Sinéad liked him like.

—When you say she'd been with him, do you mean she had sexual intercourse with him?

—Yes.

—How do you know she did?

—Everyone knows it.

—Yes but how?

—It came out one night in Roundy's. That's the pub.

—Yes.

—It just came out. Little Rascal said it.

—Said what?

—That like, he'd had sex with her in the toilets.

—And was Sinéad there when he said this?

—Yes.

—And did she admit it?

—No. She pretended she didn't know what he was on about. Then he made reference to her birthmark.

—What birthmark? I know this is difficult. But it's important that we get the facts.

—The Little Rascal said he could prove it. That he'd seen her birthmark. Said it was in the shape of a V. A line of dots in the shape of a V on the inside of one of her thighs.

—And what did Sinéad say?

—Well she started crying. James was there and he heard the whole thing. She denied it. She started calling the Little Rascal a liar. Then she said he raped her.

—I see. Do you think people believed her?

—No. Sounded made up like . . . to save face in front of her boyfriend, and everyone else I suppose.

—I see. What happened then?

—Well, Teesh and a few of the lads said she'd want to be careful about making accusations of rape. That that wasn't right.

—Yes.

—She was hysterical. Someone dragged Rascal away and James escorted Sinéad out of the pub. By the next day he'd broken it off with her.

—Broken it off?

—Ended their relationship. James went back to Dublin then. He was in college in Dublin.

—Yes. I see.

Didn't happen just like that. James gave her an ultimatum to either go to the gardaí about the rape or else it was over. She said there was no way of proving it and the Rascal was gone to Spain so there was no point. She just wanted to forget about it. James said he was going to kill him and Sinéad said not to and he couldn't understand why Sinéad just didn't want him dead. But Sinéad just didn't want James getting in trouble with the gardaí. And she didn't want anyone knowing. She asked James what his father would think. He didn't understand why that was important to her. James asked me if I'd ever heard Sinéad use the word slapper before. I said no. He said it was weird hearing Sinéad use that word. She said to him that everyone would think she was a slapper if she went to the gardaí about it.

Was sad that night anyhow, what I seen.

—Sinéad. Sinéad, James said.

She didn't answer him.

—Sinéad. Babe. Sinéad. Sinéad.

It was like he was trying to revive a dying woman. A dying spirit.

—Sinéad. Sinéad. Can you hear me babe? Sinéad.

I had to turn around cos the tears started streaming down my face. I didn't understand what was happening. But I knew it was bad. It was too fucking horrible to be a witness of.

He just left that Sunday night and it was all over. But then he arrived back down the following day. Got a train from Dublin at half five in the morning. Said he couldn't sleep so went to the train station and waited for the first train back. He asked her to come with him back to Dublin and they'd make a new start but she started crying and said she couldn't, that she had to take care of her father. He said she needs counselling and she said she wasn't going to counselling ever. She was too ashamed. And he said if it wasn't her fault how could she be ashamed and she just started crying.

He became convinced she didn't love him and he didn't believe her story any more.

It was Monday now and he was supposed to be up in college in Dublin. His father called to the house to bring me up to him. I found him in the library. He was walking around in circles. Then sitting down. Standing looking out the window. Sitting down then again. Then getting up and circling the room again. He was talking fierce bullshit. His eyes were red from crying and he rubbing them.

—She likes that fucking prick. The rape thing is only a story. I can't fucking believe it Charlie. I thought we were for ever.

—No James. She don't love anyone else.

—You don't know that Charlie. It doesn't make any sense otherwise. She doesn't love me any more.

He sat down and started weeping.

—No James, I said.

—She thinks she's not good enough for me. That's always been there. Cos my parents are rich. She's always felt inferior. I should have done more to make her feel at home with us.

Silence then for a while but then he starts off again.

—It's her father. Her father hates me. Always has. She always deep down wants to win his fucking approval.

Next thing it was my fault.

—How could you not know anyway Charlie? It's not even plausible for fuck sake, you're always below in Roundy's when she's there. You'd know what's going on. I know you listen to everything down there.

Later he blamed himself. Saying he should've known that she'd find him less attractive if he appeared at all needy. And he did need her. And to Sinéad, this became a turn-off he reckoned. He was annoying me now with all this bollicks. I didn't understand what she done either but I wasn't talking shit and he shouldn't be either. Most of all he shouldn't. Making her out to be like that.

Little did he know how much she needed him as well though. I said good luck to him and I walked away home about one in the morning and he still pacing the floor. I knew he wouldn't go back to Dublin in that state. Was about six o'clock in the following evening and his father called to my parents' house again. He was wondering if James was with us. He hadn't seen him all day and his bag for Dublin was still in the house. He was worried. I told him I'd have a look a few places and not to worry, that he might have gone to see Sinéad but he said he tried her house too and was told she was working.

—Don't worry, I said, I'll find him.

—Send him home Charlie won't you?

—I will.

—His mother is worried about him.

I found him the first place I looked. Down by the river at Pontoon Castle.

—The man himself, he goes when he seen me coming.

—The very man, I said. Your father's worried. We'll go back.

—OK.

He didn't say anything for a while then he goes.

—Can't get the picture of them doing it out of my head.

—Jesus, I said.

—Maybe he doesn't give a shit about her and that's a turn-on for her. Her taking it doggy style. Her on top. Her going down on him. Like . . . she had to be thinking of me when they were doing it. Him on top and she looking into his eyes. Maybe he was all gentle or something. Or rougher maybe.

—Jesus James, I said.

There was silence then for a bit and next thing he goes,

—How long are you supposed to last do you think?

—James . . . stop now James. You're not thinking right at all.

The next day I called up and he was up in the library. He seemed a bit better. Eyes less bloodshot.

—Sorry about yesterday, he goes.

—Nah, I said.

—Thing is, he says looking at me all matter of fact. It's not her fault. And it's not my fault. It's just evolution. Women are evolved to find a variety of men attractive. Gives their genes better chances of survival. Biology. Simple as that.

I said nothing.

—It's like the size of your prick. Mine is pretty average. I'm above average in other attributes. Below average in others. Women need the variety for to ensure success in their offspring.

He was turning into a bit of a prick himself now with his shite talk and I was starting to feel embarrassed listening to him. It was kind of insulting to her and was annoying me. I goes,

—For that to make sense all brothers and sisters would be the same. But they're not.

That shut him up. I just told him to go and see Sinéad. Before he left for the train though he called to her. I think it was to see if he could forgive her and somehow make a go of things again. He went to knock on the door but stopped when he heard the song Sinéad had playing inside in the living room. She saw him outside and they just watched each other through the window without saying anything. Tears were streaming down her face. The song on was 'River' from a one called Joni Mitchell. I don't even want to think about the fucking words of it.

At the end of the song James turned and walked away.

—She didn't even come out after me, he said, and the tears in his eyes.

As if I couldn't have seen that for myself.

James went away back to college in Dublin then. They were finished.

James always loved Sinéad. But he began to hate the people around her. Hate was something new to him. Didn't sit well on his shoulders. Transformed him a bit, so it did. Could have contorted him if he wasn't careful.

I remember around this time I came off the bus in Ballyronan after work about six o'clock in the evening and Sinéad was coming up the street on the way to Roundy's to work for the night. I crossed the road to avoid her. Could see her out the corner of my eye stopped still across the street just looking at me walking away from her. I was never so disgusted with anyone. You think you know someone and you don't isn't it? That's what I was thinking. Maybe that's what she was thinking too.

Sinéad's Psychiatrist's Evidence

—Yes. My name is Richard Mooney and I'm a consultant psychiatrist at Cork University Hospital.

—Thank you. And could you confirm, as the victim is unable to testify, that you have been requested to testify on her behalf?

—Yes. I have been requested to do so. In writing.

—And could you confirm that you are therefore permitted, and indeed required, under the law and in line with medical ethical practice in court proceedings of this type, to testify on behalf of a patient who, for whatever reason, is not in a position to describe her mental condition around the time in which the court is interested?

—Yes, I can confirm that.

—Thank you. Could you tell the court please, Mr Mooney, when you first saw Sinéad as a patient.

—Well, Sinéad Halloran presented at first with sleeping problems and some possible concentration problems, which were deemed to be mainly due to her sleeping difficulties.

—Did you ascertain a cause for these sleeping difficulties?

—Well, Sinéad had two stressors which we believed were the main . . . the main cause of her sleeping problems, namely her father being ill and consequently losing his job and secondly she missed her boyfriend who was in college in Dublin.

—I see. Did you prescribe medication for her sleeping problem?

—Yes. A standard prescription sleeping tablet. Zolpidem. I began with a half dose and told her G.P. to increase it to a full dose if it didn't work.

—I see. And did it work?

—It did, yes. Her G.P. increased it to a full dose and it did work for a time. She remained on those for a period of months but was referred to me a second time by her G.P.

—Ahm. So on her second visit to hospital she wasn't unwell enough to be admitted either, is that correct?

—Yes, that's correct. Yes, in my judgement she was depressed. She saw me as an outpatient and I felt she would get over it in time. I was aware she'd just come out of a long-term relationship and this caused her a great deal of sadness. At this stage I changed her medication from sleeping tablets to anti-depressants.

—I see. What was she taking then?

—I put her on Prothiaden. It's a mood-lifter. Unfortunately there's a lot of trial and error involved as what will work for one patient may not work for another.

—I see. And did Prothiaden help her?

—No. Not in my estimation, no. Two months later I put her on Lexapro. This didn't help her either.

—When you say it didn't help her, can you explain? Isn't it true that even though Sinéad was no longer in a relationship with James that she still worked an average of forty hours a week as a barmaid? Was she severely depressed?

—Yes. In my view she was. Many people who are severely depressed do manage to hold down full-time jobs. In many ways these late work hours helped her as she didn't sleep well anyway and starting her shift at six or eight in the evening would be much easier than a long night at home of . . . you know, deep deep sadness. And anguish.

—I see.

—Ahm . . . then . . . a few months later her . . . her symptoms pretty much disappeared.

—How come?

—We put it down to . . . to James, this boyfriend of hers she always spoke about, we put it down to them . . . reuniting.

—Getting back together?

—So to speak, yes.

—Did she continue on the medication?

—We weaned her off the tablets. . .over a period of I think eight to ten weeks.

—I see.

Mannerisms

Went downstairs there. My sister's here again with Emily only this time Emily has a little baby sister. Aoife is her name. Sister only had her a few weeks ago. I didn't say it at the time cos it's none of your business and I wasn't writing much cos of my mother putting on Johnny Lee Hooker anyhow. One good thing about the new baby is that the mother isn't bored and annoying me when I'm in my room. She's funny to watch. Emily is. The little girl. Trying to be like her mammy or her granny. Copying everything they do. She had a little floor brush with her. Toy one. 'Tisn't even two foot long. She's busy out and then she goes,

—Now so.

That's what Irish mothers say after they do a bit of housework. And she has an apron on too even though I never seen an apron on my sister. My mother wears them all right though. Best is when she copies my mother and says,

—Jesus,

cos my mother's always saying Jesus.

It's kind of nice for the grown-ups isn't it? Like a compliment for them. That this little person thinks they're worth copying. Humans know how to fit in without even knowing it. From day one, they're training as children how to be an adult who fits in. They're complete copycats really.

I seen Sinéad copy too. When James was off in Dublin. It might have been after they broke up. Probably was. For the first time she began to adopt the mannerisms and the accent of Racey and company. She began to dress like her too.

The leering old fellas in the pub made jokes that before she'd have found inappropriate. Nowadays these joke-insults seemed to give her a sense of belonging. Heard her telling Dinky and Racey this.

—I was in the butcher's the other day, buying a steak to cook for Roundy for his dinner, you know?

—You cook for him?

—Yeah, sure he's helpless in the kitchen himself.

—OK, go on.

—And in comes Teesh you know?

—Yeah?

—And he's like, 'Christ Sinéad girl, I'd say you'd have a fair old appetite for the meat would you? What do you think of them big fat sausages?' I was like, 'Jesus I dunno!' And Teesh says, 'I'd say you'd take four of five foot of that a week, would you?' God he's one gas fucker, Teesh, the whole shop was in stitches, except Mrs Higgins. I'd say she was disgusted.

Roundy's became like a big long boring Carry-On film. Sinéad lapped it all up. Joke-insults. On her. She gave the audience what they wanted isn't it.

—Oh you'd like that all right Timmy wouldn't you.

—By Jesus girleen, I wouldn't say no!

—Ah sure there's a lot to be said for it Timmy, 'tis only natural!

—You want another packet of crisps Pete? Sure you haven't eaten the last packet yet. If I didn't know you any better I'd think you only wanted to see me bending down to get them.

—Would I? Look at my innocent little faceen, would I be that mischievous!

—From what I heard of your younger days Pete, yes! I heard you were like a wild ram around the town!

—Oho! Doubt ya Pete.

—Ah sure 'tis only natural.

That kind of stuff. Lots of it. That was her now. Sinéad. Was like they'd worn her down. And she bolstering up sad lives in Roundy's with her boobs and her bottom and her lick-arsing of bachelors and men whose wives wished were bachelors.

She kind of ignored me now. Just served me my Lucozade same as any customer.

—Hi Charlie. How are things?

—Grand. How are you?

—Sure never better.

Now that light. The light of her spark was lost now under highlights and fake tan stuff or else it was just plain gone out, same as all the other fires in the history of fire on earth. At least when someone's dead you've a body. When the fire goes you're left with nothing at all that's even a small bit like it. Only darkness. No comparison, isn't it? Black and white are more alike than fire and no fire.

Laughing and joking with them halfdrunk halfwit halfsouls. Went mad with the halves there didn't I? Everything has two halves. Opposite and the same. But Sinéad and James were two halves of the same. Something. I don't know what. No two ways about it tho. Sinéad and James. No two ways.

Anyhow I dunno who she was trying to look like but it wasn't herself.

Just went tiptoeing around the house for a bit there. Got restless and cross and uneasy and the tears and snots were coming too quick to be writing and I realised I'd no candle lighting. I need the fire now. Next best thing to Sinéad in the room with you isn't it? It's either that or the music and fuck the fucking music cos it only causes distractions that bring troubles and harm. But I have the candle with me now. Cleared away all my wrappers and rubbish cos their shadows were distracting me from the candle cos I wanted to see it as good as I could. Been looking at it now a while cos I thought I might make a better go of describing it and the little bit of fire it has but it's just as useless as it was the last time I fucked up describing it. Best thing you could do is just get a candle and light it. And turn off all the lights. And if it's daytime don't bother your hole cos you won't see it right and anyhow if it's daytime where you are now you've a million daytime things in your head like dinner and petrol and telly and people and shit so just forget about the candle.

Anyhow, I won't talk about candles or fire anymore I promise. Shouldn't have even tried. I'll just give you this picture anyhow in case you don't have a candle.

Fucking thing has me driven daft. My sister helped me put it on the computer so I could cut and paste it but I held the camera sideways when I was taking it. You can just turn the book on its side to look at it. Sinéad would have kept her fire controlled and graceful same as the candle if she'd the fucking chance. You have to be careful with fire isn't it? Mind it and cherish it and respect it. Or it could burn you. Or go out. That little flame must be the only thing that still looks beautiful through tears. Gives it other dimensions or something, I dunno. OK that's it about candles. It's just the flicker of them isn't it? Same as our lives. Yours and mine and everyone else's ever. Flickering awhile.

Anyhow so that was Sinéad in the bar. I'd have thought she was happy only for her tears. She was given a week off by Roundy to go and get herself sorted out. She used to break down crying for no obvious reason. She'd be counting change in the till or wiping the bar or reading the paper and then next thing she'd just start crying. She'd walk quickly in behind the bar or run. In the end Roundy told her she'd have to take a week off and she said she'd be fine, that there was no need and he said it was a week off or finish working there altogether. He said it made him look bad, that people might think it was him was making her cry.

The next weekend I called up to James' house and told him and what does he do? He starts crying as well.

—I'm going to see her, he said.

And he did. Next time I seen him he had a new girlfriend. A new old girlfriend. Sinéad. Could've cried myself when I seen them together. No more tears formula it was for Sinéad anyhow.

Couple of weeks later when James was back for the weekend we were back in the library. Happy as ever isn't it? They were back together. We were all back together.

James put on 'Solsbury Hill' and we were sailing away again through some other place made of a million other feelings that they had no words for but everyone would recognise them.

—What's the most healing tune?

—'Spiegel im Spiegel'. Has to be.

—Or 'The Healing Game'.

—Here I am again. That's my favourite line. That and 'Back on the Corner Again'. I love that one too. It's like you don't know if he's depressed again or if he's there again for the person who's sad.

—John Lennon's 'Love'.

—Yeah.

We listened for a long time to James playing the simple tune on the piano. Then Sinéad sang it.

—In olden times you know they used to play the chord C minor to bring ease to people whose minds were troubled.

Sinéad picked up the guitar then and started strumming 'Madame

George'. Three chords. Always returning over and over again to C. She hummed it for a bit.

—Christ yeah, said James.

—Have we got it?

I went over to the boxes and started looking through the mother's records. We got lost in 'Madame George' then for a while. Sinéad standing, moving a little with the music in her all different coloured stripey woolly socks, her own clothes again. Sinéad-style. James was lying on the floor. I leaned on the windowsill and watched the candlelight shine on the spinning record and I seen what the music did to Sinéad. Moved her, same as the air she set in motion moved the candle flame. Some laws isn't it? Sometimes she sang and hummed a little along with it too. Quietly only. Just a tease.

When it was finished she did one of her tippitoe spins and ran out down the stairs shouting,

—Come on fatasses, who wants a game of tennis?

James looked at me and we both smiled and got going, a bit more than happy to be alive maybe, the two of us.

That Sunday evening James went to Dublin but the love of his life was with him. It was just for a couple of days. I seen them off. The happiest train in the world maybe. She called up to my house Wednesday evening when she came back. My mother was delighted to see her but eventually she went off to watch *Coronation Street* and we were able to talk. She was like an excited child all talk about how they went to the Ruby Sessions and they were talking to the MC and he said to send on a demo and he'd fix them up with a slot. She was back in work on Thursday but she was happy in herself. James was coming home at the weekend for a month for Easter.

But then late that Saturday night Sinéad was off so we all went to The Snug. It was Racey's birthday too. She was nineteen. But who comes into the bar only the Rascal. He came in like he was looking for someone. Said hello to the lads but he didn't have a drink. Said he was going back to Roundy's. Sinéad didn't look at him but her face went red.

Dinky's evidence tells you what happened next. He mentions the scarf here. You know the Afghan one like the one I showed you before.

More of Dinky's Evidence

—Did anybody believe Sinéad's account of what happened?

—Honestly? I doubt it very much.

—I see.

—Especially when the Little Rascal was wearing a scarf another night that James had given Sinéad as a present. The Little Rascal said she gave it to him on another night.

—Could he not have taken it from her?

—Well, Sinéad had told James that her mother borrowed it and lost it on a night out on the town. But Rascal said she left it in his car the Thursday night before when he collected her after work. Said he took her for a spin up the woods.

—I see. Do you believe this? Do you believe what the Little Rascal said about the scarf?

—Yes. No reason not to . . . she was just . . . you know, you couldn't watch her . . . there's no watching a girl like that.

—What do you mean by that?

—Well like . . . you couldn't trust her. James couldn't trust her. She was carrying on behind his back like.

—How did James react to this, when he found out about it?

—That time in the pub, is it?

—Yes.

—He hit him like, he hit the Little Rascal, but myself and Teesh pulled him away. Told him it wasn't worth it. Teesh told him he probably needed to talk to Sinéad.

—And did he?

—Yes. He broke it off. Not there in front of everyone. Like they talked later that night and he broke it off with her.

—I thought he'd ended the relationship previously?

—Yeah. He did. But after that he got back with her again for a while. Until this time when he saw the scarf he gave to Sinéad on the Little Rascal.

—Could it not have been another scarf?

—No. It was like . . . one of them Afghan scarves. But a real thick one like, and it was faded and all. It was old like. I think it was in James' family for a long time like.

—I see. So let me get this straight. He breaks it off with her after he hears she had intercourse with the Little Rascal in the toilets after work in the pub one night.

—Yeah. Yes.

—How come he was so quick to disbelieve her? Why didn't he believe that she was raped?

—Well, he wanted to go straight to the gardaí that night he found out but she wouldn't. And the way she said it in the pub anyway sounded very dodgy like . . . a bit like grasping at straws like.

—I see. But then he got back with her, is that correct?

—Yes. After a while like. Maybe a few months. Maybe more. Can't really remember like to be honest.

—OK. So he's in a relationship with her again. For how long this time, would you say?

—Ahm. About. I don't know. Couple of months maybe. He was in Dublin like. Could've been more.

—And all this time he was in Dublin, she remained in Ballyronan. Is that correct?

—Yes.

—Even though she'd promised to go to Dublin with him, is that so?

—Yes. She stayed.

—So then on another weekend night when James was back in Bally-ronan, in Roundy's, he sees the Little Rascal wearing the Afghan scarf and confronted him. Is that so?

—Yes.

—He ended his relationship then with Sinéad finally, is that correct?

—Yes, sir. Yes, I mean.

—Thank you, Denis. That will be all for the moment.

That's pretty much how all that happened all right. I can just remember Dinky acting like he was standing up for James by telling the Little Rascal to fuck off and the Rascal only laughing back at Dinky and Dinky looking away. James stormed off out and Sinéad went out after him but she never caught up with him. She looked at me as if I could tell her what to do and I shrugged my shoulders. She went off home crying.

I was going to go home but I wanted to see what the gossip with the rest of them was. It was a long night. Couldn't face going into it now to be honest. I'll give you some court transcripts instead awhile and I'll come back to that night another time. Someone had seen me and Sinéad talking down at the river some night and this lawyer wanted to know all about it.

—And what were you talking about?

—Ahm. Talked about like them frying pans with the non-stick.

—Excuse me?

—Like . . . the ones that the rashers don't stick to when you're frying them. And the wipers that come on every now and again.

—Windscreen wipers, is it?

—Yeah . . . windscreen wipers. The ones that come on every few seconds when it's not raining only drizzling.

—And that's what you spoke about? For over two hours.

—Yeah . . . that and other stuff.

—What other stuff did you talk about?

—Other clever stuff.

—Other clever stuff?

—Yeah.

—Like what?

—Like the tin openers. The blue ones.

—Blue tin openers?

—Yeah. The new ones from the telly. Just put it on top of the tin and twist and it's open. Way easier than the old ones.

—I see. And did you talk about James?

—No.

—You answered that very quickly. Why did you say 'No' so quickly, Charlie? . . . Well?

—Objection. Completely subjective.

—Cos it's only a small word.

—Charles, when your council objects it means that he thinks the question Mr Cole has asked you is unfair. Do you understand that, Charlie?

—Yeah.

—So you don't have to answer it unless I say you need to answer it, is that OK, Charlie?

—Yeah.

—Now I want the jury to disregard Charlie's answer to that question, please. Do you all understand that? Fine. Mr Cole, I'll ask you to deal with what Charlie says not the manner in which he says it, please.

—Of course, Your Lordship.

—Carry on.

—OK, Charlie. We're nearly done for now. What else did you talk about with Sinéad, Charlie?

—Ahm. Nothing.

—For two hours?

—Yeah.

—How could you both sit there and say nothing for over two hours? What were you doing?

—Just listened like. To the river. Seen a few shooting stars. And the moon. It moved across the sky behind the trees. Couldn't see it no more but you could see it in the water. The reflection of it.

—And you left after that, did you?

—Yeah.

—Were you the first to leave or was it Sinéad's idea?

—Yeah.

—Which is it? Was it Sinéad's idea to leave?

—Yeah.

—What did she say?

—She said would I walk her back?

—And what did you say?

—Yeah.

—You said you would?

—Yeah.

—And did you?

—Yeah.

—OK. And was she upset at any stage?

—No.

—Was she crying at any stage during your talk?

—No.

—And did she seem sad?

—No.

—And did you talk on your way back to her house?

—Yeah.

—What about?

—Only a little bit.

—What did you talk about?

—Toasters.

—Toasters?

—Yeah. Long ago they had to hold the bread in front of the fire stuck on to a stick so you wouldn't burn your hand.

—OK. That's fine for the moment, Charlie.

Two Gods

One time I went to the church in the evening time to scare a fella into doing the right thing by giving him a sign. That's what I thought I was doing at the time anyhow.

Snoozie had two gods. Teesh and the Holy one. Every Sunday sure as shit the lads would go down to Roundy's while their parents were at Mass. Since they were about fifteen. Custom to them. Same as Mass was custom to their parents. Slip off out the back of the church and go down. Mostly fellas would be in their late twenties or early thirties before moving out. Maybe that's why they lived in the pub whenever they could. Anyhow, in all this there was one unlikely exception. Whatever is there that puts breath in us all and whatever it is that makes the world whatever it is, to our eyes or any other eyes or any such things creatures might have for seeing or sensing or feeling or gaining understanding of, whatever it is it did this, it gave Snoozie an unwavering belief that God was the thing. And that God is good. And that God is love. And that God is all powerful. And that if you prayed to God it helped. And that not going to Mass on a Sunday was a sin. And that sins could make you go to hell. Or purgatory. Or at least were no help at all in getting to heaven. All the mocking in the world from the other god in his life, Teesh, fell on deaf Christian ears.

—Holy Joe is in, Teesh would say if he was inside in the pub before Snoozie would arrive back from Mass on Sundays.

Funny thing then. Snoozie comes over to me at training earlier. I went down to watch the lads training with the father just to shut him up. Anyhow the father was over talking to some other fella and Snoozie comes over to me. Says he knew it was me in the church long ago. That he'd seen me. I looked at him half agog.

—I was scared that God had brought you there, that's all. That's what I was scared of. That was sign enough for me.

He stared at me looking at him slantwise.

—I dreamed something you see. I dreamed you came up to me in the church. And it was empty except for Sinéad. Sinéad was standing behind you in the dream. Crying she was. Crying. And not just sad girly little crying. Wild angry crying it was. And the eyes on her and she looking at me. Very frightening. You put something into my hand then and I looked down and it was my scapular. When I looked up, yourself and Sinéad were gone. Next thing I'm up at the church for real and who do I see only you. I'm sorry I gave you such a fright that you knocked the statue but I was shitting it.

His eyes were watering.

—Shitting it I was.

—Yeah, I said.

—Went up there to feel God's protection but when I seen you in his house I knew I didn't have no protection from him until I put my story right. So next day that's what I done. And the Lord Our God is in my heart now more than ever before. Mightn't have much friends any more but who needs the like of Teesh for a friend anyhow. God is a friend that'll never let you down. Ever. Remember that Gamal. God is with you always. You mightn't know much but God has a plan even for you. It was God brought you to the church that evening to put the shits up me so I'd tell the truth in court. And it was God had me dreaming of you and Sinéad the night before. God has us all in the palm of his hand Gamal.

—Yeah, I said.

—I thought I was with God before but it was only after all that that I knew what it meant to walk with God. We were all part of a badness. An evil. The devil was at work in us. We can be part of a force for goodness too, can't we?

—Yeah, I said.

—Dunno about you Gamal, but I seen the Light of Christ. Have you?

—Yeah.

I'd heard that he was after getting involved with some funny Christian crowd. The father said it was a cult and the mother goes it's just a different religion and the father goes it's a cult. Snoozie was there in my ear cos he thought he had it and he went on and on and on but he was really talking to himself cos I was thinking about Dr Quinn long ago when I met him for the first time and I sitting in his office in more pain than I ever dreamed a man would ever feel. Said to me that even Our Lord needed help carrying the cross. Everyone needs help sometimes to get them through their troubles isn't it? And God is there for someone when they're all alone. Dr Quinn sees himself when he gets out of bed every morning as being like the lad who helped Jesus carry his cross. Imitation is what it is really isn't it? Imitation. Except it's mad people he's helping. I haven't really done nothing out in the world to help no one. Helped myself. And I never even did that too much either. I've a lot of making up to do for my sins. And I don't mean for God. There's no God for the like of me. But I'd dislike me less if I did some good for people. Same as Dr Quinn does. And all the other good people in the world.

When I was a child, I spake as a child, I understood as a child, I thought as a child: but when I became a man, I put away childish things. For now we see through a glass, darkly; but then face to face: now I know in part; but then shall I know even as also I am known

That's another cut and paste job. It's only sixty words like so I'm not gaining a whole pile from it. It's from the Bible. Not sure if I understand the end of it. Thought I could fit it in here cos by this point in my story I really was seeing through a glass darkly and I had to put away childish things. Or at least start finding a way out of the only world that was there for you when you were the village gamal. I didn't want no part in it any more. Anyhow maybe the quote makes sense for this part of my story or maybe I'm only bluffing. Maybe the fella who wrote it first day was a bit of a bluffer too, even if Holy God was prompting him a bit. Wish he'd prompt me a bit. Save me robbing stuff off the fucking internet. 'For All We Know' sang by Nina Simone goes here then.

_____

_____

_____

_____

_____

_____

_____

_____

_____

_____

_____

Because my mother played it downstairs and fucked me up alto-gether. 'For All We Know' was to blame. Wasn't Sinéad's favourite Nina Simone song but she listened to it to understand what was happening with the piano. The singing stayed at the same tempo but the piano changed in different parts of the song. She'd never heard anything like that before. Neither have most people but they don't play it over and over, pausing it and going back over bits. At the time it all seemed normal enough. Seems silly now. Maybe Sinéad shouldn't have been so obsessed with music in her life cos there's more to life isn't it?

Didn't end up doing anything after I heard it. After the mother played it. Just lied down on the bed. Headache's gone now. And the shakes. But I haven't written anything in two weeks. Didn't get out the bed the first week sure. All over a song. I'd want to fucking harden up a small bit.

18

I put in a chapter there. Forgot about them really. Don't really give a fuck about them any more. This is the last chapter. I have to just do this or Dr Quinn will be sickening to be listening to on Tuesday.

More of Dinky's Evidence

—How did you know Sinéad?

—Well . . . like . . . I knew her all my life. I hung around with herself and James and a few more. We been friends since we were kids.

—Were you ever in a relationship with Sinéad Halloran?

—With Sinéad? No. Never. She was going out with James nearly her whole life sure.

—Isn't it true that you were instrumental in the break-up of the relationship of James Kent and Sinéad Halloran?

—No.

—I'll ask you again. Did you play any part whatsoever in the break-up of the relationship of James Kent and Sinéad Halloran?

—No. I didn't.

—Very well. You are under oath. Thank you. I'm done, Your Lordship.

—You may leave the witness stand.

Dream

I used to always have a dream for as long as I knew Sinéad. In it Sinéad would be turning away and I'd be begging her not to go. Cos it was always known in the dream that she was walking away to her death, for our sake somehow. She was just looking back at me. Her face was the same in all the dreams. Hint of a smile. As if to say it's OK isn't it? In one she was being nailed to a cross by the Romans. In another one she was being carried away by an angry mob of women who were going to burn her at the stake. In another one she was an Indian girl being dragged away from her family by the cowboys. Always the same look on her face as she looked back to me. Like she knew this would happen some day. Not even a splinter of surprise. Just looked back at me trying to tell me it was OK with her eyes. Rotten dreams them. Take me half a morning to forget about it they would.

And James. One time James was shot. In my dream. Big hole in his chest size of a football and he walking backwards away from us all saying it was OK.

Voices

—Sinéad. Are you OK? Sinéad . . . Sinéad.

—Yeah?

—Are you OK?

—Yeah I'm fine, why?

—Just. Nothing.

—Cool babe.

More of Racey's Evidence

—Now. Could you give your full name to the court registrar, please.

—Tracey Martina Aherne.

—Thank you. You knew the accused. Is that right?

—Yes.

—How did you know him?

—I knew him since secondary school. We were the same age and hung around in the same gang.

—And you had a relationship with the accused, is that right?

—Yes. On and off like.

—Could you just clarify what you mean by the phrase on and off?

—Yes. Like . . . we'd go out with each other . . . then it would be off like . . . and then we'd be back together again.

—And this went on for how long?

—Since like . . . second year in school to about a couple of years ago I suppose.

—OK. And in all this time did you ever feel that the accused, Denis Hennebry, had strong feelings for Sinéad Halloran?

—Sorry, what do you mean like?

—OK. I'll put it this way. How do you think he felt about Sinéad?

—Dunno like. I'd say he liked her. Not in that way like. But as a friend like. You know. We were all friends sure like.

—OK. That's fine. Thank you very much.

—No problem.

The other lawyer comes up then.

—Hello, Tracey. The sun is really catching you there, isn't it? Are you very warm?

—Yeah, I suppose I am.

—Can we allow the witness to move Your Lordship, into the shade a bit, maybe.

—Of course.

Racey moved into the shade. The clerk moved the microphone over a bit for her. Here Tracey expains the real names of people. But I'll put in the nicknames when I'm typing it cos the real names are a pain in the hole for you to be learning at this stage. They used the real names in the court but I'll type the nicknames in instead for you. That's all I'll change though.

—Does that feel better?

—Much better, thanks very much.

—No bother at all. Now, Tracey. You say that you and Denis Hennebry hung around in the same gang throughout your adolescence, is that right?

—Yes.

—Could you name the people that you considered to be in the same gang over those years?

—Ahm. Say. Denis. Myself.

—Sorry, could you give surnames also, just for the court record if you could, thank you.

—Yeah. Denis Hennebry and myself, Sinéad Halloran, James Kent, Snoozie, I mean, Richard Fitzpatrick.

—Who's Snoozie?

—Snoozie's just a nickname for Richard Fitzpatrick. His father's pub is The Snug.

—I see. Did you have a nickname?

—Yes. Racey.

—Why did people call you Racey.

—Not sure. Think it's because I'm a good swimmer.

—Really. Very good. Did anyone else have a nickname?

—Ahm. Yeah. Well, there was the Gamal. That was Charlie McCarthy. Ahm. There was Dinky. That was Denis Hennebry. Ahm . . . And Teesh. That was Gary O'Donovan. But Teesh and Snoozie were a bit older than us. Mostly Dinky who was friendly with them, from the football. And James a bit too, I suppose.

—What do you mean a bit?

—Well, he wouldn't have been as friendly with Teesh and Snoozie as Dinky was.

—Why was that, would you think?

—I don't know. Probably didn't have as much in common.

—OK. Is there anyone else you might think was in the same social gang?

—Well, there were others like Karen that would hang around with us drinking now and again.

Fuck You All

I used to love this one Johnny Cash song when I was small long ago. 'Sam Hall' or 'Damn Your Eyes' like I likes to call it. I like Sam Hall. Like the way he goes on. He doesn't say,

—My name is Sam Hall, pleased to meet you.

He's done with people. Damn your eyes. Damn your nose. Damn your stupid face.

Spike Milligan did a stand-up show one time in England. His best friend was an Englishman called Peter Sellers. He was a comedian too. Peter Sellers was the main act. Spike was supporting him. The audience booed and hissed Spike and roared at him to get off. Then they started chanting, 'We want Sellers, we want Sellers,' and all. In the end Spike left the stage like an embarrassed childeen. Next thing Sellers came on and the crowd gave a big cheer. Sellers smiled at his adoring crowd and stood in front of the microphone for a few seconds 'til they calmed down. Then he said,

—Fuck you all, and walked off the stage.

Fuck you all. Sometimes I wonder is that what madness is. Someone having enough. And then saying, fuck you all. No one is born thinking fuck you all. Takes some stuff for them to get like that. Or maybe they're being loyal same as Peter Sellers. Loyal to what no one knows. Sinéad said fuck you all when she lived on music. But she was never alone. She had me. And James.

Anyhow next thing in the court case that happened was this. I was after paying Snoozie that visit in the church at the weekend and then he seen the Light of Christ.

Irregular Development

—Your Lordship, may it please the court, I'd like to bring to this court's attention that we have had an irregular development.

—Continue.

—Your Lordship, a witness has come to me and has requested to testify again. I requested him to speak to the registrar of the court.

—That's right, Mr Storey, I'm aware of the situation. I'm going to explain the situation to the jury now. Now an irregular development has occurred in this trial. My registrar informed me and I had a meeting with the witness and I've informed the counsel for the accused that Mr Richard Fitzpatrick (that's Snoozie) will be testifying after lunch. As a jury you'll be asked to reconsider the witness's original testimony. . . which occurred last Tuesday. In the meantime I would like this court to continue calling any other witnesses.

—Your Lordship, I believe the counsel for the accused are due to call a witness now.

—I beg your pardon. Yes, you're calling on Gary O'Donovan (that's Teesh) again.

—Well. . . ahm. . . actually. . . Your Lordship, in light of the request made by Richard Fitzpatrick we would like to request a stay for the said testimony until after we've heard what Mr Fitzpatrick has to say this afternoon.

—In that case it looks like we've got a long lunch-break.

—Your Lordship, I'm sure Mr Fitzpatrick could be persuaded to testify now.

—Your Lordship, we'd like to object on the grounds that we need some time with our client to establish if he has any idea what Mr Fitzpatrick may have in store for us.

—Well, I'm not sure what difference it will make. Nobody will be able to make contact with Mr Fitzpatrick until after he testifies. As is standard practice in such circumstances the court will have the witness in an unknown place under police protection. Anyway his testimony may take a while so we'll break for lunch.

—Very well, Your Lordship.

—I would kindly ask our jury to be back here by 1:45. The court is adjourned now until a quarter to two, thank you.

More of Snoozie's Evidence

—Overruled. The witness will claim to have further information which is highly relevant to the case in question. Sinéad Halloran is in no position to defend herself so we'll just hear what this young man has to say.

—OK, Your Lordship.

—You may ask the witness questions after Counsel O'Hare is finished.

—Thank you, Your Lordship.

—Proceed.

—I heard Dinky telling the whole story to Teesh.

—And when exactly did you hear it?

—I overheard something well over two years ago. And I can't keep it to myself no more. Before God I want to tell the truth.

—OK. Carry on.

—The lads were staying in my house.

—Why?

—That would happen often enough because they lived with their parents. We'd stay up late after the disco playing cards or watching telly. Have a few more beers.

—I see.

—Well anyhow, this time we were watching a video.

—Yes. Could you tell me exactly who was with you?

—Yeah. Ahm. Myself, Dinky, Teesh and the gamal.

Yes I was there in that house too. I tagged along with Dinky and Teesh in a taxi out to Snoozie's house. It was the night of the Afghan scarf and James finished with Sinéad once and for all. There was electricity among the lads so I suppose I just tagged along with them out to Snoozie's to see what the gossip was.

—OK.

—Ahm. I fell asleep. Then I woke up. The telly was off. I could hear Teesh and Dinky talking in the dining room. That's like beside like the television room. There's double doors between them but they were open. They were talking about seeing the last of the settlers.

—Who were the settlers?

—The Kents. They disappeared then the time of the War of Independence. The castle was burned down that time like. But James' father came back to renovate it and live there like. Settle back to Ballyronan again like.

—I see, yes.

—They were talking about old yarns their fathers had told them about the Kents in the famine times. Evicting people off their land cos they couldn't pay the rent to the landlord.

One story Teesh told was about a girl that Old Dirty Kent got pregnant cos he was famous for preying on the poor starving young girls. He'd send for them to do jobs for him and their mothers would send them up cos they knew she'd get a bit of food or a bit of money for taking care of his lordship. Anyhow this girl's mother went up and demanded that her daughter be taken care of cos she was carrying his lordship's baby. Old Dirty Kent sent out a lackey and told the whole family to call up to the house the next day at twelve noon. They went up at twelve noon and there was nobody there. They hung around for a while but then headed off back to their cottage. On their way back they noticed a plume of smoke coming from over the valley and sure enough their houseen was up in flames and they were evicted to wander the roads with all the other evicted skeletons in the famine long ago.

Dinky told another one was about him raping a souper's daughter. The soupers were called that because they were Catholics who were supposed to have taken the soup off the Prods during the famine in exchange for changing from Catholic to Protestant and becoming the landlords' lackeys. I dunno if it ever really happened. Old Master Higgins didn't think there was any truth in it when Dinky asked him about the soupers in class long ago. Anyhow, this souper's daughter was being raped on the ground by his lordship and next thing he comes around the corner to see his daughter's violation and he says to her,

—'Lift up your arse girleen, his lordship's balls are getting all dirty.'

Then Teesh told a one that I knew Dinky had heard before but he left him tell it anyway. I could hear Dinky all lick-arsy going, 'Yeah,' 'Oh right,' 'Jesus Christ,' or 'Holy shit,' every now and again to lick Teesh's ass and he telling the story. I couldn't bother telling the story now but you get the idea. Some stories are only shit and tell more about the people that tell them than the people they're supposed to be about isn't it?

Anyhow so yeah, that kind of thing. I was in the room with Snoozie in case you're a bit slow and haven't copped it. This part could be complicated depending on if you're thick or not. I was pretending to be asleep. But I was listening to Teesh and Dinky's shitetalk too. Back to Snoozie in court now so.

And how like they made a load of money in the same century off the slaves in Jamaica until slavery was outlawed. And how the whole floor of the castle was laid with rare oak wood at an enormous cost at the time and that marble stairs were put in as well. And how this all happened from 1845 to 1850. When starvation was rife in the whole of West Cork and you'd families dying on the side of the road. And how James' great-great-grandfather was one of the worstest bastards of landlords in the whole of Ireland. Then they started saying like how they weren't going to let his great-grandson come back down here and make eejits of us all. That we should burn the foreign occupier out like we done before.

—How did all this make you feel?

—Well like . . . I couldn't believe it.

—How do you mean, you couldn't believe it?

—Well. Like James was our friend. A good friend of ours like. We played football with him. He was one of us like. He had nothing to do with anything that happened long ago. And neither had his father.

—OK carry on.

Aslhdjsh as;lk dkslj a a;lsokt tha t a;lsie slkd9ich slitha;t slit dit a a;oit a dit a acoi aosid asoiwei d a;oids a;lskkde3- qpwoe0idns a;l a;ls as;ldife eoieo0 sid iwo. A;osdiikd .doi a;lsoi. Sorry the mother was at the door there and I had to pretend I was typing. She leaves me alone if she thinks I'm typing and doesn't ask me to be doing stuff or be talking shit to me. Whatever it was I'll go down to her later. Just not in the mood now. Going back now to lie on the bed now again.

I find reading the court transcripts awful hard but I have to do it. Makes me remember horrible stuff. Nearly a photocopying paper box full. Be thousands of pages if I included the whole lot, and half the time they spent talking about very little of any importance anyway. I'm trying to limit it to what helps me to tell the story. There's stuff in the trial of people saying how I was obsessed with Sinéad and how I was inappropriate watching her always but that's crap and has nothing to do with the story. Anyhow, here's more of Snoozie's evidence.

—Teesh then like was kinda like congratulating him then, saying he never really knew if he could trust Dinky all along, cos he was such friends with James, but that like he was delighted that he saw things like clearly. How things stood like.

—Sorry, I'm not sure I understand. What do you mean exactly?

—Well like, basically Teesh was saying he was happy they saw eye to eye like. . .like about the Kents like. About James and his father I suppose. That like they didn't like them. Or hated them. They saw them like as invaders or something still like.

—I see. And Teesh was happy that Dinky was likeminded, was he?

—Yes. Like he thought all along that Dinky was James' best friend and that was it. He was surprised. And happy like. That Dinky hated James too.

—I see.

I was surprised by the next bit cos I had to keep my eyes closed cos I wanted Snoozie not to know I was hearing all this.

—They went talking about the old times then like again. I could see them through the glass French doors between the room. They're panelled doors like with like glass with designs on it like. But it was dark in the telly room where I was but they had the lights on in the kitchen so I could see them fairly clear like. Next thing Teesh starts singing 'Dear Old Skibbereen'.

Knew every word of it. Only thing he ever learned in his life maybe.
—That was beautiful, said Dinky, pure poetry boy.
—Island of saints and scholars, says Teesh.
—And patriots, says Dinky.
—True and brave.
—Patriots all. True and brave.

—OK.
—So then they kind of started hugging each other then like.
—What?
—Ahm . . . like . . . they were fairly drunk and were getting carried away with their stories about the War of Independence and all that stuff like.
—They were hugging each other?
—Well, not exactly hugging like. Teesh kind of grabbed Dinky by the two arms like and he was saying, 'Are you one of our own? Are you one of our own?' Dinky says back to him, all serious like, 'Yes. Yes. I'm one of our own. Yes I am.'
—So they were in a physical embrace, were they?

—Yes. Yes, they were.

—But not a hug.

—No.

—Could you show the court? Do you think you could show the jury if I got one of the guards to help you demonstrate.

—Ahm . . . like . . .

—Don't be embarrassed. Will you do it for the court?

—Ahm OK, yes. Like OK.

—OK.

I don't know if the judge was having a laugh to himself or what was he at but anyhow Snoozie grabbed the guard by the arms, and goes, 'Like this.' The judge asked then if Teesh did anything with his arms. Then Snoozie tells the baffled blushing guard to grab him back by the elbows. The guard looked up at the judge and the judge gave him the nod to do it. Snoozie and the guard stood there like two lovers in some old play or something, holding each other. The judge roars, 'Silence,' then cos a few in the crowd started giggling. 'That'll do,' says the judge and he thanked the guard and told him to go back to where he was standing up at the front of the court looking down at the crowd and the embarrassed face burning off the poor rookie.

—Then they started roaring stuff then like . . . like something like . . . 'Ireland for ever,' or something like that.

Actually Dinky said, 'We were here before the invaders. We'll be here after them. Our families have been in Ballyronan for generations. We saw them off before and by fuck we'll do it again.' 'You're a good man, Dinky,' Teesh goes, 'You're a good man.' Then he roars, 'For Ireland true and brave,' and bangs his fist off the table, and Dinky shouts back at him, 'For Ireland true and brave.' Anyhow, I'll let Snoozie's court transcript carry on.

—I was going to go in and tell them to shut up in case they woke the neighbours but they calmed down then. One of them went to the fridge and got another couple of cans. Ahm, I might just take a drink of water.

—Take your time. You're doing fine.

Not sure what was in the water but it helped Snoozie string a few sentences together. I think he might have taken a sec while he drank to ask his God for strength. And maybe to actually sound like English was a language he was fluent in. He sat back on his chair and looked up at the sky through the skylight of the court. Chest out. Strength. Got it from somewhere anyhow. He carried on.

—So like, then Dinky goes, 'Can I trust you?' 'With your life,' Teesh says, 'With your life.' Then he says that he has James nearly out of the picture.

—What do you think he meant by, 'Out of the picture'?

—Well, Teesh asked him if he meant he was going to kill him, and Dinky said no, just out of Ballyronan. Said he'd want nothing to do with Ballyronan after what he'd managed to do.

—After what who'd managed to do?

—Dinky himself.

—OK, carry on.

I'll take it from here cos I remember it better. Teesh says then,

—Sure he's done with the place now after the way Sinéad carried on behind his back, and more power to the girl for it.

Then Dinky says,

—Best day's work I ever done.

—What do you mean? says Teesh.

Next thing Dinky came in the door to make sure myself and Snoozie were asleep. He figured we were in a coma but we were awake as fuck. In the court when Snoozie started getting into it, he started half crying.

—That's when he started telling about Sinéad...

—Are you OK?

—Ahm... It's kinda hard to tell this...

—I know it is. Take your time. You're doing very well. If you want a break at any time, just say so. Would you like a fifteen-minute break now?

—No. I'm OK, thanks.

—Fine, have a drink of water and continue then, in your own time. And tell it chronologically if you can. Do you know what chronologically means?

—No.

—It means as time unfolds. Tell what you heard Dinky tell Teesh in the order that you heard it.

—OK, Your Lordship. Well, Dinky made Teesh swear that he wouldn't tell a soul about what he was about to tell him.

—OK.

—He said he met the Rascal one night in the toilets of Roundy's. It was a lock-in like, so there was hardly anyone else around, only a few of the lads.

—What's a lock-in?

—Like. After hours. When the door is closed. But some customers are still inside drinking. With the lights off like in case the guards would see from outside. After hours like.

—Yes, yes, I understand. So a lock-in is after hours.

—Yes, Your Lordship.

It's better if I tell it cos the judge was asking him to explain everything and it took for ever so it's pages and pages of court transcripts. So anyhow. That's what Dinky said. That he met the Rascal in the toilets of Roundy's one night late. I remember the same night cos I went into the jacks and Dinky and the Rascal were in there. But it was strange.

—How are the lads?

—How's the gamal?

—Grand. Dying for a piss.

—Doubt ya boy. Better out than in. I'll see ya Dinky. And don't go telling no one no one's business. She'd have better luck proving that the Earth was flat at this stage anyhow.

I pissed. Dinky stood staring at himself in the mirror for the full duration of my piss and longer. I zipped up and looked at him. Still staring at himself in the mirror he was.

—You all right Dinky boy? says I.

—Fuck off Gamal, says he.

Next thing he runs to the cubicle and starts puking up everything inside him that would come out. I stood listening to him vomiting as I looked at the mirror. The reflection I saw was me. The reflection Dinky saw was him. Now as I'm thinking I'm wondering is there a time. Is there a time when you have to look at yourself and decide what kind of a man you are. Or what kind of a man you're not. Is there a time when you just have to decide?

—That's a nice handy bit of pebble-dashing, I said.

—Fuck off Gamal.

Pebble-dashing is when a builder plasters a wall with a mixture of mortar and pebbles. He throws the mixture at the wall trowel by trowel until it's all covered. But it means vomiting too. Anyhow I did as Dinky asked and I fucked off and thought no more of it until I heard Dinky telling Teesh the whole story. The Rascal had told Dinky about a night a few months before after he'd played a gig in Roundy's. This is what he told Dinky. That he'd been drinking late after everyone had gone home. It was just the Rascal, Sinéad and Roundy's wife. Roundy himself wasn't around the same night.

They had a couple anyway and then Sinéad went out to clean the toilets. Eileen, according to Rascal was very drunk, drinking double brandies she was. So Dinky went on then about how the Rascal said that while Sinéad was cleaning the toilets himself and Eileen started talking about her. The Rascal was saying what a nice girl she was and all, and that the customers loved her and all. Then he said like that it became obvious to the Rascal that Roundy's wife hated Sinéad. The Rascal said that Roundy's wife started giving out about her. Saying 'tisn't as if butter wouldn't melt in her mouth and all. And how she thought she was a trollop with her long legs and the perfume on her and that she didn't trust her one bit with her husband.

Hardest thing in the world to be hearing this and having to pretend to be asleep. Couldn't even open my eyes cos Snoozie would see. I wanted to put my foot through the wall. I didn't though. I kept on breathing nice and steady same as a fella if he was asleep.

So Roundy's wife thought Roundy fancied Sinéad. And that Sinéad looked at him in a way that was a come on. Said that Sinéad wasn't the nice sweet girl everyone thought she was at all. That she was a trumped up cocky little trollop. Then the Rascal said that he kept filling her glass with the brandy and that Eileen was getting thick out with the drink in her.

—By thick do you mean stupid?
—No. I mean kind of angry like. Getting thick means getting angry.
—OK.

The judge hardly understood a word Snoozie said. That's why I'm telling it cos we'd be here all day. Plus Snoozie got a lot of stuff ass-ways. But some bits he told fine so I'll give those bits of the court transcript.

The Little Rascal said like that she was saying that Sinéad was a little bitch and a little whore and a tart and stuff and saying she wasn't as innocent as she looked. That as far as she was concerned she was trying to tempt Roundy. Trying to lure him like.

—Do you personally think there might have been any truth in that?
—Honestly? No. She was just good-looking. Very, very good-looking

but she wasn't a slut. Maybe Roundy and the wife were having their own troubles but it would have been nothing to do with Sinéad.

—OK. Carry on.

—Well anyhow. According to Dinky anyhow, the Rascal was given the impression that Eileen wouldn't mind a bit if the Rascal went and taught her a lesson.

—Just a moment now. What exactly did Dinky say that Rascal told him?

—He said that the Rascal half jokingly suggested that he should go out to the toilets and teach Sinéad a bit of manners. Or put a bit of manners on her, that's the phrase he used. According to Dinky anyway.

—Carry on.

—And then Eileen said that she'd hear nothing if he wanted to go out to her. The Rascal asked her again just to make sure and Eileen said if he went out and had his way with her that she wouldn't hear a thing. Like that she'd let him. She was very drunk and called her a tart and then the Rascal said to her that he'd go out to the toilets so to see if she needed a hand. Said he'd Eileen's full blessing.

—Ladies and gentlemen, this may be a little too unpleasant for some people to stomach so if anybody would like to leave the court, please feel free to do so now. Take a drink of water there for yourself, and take your time.

—Well. (*The witness became emotional here.*)

—It's OK, take your time. Would you like a break?

—Ahm. I think so. Just for a minute.

—Very well. We'll take a twenty-minute break now. Could the jury be back here at 2:50 please. We'll adjourn now so for twenty minutes for a bit of fresh air.

The judge nodded at his registrar to look after the witness and I suppose to make sure he would be where nobody could get at him. He didn't need to be worried because the guard who wasn't blushing any more went to the witness stand to take him in behind to some room in behind the court someplace. There was a sickened kind of silence all around the court. Some women had tears in their eyes. Nobody at all seemed to be talking.

Outside you had the sun shining on us all like some kind of a sick joke. People looked to the sky for some kind of an explanation for what they'd heard and what they knew they were about to hear in twenty minutes. Cigarettes were smoked, a few drags at a time, as if a triple hit of nicotine would help somehow. The savvy streetwise journalists were no different from everyone else. Standing in huddled silences staring at the ground. Thought people would look at each other but most people didn't have the stomach even for that. Like they associated people with how Sinéad suffered because it was at human hands isn't it? And like they were ashamed of themselves as well even. For having the selfsame human hands.

I seen two of the journalists though looking at someone. And Detective Crowley was looking at someone. And so was some motherly-looking woman of about fifty that I never seen before. They all looked at someone. And it was at the same someone they all looked. And that someone was me. I was sitting on the steps of the courthouse, the tips of my fingers met at my brow, my hands were covering my face. Could see enough though, in the weird slits of the world in between my fingers. Net curtains. Can see out but you can't see in. My father and my mother sat at either side of me and my mother rubbed my back. I know it was my mother because my father would never do that.

I've all the lights off here. Just a candle for Sinéad and the laptop screen and me against the darkness. And the odd bluebottle that comes for a read. Doesn't last long with me around. Dunno what purpose bluebottles serve but they give some purpose to newspapers anyhow isn't it? Finding it fierce slow work, this at the moment. I'd do anything else bar read what I have to read now. And this is probably my fifth time trying to get this part of the story over and done with. Sends me down it does. Way down. Dubh. The shakes first usually. Tears then. Vomiting. Then bed. Two weeks the last time. In bed like a baby. Dr Quinn just puts me on glorified sleeping tablets. Says it's important that the brain takes it easy, in order to recover. Like you have to keep the weight off a broken leg. Says I must keep the weight off my brain. And not to write the heavy stuff until I'm ready cos it would weigh me down too much and the brain mightn't be ready to be dealing with it yet.

The court looked the same as before. But it felt heavier and the air was thick and it made it hard to breathe.

—So whenever you're ready so.

—Well. This is how Dinky put it anyhow. The Rascal went out to Sinéad. Sinéad screamed and he caught her by the hair and banged her head off the wall. Then the Rascal said she was putty in his hands after that. Dinky said the Rascal said that if they're willing it takes the fun out of it.

—Excuse me. Had Teesh said anything at all during all this?

—No. He was dead quiet, far as I remember. Dead quiet. I could just see him nodding the whole time through the glass.

—I see. Carry on.

—Teesh was silent for a good while. Dinky asking him what he thought of it all, and giggling.

High-pitched giggle he has, and fast when he's excited like a fucking chipmunk.

—See, they'd both seen that James and Sinéad were pretty much finished. They'd tried to make a go of it after he took her back but the lads were kind of mocking him for it that night like, trying to kind of make an eejit of him with smart comments and stuff. But then in came the Rascal with an Afghan scarf around his neck and James went over to him and asked him where he got it and he said Sinéad left it in his car the other night. James tried to hit him but the lads were already holding him back. Then the Rascal started taunting and jeering at James and laughing at him. James just walked straight out of the pub with Sinéad running out after him crying.

So anyhow Teesh speaks then and he says that she must have been half up for it anyhow, cos she went back for more, didn't she? Then Dinky said she did not. That 'twas he took the scarf from behind the bar one night when Sinéad wasn't looking and gave it to the Rascal. He said the Rascal despised James and the Kents and wanted to fuck with his head a bit, so he was well up for it when Dinky showed him the scarf. It was all part of the plan. Teesh was stunned. Just kept saying to Dinky, 'Christ, you're some operator. You're some operator.' Then he went, 'Put it there boy,' and Teesh shook his hands. Dinky like, he explained like . . . said he was friends with James until about a couple of years ago when he started to see through him. This is what Dinky says to Teesh like. That he started to see that James thought he was above him and looked down on him and the rest of the locals. That he didn't really give a shit about anyone but himself and that Sinéad was lucky to be finished with him that he'd only break her heart. Was saying that they didn't have any loyalty. That that was the difference between them and us.

—What did he mean by 'them'?

—Ahm. The Kents, I suppose. But he said they had no loyalty because it wasn't in their blood. They were settlers and would take what they could from you and give nothing back. He said Sinéad had a lucky escape. She'd be a lot better off with her own and he said that she'd come to see that in time. Teesh agreed. Said, 'Of course she would.' And that her parents would only be happy that she be finished with him and be back with her own type.

So that's how the world got to know about what happened to poor Sinéad. In the court. Course I knew all that already cos I'd heard everything that Snoozie heard in the house that night. Just in case you're confused. It was probably more than a few months after the actual rape happened. And Sinéad and James were back together until this night. Until the thing with the Afghan scarf. And lying on the couch in Snoozie's house that night I was never so mad and sad. I was thinking about the Rascal. Tomato. Squish. Thinking of the torment of Sinéad made it hard to breath. Thinking of her wronged, pulling on her clothes and running out on to the dark, deserted village streets. Wronged. Going home. Wronged. Alone. Wronged. Snoozie went away up to his room to sleep.

Teesh and Dinky had gone up already. I slipped out the front door. I walked and ran and walked and ran again. I'd tell James and he'd comfort her and say sorry for doubting her and he'd take her away to Dublin to start a new life. Like a new song.

Hail, Holy Queen,
Mother of mercy,
Hail our life, our sweetness and our hope.
To thee do we cry, poor banished children of Eve,
To thee do we send up our sighs,
Mourning and weeping in this valley of tears.

Turn, then, most gracious advocate,
Thine eyes of mercy toward us.
And in this our exile show unto us,
The Blessed fruit of thy womb Jesus.

O clement, O loving, O sweet virgin Mary,
Pray for us, O holy Mother of God,
That we may be made worthy of the promises of Christ.

Sinéad had prayer I think. I hope to God she did anyhow.

The Walk Back
The walk back to Ballyronan was a run mostly. And I was thinking. That the past being a stubborn unmovable fat fucking mountain, this present was the best of all possible worlds. And I was going making it happen. A new present. This was good. I

knew that. I knew the truth. Against all the odds the gamal who the whole wide stupid world thought was a fool would save Sinéad and James. Nothing could stop them now. I knew that.

I was thinking about when they'd be accepting some big award. I used to think about that now and again. Sinéad spoke into the microphone and the award in her hand.

—We'd just really like to thank one person. One person who stuck with us from the beginning. Who made us believe. This is for you Charlie.

That's what was going to happen now. As soon as I get to James and tell him what I heard. He'd be straight over to Sinéad. And the music would begin again. All the shit I'd ever done in my life meant nothing now. Every idiot thing I ever did somehow led to this moment. This. This was my hour. I was crying with joy to be the bearer of such terrible news but brilliant news too. Revelation. James would take her back. It would go back to being like it was supposed to be. I walked. I ran. I walked. I ran again when my lungs would let me again. I floated. I flew. My whole life. My whole stupid joke of a life. Like I'd real value now isn't it? Sinéad and James I was going to save. All the goodness they'd shown me. All the love. Repaid now a million times over. I dreamed of what James' face would be like when I told him the truth. This I knew, he wouldn't hang around. He'd rob his father's car and race to Sinéad's house to take her back and to comfort her for the terrible wrong done to her. And he'd apologise to her for doubting her. It was fucking brilliant, I'll never forget the feeling.

The walk home. And I thinking about their lives. And my life.

Dunronan was on the left, across the other side of the river. I was thinking of their song and how when it's a famous song you'd have tourists coming to see Dunronan.

—*I loved you.*
—*I loved you too.*

Half the castle is gone now, like it was bombed by the Nazis but the Nazis never bothered with us. Or maybe they were just too afraid of us. Just time and the weather was what pulled the eastern wall of it down. But the western half of it still looks sturdy enough for another hundred or two hundred or three hundred years.

I could have gone through fields and the woods but I went on the road cos if anyone passed that knew me they'd give me lift. But no one did pass.

But I knew I was free then. I knew Sinéad would go to Dublin now. I knew she'd find a way. And I knew I'd go too. I'd get a job on the building sites and start anew. And I could be their stage manager like they promised. Like they wanted. They'd have missed having me around if I stayed home. I knew that. I cried and I laughed and I cried and I ran and I jogged and I walked and I ran again. Four miles back to Ballyronan. A winding eejit of a road. Obeying the daft youngster meanderings of the river all the way. By its side all the way. Loyal and father-like. There was tears of pain for what happened to Sinéad. Tears of joy for the joy James would bring her when he took her back after I told him all what I'd heard Dinky say last night. I knew their lives would have been shit if I'd never heard Dinky's dark words. Lost loves for ever. That they met me was good so. May as well have been dead than go on apart isn't it? I was a hero then. I knew that. A life saver. A double life saver. And just maybe my own as well would make it three. Good going.

The last time I seen an otter was the first time I seen one. Was on that walk home. Couple of hundred yards after Dunronan. Seen the head moving up river and then over to the bank and scurried up the bank on the far side. Like a rat. Only with a lot more distance between its head and its ass. Wish I could get a few pages out of describing it but I've absolutely nothing else to say about that otter. Was greyish brownish I think. And wet.

Anyhow on I went. It was a nice morning. That just means it wasn't raining. That's nice in Ireland.

Went out the back door there for a smoke just now. Three big fat slugs around a soggy little piece of green bean that somehow found its way out after dinner. Stuck to someone's shoe I suppose. The father's a sloppy fucker and he eating. We've a fairly big garden. But these three slugs found their way up out of the grass and travelled a few metres on the concrete over to near where the car is to have a suck off this soggy little piece of green bean. How they found it I do not know. Fat little pieces of shit. Still could find a soggy little piece of green bean in a quarter of an acre a lot better than I could have. We mightn't rate it as a useful talent but still. If you ever lose a soggy little piece of green bean find a slug first. And follow it. Life and death to them I suppose. Other stuff is life and death to us isn't it?

Fate is a funny blah. Little did the father know that he made a great night for three slugs cos he couldn't keep his food on the table, let alone on his plate. You'd wonder what insignificant twists of fate in the universe make or break the lives and living times of all of us. Did these paragraphs that you're reading now about the three slugs and the soggy little piece of green bean make someone miss a bus to take them to a place where they would have met the love of their life? Or did someone read it while crossing the road wondering what in the name of God I was rambling on about only to get marinated on to the front of a truck? Is there stuff that's not even imaginable to us that dictates our fates? Unimaginable things same as these sentences are unimaginable to the three slugs. What can we imagine? What can't we?

Anyhow. On I walked. I was thinking about how much they deserved this new start. This new horizon. No limit isn't it?

Horizon

N. 1. place where earth meets sky; the line in the furthest distance where the land or sea seems to meet the sky 2 *astron.*; circle on apparent sphere of sky; a circle formed on the celestial sphere by a plane tangent to a point on the earth's blah.

Horizons

Npl. range of experience; the range or limits of sb's interests, knowledge, or experience [14thC. Via Old French *orizon(te)* from, ultimately, Greek *horizon (kuklos)*, literally meaning 'limiting (circle)', present participle of *horizein* 'to limit', from *horos* 'limit'.]

Listen to this. On the telly there a young lioness killed a monkey and brought it up on a tree to where the hyenas couldn't get at it.

Next thing a tiny baby monkey comes out from under the dead monkey. Was clinging to its mammy the whole time even when its mammy was being killed and dragged up the tree by the lioness. Anyhow this was the first big kill for the lioness cos it was only young and the only thing it killed before this was squirrels. So instead of eating the baby monkey doesn't it play with it for about half an hour. Next thing it ate another little bit of its mother and went to sleep for itself. The baby monkey died of cold without its mammy. When I saw that it made me think of a part of my story so in I came to write it down and now I can't remember why it made me think of part of my story. Damn. Maybe something to do with liking people or something. Dunno. Yeah. Maybe that's it. Threat isn't it? I wonder what has threat to do with liking somebody. Maybe that was it but I'm not sure. Or what has food got to do with being nice. Eating someone isn't being very nice to them. Another programme fella was talking to an Aboriginal woman who was telling him how her ancestors survived on the miserablest bit of land you ever seen. Scorched it was. Long ago a girl got shipwrecked and the tribe looked after her cos she looked like the chief's daughter who had drowned three months earlier. Otherwise they'd have eaten her like they did with all the others. Your man asked the woman how they could have eaten them and she just said it was their culture like it was just some fucking dance she was talking about. Your man just nodded. Yeah. As if hunger didn't come into it. That definitely has nothing to do with my story. Sorry.

So anyhow I'm walking. Thinking I was. Not about the cannibals or the baby monkey. That was just now. I was thinking about signs. Signs I might have seen. I might have seen signs. Flags. Or something less even. I've noticed less. The smallest things. Indicators. That my stupid hungry brain made me forget about. The look someone had on and they forgetting themselves or the ugly clenching of their teeth and furrowed brows and the angry or ugly things they might have said or nice things they might have said that had ugly motives and ugliness is only ugliness cos it's what someone who kills you would look like. Said nothing though all that time. But I was going to talk now. I was going to talk now. And I started thinking about all the good people that they could be friends with now that they knew that gang weren't really their friends. People you don't know about cos they weren't part of the story up to now. But there was millions of them in Ballyronan. Fierce decent nice people. And people that liked Sinéad and James. Good people. They were just after getting in with the wrong gang isn't it?

Cos Ballyronan is mostly nice people. Like Sheila Hayes who rescues animals from the pound and gives them a nice home. Nice for animals. Not people. Too many animals. Peter Craig and his wife are fairly nice too. I'd say they'd definitely never kill anyone on purpose or want harm to come to anyone even. Down a bit on the same road you have the O'Briens. They're farmers. One of the sons walks with a limp cos his foot got caught in a combine harvester when he tried to kick a piece of wood that was jammed in it. But the O'Briens are fierce nice too.

The O'Connors, the Crossroads live near them. At the cross. They're nice too even though they never admitted that they won four million in the Lotto even though everyone knew it was them cos they hired a Securicor van to bring the money back from Dublin. Patricia Reardon seen Bill O'Connor, the father, get out the van in Bishopstown and a neighbour of Alice Cronin's sister in Midleton is a security guard and he knew the driver of the van that went to Dublin for the money and she told my mother that he didn't say it wasn't the O'Connors of Ballyronan when he was asked. Then the O'Connors disappeared for two weeks to Donegal and came back with a tan and no one ever got a tan in Donegal in the history of the sun. But they're nice in fairness. I'd be nice too if I'd four million but they were even nice before all the money.

This is the rest of what happened so. When I arrived up the top of the lane to the castle it wasn't much different from the way it is now except it's maybe gone a bit shabby now. No sign of life though, which is fair enough for six o'clock in the morning but there was no big old Volvo out the front either, and it was there the night before and we going out. And the owner of it was in bed and we leaving. James' father was an early to bed early to rise kind of fella. His mother would paint until late. I wondered where James' father was gone at this ungodly hour cos the garage wasn't open until half seven. I know cos I worked there sometimes washing cars long ago. Pound a car. Next thing anyhow is I see the lights on around the house like it's evening time.

I threw a few pebbles at his window. Nothing. I looked in the wobbly glass by the front door to see if there was anyone up. I leaned on the big heavy front door and it moved. Fucking thing was open. I went in quiet and up to James' room. The door was closed so I knew he was in there in a drunken sleep. All rooms with nobody in them in that house had the door open usually. I went in to him quietly but he wasn't there at all. I checked the library whose door was open like you'd expect in that house. Empty. My heart started getting kind of jumpy then. I remember being annoyed with myself for worrying about nothing. I went down to the kitchen, then out back to see if his father was out in the garden or foosthering in the greenhouse. No. Went up then to James' parents' room and I decided there was no use in being a gamal if you're not ignorant so I knocks on the door.

—Hello.

I did it again. Two more times. Nothing. I opened the door and went into a room that I wasn't in since the three of us were kids. That time it was so Sinéad could sit at the dresser with the big mirrors and we could be her manservants.

—Yes, m'lady.

His parents never knew I was in there that time and they never found out I was in there this time either cos there was nobody in there. I roared for some sign of life and nothing first, but then I heard someone answer or call out. At least I thought I did. But I was wrong. False alarm. Only a siren or something. A fucking siren? I got cold and goosepimply and weak and I listened hard. Nothing. A bird probably. My mind was at me now. Got angry with myself and I ran and ran and ran. I wanted to have Sinéad and James in front of me now more than I wanted anything ever. He was well frazzled last night after seeing the Afghan scarf on the Little Rascal. Things ended bad between them. Sinéad and James. Last night.

Down the stairs, down the lane, down the road. I ran and I ran and I ran. Fuck nature and fuck the otter and fuck the weather. I ran and I ran and I ran. A car came towards me and slowed down to look at me and drove on. I didn't know them. A couple. I got to the bridge at Ballyronan and slowed down to catch my breath. There were people at the far side of the bridge. Youngsters, they were. Bunch of sixteen-year-olds and they were crying. I asked them what happened.

—Sinéad Halloran. She's drownded.

No. No no no no no. No no no no no no. I was on my knees. No no no no no. All I could hear was the girls and the young lads crying. Then a car came. No no no no no. Someone helped me to my feet. No. Detective Crowley.

—Stop it. She's not dead. She's alive.

—What?

—They had her covered with a blanket, we seen it, says one of the girls.

—That was in case of hypothermia. To warm her. She's alive. The fisherman saved her.

I looked up. Detective Crowley was looking straight at me. He had me by the shoulders. With his eyes and a nod of his head and a smile he said he's sure of what he's saying and what he's saying is true and he said it again. The world had threatened to become hell so back to normal was heaven. All the heaven I'd ever want. Sinéad not being dead.

More of Sinéad's Psychiatrist's Evidence

—And then you saw her again about seven weeks later. Could you tell us about this please?

—Yes. It was a Sunday morning and I'd been called in to the hospital. Sinéad had arrived in through Accident and Emergency having attempted to drown herself in the Bannow river in Ballyronan.

—On this occasion she was kept in, is that right?

—Yes. She remained with us for a period of nine months.

—I see. Could you describe her condition.

—Do you mean when I saw her first on that Sunday?

—Yes.

—Well, she was in shock. I mean physically in shock and she had mild hypothermia. Her hair was wet and she was pale. Once her physical condition had been taken care of, it became quite clear that she was suffering from severe depression.

—Could you elaborate please and maybe explain her symptoms to the jury?

—Certainly. She had many classic features of severe depression, such as loss of energy, loss of interest in pretty much anything or anyone. Psychomotor retardation was another feature of her illness. This is when someone appears to be functioning in slow motion, so to speak. Her speech, her thoughts, her movements even her facial expressions had a lifeless and slowed-down quality to them.

—Could this have been caused by medication?

—No, she was on no medication at this point.

—I see. Any other symptoms?

—She wasn't able to sleep without medication. She had no interest in food, but was . . . obliging in eating the bare minimum when the nurses asked her to.

—You were her consultant at this time. How did you find her? Did she open up to you?

—Well. I wouldn't go that far but she certainly knew I was there to help and once she began to trust me I could tell she wanted to be helped. She felt extremely worthless. She blamed herself for the demise of her relationship with her boyfriend. She saw no future. She believed he wouldn't ever take her back at this point in time. She was devastated by this and was genuinely suicidal. She didn't speak at all and when she did it was to know when James was coming to see her.

—You know Sinéad don't you? Detective Crowley goes then.
I nodded.
—And you know James don't you?
—Yeah.
—Where is he?
—What?
—Where is he? Where is James?
—I don't know. He's not? He didn't?
I was afraid he went in the river too.
—No. He was here the girls said.
He turned to the girls.
—Where did James go?
—He ran off that way?
She pointed back east towards the village.
—Where was he going?
—Dunno.
—Claire told him Sinéad was dead.
—Shut up. You said it too. Ye all thought the same.
—Jesus. When did he run off? How long ago? How long ago was this?

—I dunno.

—Ten minutes?

—Yeah. I suppose.

—More I'd say, one of the other girls said. Maybe twenty.

—And he ran up towards the village?

—Yeah.

—Did he say anything else?

—No.

—Nothing.

—No, he said, 'No.' And then just ran.

—Right.

Detective Crowley got on the car radio then and asked some guard to send another guard to the hospital to keep an eye out for James. He told whoever was there that James' parents went to the hospital but James wasn't with them. That they thought he'd be there but he's not. He said for some other guard to wait with his parents at the hospital and for any other available cars to come to the station at Ballyronan. And to call in all available off duties to do likewise. He had to say that a second time cos whoever he was talking to asked him if he was sure. Then he turned to me.

—Any idea where he might go?

I shrugged my shoulders.

—I haven't an absolute clue, Detective Crowley said. Do you think you might have some idea?

—Maybe. Maybe down by the river behind the football pitch.

—Hop in, he said.

He sped off down to the gates of the pitch. He was on the radio again listing roads that needed to be searched. Bohernavar. Gortnascreena. Skewna Cross. Ballygallowen. Rathdowny. Rathnashkee. Coolnagapil. Chapel Lane. Pontoon. Four Crosses road. He gave instruction for some fella called Fitzhenry to co-ordinate the initial search.

—Do you think he'd do anything stupid if he thought she was dead Charlie?

I didn't answer cos I couldn't.

—Do you think James could do harm to himself?

I still couldn't answer.

—Run off down to wherever you think he could go, I'll follow you down.

I ran down through the second pitch to the river bank leaving him on the car radio giving instructions.

I roared the word James in a way I never ever done before. Sounded like a stranger already. I looked at the water, same as something that the look of would make you sick. I ran down along the bank. Right back to the bridge. I could see people still at the bridge looking down at me shouting. I turned and ran back through the pitch to Detective Crowley. He stopped when he seen me running back and turned around and went back to the car. He'd the passenger door open for me and the engine running. I jumped in and he shouted, 'Where else?'

—The castle.

—Has he a key?

—It's open.

—Are you sure.

—Yeah.

He was over the bridge already by the time I said, 'Yeah.' He skidded up in front of the house.

—Run to his room. Run, he shouted.

Three stairs at a time I leaped and shouted the word James again. Bedroom empty. Library empty. Bathroom empty. I tried the whole of upstairs while Detective Crowley shouted for James and searched downstairs. No go. We tried the greenhouse and the outhouse and the garden and the woods around the castle but no. We went back to the station then and Detective Crowley told me to come in. Another garda of about the same age as Detective Crowley spoke to him while Detective Crowley was dialling some phone number.

—Jesus Christ Tony are you sure this is necessary?

—No.

—You'll look like some fool if . . .

—Worth the risk. Hello . . . no sign of him no? Nothing no. OK, bye. Bollicks. Get Gretta on the phone for me there John please. Are you OK, he asked me.

—Yeah.

—And give him a cup of tea John. And me.

—He's here now Gretta, he wants a word.

—How are we doing? Yeah . . . yeah . . . how many units in all? . . . Not so bad. OK, is young Fitzhenry co-ordinating the road search? OK. I'll ring him now. Thanks Gretta, bye.

He looked at me then.

—Can you think of anywhere else Charlie?

—No.

—We'll get a cup of tea into you now, you look pale. An awful business surely . . .

—Unless Pontoon but . . . I dunno.

He walked straight for the door.

—Come on, worth a look, come on. Hold the teas John we'll have one look down by Pontoon Castle.

He could move fast for such a whale. He asked me why Pontoon Castle in the car and I told him about the walk long ago and some of the other walks since. He radioed back to the fella in the station and told him to make sure someone was keeping an eye on P.J. Halloran's house in case he'd show up there. Detective Crowley skidded the car on the road right beside Pontoon Castle. We got out and looked in the castle ruin first, the two of us calling the whole time for James. We walked down along the path. Detective Crowley levered himself back to his feet as fast as he'd fallen on his ass. His trousers were destroyed. He trotted on down the path through the woods same as we did long ago, James and me and Dinky running from the Indians with our bows and arrows or our guns. We came to the wooden bridge over the waterfall. You go ahead, he said. I thought he was afraid it wouldn't take his weight but he wanted to look under it. We came to the water's edge. The river appeared through the darkness then but we knew it was there. What we wanted was James to appear through the darkness. We looked out and shouted for him and listened and I shouted again but Detective Crowley was after turning and was panting his way back up towards the footbridge doing his best to keep air in his heaving lungs. He asked quietly more to himself,

—Where in God's name are you gone to James?

I had this feeling though. I can't really describe it. I had this feeling that things were OK. I was certain that James would be by

Sinéad's bedside in the hospital soon. The image I had was so real that it calmed me no end. He was holding her hand in his telling her everything was OK. Everything was OK now. I just knew it. And sometimes you just know isn't it?

When we got back to the car he radioed John again.

—Anything John?

—No. No luck there?

—No.

—All units are on the road. Fitzhenry is checking Sinéad's house every ten minutes himself.

—OK, we'll be back there now in a few minutes.

Next thing Gretta came through on the radio.

—All units to the Catholic churchyard in Ballyronan. All units to the Catholic churchyard in Ballyronan.

—Bollicks, said Detective Crowley. Gretta? Gretta? Nine one one two Gretta? Bollicks. No bloody reception here. This'll work.

He grabbed the big lump of a car phone in his hand just as it started to ring. He answered.

—Crowley. Talk to me . . . Oh Jesus . . . Christ . . . Cut him down . . . Yeah . . . Cordon it off . . . no the whole road, yeah . . . I'll be there in five minutes. OK.

He looked at me for a second, then looked back to the road that he was speeding through same as a rally car.

—I'm sorry Charlie. I'm so sorry . . . James is dead.

He grabbed me by the arm and squeezed it for about two seconds, same as a blind man would.

—I'm going to leave you at the station with John. OK?

He made quick work of leaving me there. He called back to John before leaving,

—Make sure to look after him, check him for shock.

—I will.

John did his best to speak to me and looked at my face like it was a puzzle.

—I'll get you some tea now with lots of sugar.

He went out the back to make it and I went out the front. I ran up the old back road and hopped the wall by the new graveyard to come into the church grounds from the back through the priest's house's garden. I ran down the priest's lane and hopped the wall behind the church to save me running all the way round. I came out the side of the back door of the church and looked down at the car park but there was no people, just a few police cars and an ordinary blue car. Another police car sped in the gate and parked. Then I saw them below at the copper beech tree. Down in the grass. Ten souls and a body.

Next thing I see James' father coming walking in the pedestrian entrance with Detective Crowley. Next thing he starts running to where his son lay on the grass. He knelt beside him and he picked him up like he weighed no weight at all. He hugged him, held his face with his hands and spoke some, then hugged him again. Like he was trying to love the life back into him. He struggled to his feet, stumbling around the place trying to get James' limp body to stand with him. They fell again. James' torso held aloft by his father who was now on his knees. The pull of the earth was too strong. James' body understood this. His father's mind did not. His father took him by the arms now and shook him. If James was alive he'd be sore from it. The next logical step seemed like this father was going to start hitting his dead son.

—No. Jesus Christ James no. What did you do, my darling boy, what did you do my darling young boy? Jesus Christ almighty no.

Next thing another squad car raced down through the church-yard like a learner driver out of control. But it came to a smart sweet halt. Out of it came Father Scully like I never seen him before. Black pants. Black shirt. Bright blue slippers. The hair on his head was wild. I'd never have believed he had so much hair cos it was always greased to the scalp like a grey swimming cap. The gardaí were still like statues. James' father was still having war with the body of his son. The priest walked through the shell-shocked gardaí. This was his domain. This churchyard. This death. He grabbed James' father from behind by the shoulders and broke up the fight. He spoke calm. Slow and quiet. Like he knew what he was at. Like he'd done this before. Sure.

—Let him go. Let him go. Let him go Paul. Let him go. Let go. That's it. Let go. Let go.

His father let him go and watched, unbelieving yet, his son's dead body find its way to rest again on the grass with the help of two gardaí. Father Scully spoke some words to James' father that no one else could hear. James' father nodded slowly. Father Scully looked at Detective Crowley and he said,

—Take hold of Paul.

Detective Crowley bent down to put his arms around James' father but then James' father rose to his feet. James' father watched Father Scully take a small gold roundy case from his trouser pocket and open it. He watched him kneel on the grass beside his son and he watched him dip his thumb in the oil and make the sign of the cross on his son's forehead. He watched the face of his dead son while Father Scully prayed over him. He looked up at the sky and his eyes were drawn north-east where what was left of the cut rope dangled from the copper beech, the wind gave it precious life. A timeless pendulum. Mindless. Between worlds.

Lord have mercy. Christ have mercy.
Our father, Who art in Heaven
Deliver us from all evil.

O Lord, hear my prayer,
And let my cry come to Thee,
Let us pray. To Thee, Lord, we commend the soul of your servant,
James, that being dead to this world he may live to Thee: and whatever
sins he has committed in this life through human frailty, do Thou in
Thy most merciful goodness forgive. Through Christ our Lord. Eternal
rest grant unto him O Lord: and let perpetual light shine upon him.
Amen.

Fuck you anyhow James.

Course the world is getting up now. Tablets kicking in. Took one and a half of the white ones cos I want to be knocked out. They're the sleeping tablets. Usually only a half one I take. Thank fuck for them. Hard to cry when you're asleep. And you don't feel much. I'll carry on with the rest tomorrow. Cos I have to.

So there I am in the churchyard seeing all this. Next thing I see

Detective Crowley looking at me. I realised all of a sudden that I was up the top of the churchyard no more. I was down with the rest of them near the copper beech. I've no memory of walking down to them but I must have cos that's where I was now. Father Scully looked at James' father and asked him,

—Where's Carol?

—With . . . she's with Jim Higgins and Ber.

That was Old Master Higgins to you. Ber was his wife. James' father asked Father Scully then would he come with him. Father Scully looked at Detective Crowley. Detective Crowley said he'd bring them over there. He got another garda to look after me. Said,

—Bring him back to the station first. Give him a cup of tea and find out if he knows what exactly happened between James and Sinéad last night. If he doesn't want to talk don't push him. I'll bring him home myself after. I'll explain things to his dad.

The garda didn't say anything, just pointed me to the car beside Detective Crowley's. Next thing Dr Reid pulls in and a fucking hearse behind her like she was the worst fucking doctor ever. Detective Crowley walked with her to the body. She knelt down for a few seconds and looked at her watch and then got up and walked over to James' father and held his two hands and said something. Then the two undertakers went over. They were all talking then for a minute. The three young gardaí stood around James' body wondering what to do with their eyes and their hands. They scratched their chins or the back of their heads. They rubbed their necks, their cheeks, their foreheads. They folded their arms. They put their hands in their pockets. They looked at the doctor, they looked at the undertakers, they looked at James' father, they looked at Detective Crowley, at Father Scully, at the tree, at the church steeple, up the road, down the road and at James from head to toe all in no order known to me.

I heard Detective Crowley getting radioed then. It was John back at the station.

—I've lost him Tony.

—I know. He's here.

—Is he? Is he OK?

—He's fine. Peadar will bring him back now. Just make sure he's OK. He's seen everything here so he'll be shook.

—OK. Sorry about that. Went to make the tea and he disappeared on me.

—That's OK. See you later.

When Detective Crowley came back to the station he asked me what happened the night before and I told him. I told him I didn't know what it was about but they had a falling out. Now I only wanted to hear how Sinéad was. I asked him and he said,

—The news is good. Little bit of hypothermia is all.

—Cry for help, Garda John said, I suppose she wanted James to feel that she couldn't live without him.

Detective Crowley gave him a look to shut him up and carried on,

—Just hypothermia.

—Does she know about James? Garda John asked.

—No. She does not. And she won't a while I'd say. That was awful, what you saw. Are you all right?

I couldn't speak.

—Try and drink some of that tea. I'm going to get a cup myself OK?

He went in the back to get himself a cup. I could hear himself and Garda John talking.

—They'll have a job keeping the news from her.

—They'll just have to keep people away.

—And the paper.

—And the paper.

—And the radio.

—There'll be nothing on the radio.

—NWT call out the deaths and the funeral arrangements every morning.

—Not this one they won't, I've taken care of it. The doctors know the story. She's in the psychiatric ward. Nobody's let in or out of there unless they're authorised.

—When, do you think? Garda John asked.

—When what?

—When do you think they'll tell her?

—I've no idea John. In a couple of days maybe. Whatever they think is best for her.

—Jesus.

—Yeah. An awful business surely.

—But the funeral.

—What about it?

—Will she not . . .

—No. She won't be at it.

—Jesus.

Not sure what happened to me then but I kind of forgot how to breathe. I started kind of shaking. Next thing I remember is Detective Crowley trying to make me breathe in and out of a paper bag but I pushed him away. He just kept saying the word, 'Easy,' with his arm on my shoulder. Next thing I was in his car and he was pulling into my own house and the doctor was there waiting for me. I could hear Detective Crowley telling my father the story and then I fell asleep cos the doctor gave me tablets to knock me out.

High upon highlands
And low upon tae
Bonnie James Campbell
Rode out on a day
He saddled, he bridled, so gallant rode he,
Home came his good horse
But never came he
Home came his good horse
But never came he
Empty the saddle
All bloody to see
Home came his good horse
But never came he

James' Funeral

My mother came in the room and said it was time. She asked me had I any better shoes than the ones I had on. I said no. We were early enough to get a seat in the chapel. People called the Protestant church the chapel. We called our own church the church. I left the mother and father and went off on my lonesome. Outside all the lads had the blue and green armbands on. That's the colour of the football jerseys. Teesh, Dinky, Snoozie and Gregory were chief pall-bearers along with two of James' uncles. They carried him through the village to the cross where six more of his teammates took him up the hill. Then another six and then the chief pallbearers took over again at the gates of the Protestant cemetery. James' mother and father walked behind the coffin, followed by relations, followed by the entire village of Ballyronan. Everyone was reminded of Sinéad's not thereness by Sonny Shields' thereness. He was the local wedding video man and he was hired by James' father to record the funeral for Sinéad. Grotesque it was isn't it?

For the burial bit after I went up on top of the vicar's roof. I felt a bit closer to James. The thought of he having no spirit and just being dead meat in the coffin and no soul or nothing and that was the end of James for ever flashed in and out of my mind like a flying visit from the devil or a glimpse of hell. Just mean isn't it?

I watched the hundreds shaking hands with James' father and mother and sometimes his cousins and aunts and uncles and a lot of people shook hands with Dinky too cos they knew he was a great friend of James. Teesh was the main man organising the troops, with Dinky and Snoozie following him around the place, all grown-up and serious they were, a credit to the parish. And at the Mass Teesh did a Prayer of the Faithful and Dinky did one of the readings. This is Dinky's reading.

—A reading from Ecclesiastes chapter three. There is an appointed time for everything, and a time for every affair under the heavens. A time to be born. A time to die. A time to plant. A time to uproot the plant. A time to kill and a time to heal. A time to tear down and a time to build. A time to weep and a time to laugh. A time to mourn and a time to dance. A time to scatter stones and a time to gather them. A time to embrace and a time to be far from embraces. A time to seek and a time to lose. A time to keep and a time to cast away. A time to rend and a time to sew. A time to be silent and a time to speak. A time to love and a time to hate. A time of war and a time of peace. What advantage has the worker from his toil? I have considered the task which God has appointed for men to be busied about blah blah.

Can't type any more of it. Thought it might make me seem clever to include that reading but I think I'm only making the Bible look thick instead.

Anyhow if I didn't hate Dinky I'd have been very proud of him up there in the altar saying them words to them all. And himself and Teesh afterwards. All handshakes and manly organisation. Postponing their woeful grief for the common good. Travesty of devastation. Show must go on. Show.

Stoic

N. 1. person who is impassive, who appears unaffected by emotions, especially person admired for showing patience and endurance in the face of adversity 2. ancient philosopher; a member of an ancient Greek school of philosophy that asserted that happiness can only be achieved by accepting life's ups and downs as the products of unalterable destiny. It was founded around 308 BC by Zeno [14thC. From Latin *Stoicus*, from, ultimately, Greek *stoa* 'porch', referring to the Painted Porch in Athens, where Zeno taught.]

He was a fairly stoic man. James' father was. And he was a man of action. Even though his very worst nightmare had become a real thing in his life. Had become his life. He was making sure everything went smoothly. Ringing all the people who needed to be told. Showing his wife the catalogue of coffins to pick one out for their son. Talking to the choir people about what music was planned. Getting hold of the uilleann piper for beside the grave. Getting Dr Reid up to take a look at his wife and his sister who weren't coping so good. Dealing with the make-up artist at the funeral home. Making sure the marks would be covered properly before his wife would see her son. Handing in the clothes for them to put on him. Talking to the vicar. Dealing with the football club who were organising a guard of honour. Dealing with the principal of St. Brendan's about the school's own guard of honour and about the prayers and offerings they'd organised for the ceremony. Organising three teams of pallbearers to take James from the church up to the Protestant cemetery. Passing fivers to the altar boys for a job well done. Shaking hands. Thanking people.

Being a rock for his wife and everyone else who was floored by what was after happening. He spoke of his dead son on the altar that day and then he said some poem called 'Little Boy in the Morning' and only stopped once for a sec. His voice went high pitched for a sec and he stopped and swallowed. Then he coughed and carried on. His voice all deep and strong.

He will not come, and still I wait.
He whistles at another gate
Where angels listen. Ah I know

He will not come, yet if I go
How shall I know he did not pass
Barefooted in the flowery grass?
The moon leans on one silver horn
Above the silhouettes of morn,
And from their nest-sills finches whistle
Or stooping pluck the downy thistle.
How is the morn so gay and fair
Without his whistling in its air?
The world is calling, I must go.
How shall I know he did not pass
Barefooted in the shining grass?

Then he said he would be delighted if all would join him and his wife for some tea in their house after the funeral. That's the custom around these parts. I'd say pretty much everybody did go back to the castle.

He was standing at the window in the upstairs library when I seen this. He was staring out and the sun was going down on the village of Ballyronan. The river ran regardless as ever, parallel to the main street which was quietly hiding in the valley. Mute and cowering. Rathkeen Wood on the south side of the village. Parish farms and the new housing estates on the north. The football pitch his son played in was in the foreground. Only thing you could hear from him was a few deep sighs. His back straight like a soldier's.

Then the tears started to flow out of his eyes. And he couldn't stop them flowing. And the tears were there for all to see. When he tried to wipe them away it only made his crying all the plainer for the people to see.

His sister Bessy saw this first. She went over to him and put her arm around him. Then his wife did the same. The room started to go quiet then. Everyone started to shut the fuck up and look over. Then his brother-in-law the plumber from Wexford went over and placed his hand on his shoulder too. My mother went over then. Then Seán Fuck. Detective Crowley's wife Angela went over then. Then Old Master Higgins and his wife, Ber. Then Detective Crowley and my father. A few more that I didn't know went over then.

Whoever had been in the room were all gathered around James' father now. Nobody said anything. They were in a huddle. Everyone had a hand on his back or his shoulders or his arms or the back of his head. Like they were trying to pull the pain out of him. Take a small bit of it to carry themselves.

Next thing I seen his huge shoulders heave in fits and starts to the sound of his choked tormented sobs. Hands held, rubbed and caressed his shoulders, back, arms and the back of his grey head as he rocked back and forth. His sobs grew louder and stranger and everyone else started crying now too. I'm not sure when Mr Kent started grieving for his dead son but it might have been then. Everyone needs to be comforted sometimes. Even the chief of the tribe. Maybe that's why crying evolved.

Haven't had a fucking headache this bad now in a while. I'm going out for a walk. Down to the river maybe. Skim a few stones. I'll be able to see cos there's a full moon.

I Seen

I seen fierce rotten things. Your head would be fucked if you seen what I seen. See what I see. I seen Sinéad in hospital once. Brightest place I ever been. Like they think shadows would be bad for the patients or something. I was on my own in the visitor room and next thing she's wheeled in by a nurse and she in a fucking wheel-chair. Her mouth was like a baby's. Like she didn't know her tongue yet. The whites of her eyes were the whitest I ever seen. Her skin was pale and pasty. She dribbled and drooled and spoke in strange muttering words. I seen someone trying to talk who'd had a stroke one time. Like the tongue was swelled up or something. Was a bit like that. Just worse cos her eyes had no life in them. No struggle. First words she got out I'd been expecting but I wasn't prepared. They still seemed to come out of nowhere and gave me a shock. Fucking rogue wave or something. A strange horrible murmur.

—Where's James?

I'd been told what to say.

—He's above in Dublin. He's gonna wait until you're a bit better is all.

She started crying then but in a way that someone who is para-lysed might. The tears came down and her face flushed but the eyes just looked down. Steady like. Her face didn't have on a crying face at all. The muscles didn't as much as twitch. The noise she made was a constant high-pitched hoarse drone. Most horrible thing I ever heard. Would stop for a second while she inhaled. Then started again. Could say it was like a violin sound. But it wasn't. I don't know what that sound was like. Maybe nothing ever was ever like it.

I had to turn away then myself to hide my own tears.

—Why won't he come to see me?

—He's just giving you space is all.

—He'll find someone else now, she said.

—He won't, I said.

I looked out the window then and said,

—You've a nice view of the city.

The nurse came in then and said to Sinéad that it was time for a nap like she was a baby or a hundred years old, all pet this and pet that. She wheeled her out and nodded to me.

—Bye Sinéad, I said.

I'd an old fucking cry for myself then in the visiting room over by the window and then I fucked off to get the bus home. I wiped my face with my sleeve same as I just did now.

I realised then why I'd been sent for. She was told she couldn't see James so she asked if she could see me. That's why I was sent for. Only reason she wanted to see me was to ask me where James was. She'd have known I'd have been in touch with James fairly often. All made a bit of sense then. Suppose I kinda knew all along but I hoped for something else. What, I do not know.

I was working away up the new houses them days but I got the bus up to her every Saturday. Saturdays was the best cos it was the only time I wasn't thinking about her and wondering about the pain she was in but on Saturdays I got to see. She was in there for nearly a year. Well over six months anyhow. It was only in the last month or two really that she started being able to talk to me. I brought her up a walkman CD player one time and some CDs in the first few months but she never used it. I asked her about it and she couldn't even remember getting it but she didn't have it any more. I wanted to hold her. Even just her hand if not a hug. But she was in no condition to say if she wanted to be held or not. If she fell she wouldn't even raise her hands to protect herself. She'd just go head first into the ground. There was no pain the ground could offer her I suppose. She was beyond the limit now. When you think about it she was useless, as humans go. Madness makes you useless which is a mean thing about the way we're made. Her mind had taken away all her value to the world. But I knew the value of her. I knew.

More of Sinéad's Psychiatrist's Evidence

—And at this point she didn't even know he was dead. Is that correct?

—Yes.

—Did she ask you if James was going to visit her?

—Yes. I think . . . yes, after a few days she asked me where James was. As in, why he hadn't come to see her. Of course I was aware he had taken his own life and all of the staff knew that she wasn't to be told this because of the danger of her self-harming. I told her that James couldn't see her and she didn't ask about him again until her friend Charlie came to visit. We were advised by her family that she may speak to him. She asked where James was and she cried but said little else. By now she was on anti-depressant medication as well as a sedative agent just to help relax her mind.

—At what point did you decide to tell her James was dead?

—She was with us just under two weeks when we told her.

—Why did you tell her then?

—Well, there were several reasons but certainly the most pressing and urgent reason was that we feared she would somehow find out that he was dead from a member of staff or another patient. Even though her contact with the public was extremely minimal we couldn't guarantee that she wouldn't find out. Now as to why we felt she was well enough to hear the news...well. Her condition had stabilised. She was still severely depressed but she was more predictable. I consulted by teleconference four of the top psychiatric consultants in the country and one in London and one in San Francisco and it was deemed best to tell her sooner rather than later. We knew that it was only after she knew the truth that her own healing process could begin in earnest. Anything else was a stalling device at best. And at worst...well, we felt it could be damaging to her, not to tell her the truth at this stage.

—Who told her?

—I did.

—Not easy, I'd say.

—No.

—Can I ask how you told her?

The other lawyer pipes up then.

—Your Lordship, is this really necessary?

—Your Lordship, I really think it is. I want the jury to get a full picture as to the state of Sinéad Halloran's health at this time.

—Very well.

—Your Lordship I'm aware that this must be most distressing for Miss Halloran's family and friends, but I'm sorry, I really do feel it is in the best interests of the court.

—If anybody, family or otherwise wishes to leave, please feel free. You may continue questioning Mr Mooney.

—Thank you, Your Lordship, and thank you, Mr Mooney, I appreciate this is not easy for you either.

—It's fine.

—Now. Yes . . . how did you tell her about James?

—I simply told her that James was dead. That the morning she jumped in the river somebody misinformed James that she had drowned. That he believed this and he hanged himself.

—What was her reaction?

—The shock symptoms that she had recovered from after her suicide attempt returned. She also started vomiting. Well, mostly retching. She was sedated then and within a few days her physiological shock symptoms were completely gone but she had gone into a state of psychological stupor.

—Could you explain what stupor is, please?

—Certainly. Basically it is a state of immobility and mutism. People in a stupor are generally completely lifeless and unresponsive. Eye movements are about all you'll notice. Generally in psychiatry we speak about it in terms of retardation of speech and movement. But when there is no speech and no voluntary movement we use the term stupor.

—I see. And how long was she in this stupor?

—Well, she started to show the initial signs of improvement after about five months.

—Five months? She was in a stupor for five months?

—Yes.

—Seems an inordinate amount of time, is it not?

—No. Not at all. Even if Sinéad wasn't severely depressed she would have been very withdrawn. That is normal when grieving for somebody close and would be quite common for young women to be withdrawn in this way after someone close to them has died tragically. Now Sinéad was also deeply depressed; suicidal in fact. And on top of the normal feelings of guilt and regret that go along with grief, Sinéad had much more severe feelings of guilt and regret because her suicide attempt led directly to the death of the person she loved the most. So yes, the five months in stupor would be quite normal. Sinéad's troubled mind needed time to readjust to the harsh realities of her new world and her consciousness would need to focus solely on that. On coming to terms with it all and assimilating the awful facts. Literally, her brain needed to prioritise, and small talk and even things like dressing herself were of little importance. Stupor enables the brain to focus only on dealing with the urgent psychiatric issues which have befallen the patient. We provided a safe secure environment where Sinéad didn't need to focus on anything, where her mind was free to concentrate on remapping her new more difficult world whereby she could negotiate a life for herself in the future. She needed the time.

—What is post-traumatic stress disorder, Mr Mooney?

—Post-traumatic stress disorder is a syndrome that follows exposure to an incident or incidents which cause massive stress to the patient. It's seen quite commonly in war veterans but also in accident victims or rape victims.

—And in your opinion was Sinéad suffering from this disorder at this time?

—In the hospital, is it?

—Yes. For those five months in which she was in a state of stupor. Was she suffering from post-traumatic stress disorder?

—No. Although she suffered certain elements of it, no, she certainly didn't have post-traumatic stress disorder at this time. She didn't fulfil the diagnostic criteria. The diagnostic criteria are quite specific for this. It is generally only when one returns or tries to return to everyday life that somebody can be diagnosed with post-traumatic stress disorder. It causes inability to function normally through a variety of ways. Sinéad was suffering from deep depression made much more severe by a traumatic event which caused her mind considerable added stress, but she didn't have post-traumatic stress disorder, per se.

—I see, thank you. Could you tell the jury when she started to come out of this state of stupor she was in for five months, please? And how she appeared to begin to improve?

When she did finally emerge after everything she was like a woman mortally ashamed of her own self – a scarlet woman.

There was no way of keeping Racey away from her. Sinéad came home for a weekend first to see how she got on. She shouldn't have been going any place. She got out the Friday and Racey took her to The Snug on the Saturday even though Sinéad was in no condition. She was quiet and withdrawn in herself and Racey had dragged her out with false niceness. Loving the thought of parading herself as the loyal friend and parading Sinéad in her drugged state as the main attraction of the night. Of the month for that matter. Free spirit Sinéad reduced to a drooling pale sleepy-eyed shadow isn't it? Fucking drinking a glass of orange juice. She raised it gingerly to her lips with a hand all trembly. Her eyes looked around all sheepish and caught a glimpse of a turning fascinated head or two who happened to have a look over at that particular moment. Passers-by at a fucking car crash. She'd look up again a minute later, and someone else would be staring at her. She did that all night.

In came a fella called Liam Durcan with his brother who was home from Boston with a buddy and a cousin. They'd be around on the piss for the week so 'twas important to introduce them. To give them standing in the village while they were home. That they'd be let in isn't it? That each would be treated like one of our own. Liam was about thirty now. He was a reasonable footballer, but had given up on account of taking over the father's big farm. He introduced them all by name, and all of us by name back to them. Dinky, me, Racey, Karen, Snoozie and Ciara and then he skipped Sinéad and went on to introduce a few of the old men who were close to us at the bar.

I saw this one Ciara looking down and shaking her head to herself. No one else seemed to notice, even though it was hard not to. I was there for the night, and even when the girls had left, no one mentioned anything. The only other thing that stands out was the way they left, with Racey holding Sinéad's arm all the way out the bar, and asking her loudly if she was OK. There was no need to do either of course, but Racey was a great friend and a martyr and would do anything for her. Her destruction.

—She was always fucking tapped!

That's what Liam Durcan said later, and he pissed out of his head.

—Didn't stop you trying to have your way with her a dozen times though did it?!

—Ha, haa! Doubt ya kid.

—Durkey boy!

—The bould Durkey horse!

And they all laughing mad and slapping their knees.

—Amn't I the lucky fucker that she was having none of it. And she a raving fucking headcase.

The lads nodded in agreement and drank their pints in silence for a second.

—A standing prick has no conscience!

So that's what Liam Durcan said. I fucked off home then. Anyhow you don't want to be hearing any more of their old shite, and I don't want to be writing about it or remembering it either.

What troubled me wasn't what those eejits were saying about Sinéad. Pigs grunt. Only the way Sinéad was looking around all night like a scared child scared the living shit out of me. I never seen her like that before. Soon she was let go home for good out of the hospital. I used to visit her and put on music for her and she'd say,

—Thanks Charlie, that's nice.

You'd say something to her and then a second later she'd realise you said something to her and then she'd look at you wide-eyed and serious and try and concentrate but the world she was trying to come out of was a bit too hard for her to ignore.

Of all the upset I been in the most was probably the time I first ever seen Sinéad myself and she right proper crazed out of her outcast mind insane. The whites of her eyes were glassy-white again. She looked more beautiful and alive than any Greek goddess or Egyptian queen. Vivid or something. She spoke and moved and thought but not in the same seconds, minutes and hours as the rest of us. She was operating on a different clock and it didn't fit our world. And the distress of it was plain as day once you looked behind the fuckyouallness in her eyes. She was after losing her own grip on the person she was. Scared and scary. She talked too fast and too different and she cursed,

—Jesus Christ Charlie about fucking time for ya I've been waiting here for ages I knew you'd be coming cos James came to me in my dream and said you'd be getting the bus home and to warn you walk with me I don't have all day but I've stuff to tell you stuff that will be music to your ears come on will ya I've tonnes of shit to do walk faster basically you can stop your grieving cos James isn't dead at all he is alive very very very much alive. I know isn't it the best ever?

Her smile was more like one frozen in a photograph than one in real time. Her eyes didn't stay long on mine once they saw mine looking back at them.

—He got word to me and I can't tell you how but he told me you're the only one around that I can trust cos all the others were trying to kill him and me too you're the only one we can trust James is in America.

—How do you mean he's not dead? Sure

—Shut the fuck up will ya keep your voice down.

Her voice went quieter now and she covered her mouth with her hand.

—They've everywhere bugged everywhere I had to take wires out of my coat and two pairs of shoes and the two remote controls at home so keep your voice down and cover your mouth cos they have lip-readers and obviously you can't breathe a word of this to a soul so try and continue pretending you're grieving walk with me will ya.

I was after slowing down at my house but she was having none of it.

—We can't go into your house your parents are more than likely in on it your mother definitely is and probably your father too and even if he's not you can be sure they've your house bugged as well cos they know you're the closest to James and myself so let's just keep walking and keep the heads down here comes Mrs Higgins pretend nothing play it cool we'll just say hello like normal the backstabbing fucking bitch.

—Hello Mrs Higgins.

—Hello Sinéad and Charlie how are you both?

—Ah sure you know, coping the best we can, said Sinéad.

—I know, goes Mrs Higgins. It must be very hard for you, you poor creatures. Just put your love and trust in the Lord, that's all we can do. God is good. God is good.

—He is Mrs Higgins, goes Sinéad, he's fucking brilliant.

Off we walked up the hill and poor Mrs Higgins looking after us and Sinéad telling me what a sneaky evil fucking bitch she was and how she was sent out to see if she could hear what we were talking about and was going down in behind the post office now cos that's where the transmitters for the listening equipment and the intelligence agents were and that's where she'd report to the agents about anything she'd found out from us. She was going on with all this bullshit like the words couldn't keep up with her brain and having to breathe was an inconvenience that slowed her speech down. When we turned into the churchyard I looked back and could see Mrs Higgins still looking up at us and she looked like she was the mad one and she standing legs apart facing up the hill and her hands joined in prayer. Sinéad didn't even shut up at James' grave except when she started crying and I put my arm around her,

—Good man that's good pretend you're crying now too if you can it's crucial they believe we're genuine I'm whispering cos there'll be bugs everywhere here the flowers are nice on the grave aren't they the fresh ones are from his parents they're not in on it far as we know but we can't be certain so they have to suffer on for the moment but all will be revealed in time in all likelihood the first time they realise he's alive is when they hear us singing on the radio yeah James is in Seattle and he reckons he's met a few musicians that are perfect for the sound we're going for one of them was a good friend of Cobain's that's really impressive Charlie come here for a hug this looks real as fuck well done real tears and everything James will be delighted when he hears this you'd get an Oscar for this.

My tears were as real as tears get and her hugging me only made me worse I couldn't stop sobbing like a baby.

—OK Charlie, that's good but we don't want to overdo it in case they become suspicious. I'm gonna head off now down Bohernavar cos I've arrangements to make you'll be seeing me again soon when we've the plan of action completely sorted out and Charlie?

—Yeah.

—Trust no one.

When she left me she gave me a kiss on my cheek. That was something she never did really, and I thought about the moisture from her kiss mixed with my tears and I walking home.

The pound shop candles are the longest but they burn faster than the dearer ones. Sometimes when I'm tired the candle burns slower. This isn't just something I think. I've timed it and its true I think. I never stop working until the candle's finished burning and the wax is gone wherever it goes. That's true as well I think.

Sitting on the Grotto Wall

Soon after I heard she was sitting on the grotto wall once across from the garda station staring into blank space and all the lorries were hooting their horns at her because she was only wearing a nightgown and her boobs were showing.

Detective Crowley put a blanket on her and sat with her until two local women came along and then they took her across to the garda station. It was a Tuesday morning about half seven. I know because my mother was talking to Old Master Higgins' wife and a woman from the new houses. Told the mother she was singing the Randy Sparks song 'Today'.

_____

_____

_____

_____

_____

_____

_____

_____

_____

_____

_____

_____

Yeah so anyhow. That was her. All the lorries and vans were hooting at her and they passing. Her naked boobs were out where they shouldn't be and her mind was some place else unknown. And out of bounds too, isn't it?

More of Sinéad's Psychiatrist's Evidence

—Well the first thing was she showered and dressed herself independently and of her own accord. She began to speak. She started to come to life a bit, so to speak. She began to interact with staff and other patients. Very gradually, but she did. Over a period of about six weeks. But she did make excellent progress. She even sang at a Christmas Mass we had with the patients. Their families and all the staff were there too. It's something we do every year.

—Very nice. And was this pre-planned?

—No, it was quite spontaneous.

—So she just started singing in the middle of the Mass? Was it not arranged beforehand?

—No. It was during communion. She just started singing when everyone was going up for communion. There weren't many at the Mass so people were finished getting communion and she was still singing for a while. The priest just waited at the altar for her to finish. I think he was moved quite a bit by it. Same as everybody else who was there.

—Could you tell us what it was she sang?

—Yes, it was a song called 'If It Be Your Will'.

—And did anyone try to stop her?

—From singing? Gosh no. I think everybody thought it had been arranged by somebody and they just hadn't been informed.

—You would think though that the staff might have tried to quieten her, as she was a patient with psychiatric difficulties?

—Well, it was really very beautiful. Quietening her didn't come into it. I was sitting beside an elderly patient. These things make a difference to people's lives, you know. Especially people who are confused or in pain. It was quite extraordinary. She sang with such power. She'd become frail by now, you know, on account of her not eating much. But this voice. The strength of it. I mean. I'd barely heard her speak. And here she was. This. Like. It was like this girl who had been dead to the world was being brought to life by her own voice. Raised up by her chest. The music gave her strength somehow. Her powerful voice seemed to give her frail body strength.

—Let's fast forward then a little, please. Do you think Sinéad made a full recovery?

—I do. Insofar as someone could recover, yes, I think she did. She had some very severe setbacks but made an excellent recovery.

—Could you tell us about her setbacks, please.

—Yes. She became delusional shortly after her release from hospital. She was in denial about the death of James and she believed he was waiting for her in America.

Dr Quinn was telling me that some Einstein shrink once said that people are only considered sane by common consent. Majority rules. The odd one out is mad. Public nakedness on the bridge by the grotto in Ballyronan is mad. Sinéad went mad.

Mad

Adj. 1. very angry; affected by great displeasure or anger 2. offensive term; an offensive term meaning affected with psychiatric disorder 3. very unwise or rash 4. wildly excited 5. frantic; done with great haste, excitement, or confusion 6. exciting; very exciting or boisterous 7. seized by uncontrollable emotion; overcome with violent emotion 8. passionate about sth.; very fond of, enthusiastic about, or interested in sth.; often to the exclusion of sth. else 9. abnormally aggressive; used to describe an animal that is abnormally aggressive or ferocious 10 rabid [Old English *gamaed* 'deprived of reason', that was formed from *gemad* 'irrational', from, ultimately, an Indo-European ancestor meaning 'change' (source of English *mutate*).]

Insane

Adj. 1. *psychiat.* legally considered as psychiatrically disordered; legally incompetent or irresponsible because of a psychiatric disorder 2. lacking reasonable thought; showing complete lack of reason or foresight [Mid-16thC. From Latin *insanus, from sanus* 'healthy, sane'.]

Reasonable

Adj. 1. Rational, sensible and capable of rational judgement 2. In accord with common sense [13thC. Via Old French *reisun* from, ultimately, Latin *ratio* 'calculation, thought'.]

Rational

Adj. 1. reasonable and sensible; governed by, or showing evidence of, clear and sensible thinking and judgement, based on reason rather than emotion or prejudice 2. in accordance with reason and logic 3. able to reason [Early 18thC. Via French from Spanish *racion*, from Latin *ratio* 'calculation'.]

Sense

N. 1. physical faculty 2. feeling derived from the senses 3. ability to appreciate sth. 4. moral discernment; an ability to perceive and be motivated by moral or ethical principles 5. intelligence 6. point; useful purpose or good reason 7. reasoned opinion 8. main idea 9. meaning [14thC. Directly, and via Old French, from Latin *sensus* 'feeling, perception', from *sens-*, past participle stem of *sentire* 'to feel'.]

Common

Adj. 1. shared; belonging to or shared by two or more people or groups 2. for all; relating or belonging to the community as a whole 3. everyday 4. widely found 5. non-specialist 6. general 7. ordinary 8. of an expected standard 9. vulgar 10 *math.* with equal mathematical relationship 11. *poetry* a syllable that can be either long or short 12. *Chr.* useful for several religious festivals

I just vomited up my coffee and biscuits. I think it was looking up them words in the dictionary did it to me. It's disgusting what some words we have say about us isn't it? And how stuck we are with them and still they all do be talking about freedom. And anything tastes better than puke. Even mustard. I think it's the height of tiredness. Didn't sleep at all last night. And last night is more than thirty hours ago cos I never went to bed tonight. My brain feels fizzy. Anyhow the most astonishing thing about my story. The most astonishing thing that I realised about being a human being in the middle of all this is this. We can lose our minds. That's not normal. We think stuff is normal cos we're stuck inside in the middle of it. But that don't make it so. The tears are streaming down my face and I writing this now but I'm going to keep writing cos otherwise I might forget. Madness is nature's punishment for not fitting in. Cos there was a time when this had to be so. Otherwise the groups would all be splitting and everyone all following all different leaders in all different directions and the group would get weak. Weak is not good. When everyone is pulling together. That's when the group is strongest. Strong survives isn't it? Nature made it so that people like that would go mad or be leaders. Never an in between. If people don't follow them then they destruct themselves. The status quo worked cos people were isn't it? That was proof that it worked for them. Cos they were. All of them. Madness was essential. Essential. I seen. You know? I seen. Poor poor poor Sinéad. I must tell you. I must tell you before I go back to not knowing. I must show you what happened to her. How it happened. True and slow and sure and tortuous and damaging and relentless. I hope I can. If I could tattoo the feeling, the knowledge my brain has right now about madness I would tattoo it big and bold so I'd be reminded of it tomorrow.

Cos I'll have this knowledge forgotten when tomorrow comes. I know I will. It's like it's not for us to know. Like our brains won't take it. But I'm going to do it. I won't let sleep mess it all up now like it does with the rest of ye always. If it kills me I still won't. Nobody is born mad. If only Sinéad could've seen that they were only stupid. Stupid monkeys who didn't even know what they were doing is all they were. They didn't even mean no harm and couldn't even see really what it was that they were doing. Sinéad got brain damaged. She got a brain injury. No she didn't. Actually she got loads of brain injuries. Hurts. Brain strains. And they all built up to be a serious brain injury. There's muscles in the brain. Tiny muscles. And if they get strained a lot they can snap. A muscle in Sinéad's brain snapped. That's the way nature made it happen to people who were different cos we don't kill people we love so they have to destroy themselves cos difference is too dangerous to the group. The person who undermined the dance of the group put their loyalty to each other at risk. When the group is strong each and every one survives. Nature disposes of troublemakers. Nature saw Sinéad as a troublemaker. I seen it with my own two eyes. Everyone's always on about how great nature is. I fucking hate nature cos it made us the way we are and we didn't even have a choice. Like fucking cancer. Maybe cancer is there to kill one of us off at random so that the rest of us will all be friends and work together and not be fighting or every fella doing his own thing. Death brings the people left behind together isn't it? Nature is the fucking enemy. Our nature. We must fight against our stupid nature isn't it?

Anyhow it was against all the odds. That Sinéad was kept well. Only thing was the love she got. But then he wasn't there any more.

I have to go to sleep now. My body and my brain is closing down. I had a dream once that everyone thought Sinéad was mad cos she wasn't sticking pencils up her nose. Everyone else was going around with pencils up their nostrils but Sinéad didn't see the sense of it. She was banished. Anyhow my eyes are fucked and the light from the screen hurts and the tears are stinging so goodnight and sweet dreams.

Not really sure what all that stuff you just read was about really. Was awful tired last night and was fierce upset and went a bit rambly. Anyhow. Yeah. Sinéad became unwell. Could delete all that stuff I wrote last night but I won't cos it's a lot of words and I'll need them all to make a book if you don't mind.

Tell Sinéad

Sinéad was put back in hospital after her thing at the grotto. I did a lot of thinking then. Whether to tell Sinéad what I knew or not. Or whether to just tell the gardaí. That I found out what happened to her in the toilet in Roundy's. That the Little Rascal did what he did. That Dinky had known all along. That Dinky had stolen the Afghan scarf to destroy them. That the whole thing was rotten and rigged. I just wanted her to be able to decide what I should do. She deserved the say isn't it?

In the end she came back out of hospital after a month or six weeks. I still didn't know if I should tell her what I knew or not. I was afraid it would be the end of her. Then I was thinking there wasn't much of her there now anyhow. We sat on the river bank, the two of us, one evening then.

—But like . . . how could he believe that I'd be capable of doing it? she goes.

—There was silence for a long time cos I knew no answer. She asked what was going on in his mind. I told her about his sufferings.

—I dunno, I goes.

—But he must have said something to you Charlie.

—He just thought like. Same as the music. You needed to try things. To taste the world. We didn't really know what was in your head.

—Did you not tell him it was ridiculous Charlie? Taste the world? Did you not tell him it was stupid?

I didn't say anything so she asked again so I answered.

—Yeah.

There was silence then for a bit and then she goes,

—It was that scarf. Why did I say my mother stole it and lost it? Why did I say that to him?

Silence then again for a long time.

—How did the Rascal get his hands on my scarf Charlie?

After a while of staring at the water she looked at me. I wondered was there a chance she thought I robbed it? That the Rascal put me up to it. I got sickened in my stomach thinking that she could think that. Could she have? Her brain was in a bad state if she did. It was then I realised that I had no right not to tell her the truth. Only question was when she'd be strong enough to hear it. Dunno if humans ever get strong enough for the like of that. I just stared at the water and let the silence eat my broken thoughts. After a while she spoke again.

—Surely you told him I couldn't have cheated on him. I loved him. I loved him so much. It doesn't matter about tasting the world. He was my whole world. My whole world. All I ever wanted.

Her voice broke into a cry and we both cried silently and hard for a long time and I never felt so useless. She tried to talk a few times over the next while but she couldn't. She was just sitting there all hopeless on the gravel beside me and she was wringing her hands with a weird force as if she was trying to rub her own skin off. Her head was down like a bold shamed child the whole time. I was just looking at the river that was all the wetter and unmerciful with the tears in my eyes. It was starting to get dark then and I goes,

—I heard someone talking Sinéad. Dinky stole the scarf from Roundy's when you weren't looking.

She didn't say anything, just kept staring out at the water. So I just went on.

—I heard Dinky telling Teesh. Dinky knew everything. The Rascal told him what he did to you. I was in Snoozie's one night pretending to be asleep and I heard Dinky talking to Teesh.

I told her the whole thing. And how I never caught up with James on time to tell him and then he was gone. She just sat there still looking at the sky's darkness on the river. I was ready to grab her in case she ran into it. But she didn't. After a bit she just straightened up her back and turned to me and goes,

—Can we meet again Charlie? Maybe tomorrow evening when you're finished work.

—OK. You won't do harm to yourself tonight sure you won't? I said.

—I won't Charlie, no, she said quietly, already getting up to walk back to the village.

Next evening I walked up to her house and I could see her in the living room standing looking at me. She'd been waiting and was coming out the front door by the time I'd reached it. She said,

—Hi Charlie, and she had a kind smile on her face.

—Hi, I said.

She walked faster than I was expecting so I'd to speed up a few steps to catch up.

—Where we going? I said, the river?

—Yeah. Will we? she goes.

—Yeah, I said.

We spoke about lots of stuff. Some of it was private and some of it wasn't. We were there for hours and hours. I'd told her earlier how I'd kill Dinky, that I didn't think the gardaí would take care of it right. She wouldn't let me kill him. You might think it's only talk but she knew I'd do it if she wanted. I think the world is made up of people who think that the police and judges can be trusted to get fair play. And then other people who don't think that. I think the only thing wrong with the death penalty is that you're not allowed to torture them for a bit first. She held my hand for most of what we spoke about. She asked me one time when I was crying, she goes,

—Would you do anything for me Charlie?

and she starts crying herself then too, but like kinda smiling too and looking at me nodding, and I was crying mad and I goes,

—Yeah,

and she squeezes my hand real tight for a long time and we both crying and then she hugged me and I hugged her. Then later on a lot of what she was talking about was what I could do with my life after. After going away I mean. She said America was probably the place to go cos America was always good to music.

I'm still having problems talking about the happy memories. You might have realised this yourself at this stage. It's just that they've lost something along the way. Meaning or something. Or reality. They've lost realness I think. Those memories. Something happened to the happy memories when the shit happened. They got a spattering of it too. Stench of hurt.

Pallet of Blocks

'Twas around this time I went up to the building site of the new houses where I was doing jobs only to be told that there was no work today. I says will I get paid and the foreman told me to go away and have a good shit for myself. I asked him why there was no work and he says there was an accident now fuck off home out of it.

I looked up and I seen a garda car and an ambulance up at number three. All the houses had numbers even though most of them weren't even half built yet. I could hear the foreman inside cancelling a delivery of concrete and then he came out and walked up towards number three where the boss was talking with a couple of gardaí and two other fellas in suits.

—Are you gone yet? he said.

—What happened? I said.

—Go home now Gamal if you know what's fucking good for you.

I watched him go but he turned around and walked back towards me. I said I'm going and took a few steps back but he walked back into the portacabin and came back out wearing a shiny yellow hard hat.

—Where'd ya get the grand new hard hat? I asked him and he walking up towards number three again. No answer.

So no more building or singing or raping for the Little Rascal. Justice is mine said the Lord. It is in my hole. If there's a life after this one Rascal better hope he doesn't end up in the same place that James is or he'll be wishing he was alive and not after pulling a pallet of blocks down on top of himself and smashing his earthly skull.

I like to think Sinéad thought it was the ghost of James who knocked those blocks down on top of the Rascal. In a way I suppose it was. We never spoke about it. But the inspectors from the health and safety crowd figured he pulled them down on top of himself. He slipped off the ladder and grabbed a rope but the rope was tying twenty-four blocks together in a nice heap so grabbing the rope only slowed down his fall for a little bit but then his weight pulled the twenty-four blocks down so when he landed on his hole on the ground the blocks rained down on top of him. Nice surprise for him at seven o'clock in the morning.

Only other thing was that they put the little fucker in a child's coffin and 'twas the talk of West Cork.

Nobody

Nobody had the heart for nothing after James died you know. Nobody. And then life goes back to normal. A match. A wedding. Some accident where a local farmer got his leg taken off by a combine harvester. Someone else got cancer. Someone else's marriage went on the rocks. Someone won the Lotto. News. That's the way it happened. That's how I remember it anyhow. People found their heart again. Misneach isn't it?

Moonlight Runner

In Ballyronan about fifteen years ago a horse called Moonlight Runner won Cheltenham or the Grand National or some big massive horse race that was from Ballyronan or the owner was from Ballyronan I'm not sure which. There was a free bar in Roundy's and The Snug for two nights running. There was TV cameras and news crews and radio people and the whole lot sure. In our own little Ballyronan. Old Master Higgins was on the six o'clock news on RTE. Roundy was on BBC radio talking from Roundy's where half of the village were fully legless. The Snug had the other half legless over in his own place. The whole village was happy. Even after it sobered up. For a long time. Spring in the step isn't it? But now the whole village was gone gaunt and sickly. Made the horse racing seem like the village's childhood memory. Made the happiness seem awful silly.

Ballyronan was in the news again now and it wished the world never heard of it. Just wanted the old days back and to be left alone. You might think what does a place know? But a place gets to know its people doesn't it? There's nothing worse than someone being made to see that their happiness is silly.

I remember watching my cousins when I was small. I was sitting on the windowsill outside my cousins' house at a birthday party. I usen't play with them at all. Just watch them and tell them fuck off if they came near me. But my cousin Séamus anyhow was playing house. He was the same age as me. About nine or ten. So he's playing house with the other cousins. Three girls and two boys all between about three and seven. Next thing his older brother and cousin who were about twelve came along. They started laughing at Séamus for playing house. Séamus went red and said that he wasn't really playing house, that he was just minding the younger ones. He left the house made of boxes then and followed his older brother and cousin around the place instead.

—I was only helping them to make it cos the boxes were too big for them.

—Oh really? Were you the mammy or the daddy?

—The daddy, said Séamus and went all red again.

One of the younger ones kept trying to follow Séamus around then until Séamus gave him a dead leg and told him to fuck off.

The village became bitter of the world. Embarrassed that they were watching them when they were being so childish. Runs deep what people think is good and what you think is good yourself. In life.

Sometimes I think James and Sinéad did this to Dinky and Teesh and Racey and them. Just by being. That they did that. Made the merry happiness in the pub seem silly. And all the posturing and the laughing at the laughable. Sinéad and James made it all seem like children's play. Caused a kind of wild seething fury and gave Dinky and Teesh terrorists' eyes cos I seen pictures of terrorists' eyes. Be careful your existence doesn't insult anyone's way of life.

So anyhow back in Cape Clear island once James sang this one. This is called a flashback Dr Quinn tells me. Gives out to me when I don't tell things in order. Says I must make it clear. Flag it he says. Flag that it's a flashback. I'm flagging now. We do need a song. And James sang this one on a night on Cape Clear one time. James seemed to only get angry when he was singing an angry song. Like 'Country Feedback' he sang that time. He sang it shit but no one cared. They still enjoyed it.

People love to look at each other when they're laughing. Oh I find that very funny and so do you, the two of us are the same, not like that silly clown we're laughing at. You know it's true. You know it. Wolves hunt in packs and people laugh in packs.

Sinéad and James sang this song in a strange kind of harmony. Give you the holy spooks.

There were two sisters walking down by a stream
Oh the wind and the rain
The older one pushed the younger one in
Oh the dreadful wind and rain

Pushed her in the river to drown
Oh the wind and the rain
Watched her as she floated on down
Oh the dreadful wind and rain

And he made a fiddle from her own breastbone
Oh the wind and the rain
The sound could melt a heart of stone
Oh the dreadful wind and rain

The only tune that fiddle would play
Oh the wind and the rain
The only tune that fiddle would play
Oh the dreadful wind and rain

Sinéad played us a Bob Dylan song once that she said was like it. About a fella whose friend killed people by accident in a car crash. Turn, turn, to the rain and the wind, it goes. He says he stood up fierce slow cos the room was gone funny. That's shock. You'd know what that meant if you were at the court case I was at. Everyone who was there would know. People stood up slow after hearing parts of it. Knees go shaky isn't it?

More of Sinéad's Psychiatrist's Evidence

—And tell me, were you surprised by this development?

—Ahm . . . a little but not entirely. I just don't think she was quite ready to accept it.

—Would you say you predicted this?

—No. Nobody could have predicted this.

—Thank you. Yet you say that she made an excellent recovery and became mentally a healthy person. How can you really be certain of this? Given the fact that you were surprised by her previous setback where she became totally delusional, can you really now say that you are certain, absolutely certain that she was in good mental health at the time that she died?

—Of course I couldn't be certain. Nobody could. All I can provide is my best medical opinion.

—But you are willing to accept that your medical opinion was completely wrong in the past, are you?

—I would have to accept that to be the case, yes.

—So tell me please, Mr Mooney, can you be certain, absolutely one hundred per cent certain that Sinéad was not suicidal at the time she died?

—No. I cannot be sure.

—Thank you, Mr Mooney, for your honesty. That's all, Your Lordship, thank you.

Dr Quinn said to me today that he's noticed the last six weeks or two months that I'm the whole time biting my lip. Never noticed except just that they're red raw and sore. I just said it was the cold weather and he said it was only October. Another time he was on about the skin that joins the bottom of your thumb to your pointing finger. I know its called index but that's stupid. It's the bit of skin that can stretch. Bit webbed it is. I rubbed mine so much it bled and went scabby and would rub off the scab again until the skin went all hard like the heel of your foot and it would crack and tear when I stretched out my hand. Dr Quinn said it was a nervous thing. I said I wasn't nervous. Just realised now this second that I been biting my lip this whole time. Nice when you get a bit of skin between your teeth and when you move your lips the skin comes away and you can keep doing it until it hurts and even then you can keep doing it and you can suck the blood out of your lip and bite it off and suck the blood back to the side of your tongue where you can taste it best all sweet and salty and metal and your eyes watering with the lovely pain.

Teesh in Court

Teesh stood up in court that time in the middle of Snoozie squealing on him.

—You're fucking dead. You're fucking dead Snoozie. You're a fucking dead man.

Tim Buckley's song 'Valentine Melody' goes here. It was a fairly big part of Sinéad's mind for a while, this song was.

_____

_____

_____

_____

_____

_____

_____

_____

_____

_____

_____

_____

When I took the tablets for an dubh I didn't like my favourite song any more. That's why I swore to Dr Quinn that I'd slit my wrists before another one of them pills crossed my lips. We've listened to it a trillion thousand times me and Sinéad and James but we still never figured out the words. I think Eddie Vedder might have made up some of the words cos real ones didn't fit.

I remember Sinéad singing the song. All timid and sweet the first couple of times and then whatever pain and anguish was in her came through the third time and she was crying at the end of it and James went over and held her in his arms. Then after a bit she went over to the tape recorder and went to the bit where it goes,

Tongue twisted thoughts have spin 'round my head

and she must have rewound and played it a hundred times. She couldn't get over the way Eddie Vedder sang the word, 'spin'. Said it was the whole spirit of the song condensed into a split second. Said she'd never heard anything like it. Shaking her head she was. Tears in her eyes, nearly. Moisture anyhow. When she got James to play along with her as she practised that line we began to realise what she meant. Disappointment and love and anger and acceptance were never so close than in the way hers and Eddie Vedder's voice went on that word, 'spin'. Made different words of it. For different worlds. Human breath became part of the word and the notes somehow. A baby's cry was in there too. And the roar of an angry god. Fierce and frail. Sinéad was getting very close to it but I'm not sure if her lungs were strong enough yet but she would get it. I was certain of that. Hardest thing is seeing a peak like that, 'tis so far above us. But she knew where it was and she'd get there.

The State Pathologist's Evidence

—The victim was lying with her back to the ground naked from the waist down under the bridge at Ballyronan.

—Was she under the middle part of the bridge or . . . ?

—At the part nearest the bank on the eastern side of the river. Under the arch closest to the bank.

—I see. Was she under water?

—No. Her head and her upper torso were in a little water, but her waist and legs were quite dry. There was no water running through this part of the bridge as it was summer and the river was low. Just a couple of pools.

—I see. And she was naked from the waist down, is that so?

—Yes. She was wearing a beige blouse and nothing else. No underwear.

—Was there anything else about the scene of note?

—By the time I'd arrived the forensic team had highlighted certain aspects of the scene to me. Extensive photographs were taken. On the river bank the victim's underwear was found. Her knickers were on the ground and her bra was hanging on the branch of a tree. It appeared to have been thrown there. Her handbag was washed up on the river bank down river and had probably been thrown into the river at the scene of the crime. Also found at the scene was a silver piece of torc neck jewellery belonging to the victim.

—I see. You later carried out the post-mortem examination, Dr Gleeson. Were you able to establish how Sinéad died?

—Yes. The post-mortem showed that she had died from asphyxia due to strangulation. Her larynx had been broken, most likely during strangulation. There was considerable bruising to the front and sides of the victim's neck. Also the presence of petechiae in the eyes would strongly suggest strangulation.

—Could you explain what that is please, Dr Gleeson?

—Petechiae are broken blood vessels, in this case appearing in the eyes. This is caused by the pressure created within the skull by strangulation.

—I see. Was there other evidence of foul play?

—Yes. There was evidence to suggest foul play. Firstly her body appeared to have been dragged to where it was found. This is seen by scratch marks on the front of her body, which would have been dragged along the river bank to where it was found. Also there was a slight build-up of earth along the left side of her body, particularly her left thigh and left shoulder. This build-up was probably caused by dragging her body to the location where it was found.

—Do you believe then, Doctor, that somebody moved her body after she died?

—I do, yes.

—Was there anything else to suggest foul play?

—Yes. The presence of skin and blood under several of the victim's fingernails would indicate that she had tried to fight off her attacker. She had broken two of her nails, presumably in this struggle. The presence of two of another person's pubic hairs on the victim's vaginal area as well as semen in the vagina would indicate that her killer had raped her, particularly as the DNA of the skin under the victim's fingernails matched that of the pubic hair and the semen.

—Sorry, Dr Gleeson. Just to get this clear. Could it be argued that the skin found under the victim's fingernails was there because of a passionate sexual encounter?

—The skin of someone could be scraped by long fingernails during a vigorous sexual encounter. This is certainly true. However, the quantity of skin and blood under the fingernails of Sinéad Halloran . . . would indicate a considerable struggle on her part. The person she presumably attempted to fight off would have had quite severe scratch marks on his person, some of which would have bled.

—Thank you. Finally, Dr Gleeson, were you able to establish a time of death?

—Not very accurately, unfortunately. Because part of the victim's body was in cold water her temperature would have decreased quicker than usual. This complicates matters because it would have delayed rigor mortis. But judging by the food in the victim's stomach, which was a handful of french fries apparently eaten at one a.m., from a local mobile chip van, and taking into account an accelerated reduction in body temperature, I was able to estimate the time of death to be within a two-hour time-frame. It was almost certainly between the hours of three a.m. and five a.m. of the morning she was found. I couldn't establish a time of death more accurately than that, unfortunately.

Forensic Scientist's Evidence

—DNA doesn't lie.

—Objection.

—You need only answer the question.

—Well, in fairness, Your Lordship, I think he was answering it.

—In any case you may continue.

—Thank you, Your Lordship. Now, Dr Morlay, as we know, the defendant never came forward. He was arrested after

—Objection.

—Your Lordship, I'm only trying to get to the point a bit quicker.

—Don't.

—OK, Your Lordship. Dr, Morlay could you tell us please how your
laboratories became involved in the case?

—Well, I took a call from Detective Crowley and it was he who asked
us at St Anne's Hospital laboratories if I could accept samples of DNA
for forensic analysis with the purpose of looking for a match found with
the DNA of the semen . . . which was taken from the body of a suspected
murder victim.

—How many samples were you expecting?

—In all we received over a hundred. A hundred and nine in all.

—And who were these samples from?

—They were mostly from men from the area between the ages of
eighteen and forty and there were also some samples of men on the sex
offenders' register in the county of Cork.

—And could you tell me whose blood sample the DNA of the semen
belonged to?

—Denis Hennebry's blood was a perfect match for the semen found
on the victim.

You know that's Dinky.

—And could you tell the jury, please, was there any way that Denis
Hennebry could have denied that the semen taken from the body of
Sinéad Halloran was his? Could he have denied it was his?

—Objection, Your Lordship, Denis never denied the semen was his.

—Your Lordship, I want to establish the situation Denis Hennebry found himself in.

—Very well, carry on.

—Thank you, Your Lordship. Right, Dr Morlay, thank you for your patience.

—Not at all.

—So tell the jury, could Denis Hennebry possibly have made any plausible case that the semen taken from the victim's body wasn't his?

—Well, obviously, he could have tried. But quite honestly, it would have been useless. Solid DNA evidence like this has never been successfully contested.

—How is DNA so reliable? How is the evidence it provides so incontrovertible?

—Basically, because the chances of another match being found is in the regions of billions to one.

—Is that why it's called DNA fingerprinting?

—Yes.

—Now Dr Morlay, could you tell the jury please, do you think most people know about DNA? Do you think it's common knowledge that DNA is nowadays a very useful and reliable forensic evidence?

—Objection, Your Lordship. Dr Morlay's area of expertise does not include knowing how much the general public know about DNA evidence.

—Sustained.

—Very well. Thank you, Your Lordship. I'll say it myself then, and you can decide youselves if you think I'm being reasonable. I think that the general public know that DNA testing is hugely useful as forensic evidence. At least people who read the newspapers or watch television.

I think that's probably most people, to be fair. Now, Dr Morlay, are you aware of any other cases where the defendant changed his story after DNA evidence linked him to the crime?

—Objection. Your Lordship, I must object to this now, this is most unfair. This case is far from closed.

—Your Lordship, I never said for a second that the case is closed. I merely asked if Dr Morlay was aware of any other cases where the defendant had changed his story after DNA evidence linked him to the crime.

—Links him to what crime, Your Lordship?

—Denis Hennebry changed his story, Your Lordship, that is simply a statement of fact. And the jury must know the facts.

—Denis Hennebry did change his story. But he is not guilty of any crime until this court says so. The objection is sustained. I will ask you to be more precise in terms of your language in my court, please.

—Well, of course, Your Lordship. Thank you.

—Proceed.

—So. We've established that the defendant changed his story when confronted with the evidence that his semen was taken from the body of the victim. Having been confronted with this evidence by the gardaí. By the men and women who have the job of finding criminals.

—Your Lordship, I'm sure the jury know who the gardaí are.

There was a fierce laugh in the court then. People needed a laugh. At least.

—What I mean, Your Lordship, is to emphasise the seriousness of the job at hand.

—OK, move it along now, please.

—Well, these men and women who were working tirelessly to appre-
hend the merciless, cowardly, utterly heartless rapist and murderer were
told by Denis Hennebry, when confronted with the DNA evidence, through
his lawyer, that he wanted to change his story. Now, Dr Morlay, could you
tell me, please, is this common? Is it common for . . . a suspect . . . a prime
suspect . . . Is it common for a prime suspect who is later found guilty . . . is
it common for such a suspect to have changed his evidence, to change
his statement, when confronted with DNA evidence?

—It's not unheard of in murder trials and rape trials. It has happened
on numerous occasions in Ireland but probably thousands of times
abroad.

—There you are. Thank you very much for your expertise, Dr Morlay.

—You're welcome.

—Mr Healy, have you any questions for Dr Morlay?

—No, Your Lordship, thank you.

—Then you may leave the witness stand. Thank you. Now I think everybody needs their lunch break at this stage. We'll resume at two fifteen.

—All rise.

I remember one time in school when we were only very small
they were all teasing this one boy who was only in the school for
a few months. We were making Easter cards for our mammies and
daddies. Happy Easter To Mammy and Daddy I love you. This
boy's daddy didn't live with his mammy and him so he had to
make two different cards. And they all ganged up on him teasing
him cos this made him the odd one out. Like it was the most
natural thing in the world. Like the kids hated him cos he was
different and they wanted him to suffer for it.

Sinéad cried too once when she chose to be the odd one out by singing and people teased her. Made it hard for her to choose. Sometimes it's best to stay quiet and not to be drawing attention to yourself. Ask the animals. The boy and his mammy moved on to some place else anyhow. It's a lonely kind of crying I remember him for, with the head down looking up at the pairs of eyes in the gang every now and again for only a sec. Disbelief isn't it? Hard to choose standing out, seeing as how we are and all.

The Frank and Walters' song 'This Is Not a Song'.

_____

_____

_____

_____

_____

_____

_____

_____

_____

_____

_____

_____

_____

The Frank and Walters were encoring. We were all locked together arm in arm singing. The whole lot of us. I broke free letting on shyness. I seen Sinéad in slow motion singing and laughing and wipe some beads of sweat from her forehead and move some hair from her brow to behind her ear. I'd never seen her sweating like that at night-time. Only in daytime when she played tennis. Was different now with the light. This light was more selective, finding her glowing eyes and her cheekbones and her soft shining lips. Her laughing smile revealing her white teeth in a flash of perfection, caught in tiny time fragments by the clueless disco lights above. Even caught the glisten of her collarbone once. That's all what I seen. Two seconds worth living for. Went back to real time then again. Or usual time. Time we think in isn't it? The Frank and Walters were after making one of the whole lot of them in the hall. Thousand to one. One body. Carefree. Happy. I think they knew these moments would be rare. They'd seen our parents. Our uncles. Our aunts. Our neighbours. Ourselves in the everyhour of the everyday. Made it all the more special though isn't it?

Every mouth sang along. A wild teenage choir led by a few Cork lads who had come home after being carried around the world on the wave of this new song of theirs. And now to welcome them home a thousand teenagers sang the song they knew as well as the band did. A thousand teenagers. All their pretend cynicism banished to reveal the truth of their teenage hope. So much shit as yet unlearned. Kind of shit that makes shit of people. When it's shared. Music. I seen it then. Some reaction. Thousand to one. Whole. Happier than the sum of their parts they were. And stronger somehow. Unison. They sang.

We listened to Dolly Parton too this one evening I think it was eleven times. 'I Will Always Love You'.

—I imagine her singing in the forest and a big strong handsome woodcutter like Little Red Riding Hood's father hearing her and following the music, said Sinéad.

—Ha!

—And then he finally sees her.

—Sure how could he miss them?

—A vision.

—Two visions.

—He falls totally in love with her and she with him. They make love there and then cos they just can't resist each other.

—Dirty thing.

—Sure she couldn't resist him.

—Not her, you.

—Ah sure you can't really help what you think. My brain is in charge of what I think. I don't have a say.

—Dirty mind.

—And he minds her and protects her all the days of his life. And all the best days of hers.

—Does he now?

—He does. Cos he loves her.

I headed off then cos I could tell by the way she was looking at him that she'd have asked him to kill me if I didn't. Anyhow whatever they did, they wouldn't have been able to do it if I stayed there. I'd say they probably went for a walk in the woods.

An Awful Business Surely

It was Detective Crowley came to tell the mother and father. He'd have known I used to hang around with her a lot of course. I was above in my room getting dressed after being called for Mass. Every Sunday morning I used to have to get up and get dressed for Mass.

—When you live in this house you abide by the rules.

Usually my parents went to the nine o'clock but sometimes they had a lie-in which meant I could sneak back in to the empty house after the later Mass had started. When the mother came back she would ask about the sermon and which priest had said Mass. It was a guessing game.

—You'll have no luck for it, so you won't.

—How can you expect to have luck in this world if you insult Our Lord every Sunday?

—You wouldn't be having these troubles if you'd let the Lord into your heart.

—I am the way, the truth and the life.

'Twas no laughing matter with her either. She'd be roaring it sometimes with tears in her eyes. It was the thought of me burning for all eternity in the fires of hell that drove her demented. When they went to early Mass I usually went for one of my walks along the river instead of smoking and talking shit out the back of the church with the other eejits. Course James was never there cos he was a Prod and Sinéad was never there cos she was Sinéad.

So anyhow, there I am above in my room and I sees Detective Crowley climb out of the car that was too small for him. The whole side of the car rose like a sigh of relief when his dead weight got off the suspension. The car could breathe again.

—You can come too.

Some light young lad got out of the passenger seat after, saying nothing. There was no sigh of relief this time. The car didn't even know this little fella was there. Seemed like Detective Crowley hardly did either. Probably some local politician's nephew or something to be given a detective job so young. Detective Crowley stood with his hands on his hips and his fat belly stuck out even more as he stretched his back. He looked around at his ease. Looked at the house like a builder surveying a job for a price quote. I don't think he could see me behind the net curtains. But I don't know. Without as much as a word or a 'come on' nod of the head to his young partner, Crowley made his way to the front door. When the young lad caught up with him Crowley muttered one word. With that, the young lad turned, speed-walked to the car and returned with a notepad.

The mother was ready for Mass and was waiting for her husband who was pissing the three or four cups of tea he has on Sunday mornings.

—Hello Detective Crowley, is everything OK?

Her voice cracked like an upset child's.

—I have bad news Margaret.

Margaret, that's my mother's name by the blah. Don't think I mentioned it. It didn't come up really. She's a grand mother.

—Oh.

—Is Charlie in?

—He is. He's getting ready for Mass. Charlie!

—Yeah?

That's me.

—Come down.

That's my mother.

So I come down. Dressed but not washed. Sometimes I washed myself after dressing myself. Sure I'm the only one that would know. Wet my face and hair, squirt of deodorant under my arms and who'd know if I'd a shower or not? No one. That's who.

Anyhow. So down I comes.

—Hello.

—Hello Charlie. Will you sit down for a minute please, I've bad news for you I'm afraid.

'Twas in the sitting room they all were. So that's where I sat.

—Your friend Sinéad is dead. She was found below under the bridge this morning. I'm sorry Charlie.

Even though I was numb that morning I could tell that Detective Crowley was studying my reaction and behaviour. His eyes were on me like an X-ray machine. Subsurface. Boring into me. I didn't see it. I felt it. The stone cold sober stare. This man wasn't going to miss a fucking trick. This Detective Crowley will catch the bastard I was thinking to myself. My mother started weeping. My father strained to keep the emotion in his stomach so he could use his throat to speak. His voice broke a little on the S word though.

—Jesus . . . was it suicide?

—We don't know yet. So we're just going through the motions for the moment. Treating it as suspicious, until the coroner tells us not to.

He still hadn't taken his eyes off me.

—Charlie? Are you OK? It'll take a while to sink in you know Charlie. And I'm very sorry for you. Do you mind if I ask you a few questions Charlie?

I heard him but I couldn't speak. This was real. This was real. This had happened and it was real. I did OK. I couldn't talk or do anything now, but I did OK I think.

—He's gone pale as a ghost, Detective Crowley said.

—Charlie are you OK love? the mother asked as she sat on the couch and put her arm around me. I'd gone into a black hole and I didn't care if I never came out of it. Sinéad was gone now.

—OK Charlie, I'm just going to have a little word with your dad outside OK? I'm going to ask him to get the doctor down to have a look at you because I think you're in shock. Keep him warm, he said to my tearful mother quietly, and said God bless to her then nodded for his young partner to lead the way. Then he gestured for the father to go outside, then he followed himself. Outside the door Detective Crowley spoke loud, making sure I heard every word. State and all as I was in, I was starting to like this Detective Crowley's style.

—Just a couple of routine questions John.

—Fire away.

—Did Charlie sleep here last night?

—Jesus Christ Tony, is Charlie a . . .

—A suspect? He is. And so are you. The only one who's not a suspect to my mind this minute is myself. And that's the way 'twill be until I'm sure what we're dealing with. We *might* have a murder on our hands, so I'll deal with it as such. Was Charlie here last night?

—He slept here yeah.

—All night?

—Yeah. Since he got home like.

—Got home from where?

—From being out like. For the night with all the rest of them. They go out every Saturday night sure Tony, Jesus Christ.

—I'll be asking everyone around the same questions. It's only routine John.

—I'm sorry. I'm worried about him, that's all. And I can't believe that poor beautiful girl is dead.

Could hear the father letting himself down and going all teary in front of Detective Crowley.

—I'm sorry.

—That's alright John. Isn't it as well you're not used to this lark like I am. Listen, does Charlie take a drink?

—Christ no. Never. One blessing we have with him at least.

—Were you awake when he got home?

—No. I never am. Margaret usually wakes up though. Will I get her?

—Stay where you are a minute anyway.

An order it was. A policeman's order. Not a friend's request.

—Charlie was good friends with her was he?

—Jesus Christ. She was good to Charlie like you know? Fond of him.

—Fond of him?

—Yeah. You know Charlie is . . . well he's a bit special.

—Yeah.

—Well she looked out for him. Along with James Kent. They were very good to him you know. Involved him when others would have left him behind.

—Yeah.

Next thing my bleddy father started sobbing like a girlygirl again.

—It's OK John.

—Jesus Christ 'tis all so sad, the father wept.

—Will you call that doctor so John?

—I will.

—I'm going to head back in if you don't mind.

—Of course.

—Sorry for the interruption again.

My mother nodded that 'twas fine. He came over and knelt in front of me.

—You'll be OK Charlie. You're after getting an awful shock.

He'd his big strong shovel of a hand on my shoulder, then he patted my head. Well not patted really. He leaned in close so that his forehead touched mine. He worked his fingers right into my scalp, saying 'You'll be all right Charlie. You'll be all right.' He was checking to see if I'd had a shower cos he took a sniff of my fucking hair to see if 'twas washed as well, before slapping me softly on the cheek and saying,

—You'll be all right Charlie. You'll be OK. I'll call into you again soon. Look into my eyes Charlie . . . Yeah, the pupils, he's in a fair bit of shock I'd say. You better ring the doctor right away John.

—OK.

—I'll be leaving ye so. There's been no formal identification yet but half the parish were below around so ye needn't be telling anyone I called because they'll only be thinking Charlie did it. I just didn't want ye finding out over at Mass. Sinéad's family have

been told obviously. The body is still at the scene while the foren-
sics are finishing. Goodbye for now, and again, I'm very sorry to
be the bearer of such news.

—Goodbye and thanks Tony.

—Bye, my mother said too.

The door closed and opened a sec later.

—Sorry again, there was just the one question. Margaret if you
could just for one second.

My mother went out to him as she was asked to. This time he
left the door open and watched me when he was talking.

—Do you know what time Charlie came in last night? The
mother went thinking for a minute. She bit the fingernail of her
small finger.

—'Twas about half twelve I'd say. Maybe before it. I was still up
watching telly.

—What were you watching?

—Ahm . . . oh . . . *Columbo*.

—Was it any good?

—Yeah . . . not bad.

—What channel was it on?

—Ahm . . . BBC I think.

—Grand. One other little thing. Was Charlie wearing those
clothes last night?

She looked in at me.

—Why do you ask? Yes. The shirt anyway cos I ironed it for
him. I made him wear it to be respectable-looking. He'd go out in
his work clothes if you let him.

—And the shoes and the jeans?

—I don't know, you'd have to ask himself.

—He can't talk.

—Well I don't know. Well they're the only shoes he has so yes he'd have worn them I suppose yes. The only other things he has are his work boots.

—Can I see them?

My father interjected then.

—Jesus Christ Tony.

—I'd like to be able to eliminate your son as soon as possible because people are talking.

—Let them talk. What if I don't show you the boots?

—I'd just put that in my report. But you don't have to show them to me. I've no warrant or anything to search or take property or anything like that at this stage.

—Well Tony, with all due respect, listen to me now. That boy in there adored that girl. Adored her. And by Christ he'd never let harm come to her, let alone hurt her himself.

—Let me see the boots so John.

My father stormed off to the utility room and came back with my filthy work boots and my runners which were clean.

—Now. They're his boots. They're his runners. He's wearing his shoes.

Detective Crowley opened the front door.

—Throw them down there on the footpath.

My father did. The detective took a quick look.

—Have you any work boots yourself? Or runners?

—I've Wellingtons. And runners yeah.

—Get them John if you wouldn't mind.

—Jesus Christ Tony I can't believe this.

—A quick look is all I want.

I could see my mother hugging herself and looking at the ground scared. Then she came in and sat by myself. My father came back with his runners and Wellington boots and dropped them on the footpath with the others. Detective Crowley picked up one welly and one runner and said, 'They're fine. None of that earth is fresh.' With that he turned and walked straight back into the house.

—Just want to see how Charlie is. It's possible he'd come out of it fairly quick.

My father followed him back in. Getting agitated my father was now.

—How is he now? Any change?

—He's pretty much the same I'd say.

—There are several different types of shock. Did ye ring the doctor yet?

—No.

—Do it now sure.

—My mother went out to the hall to ring.

Detective Crowley stood and faced my father telling him some big long yarn about how he'd come across the type of shock I was in loads of times. 'Can happen to victims, culprits and witnesses,' he said, 'Or close friends or relatives of the victim on hearing the bad news.' He kept talking and his eyes glued to me.

—I remember one time, when I was working in Dublin there was a lad about the same age as Charlie and he killed his girlfriend in some mad fit of jealous rage. The first words he spoke was,

'Thank you,' and that was to the judge who'd just sentenced him to twenty-five to life in the court case which was over two years after the crime. Can be a serious thing, this type of shock. Post-traumatic shock they call it. I think Charlie's is just standard shock though. You can die from it you know. The reduced blood flow. I think Charlie is OK. He might faint is the only thing. If 'twas medically serious he'd have palpitations or his lips would go blue. It's just a psychological shock. But that can present its own difficulties. The doctor will be filling you in. Tell the doctor if he's on any medication or anything. Is he generally on medication no?

—No. Nothing.

—No anti-depressants ever or anything like that?

—No. Nothing like that ever no.

—OK. I better be off. I hope you won't take all the old questions personally John.

—Ah sure . . .

—It's business John. It's only business.

My mother came back in then.

—Doctor Reid will be here in a few minutes.

—Will she? That's good. Stay with him and keep him warm. Don't give him anything to eat or drink. The doctor might send him up to the hospital you know. I was just saying to John, Margaret that I'm sorry about all the old questions. I just want to get Charlie out of the loop as quick as possible because his name is only being bandied about unjustly.

—OK Tony.

—Take care for now.

—Bye.

He was finally ready to go now, not because he'd needed to say all that stuff, but because his partner was finished taking samples of earth from the assorted footwear outside on the footpath unknown to my poor good ignorant parents. Maybe this young detective they had working with Detective Crowley wasn't such a fool after all. Crowley knew I could see his partner's handiwork from where I stared out the window in a trance. His green X-ray eyes watched me like a fucking hawk while he spun my father the spiel about shock to bide his partner time to fill the evidence bags with the little bits of earth from the boots and wellies and runners. You couldn't be up to them.

—Goodbye and God bless, said Detective Crowley, and he turned to face my parents one last time, ' 'Tis an awful business surely,' he said.

More of Dinky's Evidence

—So you left The Snug, the bar, at approximately 2:30 a.m., is that so?

—I think so, yes.

—You had been talking to Sinéad for much of the night and you got her coat for her as you were leaving, is that correct?

—Yes.

—Did she ask you to do it?

—No, I don't think so, but I knew what it looked like and when I got mine I got hers too.

—I see. And was she waiting for you?

—No. I think she'd gone to the bathroom so I waited for her.

—Were you waiting on your own?

—Yes.

—I see. And did she ask you to walk her home?

—Yes.

—Can you remember her exact words?

—I think she said, 'Will you walk with me?'

—I see. And tell me what happened when you reached the gate of her house?

—She kept walking.

—To where?

—Past it. I said nothing, I just walked with her.

—Did you feel at this point that you might have an opportunity to kiss her?

—Ahm...I don't think so, no. We were getting on well like, just talking about old times and James and stuff. And like the future and stuff, she was telling me she was planning on trying to get a place of her own in Ballyronan and I was telling her about my plans to build a house too.

—I see. And you walked down along Pontoon road, is that correct?

—Yes.

—And at what point did you leave the road?

—Well, she walked into the woods and I walked with her.

—Were you surprised by this?

—Not really. It was a nice night and we were having a nice talk.

—So where did you both end up?

—Down by the river. On the bank near the bridge. She sat down first and then I did. She cried a little then and I put my arm around her.

—Did you try and kiss her?

—No, she kissed me.

—She was crying and she kissed you? Is that what you're saying?

—Pretty much.

—Pretty much? Yes or no?

—Yes.

—And what happened then?

—She took off her blouse and her bra.

—Really?

—Yes.

—And then?

—We had sex.

—Where exactly?

—On the river bank.

—Was it consensual?

—Yes. Totally.

—In your statement to the gardaí you said it was all over quite quickly and that it was, and I quote, 'gentle'. Could you explain what you meant by 'gentle'?

—Ahm. . . that was a lie. I didn't want them to think there was any force involved because I knew Sinéad was dead and that I was under suspicion.

—And now that so much of your blood and skin was found under the victim's fingernails, you have changed your story to what?

—Objection, Your Lordship.

—Sustained. Ask specific questions please.

—Very well, Your Lordship. Tell me. How do you explain so much of your skin and blood being found under Sinéad Halloran's fingernails?

—She was scrawling me very hard during sex.

—What parts of you?

—My chest and neck and face.

—Did you think this was strange?

—Yes.

—Was it painful?

—Yes, but it was just passion, I thought.

—Did it ever cross your mind that Sinéad didn't want to have sex with you?

—No.

—I put it to you now that you raped her. And afterwards, realising what you'd done you knelt on top of her and strangled her.

—I didn't.

—How then, were your fingerprints and palm prints all over the torc necklace of the victim that was found at the scene?

—Because she asked me to take it off her.

—Why wouldn't she just take it off herself?

—I don't know.

—Despite all this evidence you still deny that you raped and murdered Sinéad Halloran, is that so?

—Yes.

—You seem very calm, Mr Hennebry. If I was wrongfully accused of something I don't think I'd be so calm.

—Objection, Your Lordship, totally irrelevant.

—Sustained. Please stick to the facts only in my court.

—Very well, Your Lordship. Is it true that when the gardaí interviewed you first, that they found that you were wearing make-up on the cuts you had on your face and neck?

—Yes.

—Where did you get the make-up?

—My mother's room.

452

—Why did you want to wear make-up, though? I don't understand. Wouldn't an antiseptic cream be more useful?

Dinky's voice started to go all shaky now.

—I did it to cover up the scratches.

—Cuts. That's what the police called them. Cuts. Can we return, please, to photograph 15 in exhibit 6, item 3. As you can see the deceased put up quite a fight to protect herself.

—Objection.

—Sustained.

—These appear, as indicated by Detective Crowley and the forensic pathologist, to be consistent with cuts and scratches inflicted on an attacker by a fit and able-bodied young woman. And we saw other examples of rapists and murderers who had been injured in very similar ways. Now if I could continue. Let us look in particular at the severity of the cuts. The cuts are quite severe, including two particularly nasty ones on his left cheek. Mr Hennebry, what did you decide to do about these cuts the next morning?

—I put my mother's make-up on them. I didn't want her to think I was in a fight.

—Interesting. So you admit now that these were not merely a little scratch or two. These are in fact evidence of a fight.

—No.

—A fight for life.

—No. I didn't do it. I didn't kill Sinéad.

—You were jealous of James and you wanted his girlfriend. You set about their destruction in the most evil of ways.

—I admit that I did know long ago that she'd been raped by the Little Rascal and what I did was wrong. I admit that. And I don't know why I did it. But I swear I don't know what happened Sinéad. I just don't know why I did those nasty things like I did.

—You don't know. Prisons are full of murderers who don't understand their own motives, ladies and gentlemen.

—It's not like that.

—What is it like, Mr Hennebry? Tell us.

—Yes. Like, I took that scarf that time. And I knew what I was doing when I gave it to the Rascal. And the damage I was doing to Sinéad and James. It was pure rotten and I'm ashamed I done it. And I know it makes me look pure rotten. I can't understand it. Why I did it.

—A sociopath is someone who lacks empathy with people. I think you're a sociopath, Mr Hennebry, and I'll tell you why. You set about the destruction of a young man who regarded you as his closest friend. You allowed James to think Sinéad was unfaithful to him when you knew otherwise. You covered up the actions of a violent rapist, causing his victim untold suffering. You framed the poor girl further by stealing her scarf and giving it to her rapist in order to put the nail in the coffin of the relationship of Sinéad and James. This, again, caused them untold suffering. I think you raped and murdered Sinéad. And during this trial you have tried to frame poor Charlie McCarthy by saying he killed her. How much pain and suffering are you willing to cause people, Mr Hennebry? I'll answer that for you. There is no limit to the pain and suffering you are willing to cause. Because the pain and suffering of others means nothing to you. You are a liar. You are evil. You are a rare and cold-blooded creature. You are a killer. What do you say to that, Mr Hennebry?

—Well...I'm not. I'm not evil. And I don't know if Charlie

McCarthy had anything to do with it either. Or if there was a pact or if Sinéad wanted to set me up and Charlie went down after and choked her. Or if it was some straggler or some fisherman or I dunno. But I didn't kill her.

Dinky starts crying then and I could hear his mother crying below too.

—It wasn't me. I swear to God. I swear to God. I did some bad stuff but I didn't do that. Please. Please. Ye can't. . . I didn't. . .

The judge scratched his cheek and the lawyer continued.

—All of the evidence says otherwise. I think you are a liar and I think you are a coward for not admitting what you've done and apologising to the deceased's family. Shame on you, Mr Hennebry. Shame on you. I'm done, Your Lordship.
—We'll take a recess for fifteen minutes.

Dinky was sobbing and sniffling and he staggering out of the witness stand, with the garda's hand on his arm, leading him out.

My visit to Dr Quinn today was different. He thinks I'm the best fella ever now. Instead of the office we walked around the grounds of the hospital for an hour. He was thanking me for engaging with the process as if I engaged with the process. He's a fierce fan of the process like the hippy one in school long ago. And he was thanking me for trusting him as if I trusted him. And he was saying how he was amazed with the progress I was after making as if he knew the thoughts in my head.

Afterwards I got the bus into the city centre for a walk around. Walked up towards St Francis church and I could see they'd balloons and bunting and signs and all kinds of shite up and when I got to the church I heard music so I went in. On the poster at the back of the church it said Cork Culture presents The Sirene Ensemble. Bit like Sinéad. The Sirene Ensemble. 'Les Béatitudes' was the one I heard cos I robbed a programme at the back of the church. Last song it was. I missed the rest but I heard this one. So I was happy I heard this one. Would have heard more if Dr Quinn shut his hole. This music made me sick. An old man came up to me outside the church telling me to move on and I told him to fuck off and I vomited again. He thought I was a bum. The bums hang around the churches in Cork for warmth. After I finished vomiting I hung around and watched these foreign ones packing up after. The singers. Then they went away in a van and two cars to some place else on their music travels that wasn't Ireland and I suppose I half wished I was with them. Not sure why it made me think of Sinéad so much but it wasn't the voices. Might have been the hairs on the back of my neck. Give you the creeps like a ghost story.

'Les Béatitudes' goes here. I dunno what language it was. There's a million different ones on the internet. But it was one I didn't understand the words of so you must write out one from a language you don't know. Find it and listen to it. The words won't distract you from the music too much cos you won't know what they mean. Blessed are those who never met me.

_____

_____

_____

_____

_____

_____

_____

_____

_____

_____

_____

_____

Voices. No instruments only voices. Plenty of them singing. Like your man that Sinéad liked. On the Holocaust memorial from the telly. Fat fella singing with a crowd around him. The others were dark-skinned and black-haired but this fella was the odd one out. This fella was pushed around on the playground. Fat pink head on him with funny teeth and goggly eyes. And gingery hair. A freckleface in a land of no freckles. He was up at the mic and the lads who might have bullied him were singing along with him. Or sounded like it was against him sometimes. Those were the best bits, Sinéad said. The pink head on the odd one out was gone purple by the end of it. Make you think of. Of nothing. Just listen like. Your fucking ears became your brain. Or your brain became your ears. Went on for the bones of fifteen minutes. I don't know where the video of it is now. It's not in the castle any more anyhow. But if you had it. If you had this video where James' mother had the commemoration thing recorded, the picture would go to shit when you reached the odd one out singing. The tape was worn out. James just lied on the floor next to it and would rewind for Sinéad every time the odd one out came to the end of whatever strange cry of a song it was that he was singing. If I had to guess how many times we watched it over that Christmas holidays I'd say about one hundred and seventeen times. Sinéad knew the most of it anyhow by the end, whatever language it was.

Makes me think of the Russian Creed too. That was a record. Big old crackly one. Must have been James' father's. Or maybe his grandfather's. One time James had the wrong time for a match cos Dinky told him it was on at half seven but it was really on at half six. I knew it was half six it was on but I wanted to see what Dinky was up to cos I knew they wouldn't play the match without James cos it was on in the local pitch. A stone's throw from the castle. Dinky had been up the day before and thought they were bonkers listening to the Russian Creed up full blast over and over and over. So anyhow I could see them out the window of the library. The whole team was out on the pitch and they trying to shout for James but all that could be heard out over the eastern fall of the valley that evening was the Russian Creed. In the end they stopped shouting, just looked up at the castle to us between the kicks of the ball in the warm-up. It was the trainer that had to get James. The doorbell wasn't heard so he came in the front door and up the stairs into us. The look on James' face and the trainer's face was the same. They were shocked. James turned off the music and the trainer goes,

—What in the name of sweet suffering fuck are you up to James? You've a fucking match below now.

James looked up and smiled and gave us two big thumbs up from the window of the car and the trainer speeding off down the drive. Sinéad put on the song once more before we left. She said it was intimacy. That music. That's what she said about it. Intimacy. For the people singing it and hearing it. No going back after sharing something like that she said. Intimacy.

The State's Case

Now, ladies and gentlemen I am invited to argue the case on behalf of the Irish state. But I'm not going to argue with you, ladies and gentlemen. What I'm going to do, in summing up, is discuss the reasonable conclusions which can be drawn from the evidence we have heard.

Mr Cole's summing-up was excellent, I'm sure you will all agree. A very skilled speech which opened up many possibilities – among them the possibility that his client, Denis Hennebry, may be innocent. My summing-up will be very different from Mr Cole's. Mainly because my summing-up will not be based around conjecture and 'what ifs'. No. My summing-up will be entirely based around fact. And what we call, in the very serious business of criminal law, hard evidence. Hard evidence and facts, ladies and gentlemen. Hard evidence and facts.

Now I'm not sure if I have Mr Cole's eloquence. I'm not sure if my voice is as pleasant to the ear of the listener. And as I listened to him carefully yesterday, and saw how attentively you listened to him ladies and gentlemen, I could not help but hope that I might have your attention in the same way – despite my . . . well, my less honed oratory skills and my gravelly voice . . . and my old suit . . . and my age.

They say image is everything nowadays. If it is, I'm at a disadvantage. However, ladies and gentlemen, I believe that those who say image is everything are wrong. Justice, ladies and gentlemen, justice is everything. Image, varnish, gloss, depiction, portrayal, speculation, inference, assumption, guesswork, imagining, shot in the dark, conjecture, 'what ifs'. They all come to nothing beside facts. Evidence and facts, ladies and gentlemen. Evidence and facts. Justice is everything. Evidence . . . and facts. The rest, ladies and gentlemen, is distraction. Skilful distraction. Cynical distraction. But the old school taught us that evidence and facts alone will bring us justice. My wife always tells me on my way out to a big court case, she says, 'Justice is good and God is good.' Justice. Facts and evidence. Evidence and facts. Don't let your view be clouded by anything which is not evidence. Don't let your view be clouded by anything which is not fact. Justice, ladies and gentlemen. May justice prevail.

Ladies and gentlemen of the jury. In the science of medical diagnosis, doctors have a term for when you diagnose something quite common as something extremely rare and unusual. They call it a zebra. If something looks like a horse. Sounds like a horse. Feels like a horse. Acts like a horse. Then it's probably a horse. Not a zebra. What we have here, ladies and gentlemen, is the equivalent of the zebra diagnosis in the world of criminal law. But do not let this analogy deflect from the seriousness of this situation. This is a very calculated, sly and bold move by the defendant and his counsel to put doubt in your minds as to his guilt. Remember to always keep in your mind the key words for justice – evidence and facts.

What exactly are they suggesting? Are they really suggesting that poor innocent, harmless, hapless Charlie McCarthy had entered into a pact with Sinéad and strangled her? Is this really plausible? In light of the physical forensic evidence? In light of the character witnesses that have spoken on Charlie's behalf? Is this plausible? Is this a reasonable suggestion? The answer, of course, is no. We have heard many despicable things in this trial. But this, unfortunately, in this court case of law, is yet another abomination. A disgrace. Trying, in desperation, grasping at straws, a shot in the dark, trying, in one last throw of the dice to try and implicate poor harmless Charlie McCarthy in the murder, or so-called assisted suicide. . .of Sinéad Halloran is nothing short of scandalous.

Let us now examine the facts and the evidence that Denis Hennebry's counsel have put forward to support this silly notion. Well, what have we got? Nothing. Not a thing. Not a single fact. Not a single iota of evidence to back up this so-called theory. But theory is too good a word. It's fantasy. It's a big elaborate parcel with absolutely nothing in it. All the fancy language and ideas in the world won't deflect us. No evidence. No facts. Nothing. Absolutely nothing.

I implore you to respect our legal system as much as I do and banish such an outlandish and ridiculous thought from your minds. Evidence and facts, ladies and gentlemen. And excuse me if I appear angry. My profession are trained and expected not to let emotion govern our thoughts and words in the courts of law. Today. . .for the first time in my long professional life. . .I find it very difficult to control my fury. My anger. My outrage at this cynical, unjust and despicable ploy by Denis Hennebry and his counsel. Let us do a good job, for God's sake and for goodness' sake, for society's sake, for all our sakes, for Sinéad

Halloran's sake. We are all part of the Irish justice system today. I implore you to make a judgement which is morally correct. I implore you not to be distracted from the issues at hand. The guilt or innocence of one Denis Hennebry. That's what the issue is here. Let us call it as it is. A horse looks like a horse. Fact. A horse sounds like a horse. Fact. A horse behaves like a horse. Fact. Ladies and gentlemen, a horse is not a zebra. A horse . . . is . . . of course . . . a horse. May justice be served. Evidence and fact. Evidence and fact. Everything else is froth. We'll forget about fancy talk and ridiculous notions. The facts and the evidence are everything. Evidence and fact. Justice is justice. Rape is rape. Murder is murder. Evil is evil. Guilt is guilt.

That was the day before yesterday I wrote that. But yesterday something kind of weird happened to me. A three year-old-girl made me cry. Emily. My sister and her two children are staying here this weekend cos my sister's husband is away for the weekend with work. Anyhow they were giving Emily a bath. The bathroom is next to my room and I heard her singing with her own mother and my mother and she splashing around in the bath.

One. Two. Three. Four. Five.
Once I caught a fish alive.
Six. Seven. Eight. Nine. Ten.
Then I let him go again.
Why did you let him go?
Because he bit my finger so.
Which finger did he bite?
The little one upon the right.

I didn't get the shakes or go numb or nearly vomit like the other times I hear music. I just cried and cried and cried. And I didn't want to block my ears or stop the music. I wanted her to keep singing. And she did cos it was the only song she knew. And I cried and cried and cried, just lying on my bed listening to her beautiful little voice singing the song all clueless and happy and the random sounds of her splashes and my sister and mother saying kind happy things to her and her laughing and them laughing and then she singing away again and they joining in for bits when she'd forget the words. I went out then and I walked to Newport and back again. Eighteen miles altogether. And last night I slept. Without tablets. For the first time in a long time I slept at night and when the morning came I got up.

I bought matches again. Does a song stop being a song if it's never sung again? If anyone who ever heard it or played it or sang it or hummed it is dead? Does the tune of it go some place? Anyhow it wouldn't be right for people to have Sinéad and James' tunes cos it's the selfsame people killed them. We don't deserve them isn't it? The tapes melted and the pages burned away. If I make money with my book I might go away to America. I might find someone else with the music in them only this time I'll mind them better isn't it? I keep it in my bedroom. The map I got off Sinéad long ago. That she sent me in the post. I have it in my hand now. I just put it back in the drawer where it's been all the time.

My bedroom is my world now a long time. I know sometimes and I up in my room what people are thinking. I see them walking up the road and look in at the house for a minute and wonder which room is mine and they just look on up the hill then and keep walking. But I know. I know they still wonder was it me. They don't look in at the house and wonder when they're on their way down to the village at all. Only when they're coming back up from it cos they've their business done in the village and have nothing else to be thinking about only me and if I did it. Struggling up the hill with their tired legs and their heavy thoughts. Sad puzzled brains on them. You'd like to make them happy but there is no way. Only another hill after that one. And another puzzle to keep them sad isn't it? But Sinéad could have made them happy. Of all the distractions I ever seen, Sinéad was the best. She said one time that music was like the way life was supposed to be. Like when you knew the song. You knew what was coming always and you were never disappointed. But in life you had to do whatever you figured was best and then just hope.

And this is where we are now isn't it?

Cos long long long long long long ago some place on Earth small fires started to appear speckled around the land in the evening time. If there was a God maybe he'd have thought he seen some-where on the dark side of this one planet, a light shining in the dark. A glow. Where there should have been no light at all, only darkness and he goes,

—What the fuck?

And he goes for a closer look and seen that there is life and he seen these strange two-legged animals all sitting around this fire and noises coming from their mouths at each other and they passing bits of burned animal around and eating it.

Then he seen them say.

He seen them say words. And the words were all different and they were for all the different things around this animal. And they all came to know the different words for all the different things.

Then he seen them using these words for imaginings and for no reason except to pass the night away and they sitting around this fire.

He seen them laugh and gasp and look at each other and shake their heads in awe and wonder.

He seen them cry.

He seen them draw on the walls of rocks and caves. Images of each other and images of other creatures and images of strange designs of their own conjuring.

He seen them then and they making sounds. And the sounds were soundings into the space they had and the time they had. Exploring the world unseen isn't it? Inside themselves and outside themselves. Together and alone.

He seen them listen.

He seen them dance.

He seen them looking into the night's sky and wonder.

He seen them maybe and he felt lonely maybe not being with them and maybe he seen himself and how he was like them and he wondered then maybe was he only an imagining of theirs. And maybe he thought if he really was a god of theirs he would die for them so awesome and beautiful were they and all the things he seen them do.

I can hear the baby crying down stairs now and it made me remember something Sinéad said about the way Bob Dylan played guitar on his song 'I Was Young When I Left Home'. Said it was soothing cos it was like a baby crying. I won't leave space for the words of it. You'll just have to listen to the song cos that's what I'm going doing now.

When I'd the song on that time I looked out my bedroom window and they were leaving and Emily had on a little red coat and I cried for a small bit.

My father just shouted up at me now was I going to the match. I said,

—I'll be down now.

—Hurry up, he said.

Anyhow I've 114,124 words done so that's the end of my book.

ACKNOWLEDGEMENTS

Thank you to my wonderful, supportive and encouraging wife, Sandra, who was first to read *The Gamal* in its becoming. Thank you to my amazing, darling daughter, Róisín, who enriches our lives immeasurably. To my outstanding and selfless parents, Seán and Mary, to my brothers and sisters, relatives, colleagues and friends, thank you all for your support and friendship.

I'd like to thank my agent Jamie Coleman of Toby Eady Associates, for seeing what I was trying to achieve from day one and for seeing me through the first few drafts. Thank you to my excellent editor at Bloomsbury, Helen Garnons-Williams. Thank you very much Erica Jarnes, Ellen Williams, Audrey Cotterell, Anna Simpson and Oliver Holder-Rea and all at Bloomsbury who had an input. Thank you to Nancy Miller and Lea Beresford at Bloomsbury USA for helping to bring the book across the water and to Birgit Schmitz for bringing *The Gamal* to German readers. I'm also very grateful to jacket designer Greg Heinimann for creating such an attractive-looking cover.

I appreciate the helpfulness of the information desk staff at the Central Criminal Court, Dublin. I found Michael Sheridan's book on crime scene investigation in Ireland, *Bloody Evidence – CSI: Tracking the Killers* (Mentor, 2006), extremely useful. Another invaluable book I picked up was *Psychiatry in Medical Practice – Third Edition* by David Goldberg, Linda Gask and Richard Morriss (Routledge, 2008).

READING GROUP GUIDE

These discussion questions are designed to enhance your group's conversation about *The Gamal*.

About the book

Charlie has always been, as his father says, a man apart. The only people who ever really accepted him were his friends Sinéad and James, who saw a life for him beyond the restrictive judgments of their home, Ballyronan. When Sinéad and James die, Charlie is left utterly alone and unable to function in day-to-day life. He can't sleep, he suffers from severe headaches, and he rarely leaves his house. His psychiatrist, Dr. Quinn, suggests he write his story down, as a means of processing his grief, and it is through this exercise that *The Gamal* comes to life.

The Gamal is set in an Ireland defined by its national pride, a place where fitting in and maintaining the status quo is akin to patriotism. The story that Charlie shares in these pages is about three people who break the mold: Sinéad, James, and Charlie himself. Each in their own way, they challenge the world around them, suggesting that it is inadequate. It is through that inadvertent defiance that they strike fear and distrust in their peers and elders, eventually bringing great tragedy to them all. But as Charlie shares their story, we see them as more than their horrific and untimely deaths: we see the joy and beauty they brought to those who opened their hearts to them, the power they wielded by daring to devote their lives to their love for each other.

For discussion

1. Charlie tells his readers early on that they won't like him. Do you like Charlie? Why do you think that he's so sure that you won't?

2. Charlie hates descriptive writing, and when he tries to write his own descriptions, he becomes very self-critical. Why do you think that kind of writing is so troublesome to him? Why is he so biased toward unadorned, fact-based writing?

3. How do James and Sinéad take care of Charlie? How does he take care of them? How would you characterize his relationship with them?

4. On page 222, Charlie writes, "Sound was freedom. Sound was everything." Did music free Sinéad and James? Did it free Charlie? How was music a catalyst for the tragedies of the novel?

5. Fitting in with the group is a central theme in *The Gamal*. How does that play out on the different societal levels portrayed here? Compare the sense of national pride with the sense of familial—or clan—pride. How do they differ? Does belonging to any of these groups make people happy?

6. Charlie is fixated on the idea of madness. Throughout the book he has several different theories on what madness is, and why we, as a society, label certain people as mad. What do you think of his ideas? Do any of them resonate with you?

7. How would this novel be different if it had an omniscient narrator or if it shifted narration between characters? What does Charlie's perspective add to your understanding of the story? Does it detract from your understanding at all?

8. The idea of the outsider is a common theme in some of our greatest literature. Why do you think this is so?

9. In his play *The Glass Menagerie*, Tennessee Williams writes, "The play is memory. Being a memory play, it is dimly lighted, it is sentimental, it is not realistic. In memory everything seems to happen to music." How does this relate to *The Gamal*? How does the aspect of memory affect the story, especially taking into account Charlie's almost supernatural auditory memory? How do music and memory connect in the book?

10. Religion plays a big role in Irish society. Where do you see religious imagery in *The Gamal*? How do you feel about the portrayal of the martyr in the novel?

11. Sinéad was a light in the darkness for Charlie. How does he carry that light with him at the end of the book?

12. Based on what you've seen in *The Gamal*, how do the Irish honor their history? What aspects of contemporary society seem to stem from historical conflicts with the English?

13. How are women portrayed in this novel? Based on what you see in this book, what roles do women play in Irish society?

14. At the end of the novel, the state's lawyer suggests that Dinky is a sociopath. Do you agree with his assessment? Why or why not? If not, what motivated his actions?

15. Snoozie's character—and to some extent, Charlie's, as well—both deal with guilt due to complacency. Do you think this is justified? If so, do they atone for their inaction?

16. What message are you left with at the end of this book? Is it a hopeful ending? Why or why not? Was, as the state's lawyer so badly wanted, justice achieved?

Suggested reading

Mark Haddon, *The Curious Incident of the Dog in the Night-Time*; Jonathan Safran Foer, *Extremely Loud and Incredibly Close*; Dermot Healy, *Sudden Times*; Patrick McCabe, *The Butcher Boy*; J. D. Salinger, *The Catcher in the Rye*; Sabina Berman, *Me, Who Dove into the Heart of the World*; Carson McCullers, *The Heart Is a Lonely Hunter*; Patrick McCabe, *Breakfast on Pluto*; John Banville, *The Sea*; Seamus Deane, *Reading in the Dark*; Robert Kee, *The Green Flag*; Roddy Doyle, *Paddy Clarke Ha Ha Ha*; Sean O' Faolain, *The Finest Stories of Sean O'Faolain*; Flann O'Brien, *The Third Policeman*

About the author

Ciarán Collins was born in County Cork in 1977. He teaches English and Irish in a school in West Cork. *The Gamal* is his first novel.

A NOTE ON THE TYPE

The text of this book is set in Bembo. This type was first used in 1495 by the Venetian printer Aldus Manutius for Cardinal Bembo's *De Aetna*, and was cut for Manutius by Francesco Griffo. It was one of the types used by Claude Garamond (1480–1561) as a model for his Romain de L'Université, and so it was the forerunner of what became standard European type for the following two centuries. Its modern form follows the original types and was designed for Monotype in 1929.